Bertha von Suttner, Alice A. Abbott

Ground Arms!

The Story of a Life

Bertha von Suttner, Alice A. Abbott

Ground Arms!
The Story of a Life

ISBN/EAN: 9783337186746

Printed in Europe, USA, Canada, Australia, Japan

Cover: Foto ©Andreas Hilbeck / pixelio.de

More available books at **www.hansebooks.com**

"GROUND ARMS!"

THE STORY OF A LIFE

"GROUND ARMS!"

THE STORY OF A LIFE

BY

BERTHA VON SUTTNER

TRANSLATED FROM THE GERMAN

BY ALICE ASBURY ABBOTT

CHICAGO

A. C. McCLURG & COMPANY

1892

TRANSLATOR'S PREFACE.

The author of "Ground Arms!", Baroness von Suttner, is an Austrian of the upper class, the daughter of an Austrian general. Before the appearance of this work she had written several witty and tender society novels—she is a sentimentalist of the German type—but she had given no evidence of greater power. She is a handsome, brilliant woman of the world, who has become thoroughly imbued with the importance of the higher education of women. In "Ground Arms!", where she stepped at once upon a higher plane than she had occupied in any previous work, she emphasizes the necessity of this better training for women if the highest degree of civilization is to be attained by the world at large. She reasons, like Mr. Herbert Spencer, though she does not clothe the thought in his words, that if woman is to perform all the duties of her station, the era of universal peace, secured by international arbitration, must first be secured.

To hastening the advent of the rule of justice obtained without force she seems now to have largely devoted her life. Recently, as Vice-President of the International Peace Congress at Rome, she stood on the rostrum to address a most brilliant and distinguished assembly—the first woman since Corinna, whose voice has been heard within the walls of the famous capitol.

The success of "Ground Arms!" in Germany has been amazing. In the Austrian Parliament grave ministers of finance have commended its reading; all ranks of life

have been profoundly impressed by it, and able critics
have compared its influence in Germany to that of
"Uncle Tom's Cabin" in the United States.

This effect is largely due to the terrible tension of the
public mind in Europe, caused by the daily and hourly
anticipation of war. Baroness von Suttner is keenly
alive to the spirit of the times, and she has written this
book with a hot heart and a burning pen. Naturally she
has not escaped the attacks of the believers in the justice and prudence of the present condition of things, and
is accused of belonging to the sentimental company of
apostles and owners of patent rights to reform and regen-
erate the world. The book is a crusade against war, and
its whole object is to present the claims of the individual
and the family as superior to those of the state; as an
individualist she presses the claim of every human being
to the ownership and control of his own life. Then,
regarding the family as the social unit, she emphasizes
the claim of wife and child as far superior to that of
church or state.

Though "Ground Arms!" is apparently a very simple
story, its philosophy is profound; but so quietly and un-
pretendingly is it unfolded, that we are continually surprised by the strength of the author's logic. We are
sometimes oppressed by her method, which is often painfully realistic, and in other respects is similar to that of
many of the noblest spirits of our time—the method
prompted by the *Weltschmerz,* the groan of the world,
which too often cripples our efforts because of its good-by
to hope, but in her case inspires to work of a very noble
character.

This cry of a weeping, passionate woman is but an echo
of the conscience of the times. So long as it remains
true that, in the main, diplomatists and kings plot wars,

not always with the special aim, but certainly with the result of arresting the social development of humanity— it being with them a struggle to ignore as long as possible the individual rights of man—so long must such books as this aid in the advance of justice. It may not be to-day or to-morrow that this influence will prevail, but it is certainly in the trend of modern thought, and tends to aid the tremendous social and moral revolution which all reflecting minds must see approaching.

Any progress in the development of states through war and revolution our author regards as entailing such heavy misfortune, retrogression, and demoralization to the individual as seriously to retard the general welfare of humanity. This is the natural standpoint of the evolutionist, who applies his principle to sociological problems, and in so doing antagonizes the revolutionary ideas of radical socialism.

There may be some who will be offended at the half-cynical way in which Baroness von Suttner exposes the egotism of man, in ascribing to the Christian God convenient sympathy with conditions which are relics of barbarism ; but such should bear in mind that she has no contention with the principles of the founder of Christianity, only a very serious quarrel with the misinterpretation of these principles, and with the practical neglect of their application. In this countless numbers, within and without the pale of the church, will agree with her. Everywhere society is rebelling against the abuse of the principles of Christian philosophy. Among all sects, keen-eyed clergy are despairing of past methods, and from them comes often enough an arraignment of the church for its failure in the practical application of the principles of its faith. Even the non-believer in the miraculous origin of the Christian religion is sturdily fighting for the application of its ethics while stemming the force of time honored precedents. The main feature of Christ's life and teaching, it is now everywhere acknowledged, is to fit man to live with man, not to prepare him for the hereafter—unless the doing of the one may be considered an assurance of the other. The author of "Ground Arms!" is right when she practically asserts that when in the development of society Christ's tender philosophy controls the world, there will be an end of war.

A. A. A.

CONTENTS

"GROUND ARMS!"

FIRST BOOK.

1859.

AT seventeen I was a curiously overwrought
being. It would be impossible for me at this
date to comprehend my girlish peculiarities, were
it not for the diffuse and pretentious diaries which
have been carefully laid away, thus marking the
progressive stages of my life. There lie, cruelly
impaled, my long-lost enthusiasms, convictions of
which not a shadow remains, views no longer in-
telligible, sympathies dead and buried and gone
to judgment. I am thus, though somewhat bewildered, able to get some inkling of the character
of the vacuity of the silly, pretty head writing all
this rubbish. Even of this beauty I now find but
little trace, anxiously as I may study my mirror,
though old portraits are my surety for its existence.
   I can well imagine what an enviable creature
this Countess Martha Althaus must have been.
Young, handsome, popular and petted. But sin-
gularly enough these red-bound diaries indicate
more melancholy than joy in life. Can I actually
have been so silly as not to realize the advantages
of my position, or only so unbalanced as to believe
that these sorrowful sentimentalities were interesting and particularly valuable if expressed in somewhat poetical prose? My lot appeared unsatisfac-
tory, for I find in one of these precious documents:
"Ah, Joan of Arc! heaven-blessed heroic virgin,
could I but wave the oriflamme of France, crown
my king, and die for country—my dear country!"

The opportunity to gratify these modest ambitions appears to have failed me. The noble army of Christian martyrs seems next to have been regarded as worthy of emulation (date, 19 September, 1853), though this *rôle* also proved to be equally difficult of imitation. I evidently was forced to the realization that all these glorious opportunities for action, after which my soul thirsted, were forever closed to me, that therefore my life was a failure.

"Oh, why did I not come into the world a boy" (this was a frequent form of denunciation of fate, delivered in melodious measure at spasmodic intervals). Then fortune would have been kind and opportunity golden. Of feminine heroism history inscribes but few examples. How few of us appear to have Gracchi for sons! How seldom it is our mission to carry our husbands through the Weinsberg Gates, or to cause fierce, saber-swinging Magyars to shout: "Long live Maria Theresa, our king!"

But when one has the advantage of masculinity one can buckle on the sword and dash abroad to win fame and laurels, capture a throne, like Cromwell, or an empire, like Napoleon. I remember distinctly that the very highest type of manhood seemed to me embodied in a military hero. For learned men, poets, and adventurous discoverers of new countries I had some slight respect, but admiration, simon-pure adoration, I laid at the feet of the military hero and winner of battles. Such are the makers of history, the leaders of the fate of empires. In grandeur of character, in nobleness of motive, in all but god-like attributes, these excelled all other human beings as Alpine or Himalayan peaks tower above the grass and wild flowers of the valley. From all of which it appears that I possessed what is popularly considered an heroic nature; while the truth was simply this: I was enthusiastic and passionate, and these peculiarities were naturally diverted into this channel

by the character of my education and my environ-
ments.

My father was an Austrian general, who had
fought at Custozza under "Father Radetzky,"
whom he absolutely adored. What have I not
heard in the way of stories of camp and field. He
was so tremendously proud of his military adventures, and so thoroughly enjoyed the relation of
his campaigns, that I actually pitied other men who
lacked a similar experience. What a fearful dis-
advantage to woman that she is forever cut off
from the opportunity of such service to her country,
to honor and duty. At that period we heard but
little of the emancipation of women, and though
the precious little we did hear was coupled with a
covert sneer, I grasped the emancipation idea from
one side only. I was determined women should
have the right to go to war. How enchanted I was
with the story of Semiramis or Catherine II: "She
made war upon this or that neighboring power —
she conquered this or that kingdom."

History is responsible for this training of youth
to the idea of the glory of war. From baby days
it is stamped upon the impressionable childish
mind that the God of Battles has ordained wars,
and that this divine ordinance regulates the history
of nations; that these are engaged in the fulfillment of immutable decree, a law of nature, like
tornadoes and earthquakes, which from time to
time will not be stemmed; that though atrocities and wickedness, sorrow and heart-breaking
anguish are bound up therewith, these cannot be
avoided, and must be recognized as a portion of
the inevitable. The magnitude of the result
attained for the advantage of the many justifies
the sacrifice of the happiness, the interests, or the
very life of the individual. Is there a nobler death
than comes in the line of duty on the field of honor
— a more enviable immortality than that of the
heroic soldier?

Lo! There it all stands clear as sunlight in all

the primers and readers for the use of schools, where, instead of a genuine history of the development of nations and humanity there are only long lists of battles, and wonderful and entrancing stories of the military prowess of individual heroes. It all belongs to what is popularly considered a necessary system for the development of patriotism. That every child shall be made a fit and willing defender of his country, his enthusiasm for this first duty of the citizen is most carefully cultivated. His natural sympathy with humanity, his instinctive horror of inflicting suffering upon others must be as carefully repressed. The inborn divine impulse of hatred for the barbarism and inhumanity of war becomes so warped by careless and superficial treatment of this part of the story that only the impression of the old national ideals, so useful for the aggrandizement of nations, can remain. And we succeed thereby in building up a valorous and war loving race.

The girls—who are not allowed to go into camp —being drilled out of the same books and subjected to the same system, develop a like admiration for war and the military service. Delightful pictures for gentle women—for we are told we must be tender and gentle—are delivered to us in frightful stories of carnage and rapine of all the battles of the earth from the Biblical and Macedonian and Punic down to those of the Thirty Years' and the Napoleonic wars. Naturally through such repetition one's perception of the horrors of the thing become calloused. Everything which according to the rubrics of war must be expected is no longer judged from the standpoint of humanity, but receives a quite special, mystical, historical, political sanctification. It must be—it *is* the source of highest dignity and honor. The girls have not learned all the military odes by heart for nothing. And so we hear of that stronger race, the Spartan mothers, and the women who present battle flags and regimental colors, and the numerous admirers

of brass buttons, who make the officers' corps play
the *rôle* of happy belles by their invitations during
the "German."

I was not educated in a convent, as is generally
the case in my rank of life, but had tutors and a
governess at home. I lost my mother early and
her place was in a measure filled to the children—
there were four of us—by an aunt. We spent our
winters in Vienna, our summers on the family estate in Lower Austria. Being an ambitious scholar,
blessed with a good memory, I was the joy of my
teachers. Since I could not attain the coveted
career of an heroic female warrior, I excited the
admiration of all around by my enthusiastic essays
upon those of either sex who had thus made the
world's history. French and English I acquired
perfectly. Of natural history, astronomy, and
physics I mastered all that was then considered
adapted to the feminine comprehension, but to the
history of nations there was no limitation, and I
devoured everything within reach in my father's
library. But for piano playing I had an unconquerable aversion. Long and earnestly I pleaded
to be excused from such a waste of precious time,
and finally by my obstinacy induced my father to
grant me immunity from this torment contrary to
the scandalized conviction of my aunt, that in so
doing I ignored the chief and most important part
of education.

On the tenth of March, 1857, I celebrated my
seventeenth birthday. " Already seventeen," I find
set down under this date. This "already" is a
poem. Without further commentary it seems to
signify "and nothing done for immortality."

It was arranged that during the approaching
carnival I should be introduced to society. This
gave me no such pleasure as is generally felt by
girls. I had some higher aims than ball-room conquests. What were these? I had frequently
asked myself this question without being able to

answer it. Possibly it was love I was unknowingly,
blindly waiting for. All these glowing aspirations
and ambitious dreams which swell the human
heart during the youth of either sex, and which
under all forms thirst for knowledge, for travel,
for action—seek gratification, are mostly only the
unrecognized struggles of an awakening desire for
love.

During the summer my aunt was ordered to try
the springs at Marienbad. She found it convenient to take me with her. Although my official
recognition in the social world was not to take
place until the following winter, I was allowed to
attend several small dancing parties—as a sort of
practice in behavior, so that I should not appear too
shy and awkward when that time came. But what
happened at the very first of these "re-unions?"
A serious, impassioned attachment. Of course the
object was an officer of the Hussars. Naturally I
had no eyes for civilians when the military were so
largely represented. Among the most brilliant of
this dashing branch of the service Count Arno
Dotzky was the leading star. Over six feet in
height, with black, curly hair, gleaming teeth, dark
eyes, piercing and tender—in short, upon the
question: "Can you give me the cotillion, Countess?" I was satisfied there were triumphs as
glowing as waving the oriflamme of France or
carrying the sceptre of Catherine II. And he, the
two-and-twenty years old lieutenant, dancing with
the prettiest girl in the room (after thirty years one
may be allowed to say so), flying down the hall in
waltzing time, doubtless thought: "For you, my
sweetheart, I would not exchange a marshal's
baton."

"But Martha, Martha!" scolded my aunt, as I
sank breathless upon the sofa at her side, covering
her with the swaying clouds of tulle of my dress.

"Oh pardon, pardon, Auntie," I exclaimed. "I
cannot help it."

"How can you conduct yourself in such a manner with that Hussar—and to look at a man in such a way!" she exclaimed. I reddened deeply. Had I behaved immodestly? And what would the incomparable creature himself think about it.

From these dismal doubts I was relieved during the evening when my adorer whispered anxiously:

"You must hear me—now, this evening: I love you."

That sounded rather different from the famous voices heard by Joan of Arc. But we were dancing and I could not answer him. He led me into a corner and eagerly continued:

"Answer, Countess, what have I to hope for."

"I do not understand you," I replied.

" Do you not really believe in love at first sight?"

Up to the present I had had grave doubts upon this subject.

"I throw myself upon your mercy," he exclaimed; "you or no other. Decide for life or death. Life is not worth having without you. Will you marry me?"

To such a furious and direct attack I was forced to answer. I should have liked to invent some diplomatic, dignified reply, which might leave him a fragment of hope and yet preserve my dignity, but could master nothing more than a very abashed "yes."

"Then I can call upon your aunt in the morning and write to Count Althaus."

Again "yes"—this time more courageously.

"What a happy man I am! So you loved me at first sight?"

This time I answered only with my eyes, which, however, uttered an unmistakable "yes."

We were betrothed on my eighteenth birthday, after which I was presented at court. Upon our marriage we undertook an Italian journey, for which purpose Arno was granted a long leave of absence. Of retirement from the army there was never a thought. True, we each possessed a handsome fortune, but my husband loved the service,

as I also did.   I was proud of my elegant Hussar
and looked forward to his certain promotion—to
be a captain, then of course a colonel, possibly a
military governor, or, who knew but he might become a field-marshal should glorious war give him
the opportunity to serve his country.

My note-books fail me entirely as to events during our honeymoon.   In truth, there are no notes
whatever of the happy periods of my life. I appear
in those long-lost years to have thought happiness
unworthy of record, while for every ail or peevish
humor of my past I found time to waste pen and
ink. As if when one went down into a rose garden,
one brought back naught but weeds and noxious
insects.

But I can remember it was a fairy story.   I had
all that woman's heart could wish—love, riches, rank
and health. We loved each other passionately, and,
as it chanced, my dashing Hussar was in addition
a manly, noble-hearted soul, with cultivated manners and a merry nature.   It would not have been
strange if he had turned out an evil and coarse man,
but heaven was kind.   I, on my part, might have
proved the most peevish, discontented of my sex,
but fortunately I was a cheerful, loving woman. It
was not our own discretion which preserved us from
a mistake.

At last I find one happy event set down—my
delight over my new dignity as mother.   On the
first of January our son was born.   Naturally this
event aroused as much astonishment and pride as
if we were the first pair to be so honored.   For a
time my journal was full of comment upon the
mystical and sacred province of a mother.   It is
the special aim of certain social rubrics entitled
"maternal love," "maternal happiness" and
"maternal pride," to magnify the office of a
mother. There is a class of literature and art carefully cultivated to this end, such as collections of
poems, baby songs, illustrated journals and picture
galleries, just as in another direction school books

are arranged for the fostering of an admiration and love of war. Next to hero worship comes baby worship. But ah! my son—my manly, noble Rudolph—the love of your and my mature years as far exceeds that baby worship as the character of the developed man excels the nature of the nursling.

The young father was not a little proud of his successor and planned the sunniest future. "What shall he be?" Of course, a soldier. Sometimes the mother would protest: "But he might be killed in battle." "Nonsense; and if he were, one dies but once, and where it is appointed one to die. We cannot help it." Besides, we should have other sons. Rudolph must be the soldier, like his father and his grandfather before him. So it was settled. At two months of age his vocation was marked out for him. His father saluted whenever he was brought into the room, and on his third monthly birthday he was promoted to the rank of corporal. On that same day a great anxiety darkened my life and I flew to my note-book to mark how heavy my heart had grown.

On the political horizon there had risen certain suspicious, black clouds, commented on daily by the press and wherever people congregated.

"There is going to be trouble with Italy," my father, my husband, and their military friends had frequently mentioned in my hearing. But I was too much occupied to bother myself with politics. But on that first of April Arno said to me:

"See here, Sweetheart—it will soon break out."

"What will break out?"

"The war with Sardinia."

I was terrified.

"Gracious God—that will be terrible! Must you go?"

"I hope so."

"How can you say that? Hope to leave your wife and child?"

"When duty calls."

"Then we must be reconciled. But hope—to wish that such a bitter duty——"

"Bitter? Why, such a dashing, jolly war will be glorious. You are a soldier's wife—do not forget that."

I threw myself into his arms.

"Yes, yes, I know. I can be brave. How often I have envied the heroes of history; how I have longed to go into battle. If I could only go with you!"

"All very fine, my wife, but impracticable. Your place is here, at the cradle of our child, who must grow up to be a defender of his country. Your place is at the fireside. To protect this from the attack of the enemy and secure peace for our homes and wives we men must go to war."

I do not know why these words, which in similar fashion I had read and admired, somehow this time sounded like hollow phrases. There was no advancing army; no barbarous horde stood at the door—simply a political complication between two cabinets. Though my husband insisted so enthusiastically upon going to war, there certainly was no pressing necessity to protect wife, child, and fatherland. It was mere love of adventure, ambition, justifiable ambition, a delight in bravely doing one's duty. It was very fine in him if he must go into the field, and one could still hope. This and similar reasoning and lamentation fill several pages of my note-book. Louis Napoleon is denounced as an intriguer; Austria can not endure it, and war will surely come, etc., etc.

The house was full of officers excitedly discussing the situation; my father was all fire and fury, and his reminiscences became more diffuse. The vital question, namely, what would be lost or won, what every battle would cost in untold sacrifice of blood and tears, was never for one moment considered. The fate of the individual was so entirely lost sight of in the consideration of the so-claimed general interest that I felt myself ashamed of the recurring thought: "Ah, how will victory recompense the dead, the crippled, and the widowed?"

How would it be if the enemy conquered? This question I tremulously asked one evening of our military friends and was contemptuously crushed by their rejoinder. Even the utterance of such a thought, the very shadow of a doubt was unpatriotic. It was part of the duty of a soldier to believe himself invincible. It was also in a certain measure the duty of a soldier's wife to believe the same.

My husband's regiment was quartered in Vienna. From our house we had a view of the Prater, and when one looked out of the window summer seemed at hand. It was a wonderful spring. Earlier than usual the foliage had come out, and we looked forward with delight to the drives in the Prater, which it was fashionable to begin the coming month.

"Now, thank God, the uncertainty is at an end!" cried my husband, as he returned after parade on the nineteenth of April. "The ultimatum has been issued."

I trembled. "How—what does that mean?"

"It means that the last word of the diplomatic negotiations has been uttered. Our ultimatum demands of Sardinia that she disarm, which she of course will not do, and we will soon march over the border."

"Great God! But perhaps she will disarm."

"Then there would be no war."

I fell upon my knees; I could not help it. Speechless and yet almost with a shriek from the depths of my soul rose the prayer to Heaven, "Peace, peace."

Arno lifted me up.

"What do you mean, you silly child! Do you forget you are a general's daughter, a lieutenant's wife and"—with a laugh—"a corporal's mother."

"No, no," I cried, "I scarcely know myself. I know how I used to thirst for military glory, but when you come and tell me that a yes or no decides whether thousands live or die—die suddenly, cruelly

in these bright, sunny, blessed days of spring, it
seems to me all must pray for peace—must fall
upon their knees——"

"In order to inform the Lord all about it, you
precious goose!"

The door bell rang. I hastily dried my tears. It
was my father who came in with a rush.

"Now children," he cried breathlessly, "do you
want to hear the news?"

"I have just told my wife."

"What do you think, Father," I asked anxiously;
"will the war be abandoned?"

"I never heard that an ultimatum prevented a
war. It would certainly be very wise of the miserable Italian pack if they would yield and run no
risk of a second Novara. I can see already how
our Lombardy and Venetian territory can be en-
larged by a piece of Piedmont. I can see our
troops enter Turin."

"But really, Father, you talk as if the war had
begun. Think, Arno may have to go."

"Of course—he is to be envied."

"But the danger—my anxiety—"

"Pshaw! danger! One can come home from war.
I have gone through more than one campaign,
been wounded more than once, and am still alive,
because I was not predestined to die."

The same old fatalistic notion!

"Should my regiment not be ordered out——"
began Arno.

"Is that possible," I exclaimed joyously.

"In that case I shall apply for an exchange."

"That can soon be settled," my father assured
him. "Hess is to command the corps and he is
a good friend of mine."

I was sick with anxiety, and yet I could not but
admire my husband and father. I must control
myself. My husband was a hero. I sprang up
and exclaimed: "Arno, I am proud of you!"

"That's a brave wife. You have trained your
girl well, Father-in-law."

On the twenty-sixth of April war was declared by the rejection of the ultimatum.

Arno brought the news home and I could not control my despair. I threw myself upon the sofa, burying my head in the cushions.

"My darling, courage! Things are not so bad. In a short time it will be over and we shall be happier than ever. I could not let my comrades go, and remain at home. I must pass through the baptism of fire—until I do that I scarce feel myself a man. Just think how lovely it will be if I come home with three stars on my collar, perhaps a cross on my breast."

I leaned my head on his shoulder and wept unrestrainedly. At this moment the cold glitter of stars and crosses seemed of slight consequence. Ten rewards of honor upon this dear breast would be no recompense for the dreaded possibility that a bullet might shatter it forever.

Arno kissed me on the forehead, put me gently to one side and stood up.

"I must go to the Colonel now, dear child. Cry yourself out, and when I return I hope to find you in better spirits. I shall need them to keep off anxious presentiments. Now, at such a decisive moment, my own little wife will do nothing to rob me of my courage nor hinder my return to duty. Good-by, my sweetheart."

I endeavored to control myself. His last words still sounded in my ears. It was clear; not only was it my duty not to depress his courage, but if possible I must incite his sense of duty. That is the only way we women have to show our patriotism and prove ourselves in sympathy with the fame which they may win on the battlefield. "Battlefield!"—singular how this word now presented itself to my mind with two widely different significations. At one moment with the old-fashioned, historical, pathetic, half-wondering admiration, then with the shuddering repulsion of the bloody, brutal syllables, "battle." Yes, they would

lie slaughtered on the field, these thousands of
human beings now urged into action — lie there
with open, bleeding wounds — and among them,
perhaps—with a loud shriek I gave utterance to
my thoughts.

My maid, Betty, ran into the room, frightened at
the sound of my cry.

"In God's name, Countess, what is the matter?"
she exclaimed anxiously.

I looked at the girl. Her eyes were red with
weeping. I remembered that her sweetheart was
a soldier. I felt as if I could press this sister-in-
misery to my heart.

"It is nothing, my child," I said softly. "Those
who go out may come back again."

"Not all of them, dear Countess; not all," she
began with a new outburst of tears.

My aunt came in to comfort me, she said, and
to preach resignation.

"The whole town is on fire; this war is very
popular."

"The town rejoice?" I exclaimed.

"Certainly, wherever no loved member of the
family is obliged to go there is general rejoicing.
Your father will be here soon to congratulate, not
condole with, you. He regards this as a magnificent opportunity for Arno. Upon the whole he is
right. For a soldier there is nothing better than
war; he must fulfill his destiny. What must
be——"

"Yes, yes, I know, the inevitable——"

"That which God wills," continued Aunt Marie
encouragingly.

"One must accept with resignation and humility."

"Bravely said, Martha. All will turn out as the
all-wise and beneficent Providence has determined.
The hour of death is settled for all of us as is the
hour of birth. And we will pray so earnestly for
our dear soldiers."

I was not just then prepared to analyze the
contradiction involved in the two suggestions:

that death was inexorably determined and yet that we must pray that it be averted. I had no very clear perception, in fact only a vague notion that in the treatment of such sacred themes one had better not ask too many leading questions, certainly never appeal to the reason. It is the highest breach of theological etiquette to question the rationality of any dogma. Not to think was so much more comfortable that I accepted the suggestion of intervention by prayer. Yes, during the whole absence of my husband I prayed continually for the protection of Heaven, that all bullets might be diverted from his breast. Diverted! In what direction? Toward the breast of some other man for whom some other woman was also praying? And had I not had it drilled into me by my tutors that any substance hurled at such and such a momentum would strike such and such an object? Again a doubt? It was bewildering. Away with it!

"Yes, Aunt," I said aloud, rousing myself from these contradictions, "we will pray diligently and God will hear us. Arno will return to us sound and well."

"See, my child, how in the hour of trial the soul flees to religion for comfort. Perhaps the dear Lord sends this affliction to prove your spirit and rouse your lukewarm faith."

I was again not very clear as to how it was possible that all this complication (dating from the Crimea) between Sardinia and Austria, this outbreak of grim war, should have been brought about for the purpose of testing my lukewarm faith. But to express such a doubt was not decent. So soon as the appeal to God is made and his name appended to any statement, it henceforth receives a certain sort of consecrated immunity. In regard to the accusation of my indifference to sacred things Aunt Marie was right. She was sincerely devout. I was not trained to any such observance. My father and husband were indifferent to reli-

gious matters, and the exhortations to accept all
dogma taught, without protest or question, had not
suited my reasoning nature. I went every Sunday
to mass and once a year to confession; at such
times I was honestly devout, but the whole was all
a matter of the observance of ecclesiastical etiquette, just as I danced the lancers at a ball or
made the conventional courtesy when the empress
entered the ball-room. Our chaplain in Lower
Austria and the nuncio in Vienna had no right to
reproach me, but the accusation of indifference
made by my aunt was justifiable.

"Yes, my child," continued my aunt, "in days of
happiness and health people forget their Saviour;
but when death or sorrow comes upon us, or our
own lives are in danger——"

In this style she would have run on forever had
not the door been torn open and my father, rushing
in, exclaimed:

"Hurrah! it is decided. They want a good
thrashing, the rascals—now they will get it."

It was a trying time. War had broken out. One
forgets that there are but two antagonistic forces,
and people talk as if there were some mighty third
party which set these two at each other's throats.
Hence the whole responsibility is thrown upon this
mysterious force which regulates the fate of peoples. Of a revolt against war as a system there
was at this period of my life no trace; I only
suffered because my beloved husband was forced
to go and I to remain at home. I dragged again
to light for consolation all my old carefully cultivated convictions as to the highest duty of a soldier being a readiness for service and a laudable
desire for honor and glory. I lived now in a stirring epoch. This was an inspiriting reflection.
Since times of war, from the days of Herodotus
and Tacitus down to modern historians, had been
treated as the most important in the development
of man, I consoled myself with the idea of forming

part and parcel of one of the landmarks of history. This conception of war was the general one. Nothing else was talked of on the streets or in the parlor; we read nothing else in the newspapers; we prayed for nothing in the churches save the success of our armies; wherever we went earnest faces and excited voices showed that people had no thought for other matters. Business, amusement, art—all were but secondary affairs. It seemed at times as if we had scarce the right to think of anything else while this great struggle over the world's fate hung in the balance. The frequent proclamations couched in the well-known phrases confident of victory and prophesying national renown; the glitter and clash of arms and waving of battle flags as the troops marched through; the stirring public orations and newspaper articles glowing with patriotic ardor, this eternal appeal to virtue, honor, duty, courage, sacrifice; the recurring assurances of the unconquerable justice of our cause, defended by the noblest and best of nations. All these established a sort of heroic atmosphere, which filled the whole people with enthusiasm and roused a general conviction of our being the noblest citizens of the noblest of times.

Evil passions, such as thirst for conquest, brawling, rapine, cruelty, all iniquity were regarded as a necessary adjunct, but of course these offenses were perpetrated only by the enemy, whose villainy all the world must acknowledge. Consequently, quite aside from the justice of our cause, we would do the world a service by properly punishing the perpetrators of all these wrongs. These wretched Italians—what a lazy, vicious, treacherous, volatile, and upstart nation! and this Louis Napoleon—what a combination of intrigue and inordinate ambition! When on the twenty-ninth of April his famous proclamation appeared with the motto: "Italy shall be free to the Adriatic," what a storm of indignation was roused in Vienna.

I imprudently allowed myself to assert that it seemed to me this was an unselfish and noble idea,

but was quickly brought to my senses by enthusiastic patriots, who, so long as Louis Napoleon was
our enemy, could see no jot or tittle of good in
him. But a faint doubt arose in my mind. In all
historical accounts of wars I had always found the
admiration and sympathy of the writer on the side
of that party struggling to throw off a foreign yoke
and battling for national independence. Possibly
I knew not the right interpretation of the terms
"yoke" and "freedom," for otherwise I could not but
see that Italy, not Austria, was the one struggling
to these ends. But my feeble protestations were
scowlingly received and I was given distinctly to
understand that our government—that is, the government under which we chanced to live—could
never impose a yoke upon a people, its supremacy
could not but be a blessing; that those seeking to
assert their independence of us, and demanding
their freedom, were always "rebels," and that, in
short, we, and only we, were always in the right.

Early in May—they were cold and rainy days
fortunately ; sunny, joyous spring weather would
have made a more painful contrast—Arno's regiment was ordered into the field. In the morning
at seven o'clock he was due at the station. Ah!
that night before—that dreadful night! Parting
in such sorrow, and war so terrible.

Arno had fallen asleep. Breathing quietly he
lay there with a smiling face. I lit a fresh candle
and set it behind a screen. I could not endure
darkness. For me, on this last night, sleep was
impossible. Throwing on a wrapper I lay quietly
beside him, and with one elbow supporting my
head watched him, weeping quietly the while. I
dared not stir, sleep was so necessary for him. For
six hours I still had him.

Ah! six o'clock. The orderly tapped on the
door.

Arno instantly rose and dressed himself rapidly,
cheering me up with all manner of hopeful words.

"Courage, Martha! It will all be over in two
months and I shall be safe at home again. Nonsense!

out of a thousand bullets only one hits the mark.
Other men have returned from war—there is your
father. It had to be. You did not marry a Hussar to cultivate hyacinths for you. I will write as
often as possible and report what a jolly campaign
it is. If anything were going to happen to me I
could not be so cheerful. I am going to win a
decoration, that is all. Take care of yourself and
Rudolph. It will be something for him to hear his
father talk about the war of '59."

Again the orderly tapped on the door.

"Good-by, my wife"—his voice broke—a kiss,
the very last, and he was gone.

To scrape lint, read newspaper reports, and stick
pins fastened to little flags on maps of the seat of
war, in order to locate the movements of both armies, as if it were a game of chess where Austria
was expected to say, "In four moves checkmate";
to go to church daily to pray for the success and
safety of our side—such was the entire occupation
of all of us. We ate, drank, and read; attended to
necessary business; but all in a perfunctory manner. Nothing was of any consequence save the
despatches from Italy. The only gleam of light
was when I received letters from Arno. These were
always short—he was not given to letter writing—
but they brought me the happy assurance of his
safety. Necessarily these letters were irregular;
communication was sometimes cut off, and at the
approach of action mails were forbidden. When
several days passed without hearing from him I
suffered the deepest anxiety. After a battle I read
the list of killed with the greatest apprehension.
The first time I looked through the list—I had
heard nothing for days—when I saw that the name
of Arno Dotzky was not there, I folded my hands
and softly prayed, "My God, I thank thee." Scarce
had I uttered the words when a shrill dissonance
struck me to the heart. I took up the list again.
Ah! because Adolph Schmidt and Karl Müller and

many, many others—but not Arno Dotzky—remained upon the field, I thanked God. Certainly, those who trembled for Adolph Schmidt or Karl Müller would also thank God, should they read Arno Dotzky instead of the name they dreaded to find. And why should my thanks be more grateful to Heaven than theirs? Yes, that was the shrill dissonance of my prayer: the selfishness and arrogance which lay therein and could cause me to thank God that I was spared, when Schmidt's mother and Müller's wife, reading the list, wept out their breaking hearts.

On the same day I again heard from Arno:

"Yesterday we had another serious engagement, unfortunately again a defeat. But cheer up, Sweetheart, the next time we will assuredly win the battle. This was my first great affair. I stood in the midst of a thick shower of bullets—a singular feeling; I will tell you about it when we meet; it is frightful. The poor fellows fall all around us, and we must leave them despite their piteous entreaties. When we enter Turin, to dictate terms of peace, you can meet me there. Aunt Marie can take care of little Rudolph until your return."

If the arrival of such letters formed the sunlight of my existence, the blackest shadows settled down upon my nights. When I awoke from the blessed forgetfulness of dreamless sleep the fearful reality with the more fearful possibility forbade my again closing my eyes. I could not overcome the dread that Arno might at that moment be dying in a ditch—longing, longing for a drop of water and calling despairingly on me. I could not free myself from this idea until with a wrench to recover my self-control I succeeded in imagining his happy return. Was not this as probable as his death?

My father was sadly depressed. One bad report followed another. First Montebello, then Magenta. Not he alone, all Vienna was disheartened. Every one had been so certain of victory that they already talked of decorating the houses with flags and of singing Te Deums in the churches. Instead of this

they were waving flags and the priests were chant-
ing Te Deums in Turin. There they were thanking God that he had helped them defeat the odi-
ous Austrians.

"Father, in case of another defeat do you not
think that peace would be declared?" I asked him
one day.

"Are you not ashamed to suggest such a thing,"
he exclaimed. "It had far better be a seven, nay,
a thirty years' war. We must fight until we can
dictate terms and compel them to lay down their
arms. What do we go to war for if we have to end
it as soon as possible? In that case we had better
stay at home."

"I think so myself," I sighed.

"What cowards women are! Why, you were well
grounded in patriotism, and now you value your
personal quiet more than the welfare and honor
of your country."

"Yes, because I love my Arno better."

"Family love—wedded love—that is all very fine,
but it takes second rank."

"Should it?"

The list of fatalities contained the names of
several officers personally known to me. Among
others that of the son—the only son—of an old lady
I greatly respected. I felt as if I must go to her.
Comfort her I could not—at the most I could but
weep with her. When I arrived at her house I
hesitated before I rang the bell. The last time I
had been there it was at a merry dancing party.
That night the dignified, charming old lady had
said to me: "Martha, we are the most enviable
women in Vienna. You have the handsomest husband and I the noblest son." And to-day? Have
I still a husband—who knows? Shot and shell
were flying even then, and at any moment I might
be a widow. I rang the bell. No one answered,
but the door of an adjoining apartment opened.

"You will ring in vain, Madam—the house is empty."

"Where is Frau von Ullsman?"

"She was taken to the insane asylum three days ago."

For a few moments I stood motionless and pictured the scenes which must have preceded the time when madness followed agony. And my father would have war last thirty years—for the good of the country! How many mothers would lose the light of reason?

Deeply moved I descended the steps meaning to visit a young friend whose husband was also at the seat of war. I passed the building used as a storehouse by the patriotic Relief Corps. At that time there was no Red Cross service, and this humane institution had been organized to distribute all needed supplies, which the people eagerly offered for the sick and wounded. I entered; I felt impelled to offer the money in my purse to the committee. It might save some poor fellow—and keep his mother from the madhouse. I knew the president. "Can I see Prince C——," I asked.

"He is not in at present, but the vice-president, Baron L——, is here."

The man pointed the way to the office where all money contributions were received. I passed through several rooms where upon long tables were piled up packages of linen, cigars, tobacco, and wines—but mostly mountains of bandages. I shuddered. How many wounds must bleed to need all those rolls. "And my father," I thought again, "would for the good of the country have this war last thirty years. How many defenders of their country would survive their wounds?" Baron L—— received my money thankfully and gave me much information in regard to the practical service of the relief corps. An old gentleman entered and, sinking upon a chair, drew out his purse, from which he took a hundred-florin bill.

"Allow me," he said, "to give my little toward your noble work. I am an old soldier (Field Mar-

shal-Lieut. X——, introducing himself) and know
its value. I served in the campaigns of 1809–1813
and at that time we had no patriotic relief corps;
no one sent the wounded pillows and bandages.
The insufficient supplies of the surgeons could not
prevent thousands from suffering a hideous death.
It is a philanthropic, humane work, and you can
scarce realize the good you do." And the old man
went away with tears in his eyes.

A commotion outside was explained by the announcement: "Her majesty, the Empress!"

I looked from my quiet corner at the beautiful
face of our youthful sovereign, who in her simple
walking costume was even more charming than in
the full dress of court balls.

"I have come," she gently said to Baron L——,
"because I have just had a letter from the
Emperor, who desired me to visit the Relief Corps
and assure you of the great good your supplies are
doing at the seat of war."

With lively interest she went through the building examining the supplies. She took up a roll of
linen. "See how fine it is, and how beautifully
sewed," she exclaimed. "It is a noble, patriotic
undertaking which the poor soldiers——"

I did not understand the rest. "Poor soldiers"
The words sounded deeply sympathetic. Poor
indeed, and the more supplies we could send them
the better. But it came into my head to doubt the
necessity of sending the poor fellows out to endure
all this suffering. Why not keep them at home?
I drove away the thought. We sent them because
we must. Other excuse there is none for the horrors of war than this—it must be.

I went on my way. In passing a book-store I
remembered that our map of the seat of war was
worn to tatters. A number of people were there,
all demanding the same thing. When my turn
came the proprietor asked: "A map, Madam?"

"You have guessed right."

"That is easy enough; people buy nothing else
nowadays."

While wrapping it up he remarked to a gentleman standing near:

"It is a hard time for the authors of literary or scientific works, Professor. So long as the war lasts no one is in the least interested in anything else."

"And a bad time for the nation," replied the Professor. "It results in intellectual degeneration."

"And my father," thought I for the third time, "for the good of the country, would have the war last thirty years."

"So your business is bad?" I asked.

"Not mine alone. Everything is at a standstill. With the exception of the army contractors there is no class of business men which the war does not injure enormously. Manufacturers fail and factory hands are out of employment; there are not enough laborers for the farms; large numbers of human beings are out of work and starving. Stocks fall, gold rises, all enterprise is stifled, numerous firms go into bankruptcy; in short, it is misery—nothing but misery."

"And my father," I repeated to myself as I left the book-store.

I found my friend at home. Countess Lori Griesbach was in more than one sense the sharer of the same fate as mine. She was also a general's daughter, had married an officer a short time before, and her husband as well as two brothers was in the service. But Lori was not of an anxious nature. She was firmly convinced that these members of her family were all under the special protection of the saints, and she confidently reckoned upon their return. She received me with open arms.

"Ah, how lovely of you to come! But you look pale and worried. Any bad news from the seat of war?"

"No, thank God. But the whole thing is so terrible——"

"Oh, you mean the defeat? That doesn't amount to anything; the next report will be of a victory."

"Defeat or victory, war is horrible. How much better it would be if we had no war."

"Mercy on us! What would become of the military profession?"

"Why, we should not need any."

"How can anybody be so silly!" she exclaimed. "That would be a fine sort of life—nobody but civilians. I shudder at the thought. Fortunately it is impossible."

"Impossible! Well, it may be. But I could imagine it as possible."

"What do you mean?"

"The disbanding of armies. But no, one might as well expect to prevent earthquakes."

"I cannot make out what you are talking about. So far as I am concerned I was rejoiced when this war broke out in order that my Louis might have the chance to distinguish himself. It is a good thing for my brothers also. Promotions are so slow in times of peace. Now they will have a——"

"Have you heard from them recently?" I interrupted.

"Not very long since. But you know how uncertain the post is, and after an engagement they are so tired, they do not feel like letter-writing. But I am satisfied. Louis and my brothers wear consecrated amulets. Mamma hung them round their necks herself."

"How can you imagine a war where every man on each side wears an amulet, Lori? When the bullets fly here and there are they going to be diverted to the clouds?"

"I never understand you, Martha; you are so lukewarm in your faith. Your Aunt Marie complains greatly of you."

"Why do you not answer my question?"

"Because you are deriding what is sacred to me."

"Derision! not at all. Simply a reasonable suggestion."

" You know very well that it is a sin to trust to
private judgment in things too sacred for us to
discuss."

"I will be quiet, Lori. You may be right. Reason and logic are dangerous. All sorts of doubts
arise in me, and I suffer torment in trying to solve
them. If I lost the conviction that it was absolutely necessary to begin this war, I could not forgive the one who——"

"You mean Louis Napoleon? He is certainly an
intriguer."

"Whoever it is, I am inclined to believe that it
is no human being who causes war, but that it
breaks out of itself, like a nervous fever or an
eruption of Vesuvius."

"What a state of mind you are in. Let us talk
sensibly. Listen to me. The campaign will soon
be over, and our two husbands will come back cap-
tains. I shall not give mine any peace until he
gets a leave of absence and takes me to a watering
place. It will do him good after all the privations
he has undergone, and me also; for this heat, this
dullness, and this anxiety are wearing me out. For
you must not think I have no anxiety. If it is
God's will that my husband should die—what is
more noble, more enviable than a gallant soldier's
death, on the field of honor, for God and country?"

"You talk like the latest army proclamation."

"Well, it would be dreadful for poor Mamma to
lose Gustav or Carl. But we will not talk about
it. As I was saying, we will have an amusing season—I think in Carlsbad. I was there once when
I was a girl, and had a glorious time."

"And I was at Marienbad. There I met my
Arno. But why are we sitting here idle? Get
some linen and let us make bandages. I have just
come from the warehouse of the Patriotic Relief
Corps——"

We were here interrupted. A servant brought in
a letter.

"From Gustav!" cried Lori joyfully. After read-

ing a few lines she threw down the letter with an
outburst of tears.

"Lori—dear heart, what is it?" I exclaimed.

"Read," she gasped.

I lifted the letter from the floor and began to
read. I can remember every word to this day, as
I afterwards borrowed it to copy in my diary.

"Read aloud," she begged, "I could not finish."

"DEAR SISTER:
Yesterday we had a severe engagement. There
will be a tremendous list of dead and wounded. In order
that you may prepare our poor mother, tell her that he
is severely wounded, but the truth is our brave Carl died
for his country."

I stopped to embrace my friend and then continued, tears choking my voice.

"Your husband is safe as well as myself. If the enemy's ball had only struck me. I envy Carl his heroic
death; he fell at the beginning of the battle and is saved
the knowledge that it was a defeat. That is the bitter
part. I saw him fall, for we rode close together. I
sprang off to raise him—a glance and I saw he was dead.
The ball must have gone through the heart or lungs; it
was a quick, painless death. How many others lay helpless and suffering untold agony throughout the battle
before death released them. It was a fearful day; more
than a thousand bodies—friend and foe—covered the
field. I found among the dead so many dear, well-known
faces. Among others poor Arno Dotzky."

I fell insensible to the floor.

"It is all over, Martha! Solferino has decided it.
We are beaten."

With these words my father came to the corner
of the garden where I was sitting, under the shadow
of a linden.

I had gone back with my little Rudolph to the
home of my girlhood. Eight days after the blow
which left me a widow I returned with my family
to Grumitz, our estate in Lower Austria. All
were with me as before my marriage: father,

aunt, my little brother, and two half-grown sisters. Everything was done to mitigate my grief and all treated me with a reverential sympathy which touched my heart. Next to the blood poured out by the soldiers upon the altar of their country the tears of soldiers' mothers, wives, and children are the holiest libation. There was also a certain pride in the knowledge which remained to comfort me of the conventional, heroic dignity which attaches to all who die upon the field of honor.

Particulars as to Arno's death I had never been able to obtain. They had found, recognized, and buried him—that was all. His last thought was certainly of me and our little child, and his consolation in his last moments must have been: "I have done, more than done, my duty."

"We are beaten," repeated my father, seating himself on the bench at my side.

"And the victims were sacrificed needlessly" I sighed.

"The victims are to be envied, for they do not know the disgrace of their country. But we will soon gather ourselves together, if, as it appears, peace is concluded."

"Ah, God grant it!" I interrupted him. "For me it is too late, but what may it not spare thousands of others."

"You think of nothing but of yourself and private individuals. But this is a matter for Austria."

"Well, does not Austria consist of individual human beings."

"My child, an empire, a state, has a longer and more important existence than individuals. These disappear, generation after generation, while the empire develops farther, grows in fame, extent, and power, or sinks, dwindles, and disappears, if it allows other states to surpass it. Therefore it is most important, and the highest duty of each individual, to strive, suffer, and even die that the greatness, the extent, the welfare of the state shall survive and increase."

These instructive words I impressed upon my mind, in order that I might write them down in my note-book. They sounded to me curiously like what I used to read in my school books, words which in my anxiety and sorrow I had forgotten; and I determined to hug them to my heart for the comfort and consolation they would give me when I reflected that in the loss of my husband I had done my share toward this important matter.

Aunt Marie had also other grounds for consolation to offer me. "Do not weep, dear child," she was accustomed to say, when she found me sunk in profound grief. "Do not be so selfish as to mourn for the one who is now so much better off. He is among the saints, and looks down and blesses you. Only a few fleeting years and you will meet him again in glory. For those who die on the field of battle heaven has prepared a special abiding place. Happy are they who, when performing a sacred duty, are called to its enjoyment. Next in desert to the dying martyr comes the dying soldier."

"So I am to rejoice that Arno——"

"Rejoice; no—that is too much to expect. But endure your fate with resignation. Heaven has sent it as a trial to purify your heart and increase your faith."

"So in order to purify my heart and increase my faith Arno——"

"No, no; but who can, who dare attempt to comprehend the mysterious ways of Providence?"

Although Aunt Marie's consolation was rather distracting, I managed to accept the somewhat mystical conception, and endeavored to believe that my dear victim enjoyed in heaven the reward of his sacrifice, and that his memory among men was kept alive by the glorified heroism of his death.

The day before our departure from Vienna I was present at the services at St. Stephens in honor of the dead. The *De Profundis* was sung for all who had fallen and lay buried in a foreign land. In the middle of the church a large catafalque had been erected, surrounded by hundreds of burning candles and decorated with military emblems, flags, guns, and side arms. The choir sang the grand, pathetic requiem, and the congregation—mostly women clothed in mourning—wept aloud. And each one wept, not for her own alone, but for all who had met the same fate. They had all, these poor, brave brothers, given up their young lives for us, that is, for their country and the honor of the nation. And the living soldiers who stood in the background, from several regiments remaining in Vienna, were ready and willing, without hesitation, without complaint, without fear, to follow in the footsteps of their comrades. Yes, these clouds of incense, these swelling organ-tones, these humble petitions, these blinding tears must have risen to a well-pleased Heaven, and the God of Battles must have dropped down his blessing upon the graves of those for whom this catafalque was erected.

At least that is what I thought at that time and wrote in my journal.

Fourteen days after the report of the defeat of Solferina came the news of the peace of Villa Franca. My father took all manner of pains to explain to me how necessary for political reasons this peace had become, whereupon I assured him that for my part I was satisfied to see an end of all this fighting and dying.

"You must not think for one instant," he continued, "that in making peace we compromise our own dignity. It was not Solferino which compelled us, but far more important considerations. We refrain now in order to protect later other provinces ruled by branches of our imperial house. This Sardinian robber-captain, aided by this miserable French intriguer, may venture to attack other portions of Italy. They will move against Modena and Tuscany, and probably will even fall upon Rome and the Pope—the vandals! If we now surrender Lombardy we still retain Venice, and can protect the South Italian States and the Holy See. You can comprehend, therefore, that for purely political reasons it is now our wisest course to make peace——"

" Yes, yes," I interrupted him, "I understand it all. It is a pity they had not thought of this before Magenta," I sighed heavily. Then, to change the conversation, I directed his attention to a package of books just arrived from Vienna.

" See here, the bookseller sends us among other things a work which he recommends as marking an epoch in modern thought. It is the work of an English scientist named Darwin, 'The Origin of Species.'"

"He can just let me alone," my father replied. "Who wants, in such stirring times as these, to bother one's self about such rubbish? How can a book about the origin of plant and animal life mark an epoch? Yes, the confederation of the Italian States, the consolidation of Austria—they are epoch-marking matters. They will live in history long after this English book has been forgotten. Remember that."

I have remembered it.

SECOND BOOK.

TIME OF PEACE.

FOUR years have passed. My sisters—now seventeen and eighteen years of age—were to be presented at court. I determined to take the opportunity of returning to the great world of society.

Intervening time had done its work and had tempered my grief. Despair was followed by sorrow, sorrow by melancholy, melancholy by listlessness, and this in turn by a renewed interest in life. I awoke one morning to the consciousness that I was actually in a position to be envied. I was twenty-three, handsome, rich, the mother of a charming boy and one of an affectionate family. Were these not conditions sufficient to make life enjoyable?

The short year of my married life lay behind me like a dream. I had dearly loved my handsome Hussar, his devotion had made me very happy, the separation had caused me great sorrow, his loss profound grief; but it was all in the shadowy past. Our life together had been too short for the growth of a close sympathy. We had worshipped each other like a pair of fiery lovers, but we had known nothing of that mutual respect and friendship which is felt by those husbands and wives who for long years have shared joy and sorrow. I had not been indispensable to him, for in that case he would never have felt impelled to go into the field, as his own regiment had not left Vienna. In the four years I had gradually developed into a different being; my intellectual horizon had greatly broadened, and I had attained a degree of knowledge and its attendant culture with which I felt sure Arno would have been little in sympathy.

How had this change been brought about?

A year of my widowhood had passed and despair
—first phase—had merged into a deep, depressing
sorrow. Of society I would hear nothing. I imagined my future as devoted to the education of
my son, who became the sole hope and pride of my
existence. I buried myself in the treasures of our
large library, and as before history became a passion. Since actual war had torn so much from me
and my contemporaries, my former enthusiasm had
considerably abated, but I vigorously fanned the
old passion into life. I found a certain consolation, when reading reports of noted battlefields, in
the reflection that the death of my poor husband
and my own widowhood were but a repetition of
an old, old story. Sometimes this was the case
—not always. It was scarcely possible for me to
transplant myself even in imagination to that earlier period of my girlhood when Joan of Arc was
my ideal.

I soon exhausted the resources of our library and
wrote to our agent in Vienna for any new books he
might have on hand. He sent Thomas Buckle's
"History of Civilization." "An incomplete work,"
he replied, "but so far as they go the two volumes
are a logical whole and their appearance has excited the liveliest interest in England, as also
throughout the civilized world. The author has
laid the foundation of a new conception of history."

New, indeed! After I had read and re-read the
volumes it seemed to me that I had hitherto
passed my life cramped in a narrow valley, but had
now come upon the mountain tops, from which
could be seen a broad stretch of country covered
with towns and gardens and bordered by a bound-
less ocean. I will not maintain that I—a twenty-
year-old woman, who had received only the conventional superficial education granted to her sex—
comprehended the full grandeur of the landscape
(to carry on the metaphor) spread out before me.
But I was dazzled, was overmastered by it; I realized that beyond the narrow limits of my old hori-

zon there lay a mighty world of which I hitherto
knew nothing. Years later, when trained by much
other reading, when I again took up the work, I
could humbly claim that I really grasped its broad
and noble meaning. But this much I seized at
once: the history of humanity cannot be told
through stories of kings and statesmen; nor of wars
and treaties which are the result of the ambition of
one and the chicanery of the other, but is to be
learned only through the progressive development
of intelligence. The chronicles of courts and battles, which compose the chief part of books of history, may present particular phases of the civilization of the time, but not its underlying causes.
I found in Buckle not a trace of the glamour with
which historians are accustomed to invest the lives
of mighty warriors and devastators of countries.
On the contrary, he convinces us that the respect
for the profession of arms is in inverse ratio to the
civilization of the people; the farther we descend
into the barbaric past, the more frequent the appeal to violence and the narrower the bounds of
peace; we find province against province, town
against town, family against family. He maintains
that in the progress of society not only war, but all
love of military renown engendered by the stories
of the past will cease to be. He appealed to the
convictions of my own heart, which I had often
repressed as cowardly and unworthy, but which I
now joyfully recognize as being but the faint reflection of the growing spirit of the times. I at one
time attempted to talk with my father upon this
subject. But in vain—he would not climb with me
to the mountain top—that is to say, he would not
read the book.

Then followed the year—my second phase—
when sorrow became melancholy. I read and
studied with renewed ardor, and while brain and
heart developed melancholy disappeared. There
came a time when books grew wearisome to me,
the joy in existence reawakened, and all the 'olo-

gies and 'graphies in the world could not afford content. And so it came about that in the winter of 1863 I chaperoned my sisters, and opened my house to Vienna society.

" Martha, Countess Dotzky, a rich young widow." Under this oft-repeated description I soon found myself a player in the comedy of society.

It was assumed by my family that I would marry again. Aunt Marie no longer referred in her homilies to the soldier saint above patiently waiting for me. For if in the few short years between me and the grave I saw fit to take unto myself a second husband, this fact might prejudice the prospect of a pleasant meeting there.

All of those about me seemed to have forgotten Arno's existence—all save myself. One may cease to mourn the dead, but forgotten they should never be. I regarded this silence in regard to those lost to us as a second death, and to keep my husband's memory green I taught my little Rudolph to speak daily of him, and at night to add to his evening prayer: "God keep me good and brave for love of my father Arno."

We sisters enjoyed ourselves immensely. It was really my own debut. During the short time I had seen the world and society before my marriage I was a betrothed bride, hence I had missed the chief attraction in the comedy—the love-making. But now, though I enjoyed being surrounded by a crowd of admirers, I could not easily get on with them. A barrier lay between them and me which seemed insurmountable. All these dashing young gentlemen (chiefly officers in the regular service), who appeared absorbed in amusement, horses, play and the ballet, could not have the faintest conception of the things of which I thought and read. That language of which I had but learned the alphabet, but through which I knew the men of science were solving the noblest riddles, was to these gay butterflies not merely "Spanish," but Patagonian.

Among this tribe I should certainly find no husband, and I was only concerned for the sake of
my good name that no compromising notion that
I allowed love-making should mount into their
feathery brains. But in all else—the dance, the
theatre, and dress—I played my *rôle* with a light
heart. I neither neglected my little Rudolph nor
failed to keep informed in regard to all the tendencies of the literature of the day. This latter occupation certainly did not tend toward the lowering
of the barriers between me and my fashionable
adorers. I would gladly have entertained in my
salon the distinguished men of the scientific and
literary world of Vienna. But in the circle to
which I belonged this was scarcely possible. The
middle-class element was not tolerated in Austrian
"society." This was so especially at that time,
though nowadays it has become the fashion to open
one's doors to a few rare representatives of art and
science. Those who could not be presented at court
—that is to say, could not show sixteen generations
of ancestors—must be shut out. Our friends would
have been quite unpleasantly startled to meet un-
titled people at my house, and would have found
it impossible to affiliate with them. And these
people themselves would have considered the company collected in my parlors frightfully tiresome.
What part could men of brains and knowledge,
writers and artists, have taken in the senseless
chatter of the old generals and ancient ladies-in-
waiting, the gay sportsmen and vapid young girls
who would have edified them by the account of
where we danced yesterday, and where the next
ball was to be, at Schwarzenberg, at Pallavicini,
or at court. How they would have been inspired
by the gossip as to the quality of the passion displayed by the adorers of Baroness Packer; or how
interested to learn the name of the latest unfortunate rejected by the Countess Palffy; or how
many houses Prince Croy maintained. How instructive they would find the discussion as to the

maiden name of the young Almasy—whether she was a Festetics or a Wenkheim, and if a Wenkheim could it be on the Khevenhüller side, etc., etc. That was the sort of stuff which made up the conversation of my guests. Although there were occasionally intellectual and able statesmen, diplomatists and men of note among us, they generally conformed to custom and adopted the same frivolous tone.

Often after one of my dinner parties I would have gladly joined the group of brilliant men who had escaped to a corner and were evidently surreptitiously discussing something rational. But my duties to the other guests scarcely permitted this, and even if I had ventured to approach them when they were deep in the theories of Strauss and Renan, the political situation, or the latest scientific discovery, such conversation would have ceased instantly. One and all they would have begun: "Ah, Countess Dotzky, how charming you looked yesterday at the picnic! Of course you are going to the reception at the Russian embassy?"

"Allow me, dear Martha," said my cousin, Conrad Althaus, "to introduce Lieut.-Col. Baron Tilling."

I bowed and half rose, supposing this to mean an invitation to dance.

"Pardon me, Countess," said the Baron, a slight smile showing his white teeth, "I cannot dance."

"So much the better," I answered, sinking back. "I sat down to rest a moment."

"I asked for the honor of an introduction," he continued formally, "as I had some information to give you."

I looked up astonished. The Baron had a grave face. He was an earnest looking man, no longer young, possibly over forty, and a few white hairs were plainly visible—upon the whole, a distinguished, sympathetic personality.

"What I have to say is scarcely the thing to be told in a ball-room. May I call upon you at any hour you may appoint?"

"I receive on Saturdays between two and four."

"Then I suppose that on Saturdays your house is like a bee-hive. The swarm hours do not suit me at all. I had rather see you alone."

"You excite my curiosity. Come to-morrow at the same hour, two."

The Baron bowed and left me. A little later Cousin Conrad passed. I inquired about Baron Tilling.

"He pleases you, does he? He has made such an impression that you are already setting an investigation on foot. He is to be had—that is, he is unmarried. But there is a rumor that a certain distinguished lady (he named a princess of the reigning house) has him in her silken toils, and that he consequently does not wish to marry. His regiment has been ordered into garrison here, and I have met him socially, though he is no friend to balls and the like. I made his acquaintance at the Casino, where he spends his time in the reading-room or in playing chess. I was surprised to see him here, but I believe our hostess is his cousin. After he left you he disappeared."

"Did you introduce him to other ladies?"

"No. But do not imagine that he looked at you from afar and straightway asked for an introduction. He simply asked: 'Do you know a certain Countess Dotzky, formerly an Althaus; possibly she is a relative of yours? If she is here I should like to meet her.' 'Yes,' I answered, 'there she is, in that corner, the one in a blue dress.' 'Be so good as to introduce me,' and away we went. How could I imagine that I would thereby destroy your peace of mind?"

"Nonsense, Conrad—my peace is not so easily ruffled. Tilling! What family is that? I never heard the name before."

"See how she persists! He is a lucky man. Here I have brought all my powers of fascination to bear upon you for three months in vain. This cold-blooded lieutenant-colonel comes along—for he is cold and unfeeling, I can tell you that—and walks away triumphant. You ask about the family? It is of Prussian origin, though his father was in the Austrian service ; his mother is a Prussian. You must have noticed his North-German accent."

" He speaks a charming German."

" Oh, of course—everything is charming about him." Conrad rose. "Now, I have had quite enough; I will leave you to your pleasant, deceptive dreams. I can hunt up ladies who——"

"Will think you charming, Conrad. There are plenty of them."

It is unnecessary to describe how I enriched the diary of that period with reflections upon the character of my new acquaintance, to which is added unpleasant doubts as to where he had spent the remainder of that evening. Probably at the feet of the princess, I wrote, and I rounded out my sentences by envying her—not Tilling, oh, no!—but the being loved by any one at all.

That I thought a moment, while I dressed that afternoon, as to whether violet velvet is not best adapted to set off the beauty of a blonde I will acknowledge. The Baron was announced at ten minutes after two.

"As you see, Countess, I have made prompt use of your permission to call," he said, kissing my hand.

"Most fortunately," I answered, " for I am overwhelmed with curiosity to know the nature of the information you bring."

" Then I will at once say what I meant to tell you. I was at the Battle of Magenta."

" And you saw Arno die? " I cried.

" Yes, I can give you all the particulars. Believe me, I would not have spoken of it if I had not felt sure of the relief I might bring you."

" You lift a stone from my heart. My anxiety has been heart-breaking."

"I will not repeat the commonplace phrase that he died as heroes die, because I do not know what that means. But I can give you the only comfort, that he died instantly without knowing that death was near. He was hopeful from the first. We were frequently together; he had shown me the pictures of his wife and child and invited me to visit him when the campaign was over. At the Battle of Magenta I chanced to be at his side. I spare you the scene. Men of warlike temperament in the turmoil of an engagement are scarcely conscious of what they are doing. A shell burst near us and ten men—among them Dotzky—fell together. A shriek of agony came from some of the poor fellows, but Dotzky was killed instantly. All but Dotzky were so shockingly mangled that we could do nothing for them. A charging column of cavalry rode down these wretched wounded. After the battle I searched the field and found Dotzky lying with the same pleasant smile on his face as when I first reached him after death. I have meant for years to tell you this, but have had no opportunity. Forgive me if I revive unhappy memories. It is better to be released from painful uncertainty."

The Baron rose, while I, drying my tears, thanked him warmly.

"It is a relief to know my husband died free from lingering agony. But, stay a moment; something in your tone touches a chord in my own heart. You, too, hate war?"

His face darkened.

"Forgive me, Countess," he answered, "if I cannot talk with you on that subject. I regret that I must leave; I am expected elsewhere."

Probably by his princess.

"I will not detain you," I coolly replied, and he left without asking permission to come again.

The carnival season was over. Rosa and Lilli boasted a half-dozen conquests apiece, but no de-

sirable match among them. I wrote disconsolately
in my diary: "I am glad dancing is over; it began
to be tiresome. Always the same dances and the
same dancers. The same grimaces, the same sighs
and killing glances. Not one interesting man
among them. The only one worth knowing apparently belongs to his princess. She is a pretty
woman, but thoroughly heartless."

Although Lent had commenced, there were certain canonical species of gaiety mixed in with our
religious duties, such as dinners, concerts, and receptions; we were also promised a new play after
Easter. Aunt Marie considered us all unruly sin-
ners and dragged Rosa and Lilli about with her
to hear all the famous preachers. The girls were
quite willing, as they met all their coterie at church
and continued their flirtations. Certain noted
priests, such as Father Klinkowström among the
Jesuits, were as much the fashion as Murska was at
the Opera House.

"My dear, I have a favor to ask of you," said my
father one morning, as he entered my breakfast-
room. He carried a paper-covered parcel in his
hand. "Here is something for you."

"A petition and a present?" I laughed. "That
is bribery."

"Then hear my petition before you open the
parcel. I am going to have a most tiresome dinner-
party to-day——"

"Oh, I know; three old generals and their
wives."

"And two cabinet ministers with theirs; in short,
a stiff, sleepy, state affair. I want you to help me."

"Where is Aunt Marie?"

"She has one of her headaches."

"So you will sacrifice your daughter like the
ancient fathers. For instance, as Agamemnon sacrificed Iphigenia. Very well; I submit."

"I thought I would add a younger element. Doctor Bresser, for one, who treated me so well in my

last illness that I would like to be polite to him, and Lieut.-Col. Tilling."

I began to open the package.

"It is nothing for you. It belongs to Rudi."

"Yes, I see; a box of leaden soldiers. But, father, that four-years-old child should not——"

" Now, now, what nonsense. I played soldier when I was three years old—one cannot begin early enough. My earliest recollections are of drums, sabers, learning to drill and march. In this way we arouse a love for the profession."

"My son, Rudolph, shall never be a soldier," I interrupted.

" Martha! I know well what his father's wish would have been."

" Rudolph belongs to me now, and he shall not."

"Shall not adopt the noblest, the most honorable profession? "

" The life of my child shall not be risked on the battlefield."

"Why, I was an only son and *I* became a soldier. Arno had no brother, and your brother Otto is an only son, and yet I have sent him to the military academy. The traditions of the family demand that the child of a Dotzky and an Althaus should devote his life to the service of his country."

" His country needs him less than I do. Are there no other ways of serving his country? "

" Luckily all mothers do not think so."

"If they did there would be fewer parades and grand reviews and fewer men for cannon fodder, as it is now the fashion to call the rank and file. That would be no misfortune."

My father looked very much provoked.

"Oh, you women! How you mix up the ethics of the family and of the state. Fortunately the youngster will not ask your permission; soldiers' blood flows in his veins. He will not be your only son, Martha. You really must marry again. What has become of all your admirers? How is it with Captain Olensky, who is dead in love with you?

He has lately been pouring forth his protestations to me. I should like him very well for a son-in-law."

"I should not like him for a husband."

"Then there is Major Millersdorf."

"You might offer the whole army roll—I want none of them. At what hour do you dine?"

"At five. Come a little earlier. Give my love to Rudi—the future field-marshal of the imperial army."

It would have been a tiresome ceremonial dinner for me, had it not been for the presence of Tilling. While at the table I had no opportunity of speaking to him, but after we had risen from dinner he joined a group in one corner of the long drawing-room, where smoking was allowed. The old ladies withdrew into a recess at the lower end. I lighted a cigarette. The two old gray-headed generals who had been seated by me at dinner remained faithful attendants as I sat at my little table serving the black coffee.

"I wonder if we may not expect an outbreak soon?" said one of the old gentlemen.

"H'm," replied the other. "The next war will be with Russia."

"Must there always be a next war?" I murmured; but no one noticed me.

"It is far more likely it will be with Italy," replied my father. "We must get Lombardy back some way. I want to see a march into Milan like that of '49 under Father Radetzky. It was a bright, sunny morning——"

"Oh," I exclaimed in a panic, "we all know the story of the march into Milan."

"All about the brave Hupfauf also, I suppose," answered my father laughing.

"Yes, yes, and it is horrible."

"Let us hear it, Althaus. We have not heard it," one of the group said diplomatically.

My father did not need a more pressing invitation.

"This man Hupfauf belonged to a regiment of Tyrolean Jägers; he was a native Tyrolean and the best shot you ever saw; he always carried off the prizes at the shooting matches. When the Milanese rebelled, he asked permission to climb to the roof of the cathedral; he proposed to take four comrades with him and shoot at the rebels. He was allowed to do it. The four did nothing but load their rifles and hand them to him; he hit his mark every time and killed ninety Italians."

"It was abominable," I exclaimed. "Every one of those poor fellows had a mother, wife, or sweetheart at home, and a right to his own young life."

"They were our enemies, child; that alters the point of view."

"Quite right," said Doctor Bresser sarcastically; "so long as the idea of enmity being justifiable is sanctioned among men, based solely upon the fact of your being on one side of the boundary line of a country and I on the other, the law of humanity will receive but slight recognition."

"What do you say, Baron Tilling," I asked.

"I would have given the man an order to decorate his gallant breast—from the standpoint based upon the ethics of war—and would then have put a bullet through his flinty heart; both were well deserved."

I looked up at the speaker warmly, gratefully. The remarks, however, evidently jarred upon the conventional class sensibilities of the others, and there was an awkward pause.

"Have you seen the new book by the English naturalist, Darwin," asked the Doctor, turning to my father.

"I know nothing of it."

"Why, Papa," I exclaimed, "you do not remember; our bookseller sent it to us four years ago, and you then predicted it would soon be forgotten by the world."

"So far as I am concerned that is true."

"The whole world is turned upside down by it," returned the Doctor. "Everybody is discussing the new theory of the origin of species."

"Ah, you mean the monkey theory?" exclaimed the old general at my right. "I heard them talking about it at the Casino. The learned gentlemen have reached a strange conclusion—that man was originally an orang-outang."

"Upon the whole," the cabinet minister began—when our old friend opened his orations in this style, we quaked in our shoes—"the thing sounds absurd; but it really cannot be treated as a joke. It is a theory built upon diligently collected facts and ingeniously elaborated. To be sure it has been attacked by men of repute, but like many speculative ideas distasteful to us it has produced an effect and has warm defenders. We shall soon hear the word Darwinism, which will survive long after his theory has been abandoned. It is a great pity that people display so much temper in discussing this singular Englishman. Of course the clergy object to the destruction of their story of the creation of man after God's own image;—no wonder they denounce it as a scandalous attack. But the condemnation of the church can no longer prevent the spread of a theory presented under the cloak of science."

"What folly!" exclaimed my father, beginning to be anxious about his other guests, who looked rather bored. "Man descended from apes! One only needs a little common sense to reject such an absurd notion."

"We are not at all certain how the discussion may end," the minister solemnly insisted. "It cannot be denied that between man and ape there is a great resemblance."

"The abyss between them is immeasurable," quietly replied one of the old generals. "Can one conceive of an ape who could invent the telegraph? Language itself lifts man far above the brute."

"Pardon me, your Excellency," said Doctor Bresser. "Language and the capacity for technical discovery were not originally born with man—a wild man could not to-day invent the telegraphic

instrument. That is all the result of slow development and evolution."

"Yes, yes, I know, Doctor," answered the general.
"Evolution is the battle-cry of the new school, but
one cannot evolve a camel from a kangaroo. Why
do we not find apes to-day developing into men?"

I turned impatiently to Baron Tilling.

"What do you say? Do you march with the
defenders or the opponents of Darwin?"

"Although I have heard much of the subject,
Countess, I can have no opinion. I have not read
the book."

"Nor I," the Doctor acknowledged.

"Nor I—nor I—nor I"—chorused all the others.

Amid the general laughter the Minister of Finance
apologetically added:

"After all, the battle-cries of the system have
become so well known that we acquire quite a good
idea of what it all means and can join either army
of combatants. 'The survival of the fittest,' 'natural
selection,' 'evolution,' are expressions familiar as
the alphabet. You find defenders of the advanced
ideas among all the destructive spirits who are
always running after a new thing, while the cold-
blooded, critical people, who insist upon positive
evidence, are found on the other side."

"The opposition to every new idea, of which
we everywhere hear the chorus," said Tilling, "is
usually based upon the falsest and most cowardly
grounds—and it would be impossible for one to
echo it. Even when new scientific hypotheses are
proved, they continue to be assailed by conservative
people. I shall undertake to read the book, but
not to pass judgment upon its scientific theories,
as my knowledge in that line is very limited. I
acknowledge, however, that a theory which so violently antagonizes all preconceived opinions prejudices me in its favor for that very reason."

"Oh you clear-headed, courageous soul!" I silently apostrophized the speaker.

About eight o'clock the party dispersed. My father politely urged delay and I mildly murmured: "At least a cup of tea?" Each had his excuse: one was expected at the Casino, another was going to a concert; one of the ladies had a box at the opera and wished to see the fourth act of the Huguenots; the second expected guests; in short, all quite willingly, though with polite assurance to the contrary, left the house. Tilling and Doctor Bresser lingered and needed but slight urging to remain.

My father and the Doctor were soon seated at the card table playing picquet, while Baron Tilling joined me before the grate.

"I must really reproach you, Baron Tilling; why have you forgotten the way to my house?"

"I was not invited to repeat my visit."

"Why I told you that I received on Saturdays."

"Yes, between two and four; you must excuse me, Countess. I know nothing more abominable than these conventional receptions. You enter a drawing-room filled with strange people, bow to the hostess; then you are pushed to the outer edge of a half-circle. You hear remarks about the weather, and if you chance to see an acquaintance may discuss the same subject. If you make a desperate attempt to exchange a word with the hostess, you are pushed away by some later arrival, and back you go to the half-circle, and—being of the opinion that the subject is not yet exhausted—you begin again with somebody about the weather. Then after ten minutes, when the crowd increases, perhaps you are crowded out by a mamma with four marriageable daughters who cannot find chairs. You make your escape the best way you can. No, Countess, that is more than my weak capacity can endure."

"You appear to dislike society. I see you nowhere. Perhaps you hate your kind. No, I do not mean quite that. I am sure, from what I have heard you say, that you love all men."

"I love humanity, but all men—no. There are too many coarse, wicked, cold-blooded wretches

among them. I cannot love such men, however I
may regret that education and environment have
prevented their becoming worthy of any love at
all."

"Education and environment? The character
depends chiefly on hereditary tendencies, does it
not?"

"What you call inherited tendencies are usually
nothing more than environment—inherited environment."

"Then you hold that a bad man is not responsible for his wickedness, and should not be shunned
on its account?"

"One does not follow the other. He may not
be responsible, but still must be avoided."

There was a pause for a moment.

"Why did you become a soldier, Baron Tilling?"

"Ah, there you show how you have read my heart.
But it was not I, not Frederick Tilling, now thirty-
nine years old—the man who has seen three campaigns—who chose the profession. It was the ten
or twelve years old Fritz, whose babyhood was
spent among wooden cavalry and leaden soldiers.
It was the boy whose father, a general, decorated
with many orders, and whose uncle, a lady-killer of
a lieutenant, were always asking, 'Youngster, what
are you going to be?' Of course the boy always
answered, 'A real soldier with a real saber and a
live horse.'"

"A box of leaden soldiers was brought to my
house to-day for my little Rudolph, but I shall not
give them to him. But why after Fritz had developed into Frederick did you not abandon a calling hateful to you?"

"Hateful? That is saying too much. I hate the
condition of things which requires of men such
dreadful duty as the conduct of war; but as this
condition exists and is not yet unavoidable, I cannot hate the men who accept these necessary duties
and conscientiously fulfill them. If I left the military service would there be less of war? In my

place another would risk his life. That I can do as well as he."

"Could you not better serve your fellow-men in some other way?"

"I do not know. I have not been taught anything but the art of war. In any station a man may be of service to his fellow-men. I have opportunity enough to lighten the burdens of those who serve under me. I appreciate the respect with which the world regards my rank. I have had a fortunate career and enjoy my success. I possess no private fortune and as a civilian I could be of no use to myself or others. Why should I abandon my profession?"

"And yet the destruction of human life is abhorrent to you?"

"When it comes to defense of one's own life personal responsibility ends. War is often called wholesale murder, but the individual soldier does not regard himself as a murderer. It is true that the suffering and atrocities of the battlefield fill me with pain and disgust. I suffer, suffer intensely; but so must many a seaman during a storm suffer from sea-sickness; yet if he is but half way a manly fellow he remains on deck and defies and masters his surroundings."

"Yes, if it must be. But must war be?"

"That is another question. But the individual must serve, and that necessity gives him the strength to fulfill his obligation."

We continued our conversation in a low tone that we might not disturb the players. Tilling told of some of the episodes of war, and I quoted Buckle's opinion that with the advancement of civilization the military spirit would decline; but such talk would not have pleased the ear of General Althaus.

"What are you two whispering about?" my father suddenly called out.

"I am telling old war stories," answered the Baron.

"Martha is used to that from her childhood. I even go over a few nowadays."

I rose and glanced at the clock.

"I must say good-night, Papa," and I withdrew, Tilling accompanying me to the carriage.

Within the next few days I visited my old friend, Lori Griesbach, with whom I was intimate, though in many respects there was not the slightest sympathy between us. She could not have comprehended many of my ideas of life and duty. How rarely do we find a human being to whom we can show all of our nature. Our friendships are but one-sided and our misconceptions of each other manifold.

Lori's boy, Xaver, was of the same age as my Rudolph, and they were playfellows; and Lori's ten-months-old baby, Beatrice, we had jestingly set apart as the future Countess Rudolph Dotzky.

"Are we really to see you again?" exclaimed Lori as I entered. "You have become a hermit. I have not had the honor lately of seeing my future son-in-law. Beatrice will be very much offended. What have you been doing? How is Lilli? My husband came home from the club with a fine report about her. It seems somebody is in love with her whom we have all supposed was courting you. What a lovely dress! Francine made it of course."

She chattered on and I replied in kind, at last taking occasion to inquire whether she had ever heard the gossip about Tilling and the princess.

"Oh that is ancient history," she replied. "It is well known nowadays that the princess is devoted to an actor at the Burg Theatre. Are you interested in Tilling? Better confess. You have been frosty and unfeeling long enough. It would do me good to see you in love. But he is no match for you. Of course you have money enough for both, but you have had brilliant opportunities. Have you heard about Frederick Drontheim, the same one who squandered his fortune on the ballet dancer, Grilli? He is going to marry a rich banker's daughter and become a nobleman. Of course no one will visit her. Are you going to the English Embassy this evening? No? Quite right. You never know whom you are going to meet there. It is positively shocking; there are so many queer people, you are not at all sure they are *comme il faut*. Every Englishman who brings letters to his embassador is invited even if he is only a rich commercial man. I cannot endure the English—except in the Tauchnitz edition. Have you read "Jane Eyre?" Lovely, is it not? As soon as Beatrice begins to talk I shall get an English maid. I am not at all satisfied with my French one. Just imagine, I met her lately on the street when she had taken the baby out, whispering very confidentially with some young fellow—looked as if he might be a clerk. You ought to have seen their consternation when I suddenly appeared before them. Such people are a nuisance. And my dressing maid has had the assurance to tell me she is going to be married. Then I shall have to have a stranger about again. What, are you going already?"

I was rejoiced to see Tilling's cousin enter my parlor on my next reception day.

"I have a message for you," she said at once. "Cousin Frederick sends his compliments. He left yesterday." I felt my cheeks grow pale.

"Left! Has the regiment been ordered away?"

"No, he was obliged to ask for a leave of absence. His mother is very ill and he has gone to Berlin."

Two days later I received a letter in an unknown hand from Berlin. I knew it was from Baron Tilling.

BERLIN, Frederick St. 8.
30 March, 1863.
1 o'clock, midnight.

MY DEAR COUNTESS:

I must write to you of my deep trouble. Why do I turn to you? Have I the right? I do not claim it; it is only the irresistible impulse. You will sympathize

with me, I am sure. If you had only known you would
have loved my mother. And now this tender heart, this
clear intellect, this cheerful temper, this sweet dignity
must soon pass into the grave—there is no hope. I have
spent the whole day at her bedside and shall be by her
side this last night. She has suffered much. She is now
quiet, for Nature's powers are benumbed, her pulse has
almost ceased to beat. The physician and her sister are
with me. Ah! this terrible destruction, this death. We
all know that we must die, yet we cannot comprehend
why those we love should be taken from us. What my
mother has been to me I cannot express to you.

She knows that she must die. When I arrived this
morning she received me with a cry of joy. " My boy, I
feared you would come too late." " You will get well,
Mother?" I cried. " No, no, it is not possible. Do not
waste the sanctity of our last parting by the usual sick-
room commonplaces. Let us say good-by."

I fell weeping on my knees at her bedside. " You weep,
my son? See, I do not repeat the customary protest. I
am glad that the parting from your best old friend
grieves you. It assures me that you will remember me."

" So long as I live, Mother."

" Remember, then that you have given me much happiness. Excepting the natural anxiety which your childhood cost me, and the dread of losing you during the
time of war, you have brought me only happiness, and
have shared all that fate has brought me of other trouble.
I bless you for that, my child!"

Then came one of her dreadful attacks of pain. Her
groans and gasps were enough to break one's heart. Yes,
he is a frightful enemy—this death, and the sight of her
suffering brought back to memory all the agony I had
seen in the battlefield and in the hospitals. When I
reflect that we drive men on to meet death joyously; that
we urge full-blooded, happy youth to sacrifice themselves
to death, against which weary and enfeebled age protests,
I see how base we are.

This night is frightfully long. If the poor soul could
only sleep! but she lies there with open eyes. Every
half hour I kneel motionless beside her; then I come
away to write a few lines to you—then go back to her.

It is four o'clock. I have just heard four strokes from
every clock tower. Ah! it seems so relentlessly cold and
heartless that time strides on for all eternity, while soon
for one passionately loved soul time shall cease—for all
eternity. But the more this outer world turns from our

pain, the more longingly we turn to that other human heart where we hope for consolation.

Seven o'clock. It is all over. "Farewell, my boy," were her last words. Then she gently shut her eyes and fell asleep. Grieved unto death,

Yours,

FREDERICK TILLING.

This letter I have still. How worn and faded the page now looks. Not only the wear of twenty years has caused this decay, but the tears and kisses with which I then received it. All doubt was laid at rest, and I was sure of this man's love.

Three weeks had passed. Conrad Althaus had offered himself to Lilli and had been rejected. He took it far from tragically and was as persistent a visitor as before, and devoted himself assiduously to us whenever we met in society.

I once expressed my surprise at this loyalty.

"I am delighted that you are not offended," I said; "but it only proves to me that your attachment for Lilli was not very serious, for despised love is usually malicious."

"You are mistaken, respected cousin, I love Lilli frantically. At first I thought I loved you, but you were so cold-blooded that I next bestowed my affections upon Rosa; but finally I discovered that Lilli was the one, and by this decision I mean to abide to the end of my days."

"That is very probable."

"Lilli or no one!"

"But if she will not marry you, Conrad?"

"Do you suppose that I am the first man who after receiving the mitten the first time is discouraged by its presentation a second, a third, or a fourth—why, she will marry me to get rid of me. Lilli is not a bit in love with me. But it has delighted me that she has refused several good matches, and I am more in love with her than ever. By and by my fidelity will touch her and excite some return; for you are bound to be my sister-in-

law, Martha. I hope you will not use your influence against me."

"On the contrary, I approve your plan of perse-
verance. That is the way a woman should be won.
But our modern young gentlemen want to secure
their happiness by idly plucking it like a flower
by the wayside."

Tilling had been in Vienna ten days but had not
been near me. I was depressed and unhappy and
Aunt Marie reproached me for my low spirits.

"Have you tickets to see the Foot-Washing?" she
asked one day. "To-morrow is Maundy Thursday."

"Yes, Papa brought us some. But I really don't
know whether I care to go."

"Oh, you must. There is nothing more sublime
than this touching ceremony—the triumph of
Christian humility. Emperor and Empress stoop-
ing to wash the feet of those poor old people sym-
bolizes how small and insignificant earthly majesty
is compared with the Divine love."

"You must actually feel humility in order to
represent it by throwing yourself on your knees.
This ceremony only says: 'What God's Son was
in relation to the apostles, that am I, the Emperor,
in my relation to these paupers.' It seems to me
that this does not express humility."

"You have such curious notions, Martha. During the three years that you have lived in the
country, reading bad books, your ideas have become completely warped."

"Bad books!"

"Yes, that is just the word. The other day when
I innocently mentioned to the Archbishop that I
had seen on your table a book called the 'Life of
Jesus,' by one Strauss, he threw up his hands and
cried: 'Merciful heaven, how did you get hold of
such a vicious book?' I blushed fiery red and assured him I had not read it, but had only seen it on
the table of a relative. 'Then appeal to this relative, by all her hopes of salvation, to throw that
book into the fire.' I beg you now, Martha, to do it.
Will you burn the book?"

"If we had lived two or three hundred years ago we should see not only the book but the author thrown into the fire. That might have been effectual—temporarily effectual—but only temporarily."

"Why do you not answer? Will you burn the book?"

" No."

"So short as that—no?"

"What is the use of talking. We do not understand each other at all in this matter, dear Aunt. Let me rather tell you what Rudolph said yesterday."

And the conversation was happily turned upon a theme of which my good aunt never tired.

I determined the next day to witness the Foot-Washing. About ten o'clock, dressed in black, as is usual in Holy week, my sister Rosa and I went to the palace to witness the great ceremony. Upon a platform places had been reserved for the members of the aristocracy and the diplomatic corps. We were thus again safely set apart by ourselves, and exchanged greetings right and left. The gallery was also filled by those for whom seats had been reserved, a somewhat mixed crowd, not the cream, as we were. In short, the old caste distinctions and privileges must countenance this festival of symbolic humility.

I do not know whether the others were in the proper religious mood, but I awaited the ceremony with exactly the same feeling with which I anticipated a new spectacle at the theatre; excited just in the same way as, after exchanging greetings from box to box, we await the rolling up of the curtain. I watched the point from which the choir and solo singers were to appear. The decorations were already in place, that is to say, the long table at which the twelve old men and twelve old women were to be seated. I was glad I had come; it was something new—always a pleasant sensation—and for a time obliterated all melancholy thoughts.

At the moment when I had forgotten him my eye fell upon Tilling, who entered with the generals and their staffs. He took his place opposite and I endeavored by persistently keeping my eyes on him to attract his attention—but in vain.

"They are coming, they are coming!" cried Rosa. "How lovely! What a picture!"

They were the old men and women, clad in an obsolete German fashion. The youngest of the women—so the papers had announced—was eighty-eight; the youngest of the men, eighty-five years old. Wrinkled, toothless, bent—I could not apply Rosa's "charming." What pleased her was the costume. It was admirably adapted to this ceremony of the Middle Ages. The anachronism was in our presence, our modern clothes, and our modern ideas—we were not a consistent part of the picture.

After the twenty-four old people had taken their places at the table, a number of decorated and distinguished individuals, mostly old men, privy councilors and gentlemen-in-waiting, came in,—all well-known faces,—Minister "Upon the Whole" among them. Last came the clergy who were to officiate at the ceremony.

Now came the most important figures in this pageant—the imperial couple—certainly the handsomest pair on the continent. They were attended by a brilliant group of archdukes and duchesses. The ceremony could now proceed. Stewards and pages brought in bowls filled with food, and the Emperor and Empress placed them before the old people. It was more of a picture than ever. The utensils, the character of the food and the attire of the pages reminded one of certain famous pictures of festal occasions painted in the Renaissance style.

Scarcely were the dishes set before the people when the table was again cleared, which work, as a lesson in humility, was performed by the archdukes. Thereupon the table was carried out and the scenic effect proper of the play—the Foot Washing—begun. In truth it was but the counterfeit presentment of washing, as the meal had been a counterfeit one. Kneeling upon the floor the Emperor lightly rubbed a towel over the feet of the old men, after an attendant priest had pretended to pour water out of a consecrated vessel. Slipping along the floor from the first to the twelfth, the Emperor continued, while the Empress in the same humble position followed this procedure with the old women. The proper music followed the reading by the Court Chaplain of the Gospel for the day.

How gladly would I for a few moments have exchanged places with one of the old people in order to experience the effect upon them of this quaint old costume, this brilliant gathering assembled to witness their Majesties at their feet—to get their point of view, in fact. Probably it was only a bewildered half dream, a little pleasure and confused pain, or a complete suspension of strength which was experienced by the poor, feeble old souls. The only real things about the whole affair were the red silk purses with thirty pieces of silver, thrown round the necks of the old people by their Majesties to conclude the ceremony, and the permission which was given to carry home the bowls of food.

The ceremony was soon over and was followed by a whirl of greetings, congratulations and polite nothings, after which the guests hastened away. We found Tilling waiting to see us, and he thanked me for the funeral wreath I had sent to Berlin. I offered him my hand, and as we were seated in my carriage I leaned forward to say, though with the greatest effort:

"I shall be at home Sunday, between two and three."

He bowed silently and we drove away. When he came, the following Sunday, he was reticent and cold, formally apologized for his boldness in writing from Berlin, and when gently questioned spoke somewhat of his mother's life, but of what I hoped to hear—not a word. We parted with restraint, and I found poor consolation for my disappointed, troubled spirit in declaring to my journal that I had deceived myself.

Easter Monday was favored by Heaven with the loveliest of skies, and the usual drive through the Prater—which it was customary to make a sort of social inaugural of the great first of May Corso— was more than ordinarily brilliant. All this brilliancy, this joy in mere existence and in the fresh springtime which inspired the beautiful and dashing occupants of the numerous carriages, intensified by contrast the sadness which depressed my spirit. And yet I would not have surrendered this melancholy in exchange for the light heart of two months earlier—before I met Tilling. For even if my love should prove—what from all present prospects it promised to be—an unhappy one, still it was love, that is, the climax of life's intensity.

Some days later, when my parlors were filled with other guests, Tilling was announced. My delight in seeing him was speedily clouded by the announcement that this was a final visit, as he expected to leave Vienna in a few days for another post in Hungary.

"That is a rash conclusion. What has Vienna done that you wish to leave?" I asked, with an effort at self-control.

"It is too gay and pleasure-loving. I am not in the mood to join in it and it depresses me."

"The best thing to shake that out of you, Tilling," said my father, "would be a right fresh, breezy war; but unfortunately there seems no prospect of one."

"Chance is always in your favor, Colonel Tilling," said a cabinet minister present; "not that there are any dark clouds on the horizon now, but it takes but a little, in the present condition of European politics, to cause an outbreak. As Minister of the Interior I am naturally anxious for peace, but I am willing to recognize the different standpoint from which military men regard it."

"Allow me to assure your Excellency," interrupted Tilling, "that I am far from desiring war, and I protest against the idea that the military standpoint should be any different from that of the humane one. We are here to defend our country when attacked, just as the fire department stands in readiness to put out a fire. Both war and fire are misfortunes with which no humane man could wish to afflict his fellow creatures. Peace is the highest good, or rather it is the absence of the greatest evil. It is the only condition which conduces to the welfare of the whole nation, and yet you would recognize the right of a portion of the people—the army—from motives of grossly personal ambition, to desire to precipitate the greatest misery and suffering upon all. To carry on war in order that the army may be kept busy and satisfied is like applying the torch to houses in order to employ the fire department."

"Your comparison is not apt, Lieutenant-Colonel," said my father, laying stress upon the title, as if wishing to remind Tilling of his military duty. "Fires cause only disaster, while wars tend to increase the power and glory of the country. How could nations otherwise develop and extend their territory except through conquest? Personal ambition is not the only motive of the gallant soldier; above all it is the national, the patriotic spirit which leads him to desire war."

"Oh, this love of country!" exclaimed Tilling impatiently. "I do not see by what right the military profession should claim patriotism as their own special and peculiar quality. Every one loves the soil upon which he has taken root; all wish, ardently wish, for the happiness, development and glory of their native land. There are other ways to fame than through violence; we can be proud of other things than feats of war. Personally I admire Anastasius Grün more than any commanding general I can remember."

"How can you compare a poet and a soldier," exclaimed my father.

"The bloodless crown of laurel is, undoubtedly, the finer," answered Tilling.

"But, Baron Tilling," expostulated Aunt Marie, "I never heard a soldier talk so. What would become of the martial spirit?"

"When I was a nineteen-year-old boy, making my first campaign, I was filled with it. After I had seen the reality of the slaughter, and witnessed the brutality of war, that martial spirit died out and I entered upon every other campaign with loyalty, but with no martial ardor."

"Now, see here, Tilling," replied my father, "I have been through as many campaigns as you and witnessed all their terrors, but I went into the last, even when getting to be an old man, with the same zeal as the first."

"Pardon me, Excellency, but you belong to an older generation, a generation when the martial spirit was much stronger than with us, and to a time when that sympathy with humanity which now permeates all society, and anxiously desires to ameliorate all misery, had not yet been born."

"What can you do? Suffering must exist forever. You cannot get rid of it any more than you can banish war."

"There, Count Althaus, with those words you define the old attitude, now fortunately untenable, with which the past met every social evil—that of *resignation* to what it deemed unavoidable and founded on the nature of things. But so soon as the heart begins to question, 'Is it necessary?' no longer can that heart cold-bloodedly contemplate it. With sympathy grows up a sort of penitence— not personal, but which one might define as the reproach of the conscience of the times."

My father shrugged his shoulders.

"That is too lofty for me. I can assure you that not only we grandfathers look back with pride and joy on all our past campaigns, but the very youngest of our soldiers to-day, when asked if he goes into the field willingly, would reply: 'Willingly—yes, joyfully.'"

"The youngest—that is true. Have we not drilled enthusiasm into them at school. And of the others many would reply 'willingly' for fear of the reputation of cowardice did they speak the truth."

"Yes," said Lilli with a shudder, "I should be afraid. It must be horrible to stand with bullets flying around you, any moment awaiting death."

"That all sounds very natural from girlish lips," answered Tilling. "But we must repress all instinctive feeling. Soldiers must deny all sympathy for the suffering of friend or foe, for next to fear, every sentiment of tenderness or mercy is a like reproach."

"Only in war, dear Tilling," said my father, "only in war; in private life, thank God, we have tender hearts."

"Yes, I know; that is a sort of hocus-pocus transformation. So soon as war is declared one hears of all atrocities with a careless 'it is to be expected—it matters not.' Murder is no longer murder; robbery is no longer robbery—but requisition; burning villages represents only 'secured position.' Of all defiance of the moral law, of humanity, or of decency, we hear only so long as the contest lasts, 'It is of no consequence.' 'It is to be expected!' But when in the abyss of such general demoralization there arises the consciousness that it does matter to be rid of this mass of crime and misery, and responsibility in its existence, one would almost welcome death."

"Certainly it is true," said Aunt Marie reflectively. "Such commands as: Thou shalt not kill—Thou shalt not steal—Love thy neighbor as thyself—Forgive thine enemies——"

"Do not apply," said Tilling. "And those whose profession it is to teach these laws are the first to consecrate our banners and call down the blessing of Heaven upon our slaughter fields."

"And with justice," said my father, "for the God of the Bible is the God of Battles, the Lord of Hosts. It is he who has commanded us to draw the sword; it is he——"

"Whose decrees men are always construing to suit their own convenience, and to whom they then ascribe the great law of love. Just so vindictive, exactly so inconsequent, exactly so childish as themselves, is the imaginary God whom human beings have set up as the embodiment of even-handed justice and mercy. But forgive me, Countess," said Tilling rising, "that I have caused so wearisome a discussion. I must say good-by."

I was overcome with emotion. How could it be possible to allow this man, dearer to me than ever, to go from me without one word of protest.

I rose with him and walking slowly down the room said quietly:

"I must show you the photograph I told you about the other day."

Tilling looked surprised, but followed me to a table at a distance from the other guests.

"I cannot let you go. I must speak to you."

"As you will, Countess. I am listening."

"No, not now. You must come to-morrow at this hour."

He appeared to waver.

"I insist. By the memory of your mother whose loss I mourned with you."

"O Martha!"

We understood each other, and bowing to the company Tilling withdrew.

I looked forward to the meeting with a mingling of impatience and apprehension. Suppose Tilling were to propose the critical question, "Now then, Countess, what did you wish to say to me?" I could not say to the man: "I have to inform you that I am in love with you; therefore I desire you to remain." While I was reflecting upon this difficulty Tilling was announced.

"I am happy to see you, Baron Tilling."

"And I am happy that you invited me to come in the name of my mother. I have determined to tell you all that troubles me. I—"

"Well—why do you hesitate?"

"It is more difficult to speak than I thought."

"You showed some confidence in me when you wrote during that sad night when you watched by your mother's deathbed. How does it happen you have no faith in me now?"

"In that dreadful hour I forgot myself; since then my old timidity has taken possession of me. I see now I had no right, and for fear of repeating my offense I was going away."

"So it seems; you appear to avoid me—why?"

"Why? Because—because I love you."

I made no response and Tilling was silent. Desperately I broke the silence.

"Why were you going to leave Vienna?"

"For the same reason."

"Could you not now determine otherwise?"

"Yes, I could—the transfer has not yet been ordered."

"Then remain."

He grasped my hand—"Martha."

At this moment my father opened the door.

"You are there? The servant said you were not at home, but I told him you expected me. Good day, Tilling. After last night's farewell I am surprised to see you. I have an important family affair to report to you, Martha."

I wished papa with his family matter at the antipodes. Tilling rose.

"When can I see you again?" he asked in a low voice.

"To-morrow at nine o'clock, on horseback in the Prater," I replied quickly in the same tone.

"Now what does this mean?" demanded my father as the door closed after Tilling. "What is the family affair you speak of?"

"It is this very thing. I wanted to drive your admirer away in order to express my opinion. I regard it as a very important matter that you, Countess Dotzky, born Althaus, should not imperil your reputation."

"Allow me to tell you, Father, that the surest protection of my honor is my son, Rudolph, and to remind you that I am responsible to no one for my actions. I have no intention of accepting a lover, but I do mean to marry and to choose as my own heart dictates."

"Marry Tilling! What are you thinking about? That would be a family misfortune."

"Why, what would you have? Lately you offered me a captain, a lieutenant, and a major. Tilling outranks them all—he is lieutenant-colonel."

"So much the worse. A man with his opinions has no business to be in the army; they border on treason. Perhaps he would like to resign, and as he has no property a rich widow is an enticing prize. But I hope to God that a woman, the daughter of an old soldier who has fought in four wars and is willing to go out again, and the widow of a gallant young soldier who died on the field of honor a noble death,—will not so sacrifice herself."

I was profoundly outraged. All this repetition of hollow phrases, meeting me at every turn of life, sickened and disgusted me. It was impossible to make my father understand the ethical position of Tilling as a man and thinker, and useless to argue with him. I was fortunately free, and in my great happiness I could not allow such paltry attacks to trouble me.

It was not quite nine o'clock when I left my carriage, at the entrance of the Prater bridle path, and mounted my horse, which had been sent in advance. I had scarce ridden a hundred yards when I heard the sharp trot of a horse behind me. It was the inevitable Conrad. The meeting was not a joyful one to me. Certainly I did not own the Prater, and on such lovely mornings the bridle path was apt to be thronged. How could I have been so foolish as to expect an undisturbed rendezvous. Althaus had drawn his horse up to the gait of mine, evidently determined to be my faithful cavalier. I saw Tilling galloping in the distance.

"Cousin, is it not true I have been a good ally of yours. You know what pains I have taken to interest Lilli in you."

"Yes, noblest of cousins."

"Only last night I seized the opportunity to exploit your good qualities,—for you are a fine fellow, charming, considerate——"

"Now what do you want of me?"

"That you give your horse a good whipping and gallop on."

Tilling was very close. Conrad looked at him, then at me, and without saying a word, he laughingly nodded and flew away as if he were possessed.

"That Althaus again," said Tilling in a dissatisfied tone. "Did he leave because he saw me, or has his horse run away?"

"I sent him away because——"

"Countess Martha, do you know that the world says he is in love with his cousin?"

"That is true."

"And courts her furiously."

"That is also true."

"And not hopelessly."

"Not quite hopelessly."

Tilling was silent. I looked at him laughingly.

"Your looks contradict your last words," he said after a pause, "for your glance seems to say, 'Althaus loves me hopelessly.'"

"He does not love me at all. The object of his devotion is my sister Lilli."

"You roll a stone from my heart. This man was the cause of my wishing to leave Vienna. I could not endure to see——"

"What other grounds had you for leaving Vienna?" I interrupted.

"The dread that I could no longer conceal my

passion for you—that I might make myself both
ridiculous and unhappy."

" Are you unhappy this morning? "

"O Martha! Since yesterday I have lived in such
a tumult of emotion that I have scarce known myself. It has not been without anxiety—as when
one has pleasant dreams—that I might be suddenly
awakened to a painful reality. What prospects has
such a love as mine. What can I offer you? To-
morrow, or perhaps a little later, you will with-
draw the undeserved favor and I will be plunged
into the depths of despair. I do not know myself
when I talk in such an extravagant style. I have
been usually a cool, prudent man, the enemy of all
excess of feeling; it is in your power to make me
happy or miserable."

" Relieve me from one doubt, the princess? "

" Oh, have you heard that nonsense? "

" Of course you would deny it. That is your
duty."

"The lady in question, whose heart is now interested in the Bury Theatre—for how long no one
knows, for she is fickle—is so well known that the
most discreet of men would not feel obliged to
maintain the silence of the grave, so you may believe me. But reflect: would I have left Vienna
if the report were true?"

"Jealousy knows no logic. Is it likely I had invited you to meet me if I had expected to see my
cousin Conrad? I cannot comprehend why you
should have kept away from me."

" Because I never dared hope that I might win
you. Only when you appealed to me in the name
of my mother did I understand that you cared a
little—just a little—for me."

" So, if I had not 'thrown myself at your head'
you would not have made the attempt? "

" You have so many admirers—I did not want to
be counted among them."

" Oh, they do not amount to anything. They are
mostly only interested in the rich widow——"

"There, now, you have touched the very point which held me back—a rich widow, and I entirely without fortune. I would rather be miserable through an unfortunate attachment than be accused by the world and by the woman I worship of the motive you ascribe to your other admirers."

"My dear, my noble Tilling. It would not be possible for me to make such an accusation."

From the Prater I drove to my father's house. I realized that the announcement I had to make would be unpleasant to him, but I was determined to have it over as soon as possible. My father, being a late riser, was reading the paper while at breakfast. Aunt Marie was also present. Both looked up with astonishment at my abrupt entrance.

"I have been riding in the Prater," I explained, as I embraced them both, "where an event occurred of which I wish to inform you without delay."

"Indeed," said my father dryly as he lit a cigar, "so formal an announcement excites the liveliest curiosity."

"I have promised to marry——"

Aunt Marie threw up her hands and my father, frowning, exclaimed:

"I can only hope "—he began.

I would not allow him to continue. "I have promised to marry a man whom I love and respect with all my heart, who I am sure will make me happy—Baron Frederick von Tilling."

My father sprang up: "After all I said to you yesterday."

Aunt Marie shook her head. "I had rather have heard another name. In the first place Baron Tilling is not a good match; he has nothing, and his views are so peculiar."

"His principles and views in general are after my own heart, and I am not hunting a good match, as you call it. But Father, my dear old father, do not look so angry; do not mar my happiness by making me feel your displeasure."

"But, child," he said, in somewhat softened tone, for a little tenderness usually disarmed him, "I only desire your happiness. I could not be happy with a man who is not heart and soul a soldier."

"You do not have to marry him," remarked Aunt Marie judicially. "His soldier notions are of no consequence," she added. "But I could not be happy with a man who could speak of the God of the Bible with such lack of reverence."

"Allow me to remark, dear Aunt, that you do not have to marry him either."

"Each man's desire is his own heaven," sighed my father as he seated himself. "I suppose he will resign."

"We have not spoken of it, and I most earnestly desire it, but I fear he will not."

"When I remember that you rejected a prince," ejaculated Aunt Marie, "and now instead of rising will descend in the social scale!"

"How unkind you both are! and I had believed that you loved me. Here I come to you, the first time since poor Arno's death, with the assurance that I am happy, and instead of rejoicing you drag out all sorts of bitter reasons to reproach me with —the military service, Jehovah, social position!"

At the end of half an hour I succeeded in somewhat reconciling the two old people to the inevitable, and my father promised to come to my house the same evening to receive his future son-in-law. I invited all my relatives to tea and presented Tilling to them as my betrothed.

Rosa and Lilli were delighted; Conrad Althaus cried: "Bravo, Martha! and you, Lilli, profit by the example." My father was kind and courteous, and Aunt Marie overflowing with sentiment.

"Marriages are made in heaven," she said, "and happen just as they are ordained. With God's blessing you will be happy, and I shall pray incessantly that his blessing may descend upon you."

My son Rudolph was presented to his "new papa," and Frederick lifted him in his arms, kiss-

ing him as he said: "We will both try, my little
fellow, to make a good man of you."

In the course of the evening my father hinted at
his idea that Tilling would retire from the service.

Frederick threw up his head in astonishment.

"Resign—abandon my career! I have no other.
One does not need to be a friend of war to do faithful service in the army."

"Yes, yes, I know; just as you said lately the
fireman need not want to set a house on fire."

"I could suggest other illustrations: need a physician love cancers and typhus, or a judge have
a particular zest for burglary and murder? But
abandon my profession! What reason could I have
for doing so?"

"Reason enough," said Aunt Marie, "to spare
your wife garrison life and anxiety in case of war.
Although this anxiety is nonsense; for if a man
is destined to live to old age, he will come safely
through all dangers."

"The reasons given are certainly important; it
will be my earnest endeavor to spare my wife as
much as possible all the anxieties of life. But the
unpleasant circumstance of having a husband without profession or occupation would be worse than
garrison life. And the risk that my resignation
would be ascribed to indolence or cowardice would
be far more than the dangers of a campaign. I
have never thought of such a thing for a moment.
I trust you have not, Martha?"

"Suppose I made it a condition?"

"You would not do that? I should be obliged to
sacrifice my happiness. You are rich, I possess
nothing except my pay and the prospect of promotion; I will not surrender these. It would be a
lowering of my dignity and contrary to my idea of
honor."

"Right, my son; now I am reconciled!" exclaimed
my father. "It would be an outrage to abandon
your career. You will soon be colonel, probably a
general, and may hope to be division commander

or minister of war. That will give your wife a
notable position."

I was silent. I was little affected by the prospect
of being the wife of a division commander. I would
far rather live in retirement upon one of our estates;
still the standpoint of Frederick met my approval.

"Yes, quite reconciled," continued my father.
"For to tell the truth—now you need not look so
black—I thought you would desire to retire to private life. But so far as Martha is concerned, you
could scarce expect a soldier's daughter and a
soldier's widow to be willing to join the ranks of
the civilians."

Tilling laughed. He glanced at me as if to say,
"I know you better," but said aloud:

"Oh, I presume she fell in love with my uniform."

We were married in September of the same year.
My husband had two months' leave of absence.
We spent a week in Berlin, and our first visit there
was to the sister of Frederick's mother. I could
judge from the amiability and intellectual character
of this lady what Frederick's mother must have
been, as they were said greatly to resemble each
other. Frau Cornelia von Tessow was the widow
of a Prussian general; she had an only son who
had just become a lieutenant. I have never seen
a handsomer young man than Gottfried Tessow.
The devotion of mother and son was touching.

"How can a mother who loves her son as the very
apple of her eye allow him to adopt so dangerous
a profession as that of arms," I said to Frederick.

"There are some facts which no one considers,
some risks which no one ever contemplates. One
of these is the thought of the danger of the
soldier's life. If the idea is even suggested, one
feels as if it were unmanly and cowardly to consider it at all. It has now become so universally
accepted that this danger must be met, and at the
same time the percentage of those who fall is so

much less than of those who escape, that no one ever thinks about the chances of death. Every human being knows he must some time die, and really, what pleasanter and more reputable position can a Prussian nobleman attain than that of a cavalry officer."

We spent our time at the different fashionable resorts and I discovered new accomplishments in Frederick, that he spoke English and French well, while his refined enjoyment of music, art, and every fresh landscape added to my delight.

Upon our return we joined Frederick's regiment, then stationed at Olmütz. No congenial companionship was to be found in the place, and we withdrew entirely from society. Excepting the hours necessarily spent by Frederick in his official duties, and by myself with my little Rudolph, we devoted our whole time to each other. I exchanged the first necessary visits of ceremony with the ladies of the garrison, but would not allow an intimate acquaintance. I could not endure the scandal, servant-girl stories, and general gossip of their coffee parties, and Frederick had an equal distaste for the card and drinking parties of the officers. We had other and better things to do. The world in which we moved as we sat by our steaming tea-kettle was millions of miles apart from that of the Olmütz garrison. We joyfully took up a course of scientific reading, and with liveliest sympathy kept pace with the advancing thought of the world's earnest workers; not alone in science, but in all the social and philanthropic development of the age we took an interested part.

The Christmas holidays we spent at my father's house in Vienna. On Christmas Eve the family were joined by Doctor Bresser and his Excellency " Upon the Whole," who chanced, in answer to a casual question, to say in my hearing:

"It is true. There are heavy, dark, and portentous clouds on the political horizon."

I shrank in terror.

"What! How! What do you mean?" I cried anxiously.

"Denmark is getting too audacious."

"Ah, Denmark," I said, relieved. "The storm does not threaten us. It is in any event distressing to hear of a prospect of war, but when I am told the Danes and not the Austrians are concerned, I feel compassion but not terror."

"You need not alarm yourself," cried my father, "in case Austria is drawn into it. If we must maintain the rights of Schleswig-Holstein against the violence of Denmark, we shall not lose anything. There will be no risk of loss of territory even in the event of an unfortunate campaign."

"How can you believe, Father, that if our troops march over the border I would think of any such thing as Austrian territory, Schleswig-Holstein rights, or Danish arrogance? I should see but one thing, the danger of those I love. And that remains the same, no matter upon what grounds war is begun."

"My child, the fate of the individual cannot be considered when events involving the world's history are at stake. So soon as war breaks out, whether this or that man fall becomes of no consequence in view of the mighty question whether the cause of our own land shall be lost or won. And, as I said, should we cross swords with the Danes, nothing is lost and we may thereby extend our influence in the German Alliance. I dream continually of the time when the Hapsburgs shall recover the German imperial crown, to which they are entitled. I would regard the war with Denmark a fit opportunity, not only to wipe out the disgrace of '59, but also so to secure our position in the German empire that we could indemnify ourselves for the loss of Lombardy, and perhaps,— who knows?—so increase our power that we might reconquer that province."

I looked across the room where Frederick, unconscious of this conversation, was having a laughing wit encounter with Lilli. An agonizing pain possessed my soul; a pain which in one moment revealed a host of possibilities. War,—and he, my all, must go, to be wounded, perhaps killed. Our child, yet unborn, to be brought fatherless into the world,—our happiness, so short-lived, to be cut off,—this danger in one balance, and in the other? Austria's position in the German Alliance, the independence of Schleswig-Holstein, "fresh laurels in the army's crown of glory"—a few poor phrases for school orations and army proclamations. And yet victory or defeat remained alike uncertain. Not only my individual suffering would be staked against the pretended welfare of the realm, but that of thousands upon thousands of other individuals in my own and in the enemy's country. Ah, if it were only possible to turn aside this monstrous thing? If all united—all reasonable, just, and righteous folk—to banish this threatening, hideous evil.

"Tell me," I said to his Excellency, "has the matter gone so far? Do you diplomatists and politicians not know how to prevent this conflict?"

"Do you think, Baroness, that it is always our duty to maintain peace? It would be a noble mission, but impracticable. We are charged to guard the interests of our respective states and dynasties, to watch against any threatened infringement of their powers, and to seize every opportunity for supremacy, jealously to maintain the honor of the land, and to revenge insult."

"In short," I said bitterly, "according to the maxims of war, to injure the enemy—that is, every other state—to the utmost of your ability, and if the struggle is prospective, to maintain, stiff-neckedly, that you are in the right, even if well aware that you are in the wrong."

"Certainly."

"Until both sides lose patience and fly at each other's throats. It is horrible."

"It is the only resource. How else could a contest between nations be decided?"

"How are contests between respectable citizens settled?"

"Through courts of law. The nations recognize none such."

"Just as the barbarian does not," exclaimed Doctor Bresser. "Nations are in their mutual intercourse still uncivilized, and it will be a long time before they will rise to the sense of the justice of an international tribunal."

"That will never be," said my father. "There are things that can only be fought out, and cannot be settled by legal process. Even were the attempt made to establish such a jurisdiction, the more powerful states would never submit to it any more than two gentlemen, one of whom had insulted the other, would carry their difference into the courts. They would simply choose their seconds and settle it with their swords."

"The duel is a barbarous, an inhuman custom."

"You cannot alter it, Doctor."

"I would at least not approve it, your Excellency."

"What do you say, Frederick," said my father, turning to his son-in-law. "Are you of the opinion that after a box on the ear you should go into the courts and get five florin damages."

"I would not do it."

"You would challenge the offender?"

"Certainly."

"Aha, Martha! aha, Doctor!" cried my father triumphantly. "Did you hear? Even Tilling, who is no friend of war, acknowledges to being an advocate of the duel."

"An advocate? I have not said that. I only said, that in certain cases I would of course resort to the duel — as I have several times been obliged to do, just as I have from loyal obligation entered every campaign. I conform to popular prejudice as to laws of honor. But I do not mean it to be understood that this same code of honor conforms to my ideal. By-and-by, when this ideal attains the mastery, the receiver of an unmerited injury will not be regarded as disgraced—only upon the boorish offender the disgrace will fall. It will then be considered as immoral to seek personal revenge, as in other respects in cultivated society it is intolerable to take the law into one's own hands."

"We shall wait a long time for that," said my father, "so long as an aristocracy exists."

"That will not be forever," muttered the Doctor.

"Oh, so you would abolish the aristocracy?"

"Yes, the feudal. The future needs no nobility."

"So much the more it needs noble men," added Frederick.

"And this new race will accept a box on the ear?"

"There will be no one to offer one."

"And they will not defend themselves when a neighboring state falls foul of them?"

"No neighboring states will attack them, just as none of our neighbors attack us at our country seats, and as the lord of the castle no longer nowadays keeps his troop of horse."

"The state of the future will maintain no standing armies? What, then, will become of you lieutenant-colonels?"

"What has become of the feudal squires?"

THIRD BOOK.

1864.

WE remained in Vienna two weeks. It was no
happy time for me. This fatal prospect of
war benumbed every hopeful and joyous thought;
the instability of my happiness overmastered me.
The possibilities, which always surround us, of sick-
ness and death, of disaster by fire or flood—nature's
elemental threats—we become so hardened to that
we live with a comfortable sense of security. Why
has mankind willfully fixed other barriers to happiness and added to natural hazards, such as vol-
canoes and tornadoes, the possibility of war?

I could no longer accept this as the decree of fate.
Instead of resignation I felt only pain and horror.
Why should we concern ourselves about the constitution of Denmark and Schleswig-Holstein? Of
what consequence to us was it whether the "Protocol Prince" repealed or confirmed the constitutional law of the thirteenth of November, 1863?
All the newspapers were full of discussions of this
question as if it were the most important matter in
the world, so that people had no time to consider
whether it was worth while to expose our husbands
and sons to the risk of being shot down. Only
momentarily could I become reconciled to this view
of the thing when the idea of duty was presented
to my mind. True we belonged to the German
Alliance, and as German brothers we must defend
the rights of oppressed German kindred. The
national spirit justified the use of force; there was
an obligation from this standpoint. By desperately
clinging to this idea the oppressive anxiety of my
heart was somewhat lulled. Had I anticipated that
two years later this whole German brotherhood

would be dissolved into fragments and become the bitterest enemies, and that the present Austrian hatred of Denmark would be exceeded by Austrian hatred of Prussia, I would have even then discovered that the motives which are proclaimed as justification of war are nothing more than phrases.

On the tenth of January we returned to Olmütz. There was no longer any doubt about the war. Among the officers and their wives there was great excitement, chiefly of a pleasurable kind. The opportunity for promotion and distinction made all jubilant, whether the motive was ambition, restless desire for action, or the longing for increase of pay.

"It will be a famous war," said the Colonel, "and will be immensely popular. There will be no damage to our territory; the seat of war is on foreign soil. Under such circumstances it is a double pleasure to fight."

"What fills me with enthusiasm," said a young lieutenant, "is the noble motive: the defense of our German brothers. As the Prussians unite with us, we are secure of victory, and the national bonds will be drawn still closer. It is the national idea."

"Do not say much about that," replied the Colonel almost sternly. "That kind of a swindle does not suit an Austrian. It was just that sort of a hobby-horse that Louis Napoleon rode in 1859— 'An Italian Italy.' The whole thing is unsuited to the condition of Austria. Why talk of a band of German brothers to us? Bohemians, Hungarians, Germans, Croats,— where is there any *national* bond? We know but one motive for union, the loyal love of our own dynasty. The thing which should inspire us when we go into the field is not the circumstance that we are allies as Germans and for Germans, but that we are doing good and faithful service for our beloved ruler. Long live the Emperor!"

All rose and pledged the toast. A spark of enthusiasm filled my heart for a moment. When thousands are inspired by one and the same motive for one and the same person, there is pleasure in self-sacrifice. That is the spirit which swells the heart, whether we call it loyalty or patriotism or *esprit de corps*. It is but another name for love, and it works so masterfully that in its name the most atrocious work of deadly hate, war, is made to seem love's duty.

But only for a moment did it warm my heart, for a stronger love than that of country is the love for husband. My husband's life was to me of far greater value, and when this was at stake I could only curse all parties—whether of Schleswig, Holstein or Japan.

The days succeeding I passed in continual anxiety. On the sixteenth of January the allies demanded that Denmark revoke a certain decree against which the Holstein chambers and nobility had protested, invoking at the same time the protection of the German Alliance. Twenty-four hours' grace was allowed. Denmark naturally refused. This refusal was expected, for the Austrian and Prussian troops had been massed on the border, and on the first of February they crossed the Eider. So then the die was cast, the struggle had begun. My father at once addressed a letter of congratulation to us:

" Rejoice, my children," he wrote, " we have now the opportunity to make good the defeat of '59 by dealing a few sharp blows at Denmark. When we return from the north as victors we can again turn our attention to the south; the Prussians will remain our allies and it will not be possible for the intriguer Louis Napoleon and the treacherous Italians to defeat us."

Frederick's regiment, to the great chagrin of the Colonel, was not ordered to the north. This soon brought a letter of commiseration from my father:

" I regret sincerely that Frederick has the ill luck to serve with a regiment which is not called upon to take part in this glorious campaign.

Martha will naturally rejoice that she has her husband at her side and is spared the anxiety, but
Frederick, I am sure, though from philanthropic
motives he is opposed to war, can but regret, when
it breaks out, that he is not on the scene, as his
military ardor must surely be aroused."

"Is it hard for you to remain with me, Frederick?" I asked, when we received this letter.

He pressed me to his heart.   The silent answer
was enough.

But there was always the risk that additional
troops would be ordered to the seat of war.   With
the greatest interest I read every report and zeal-
ously hoped the struggle would soon end.   The
wish was not a patriotic one.   I would have preferred that our army should be victors; but what I
vainly hoped for was the close of the war before
the man I loved should be sent into the field, and
the very last thing I cared for was what might become of the little scrap of country concerned.
Anxious to learn what could be the "reasons of
state" to justify the interference of the allies, I
studied the history of Schleswig-Holstein.

I found that the disputed district had been ceded
to Denmark in 1027.   Then the Danes were right;
they were the legitimate kings of the country.

Two hundred years later, however, the province
was turned over to a younger line of the royal
house and was only regarded as a Danish fief.   In
1326 Schleswig was given over to Count Gerhard
of Holstein, and the Waldmarsch constitution,
which was then formulated, stipulated that never
again should Denmark claim any rights of ownership.   Why, if this was the case, then it was certainly right that we should be on the side of the
allies; we fought for the Waldmarsch constitution.
What was the use of constitutional law if the rights
so assured were not upheld?

In the year 1448 the Waldmarsch constitution
was ratified by King Christian I.   Beyond a doubt
Denmark would never again claim sovereignty.

How then did the Protocol Prince set up his claim?

Twelve years later the ruler of Schleswig died without heirs, and the National Assembly met at Ripon (it is always satisfactory to know just when and where the national chambers convene—it was, namely, in 1460, at Ripon), and there proclaimed the Danish king Duke of Schleswig, whereupon he pledged himself that the countries should remain forever undivided. This confused me again a little bit. The only thing certain is that they shall remain forever united.

With further historical studies the confusion increases, for now begins, notwithstanding the "forever undivided" clause (this word "forever" plays an enviable *rôle* in all political complications), an eternal division and subdivision of the country between the sons of kings, followed by a re-union under the succeeding kings, and the founding of new lines—Holstein-Gottorp and Schleswig-Sonderburg. These, again, cause further slicing under new lines, Sonderburg - Augustenburg, Beck-Glücksburg, Sonderburg-Glücksburg, Holstein-Glückstadt; in short, I cannot find my way out.

But look a little farther. Perhaps we can establish the historical right for which our countrymen must shed their blood.

Christian IV. took part in the Thirty Years' War, and the Imperialists and Swedes fell upon the duchy. Then a treaty was made (at Copenhagen, 1658,) by which the line Holstein-Gottorp was secured in the possession of the Schleswig province, and at last the Danish sovereignty was surrendered.

Surrendered forever. Thank God. I begin to feel that I am on safe ground.

But what happened through an agreement of the twenty-second of August, 1721? Simply this: The Gottorp portion of Schleswig became a dependency of the Danish monarchy. On the first of June, 1773, Holstein also was abandoned to Denmark— the whole becoming simply a Danish province.

That alters the case; now I am sure the Danes
are in the right.

But yet not quite, for the Vienna Congress of
1815 declared Holstein a part of the German Alliance. This, however, enraged the Danes. They
raised the battle-cry, "Denmark to the Eider," and
strove to secure the complete possession of what
they called South Jutland, otherwise Schleswig.
As a solution of the difficulty, the hereditary right of
the Augustenburg line was utilized to enforce the
German National Claim. In the year 1846 King
Christian wrote an open letter, wherein he declares
his aim to be the maintenance of the integrity of
the whole land, against which the "German provinces" protested. Two years later an announcement from the throne declared this complete union
as *fait accompli*, whereupon a rebellion broke out in
the two "German provinces." The Danes won one
battle, the Schleswig-Holsteiners the other. The
German Alliance interfered. Prussia took some
important strategic points, but this did not end the
struggle. At last Prussia and Denmark concluded
a peace; Schleswig-Holstein fought the Danes
single-handed and was defeated at Idstedt.

The German Alliance now peremptorily demanded that the insurgents suspend operations;
Austrian troops invested Holstein and the two
duchies were divided. What has become of the
"eternal union" promised by treaty and constitution?

Affairs do not yet seem to be finally settled. I
discovered a London protocol of May 8, 1852
(how lucky! we are at least sure of the dates of all
these brittle treaties), which *secured* to Prince
Christian of Glücksburg the succession to Schleswig. Now at last I know where this descriptive
title, "Protocol Prince," originated.

In the year 1854, after each duchy had adopted a
constitution, both were again appended to Denmark.
In 1858 Denmark was compelled to abrogate its
claim. This historical complication approaches the

present time, but I am not at all clear where the two provinces rightfully belong, and what is actually the cause of the outbreak of the present war.

On the eighteenth of November, 1858, the German Parliament approved the famous decree for the settlement of the common affairs of Denmark and Schleswig. Two days thereafter the king died. With him another line, that of Holstein-Glückstadt, became extinct, and as his successor prepared to claim the protection of the Alliance under the new decree, Frederick of Augustenburg appeared upon the scene. (I had almost forgotten this line.)

The Alliance at once allowed the Saxons and Hanoverians to invest Holstein, and proclaimed Augustenburg the Duke. Why? The Prussians and Austrians were not agreed as to the reason.

To this day I have not been able to comprehend it. It is asserted that the London protocol must be respected. Why? Are protocols in regard to things which absolutely do not concern us so eminently respectable that we must defend them at the expense of the blood of our own sons? Behind this probably is secreted another one of those "reasons of state." We must maintain as dogma that what the gentlemen around the green diplomatic table decide is the highest wisdom, that their aim is the greatest possible assurance of the increase of national supremacy. The London protocol of the eighth of May, 1852, must be upheld, but the constitutional decree of Copenhagen, of the thirteenth of January, 1863, must be revoked, and that within twenty-four hours. Upon that depended Austria's honor and welfare. The dogma is a little hard to believe; but in political matters even more than in religious questions, the mass allows itself to be guided by the principle of *quia absurdum;* to comprehend and reason is from the outset forbidden. When the sword is once drawn nothing more is allowable than a "hurrah," and a general struggle for victory, and the blessing of Heaven is at once invoked upon the strife. For so much is

certain: it must be of great consequence to the
Almighty that the London protocol should be maintained and the decree of the thirteenth of January
be revoked; he must so guide matters that just so
many human beings shall shed their blood and so
many villages be destroyed, in order to establish
the sovereignty either of the line of Glückstadt or
that of Augustenburg over a particular small section of this earthly territory. O, foolish, inhuman,
unreasoning world, still in the leading strings of
infancy! That was the conclusion of my historical
studies.

The most encouraging reports came from the
seat of war. The allies won battle after battle.
After the first engagement the Danes evacuated
the entire field; Schleswig and Jutland as far as
Limfjord were invested by our troops, and the
enemy was massed behind the fortifications of
Düppel and Alsen. Again we followed by means
of maps and flag-decorated pins the plan of campaign.
"If we only take the fortifications of Düppel or
capture Alsen," said the Olmütz citizens (for no
one talks with so much relish of military achieve-
ments as those who take no part in them), "then it
is over." Our brave Austrians show what they are
made of, and the Prussians do very well; the two
together are simply invincible. The result will be
that the whole of Denmark will be conquered and
added to the German Confederation. "What a
glorious result of war!"
There was nothing I more earnestly desired than
the storming of Düppel; the sooner the better, in
order that this butchery might end. If we could
only hope that it would end before Frederick's
regiment was ordered into the field! O, this sword
of Damocles! Every day I awoke with the dread
that before nightfall the order to march might
arrive.
"Accustom yourself to the thought, my wife,"
said Frederick. "Against the inevitable it is use-

less to protest.   I do not imagine that the war
will end with the capture of Düppel.   We shall be
obliged to send strong re-enforcements, and it is not
likely that my regiment will be spared."

The campaign lasted two months without result.
It is a pity such matters cannot be decided by one
battle as in the duel.   But no.   So soon as one
battle is lost another one follows, when one position
is abandoned another is secured; and so it goes on
until one or both armies are destroyed or reach the
point of exhaustion.

On the fourteenth of April, Düppel was stormed
and taken.   The news was received with acclama-
tion.   Men embraced each other on the street.   "Oh,
our noble army, gallant fellows; a wonderful piece
of strategy and courage!   We thank God."   In all
the churches the Te Deum was sung; the musi-
cians played new "Düppel Marches" and "Storming of Düppel Galops."   The comrades of my husband and their wives had a bitter drop, however, in
their cup of joy—their unlucky absence from the
field.

Immediately after this victory a peace conference
assembled in London, and I rejoiced over the prospect of a termination of the war.   How freely one
breathes when this word "peace" is uttered.   How
the nations will be relieved when the command,
"Ground Arms!" is heard around the world.   I
wrote down "Ground Arms" for the first time in
my diary.   Next to it—Utopia.

The conference dragged itself along for two
months and ended without any agreement as to
terms of peace.   Two days later came the order to
march.   We had twenty-four hours for preparation
and farewell.   I hourly expected the birth of my
child.   At the time when a wife most needs the
consolation of her husband's presence I was to be
deprived of it, and with the terrible possibility
awaiting him of death or equal disaster.   We were
too clear-sighted to console each other with any of
the hollow phrases and hypocrisy by which war

is made to seem a thing of righteous duty. The appalling magnitude of the approaching evil I would not cloak by any of the conventional patriotic or heroic masks. The prospect of being able to shoot and cut down the Danes was no compensation to him for the dread parting from his wife, for death and destruction are repulsive to any noble mind; and in case this parting should prove an eternal one, what reason of state could reconcile me to such a sacrifice. The defender of his country: that is the sonorous title which decorates the soldier. In truth what nobler duty can there be than to defend the common cause. But why should the soldier add to his oath of allegiance a hundred other military duties besides that of defense of country. Why must he go beyond this duty: to attack another country, when not the slightest danger threatens his own. Shall he, because of the love of strife or the ambitious motives of foreign princes, pledge his highest good,—life and health,—as he is only justified in doing when such danger actually threatens life and home? Why, for instance, must this Austrian army march out to set the Augustenburg upon his petty throne? Why, why? That is the question which to propose to emperor or pope is treasonable and blasphemous, and which by them would be considered on the one side impiety, on the other dangerous disloyalty, which both would scorn to answer.

The regiment was to march at ten o'clock. Not one moment of those few last hours did we give to sleep. There was always the possibility of safe return and we vainly strove to grasp this feeble hope. As day dawned exhausted nature revenged itself, and with groans and tears I realized that my hour of trial had come. Physical anguish scarce heightened the sorrow of parting, and Frederick tore himself away uncertain whether the next hour might not leave him bereft of wife and child.

The Olmütz papers of the next day contained the following account:

" Yesterday, with flying colors and beating drums the —th Regiment marched out to win fresh laurels at the seat of war, in defense of the outraged rights of German brotherhood. Joyous enthusiasm inspired each heart, patriotic spirit illumined each eye," etc., etc.

I lost my child and for weeks I lay unconscious. One day I suddenly awoke after frightful dreams of battle scenes, where I seemed to be continually pleading in the name of justice, of mercy and humanity: "Ground Arms!"

My father and Aunt Marie stood at my bedside. "Is he alive," I cried; "have letters come, or despatches?"

Yes, there were both, and after some days I was allowed to read them. There was one marked— "Not to be delivered until all danger is past." From this I take some extracts:

" To-day we met the enemy for the first time. Up to the present we had marched through conquered territory, the Danes having rapidly retreated. All around us were the ruins of smoking villages, scattered harvests, abandoned arms and knapsacks; the earth was torn up by shot and shell, and covered with dead horses and masses of graves. Such were the landscapes and accessories, through which we followed the footsteps of the victors, in order to make sure of other triumphs—that is, to burn new villages, etc.; this we have done to-day. We have captured the position of the enemy. Behind us a village is in flames. The inhabitants, fortunately, had already fled. But a horse had been forgotten in his stall. I heard his despairing stamping and whinnying. Do you know what I did? It would not have gained me a decoration—for instead of cutting down a few Danes I ran to free the poor animal. It was too late; the crib was already in flames, the straw under his hoofs, and his mane were in flames. I shot him through the head and he dropped dead, saved from horrible torture. Back I rushed into the field, into the smoke of powder, and the wild alarm of continual volleys of musketry, flying cannon balls, raging battle-cries. All around me, friend and foe, were absorbed in the tumult of contest. I could take no part in this feeling. I could think of nothing save the possibility that I had already lost you. The engagement lasted two hours and the enemy abandoned the field. We did not pursue them. There was enough to do. A few hundred steps from the village, untouched by the flames, stood a farmhouse with capacious granaries and stables. We collected our wounded and cared for them as well as possible. The dead were buried in the morning—and with them probably many yet alive, for it frequently happens with the severely wounded that a species of tetanus causes the bodies to assume the rigidity of death. Many, whether dead, wounded, or unharmed bodily, we shall leave behind us; those, too, who were overwhelmed by the falling walls of the burning buildings. The dead will slowly moulder, the wounded slowly bleed to death, and the uninjured slowly starve. And we—hurrah! We will push on in our merry, dashing war."

" The next engagement will probably be a pitched battle. From all information obtained, two great army corps will stand opposed to each other. Then the loss in killed and wounded will run up into the thousands; when the artillery has begun its deadly work, the front ranks are quickly mowed down. That is a magnificent arrangement. The pity is that some weapon is not yet invented, which each side can fire once, and which will by that discharge utterly destroy both armies. Possibly that would abolish war. Brute force could then never be relied upon to settle differences.

" Why do I write all this to you? Why do I not break out, as every soldier ought, in enthusiastic hymns of praise of the glorious results of war? Why? Because I will speak nothing but the truth, the absolute, unvarnished truth; because I hate the customary lying phrases; and because, in this hour when I may be so close to death, I am doubly impelled to tell you what lies next my heart. Whether thousands think otherwise, or feel impelled by duty to speak otherwise, I must once more say, before I fall a sacrifice, that I hate war. If every man who feels the same would say so, what a warning cry would go up to heaven. All the present hurrah accompanying the thunder of cannon would be overpowered by a new battle-cry of suffering, outraged humanity: 'War upon war.'

4:30 A. M.

" The foregoing I wrote last night. I then lay down, upon a pile of straw and snatched a few hours sleep. In half an hour the reveille will sound and I can throw this letter into the field mail. All are already awake and preparing for the march. Poor fellows! they have had little rest, after yesterday's bloody work, to prepare them for a still bloodier struggle to-day. I have just made the rounds of a temporary hospital which we must leave behind us. Among the dying and wounded were several whom it would have been charity to shoot as I did the poor horse. There was one whose whole lower jaw was shot away; another—but enough, I cannot help them. Death is the sole release and death comes so slowly. To those who beg piteously death turns a deaf ear. He is otherwise engaged tearing away the busy and the happy who vainly plead for yet a little time. My horse is saddled. Farewell Martha—if you still live."

Fortunately I found in the packet one or two letters of later date, written after the battle anticipated by Frederick.

"The day is ours. I am safe and well. Those are two favorable reports—the first for your father, the second for you. I dare not forget that for countless others the same day brought overwhelming sorrow and misery."

In another, Frederick reported meeting his cousin Gottfried.

"Imagine my surprise when I saw Aunt Cornelia's only son at the head of a detachment riding past me. The youngster is filled with martial ardor, but how his poor mother must suffer. That evening we were in the same camp, and I sent for him to come to my tent. 'Is it not magnificent,' he cried, 'that we are fighting for the same cause and are near together. How lucky I am that war should break out the first year of my service. I may win a cross of honor.' 'And my Aunt, how does she take it?' 'Oh, like all women—with tears which she strove to hide from me, in order not to dampen my enthusiasm; with blessings, sorrow, and pride.' 'And how was it with you, yourself, youngster, the first time you went into battle?' 'Oh, enchanting, delightful!' 'You need not lie, my boy; it is not the staff officer examining into your fitness for a military office, but your friend, who is questioning you.' 'I can only repeat, it was inspiring. Horrible? Yes, but grand! And with the consciousness that I was fulfilling man's highest duty, with God on my side for king and country! And then: that I met death so close—dared it face to face, and it did not touch me—that filled me with a lofty sense of the peculiar glory of war, as, in the old epic stories, I saw the muse of history guiding our arms to victory. A noble indignation filled me against the

insolent enemy who had dared to attack a German country, and it was an intense satisfaction to gratify this hate.
This desire to destroy, without being a murderer, this setting one's own life in the balance is a singular sensation.'

"So the boy rattled on. I let him talk. I had experienced it all in my first campaign. 'Epic'—yes, that was
the right word. The stories of martial heroes and battlefields, by means of which we so carefully train our incip-
ient soldiers in the schools, are the proper preparation
for the thunder of artillery and the battle-cries of the
combatants, which mount with resonant force into our
heated brains. And the extraordinary surroundings, the
incomprehensible lawlessness in the midst of which we
find ourselves, seems like an outlook from a former
peaceful, law-abiding life down into a titanic struggle
within the gates of hell. I could with difficulty readjust
myself so as fully to comprehend Gottfried's state of
mind. I had so early realized that military zeal is not
superhuman but simply inhuman; no mystical revelation
from the kingdom of Lucifer, but a reminiscence of the
period of brutality—a resurrection of barbarism.

"Only he who becomes drunk with the passion of destruction, who—as I have occasionally seen among us,—
can split open with vindictive blow the defenseless head
of a disarmed enemy, who can sink to the Berserker—
deeper still, to the rank of bloodthirsty tiger—has for the
moment enjoyed the lust of war. I never can, my wife,
believe me, never.

"Gottfried is delighted that we Austrians fight for the
same just cause (what does he know? as if every cause
is not claimed by the army orders as just) as the Prussians. 'We Germans are a band of brothers.' 'That was
proved by the Thirty Years', also by the Seven Years' war,'
I suggested in a low tone. Gottfried paid no attention.
'Together, for each other we will conquer every enemy.'
'How will it be, my boy, when to-day or to-morrow the
Prussians declare war against the Austrians, and we two
stand opposed to each other?' 'Not to be thought of.
What? after having fought and bled together? Impossible!' 'Impossible? I warn you against that; nothing is
impossible in political matters. As evanescent as the
ephemeral fly in the kingdom of nature are the enmities
and friendships of nations."

"I write all this, not that I believe in your invalid condition it may interest you, but because I have a haunting
conviction that I may not survive the campaign, and I am
not willing to take my convictions into the grave with

me. The convictions of reflecting and humane soldiers should not be falsified or buried in silence. 'I have dared,' was Ulrich von Hutten's motto. 'I have said'—: with this quieting of conscience, I will depart from life."

The latest of these letters was five days old. What had happened in those five days? My anxiety and dread became insupportable. My father was obliged to return to his estate of Grumitz, and I was out of all present danger. Aunt Marie remained and endeavored to quiet me with her conventional ideas of destiny, special providences, and the like—small comfort for the dreadful lack of news from the front. After his return home my father telegraphed repeatedly the result of his inquiries. He could get no reply from Frederick's colonel, yet on examination of the list of killed and wounded his name was not discovered.

One afternoon, when I had begged to be left alone, I lay on the sofa half dreaming of the day he left me. Aroused by a slight movement I sprang up in terror, with the feeling that anxiety had overmastered reason, and that it was in imagination only that I saw Frederick standing in the doorway. The next moment I was clasped to his heart.

When we found time for other thought than the joy of re-union, Frederick explained that he had been left wounded in a farmhouse, and the regimental surgeon could make no other report than "missing," which, fortunately, had not reached us. As soon as possible he hastened home, and the war was virtually at an end when he recovered sufficiently to be moved.

We spent the summer in Grumitz, and after much serious consultation I persuaded Frederick to resign his commission. Our interests had now, through our love, become so united, that there was no longer any feeling of hesitancy on account of my being the financial partner. He was only anxious to spare us both the horrors of another war.

My son Rudolph, now a seven-years-old little

man, began to learn to read and write. I was his teacher. I should not have been willing to turn over to any hired servant the delight (which to her would have been no pleasure) of watching the dawning of intelligence and the slow unfolding of this precious soul. He accompanied us in our daily walks, and, as is usual with children, he tested our intelligence by the waking curiosity of his own. We did not hesitate to say to him, upon questions that no human being can justly answer, "We do not know." In the beginning, when we made this reply, Rudolph was not satisfied, but carried his queries to his aunt Marie, his grandfather, or his nurse, and was, of course, gratified by no doubtful answers. Triumphantly he would return to us. "You do not know how old the moon is? I do; six thousand years—remember that." Frederick and I exchanged glances. A whole volume of pedagogic lament and comment lay in this glance and silence.

I particularly objected to the "playing soldier," with which my father and brother Otto continually sought to entertain him. The idea of an enemy and the duty of cutting him down was developed without my knowing how. One day Frederick and I surprised him beating two crying puppies with a riding-whip.

"You are a treacherous Italian," he cried, giving one of the poor little creatures a blow; "and you," hitting the other, "an insolent Dane."

Frederick snatched the whip from his hand.

"And you are a heartless Austrian," he said, laying two or three lashes on Rudolph's shoulders. The Italians and Danes ran away joyfully, while the Austrian began to blubber.

"I hope you are not angry, Martha, that I have struck your boy? I am no friend in general to the lash, but cruelty to animals I cannot endure——"

"Quite right," I interrupted.

"People can only be cruel to people, then?" whimpered the little fellow between his sobs.

" Not at all."

" Why, you yourself went out to beat the Italians and Danes."

" They were enemies."

" Then we can beat our enemies? "

" And to-morrow, or the day after," said Frederick, turning away, " the priest will tell him that he must love his enemies. Oh, logic! "

He turned again to Rudolph.

" No, we must not beat our enemies because we hate them, but because they are going to beat us."

" What are they going to beat us about?" exclaimed Rudolph, intensely interested.

" Because we—no, no!" and Frederick gave it up, " we will never make our way out of this circle. Go and play, Rudi—we forgive you, but you must not do it again."

Cousin Conrad, whose regiment was stationed in the neighborhood, made some slight progress in Lilli's favor. He made no special assaults, but was evidently bent upon a prolonged siege.

" There are various ways of capturing a fortification," he explained to me one day, " by storm, by famine; there are also several methods of bringing the feminine heart to capitulation. The surest of these is habit—the custom of seeing a fellow about. It must touch her finally to see the persistence of my love; how patiently I keep silence but so unfailingly turn up again. When I stay away a little while it will make quite a hole in her existence; when I remain long away she will not know how to live without me."

" And how many times seven years do you intend to serve? "

" I have not calculated—as many as necessary until she accepts me."

" I am struck with admiration. Are there no other girls in the world? "

" None for me. I have Lilli on the brain. There is something in her walk, in the dimple in her chin, in her way of speaking that no other can equal.

You, Martha, are, for example, ten times prettier and a hundred times cleverer——"

"Thanks."

"But I would not have you for a wife."

"Thanks."

"Just because you are too clever. You would certainly look down upon me. The cross on my collar, my saber, my spurs have no effect upon you. Lilli has a great respect for a fighting man. I know she worships the army, while you——"

"I have only married into the army twice," I replied laughing.

We often had visitors from Vienna, diplomatists and distinguished officers. I frequently took part in their discussions over present political difficulties, though always after protest on their part that I would surely feel but little interest in them. Through these I was enabled to follow to the end the Danish question which I had so industriously studied during the campaign. Certainly, after all these battles and victories, it would be decided what was to be done with the duchies. The Augustenburg—the famous Augustenburg, to maintain whose well-established rights the whole strife had been made—had he received his portion? Not at all. An entirely new pretender appeared upon the scene. It was not enough to have Glücksburg and Gottorp, and whatever all the other lines were called, but in addition Russia must step in with a fresh candidate. Against Augustenburg Russia pitted Oldenburg. The final result of the war seemed to be that none of the "burgs" were to have the duchies, but that these were to be divided among the victors.

The following were the articles upon which it was proposed to conclude peace:

(1.) Denmark must surrender the duchies to Austria and Prussia.

I was satisfied with this. The allies would naturally hasten to restore these conquered provinces to their rightful owners.

(2.)   The border must be carefully defined.

That was also very fine; if only these metes and bounds could be given the grace of durability; but it is aggravating to watch the everlasting vicissitudes of the blue and green lines on the geographical maps.

(3.)   The state debt must be divided according to the population.

This I did not understand at all.

(4.)   The expenses of the war must be borne by the duchies.

I did not exactly comprehend this, either. The land had become a desert, its harvests were destroyed, its sons were in their graves; some compensation must be offered them. Now, then, it must pay the costs.

"What is the news in regard to Schleswig-Holstein?" I asked one day to open the conversation.

"The latest is that von Beust has addressed a categorical demand to the Parliament for information as to how it can be possible for the allies to accept the surrender of these provinces from a king whose provincial sovereignty had not been recognized by them."

"Quite an intelligent suggestion," I remarked; "for it is said that the Protocol-Prince is not the legitimate heir to the German provinces, and now you allow Christian IX.——"

"You do not understand anything about it, child," said my father impatiently. "It is a piece of impudence and chicanery in this Beust, and nothing else. The duchies belong to us because we have conquered them."

"But not for ourselves; it was claimed for Augustenburg."

"You do not understand. The causes which before the outbreak of war are given by diplomatists as justifiable for action frequently retire into the background so soon as the struggle is over. Victories and defeats produce entirely new complications, and nations are forced to fresh considerations by undreamed of circumstances."

"So that after all the reasons áre no reasons at all—only pretenses?" I inquired.

"Pretenses? No." One of the generals came to my father's relief with "apparent motives—suggestions of probable events which are justified by the measure of their success."

"If I were allowed to suggest," said my father, "I would not have permitted an intimation of peace after Düppel and Alsen had been captured, until the whole of Denmark had been conquered."

"What would you do with it?"

"Make it a part of the German Confederation!"

"Why should you, Papa, who are such a patriotic Austrian, care for the German Confederation?"

"Have you forgotten that the Hapsburgs were German emperors, and may be so again?"

"How would it be," suggested Frederick, "if some other great German cherished the same dreams?"

My father laughed derisively.

"The crown of the holy Roman-German Empire on the head of a Protestant prince! Have you lost your senses?"

"It is not certain that the two powers will not differ as to the settlement of this latest question," remarked Doctor Bresser. "To conquer the provinces of the Elbe is of not much consequence—but what to do with them may prove the source of discord. Every war, whatever the result° may. be, contains within itself the seed of future wars. Naturally one act of violence leads to another, and they proceed in an indefinite procession."

Some days later a fresh piece of news was reported.

King William of Prussia visited our Emperor at Schönbrunn. The meeting and embraces were most affectionate, while the Prussian eagle floated in the breeze, military bands played only Prussian national hymns, and there was great popular

enthusiasm. I rejoiced over this account, as it
seemed to contradict Doctor Bresser's fateful prophecies. My father rejoiced because of the advantage
to be gained in using the allied forces, in case Austria wished to re-conquer Lombardy.

" Napoleon III. will never tolerate that," said one
of the generals. " It is a very bad sign, indeed, that
Benedetti, Austria's worst enemy, is now Minister
to Berlin."

" Will you tell me, gentlemen," I cried, folding
my hands, "why do not the general powers organize
a confederation?"

The gentlemen shrugged their shoulders. I had
evidently made one of those stupid suggestions
with which the fair sex are in the habit of enrich-
ing political discussions.

Autumn arrived. On the thirtieth of October
articles of peace were signed at Vienna, and the
desire of my heart, my husband's resignation, could
now be sent in. But man proposes and circumstances dispose of our plans. The house of Schmitt
& Sons went into bankruptcy, and the whole of my
private fortune was swept away. This was also
one of the results of war. Fortunately my father
was able to do something for me, but of quitting
the service there was now no prospect. We needed
Frederick's pay; it was our only means of independent livelihood. We were quartered in Vienna for
the winter, living in simple style, abandoning all
social pleasures of the gay world. It was enough
for my happiness that there was no present prospect of another war. Aunt Marie and my sisters
spent the season in Prague. As Conrad's regiment
was stationed in the Bohemian capital I somewhat
suspiciously questioned Lilli as to this singular
coincidence, to which she shrugged her shoulders
and replied: " You know I cannot bear him."

To a small circle of relatives and friends our
house was always open. The old companion of my
youth, Lori Griesbach, visited us often, in truth

oftener than was agreeable. Her conversation, even in earlier times generally uninteresting to me, I now found tiresomely superficial, and the horizon of her interests, which had always been a narrow one, seemed to have lessened astonishingly. She was handsome and gay and a coquette. I understood that in society she turned the heads of many, and it was rumored that she had no objection to love-making. It was not very agreeable to me to discover that she admired Frederick exceedingly, and I intercepted many a languishing glance which indicated her intention to occupy a niche in his heart. Lori's husband, the ornament of the Jockey Club, the race-course, and the theatrical *coulisses* was notoriously so unfaithful to her that she might be pardoned for some small attempt to avenge herself; but I preferred she should not choose Frederick as a means to that end. I had something to say about that.

Jealous—I? I grew red at the consciousness of this feeling. I was so certain of his heart. He could love no one—no one in the world as much as he loved me. Well, yes, love—but an innocent sort of flirtation, a little temporary state of amorousness. I was a little doubtful on that point.

Lori did not attempt to conceal from me how much she admired Frederick.

"Do you hear, Martha? you are really to be envied such a charming husband;" or, "Keep close guard over your Frederick, for he is surely firing the hearts of all the women."

"I am certain of his fidelity."

"Do not be so ridiculous—as if fidelity and married men were to be mentioned in the same breath. Faithful men do not exist. You know, for instance, how my husband——"

"But Lori, perhaps it is not true. Then, all men are not alike——."

"All of them, all of them; I can assure you of that. I do not know one man who will not flirt. Among those who are devoted to me are several

married men. What would you have? We are not
giving each other lessons in faithfulness."

"They know probably that you will not listen to
them. Does Frederick belong to this phalanx?" I
asked, laughing.

"I am not going to tell you, you little goose. It
is very good of me to direct your attention to the
fact of how much I admire him. I merely warn
you to keep an eye open."

"I have kept my eyes wide open, Lori, and they
have already informed me to my dissatisfaction
that you have opened your batteries upon him."

"There it is! I shall have to be more prudent in
future."

We both laughed; but still I felt that behind all
this joking allusion to my jealousy there was the
spark to rouse that passion, and that also back of
her teasing there might be a kernel of truth.

Lori's husband had not been in the Schleswig-
Holstein campaign, and the fact was an annoyance
to him. Lori was also provoked at the unlucky
circumstance.

"It was such a glorious war!" she complained.
"Griesbach would have been promoted. The only
comfort is that in the next campaign——"

"What are you talking about?" I interrupted.
"There is not the slightest prospect of one. Or
have you heard anything? Why should war break
out now?"

"Why? I never trouble myself about that. Wars
come and there they are. Every four or five years
one breaks out—that is the course of history."

"But there must always be a cause."

"Perhaps—but who knows? Not I, nor my husband. 'What are they fighting about anyway
over there,' I asked him during the last war. 'I do
not know, and I do not care,' he answered, shrugging his shoulders. 'It is only provoking that I
am not with them,' he added. Oh, Griesbach is a
true soldier. The why and the wherefore of a war
are no business of the soldier. The diplomatists

settle all that. I never bother my brain about political matters. They do not concern us women—
we should not understand them. When the storm
breaks loose then we fall to praying——"

"That the storm may burst above our neighbor,
not upon us, naturally," I replied.

DEAR MADAM:
A friend—perhaps also an enemy, but at the
same time one who knows what he is talking about—in-
forms you by this letter that you are deceived—in the
most treacherous manner deceived. Your apparently
pious husband and your innocent looking friend do not
deserve your confidence. You poor, blind woman! I
have my reasons for tearing off their masks. I do not
inform you of this out of kindness to you, for I am sure
the knowledge of the deception of these two loved friends
will give you much pain; but I owe you no special regard.
Perhaps I am a repulsed admirer seeking to revenge himself. Of what consequence is it what the motive may be?
The fact is there, and you can make the most of it.
Without evidence you will not believe an anonymous
letter. The enclosed note was lost by the Countess G——.

This astonishing document lay on our breakfast
table one fine spring morning. Frederick sat opposite me, busy with his meal, while I read and re-
read this letter. The treacherous note enclosed was
in another envelope and I hesitated to open it.

I looked up at Frederick. He was buried in the
morning paper but must have become conscious of
my earnest glance, for he dropped it and with his
usual smiling face turned his head toward me.

"Well, what is the matter, Martha? What are
you staring at me for?"

"I want to know whether you still love me."

"Oh, of course not," he answered, laughing. "To
tell the truth, I never could endure you."

"I do not believe that."

"But what is it, is anything the matter? You
look faint."

I hesitated. Should I show him the letter?
Should I first examine the evidence I held in my
hand? My head whirled. My Frederick, my all,

my friend and husband, my confidant and lover—
could he be lost to me.   Unfaithful—he!   Perhaps
it was only a momentary passion, nothing more.
Was there not enough forbearance in my heart to
forget and forgive that, as if nothing had happened?
But the treachery!   How would it be if his heart
had turned from me and he really loved the beautiful Lori?

"Speak!   Why do you not speak?   Show me the
letter which has frightened you?"

He leaned over and took the letter out of my
hand.

I retained the inclosed note.

His eye flew over the pages.   With an oath he
tore the letter to pieces and sprang from his seat.

"It is infamous!" he cried.   "Where is the so-
called evidence?"

"Here, I have not opened it.   Frederick, say the
word and I will throw the thing into the fire.   I do
not wish any evidence that you have deceived me."

"My darling!" he was at my side in an instant
and caught me in his arms, "my jewel!   Look me
in the eye—do you doubt me?   Evidence or no evidence—does my word satisfy you?"

"Yes," I said, and threw the envelope in the
grate.

Frederick sprang to catch it.

"No, no, that would not do.   I am curious.   We
will look at it together.   I do not remember that I
ever wrote anything to your friend which would
indicate the least interest in her."

"But she likes you, Frederick.   You only need to
drop your handkerchief."

"Oh, are you sure of that?   Come, let us read
this precious document.   Right, it is my hand.
Ah! see here, it is the few lines which you dictated
yourself some weeks ago when your right hand was
lame."

My Lori, come, I expect you with pleasure at five
o'clock in the afternoon.   MARTHA (still a cripple).

"The finder of the note evidently did not understand it. It is certainly a good joke. Let us be thankful that this precious evidence was not truth —my innocence is established. Or are you still suspicious?"

"Frederick, since you looked me in the eye I have not had a doubt. Do you know, Frederick, I was frightfully unhappy; but you must forgive it. Lori is a coquette, very beautiful—tell me, has she not made advances? You shake your head. Of course, you are right in that, it is really your duty to lie to me. A man must never betray the neglected or accepted favors of women."

"You would really pardon a temporary aberration. Are you not jealous?"

"Yes, painfully. When I think of you at the feet of another—kissing another woman—cold to me—passion dead—it is frightful. But I am not afraid of losing your love. Your heart will never grow cold to me, that I am sure of—our souls are so sympathetic—but——"

"But—I understand. You need not accuse me of a feeling for you like that of a husband after his silver wedding. We were married too young for that. So far as the fire of youth runs in my veins I burn for you,—though I am forty years old. You are for me the one woman on this earth. The happiness which lies in the knowledge of having kept my faith; the proud confidence with which one can say that in every respect this bond of marriage has been kept sacred—all this I consider so beautiful that I would not lose it for a mere moment of reckless intoxication. You have made me such a happy man, Martha, that I am as much raised above every temptation of passion or pleasure as the owner of an ingot of gold is above the desire to win a penny."

How happy I was made by these words? I was thankful to the anonymous letter writer who had called them out. I wrote every word down in my journal. Here is the date, January, 1865. Ah, how far back that now seems!

Frederick remained very much provoked. He swore he would find out the author, and punish him.

I discovered on the same day the origin and object of this piece of literature. The result, that Frederick and I were brought nearer to each other, the originator had not anticipated.

That afternoon I went to see my friend Lori in order to show her the letter. I wished to inform her that she evidently had an enemy who had directed suspicion upon her, and expected to laugh with her over the failure of the intention of the sender.

She laughed more than I had expected.

"So you were alarmed?"

"Yes, terribly. And yet I came very near burning the enclosed note without reading it."

"Then the whole joke would have been spoiled."

"What joke?"

"Why, you would in the end have believed that I really had betrayed you. I will take this opportunity to confess that in a crazy moment—it was at a dinner-party at your father's, when I sat next to Tilling, and because I had been drinking too much champagne—that I really, so to speak, offered my heart to your Frederick on a presentation salver."

"And he?"

"He gave me to understand at once that he loved you above everything, and would be faithful to you until death. In order that you might more fully appreciate such a phenomenon I got up the whole thing."

"What joke are you continually talking about?"

"You know very well that the letter and contents came from me."

"From you?"

"Yes, see here, turn the paper over, look at the date: the first of April."

When spring came and the usual migrations began, I refused to accompany my father to Gru-

mitz, preferring to remain in the neighborhood of
Vienna, where I could see Frederick daily. My
sisters and Aunt Marie went to Marienbad. Just
before leaving Prague, Lilli wrote me:

"I will acknowledge that Cousin Conrad begins to be
not quite so disagreeable to me. I have been in the
humor during many a dance this winter to answer 'Yes,'
if he would only repeat his question; but he never seized
the right opportunity. I have, in fact, become so accustomed when he propounds his 'Will you be my wife?' to
answer, 'I cannot think of it,' that I could scarce this
time add to it: 'Ask me again in six months.' If I cannot forget him this summer then the obstinate, persistent
cousin will have conquered."

About the same time Aunt Marie wrote (as it
happens, it is the only letter from her which I have
saved):

My Dear Child:
It has been a tiresome winter campaign. I shall
be thoroughly rejoiced when the time comes that Rosa
and Lilli shall each find their match. They have had
opportunities enough, for they have each rejected a quarter of a dozen—without counting the perennial Conrad.
The torment begins again shortly in Marienbad. I would
gladly go to Grumitz, or would join you, but instead must
take up this tiresome and thankless task of chaperon to
two pleasure-loving girls.
I am rejoiced to hear that you are well. (I had suffered a long attack of fever.) Now that it is over I can
tell you how alarmed your husband was. But your time
has not yet come, thank God! The special propitia-
tory services which I ordered at the Ursulines aided undoubtedly in bringing about your restoration to health.
The dear God will preserve you for your little Rudolph.
Kiss him for me; tell him he must learn all he can. I
send him by this mail a few books: 'The Pious Child
and His Guardian Angel'—a beautiful story—and 'The
Heroes of Our Country,' a collection of war stories for
boys. We cannot begin too soon to inspire the youth
with such glorious ideas. Your brother Otto was scarce
five years old when I told him the stories of Alexander,
of Cæsar, and other great warriors, and see how enthusiastic a lover of all that is heroic he now is—it is a delight
to me.

I have heard that you intend to remain in the neighborhood of Vienna all summer. I suppose it is on account of your husband, but I should think you owe some duty to your father. Believe me, it is not prudent for married people to stick so closely together; they should allow each other some little liberty.

Heaven protect you and little Rudi is the constant prayer of your loving   AUNT MARIE.

P. S.—Your husband has relatives in Prussia (fortunately he is not so arrogant as his countrymen). Ask him what they are saying there about the present political complication. It is rather critical.

This letter first brought the fact to my notice that there again existed a " political complication."

"What does Aunt Marie mean by 'critical,' you less than ordinarily arrogant Prussian?" I asked my husband, handing him the letter. "Is there really an unusual political situation?"

"There is—just as there always is—a storm in prospect. The present situation is particularly unstable and treacherous."

"Does it relate to the Duchies of the Elbe again? Has not that been settled?"

"Far from it. The Schleswig-Holsteiners have more than half a mind to throw over the arrogant Prussians. 'Rather Danish than Prussian,' they cry."

"And what has become of Augustenburg. Do not tell me, Frederick, that they will not have him. On account of this sole just heir, so longed for by the oppressed Danish provinces, the whole war was brought about. Give me at least the comfort of knowing that Augustenburg was installed in his rights and that he reigns over the undivided duchies. On this 'undivided' I take my stand; it is an old historical right which has been pledged for several hundred years, whose whole history I studied with such painstaking care."

"It has gone rather hardly with your historical claims, my poor Martha," laughed Frederick. "Outside of his own protests and manifestoes we hear no more of Augustenburg."

Naturally I began at once to study the political situation, and discovered that, notwithstanding the Vienna treaty, nothing was really settled. The Schleswig-Holstein question was a more formidable one to solve than ever—it would not down. After the enforced retirement of Glücksburg, Augustenburg and Oldenburg hastened to lay their claims before the German Alliance. The Province of Lauenburg petitioned earnestly to be annexed to Prussia. Each of the two great powers was accused of seeking to overreach the other.

"What do these arrogant Prussians want?" was the continual suspicious cry from Austria, the Middle States, and the duchies. Napoleon III. advised Prussia to annex the duchies up to the boundaries of the Danish-speaking provinces. But for the present Prussia pretended not to be willing to consider the suggestion. At last, on the twenty-second of February, 1865, Prussia formally announced the claims decided upon: Prussian troops were to occupy the provinces; all provincial troops by land or water were to acknowledge the supremacy of Prussia, the only exception being a contingent representing the Alliance. The harbor of Kiel was seized; the postal and telegraph systems were to be under the control of Prussia, and the duchies must join the Customs Union. These demands angered our Minister of War, Mensdorf-Ponilly—I did not see why; and at the same time —I did not see any reason for it except jealousy—the Middle States took it to heart. These last energetically demanded that Augustenburg should be at once put in possession of the duchies. Austria, however, had something to say, and said it, treating Augustenburg's claims as of no consequence. It would gladly agree to the Prussian possession of the harbor of Kiel, but would not tolerate the right to recruit soldiers or sailors.

Prussia declared that the demands made were not for absolute annexation, but solely to secure the interests of the whole of Germany. Augusten-

burg might, by recognizing the above claims, be
invested with his prescriptive right; but in case
this was not agreed upon—with an increasingly
threatening manner—Prussia might be compelled
to insist upon still greater demands.

Bitter, defiant, vindictive voices were raised in
the Middle States and Austria against this "insolent" announcement, and the public sentiment
against Prussia and Bismarck was daily intensified.

On the twenty-seventh of June the Middle States
demanded information (information is not a diplomatic custom—secrecy is the only proper thing),
but the two superior powers continued their private negotiations. King William betook himself
to Gastein, the Emperor Francis Joseph to Ischl.
Count Blome flew unremittingly between them
and upon several points an agreement was reached.
The investment should be half Austrian and half
Prussian. Lauenburg should be annexed to Prussia as it desired. As compensation therefor Austria
was to receive two and a half million dollars. I
could not feel any particular patriotic pleasure
at this. How would this insignificant sum benefit
the thirty-six millions of Austrians, even if it were
divided among them—which would not be done?
Would it make good the hundred thousand I had
lost through Schmitt & Sons by reason of the war,
or replace the loss of those for whom thousands
wept? I was rejoiced that on the fourteenth of
August a new treaty was signed at Gastein.
"Treaty" sounds so reassuring. Later I learned
that treaties are generally made to form the basis
for some future *casus belli*. One needs only to
assert that a treaty has been outraged and—with
all the appearance of justification—out springs the
sword from the scabbard.

For the time, however, the Gastein treaty quieted
me. General Gablenz — the handsome Gablenz,
for whom all womankind were fired with enthusi-
asm--was in command in Holstein, Manteuffel in

Schleswig. Of the promise of 1460, that the provinces should remain forever united, there was of course nothing more heard. And my Augustenburg, for whose rights I had so strenuously battled, had the painful experience of receiving a gentle warning from Manteuffel, when he ventured to set foot within his duchy and was jubilantly received by the populace. In strictly courteous, but no uncertain language, he was advised that incarceration in a moist, unpleasant prison awaited him should he venture there again without permission. He who does not regard this as a sarcasm of the muse Clio has no comprehension of the comic side of history.

Notwithstanding the Gastein treaty, affairs did not quiet down. By patient reading of all the political articles in the daily press I had a fair understanding of the shifting state of things. I could not believe that war would result. Such legal questions must go the way of all litigation; from careful consideration of equitable rights a just judgment must ensue. Certainly all these judicious diplomatists and privy councilors, these parliamentary leaders and politely fraternal monarchs could find some common ground to settle general differences. More out of curiosity than anxiety I followed the course of events, whose regular order I noted in my journal.

The first of October, 1865. In the Imperial Council at Frankfort the following resolutions were adopted:

1. The autonomy of the Schleswig-Holstein people must be preserved. The Treaty of Gastein was rejected as an infringement of the rights of the nation.

2. All officials should refuse to pay over to these allied powers taxes and loans ordered by the former government.

October 15. A royal Prussian edict declared approbation of the decision in regard to the hereditary claim of Prince Augustenburg. The father of the latter, for himself and his successors, abrogated all claims to the throne in consideration of the sum of one and a half million dollars.

By the Vienna treaty the duchies were ceded to the allies; henceforth the Augustenburgs can make no further claims.

There was a continually increasing protest against "Prussian arrogance," which became a species of battle-cry. "We must protect ourselves against them" was declared as authoritatively as dogma. "King William aspires to the *rôle* of Victor Emanuel in Germany." "Austria has the secret intention of re-conquering Silesia." "Prussia is coquetting with France." "Austria is courting France"; *et patati et patata*, as the French say, a species of mutual recrimination which is indulged in by cabinets as it is by the gossips round the village tea-kettle.

With autumn the whole family returned to Vienna. I would not go to Grumitz for the hunting season, as my husband could not secure a leave of absence. I was also unwilling for any length of time to place my little Rudolph under the influence of his grandfather, who was determined to instill into his childish mind all sorts of martial notions. The desire for a military career had already been awakened in my son. Perhaps it was in the blood. The scion of a long line of soldiers must naturally develop warlike tendencies. In the works on the natural sciences, which I studied more enthusiastically than ever, I had learned the force of heredity, the result of natural tendencies, which is nothing more than the pressure of the mental and physical habits acquired from a line of ancestry.

On his birthday his grandfather bought him a saber.

"You know very well, Papa," I said angrily, "that I will not allow Rudolph to become a soldier. I most earnestly beg of you——"

"Now, now, you would like to keep him tied to your apron-strings. It is to be hoped you will be disappointed. Good soldier's blood will tell. When the boy is grown he will choose his own profession—and a nobler one is not to be found than that which you deny him."

"Martha is afraid of the danger to which her only son will be exposed," remarked Aunt Marie, who chanced to be present, "but she forgets that when one is ordained to die, his fate will meet him whether in his bed or on the battlefield."

"I suppose you mean that if a hundred thousand men are fated to fall in battle, the same number would come to their end in time of peace?"

Aunt Marie was prepared with an immediate reply.

"The hundred thousand were decreed to die in battle."

"Suppose men were clever enough to refuse to go to war?"

"That is an impossibility," cried my father, and the usual combat began.

There is nothing to which the fable of the Hydra so well applies as to that monster, unreasoning conviction. Scarce have we cut off one head of the argument and turned to tackle the second, before the first is grown again and active as ever.

My father always had a few favorite arguments in defense of war, which were unconquerable:

1. Wars are the decree of God; the Lord of Hosts has himself ordained them (see Holy Writ).

2. Wars have always existed, therefore they will always continue to exist.

3. The earth, without this destructive agency, would suffer too great an increase of population.

4. Perpetual peace would relax and enervate the race, and a consequent demoralization would ensue.

5. War is the best means for the development of self-sacrifice, of heroism, in short for the strengthening of character.

6. Mankind will always differ. Complete harmony in all respects is not possible; different interests must be antagonistic; consequently to expect perpetual peace is an absurdity.

None of these wise sayings can be logically maintained when you show their absurdity; but each serves its defender as a breastwork when he sees

the preceding fall around him, and while he re-
treats from the ruins of the one he intrenches himself in the old earthworks round the other. For
example, finding number four no longer tenable,
and obliged to acknowledge that a condition of
peace is for humanity more certain of securing
happiness, intellectual progress, and financial prosperity, he will agree: "War is in truth an evil, but
unavoidable."

Then, when in reply to numbers one and two it
is proved that by international agreement, by international jurisprudence, war could be avoided, he
acknowledges that it could but should not. Then,
at number five the tables are turned, and the advocate of peace proves that, on the contrary, war
develops all the brutality and inhumanity of man.

"Well, possibly, but there is yet number three."

This argument, when brought forward by the
defenders of war, is of all the most uncandid. It
serves, in truth, far better those who detest war.
He who loves war and would retain it as a factor
of existence certainly does so from no thought of
the welfare of succeeding generations. The violent
decimation of the present generation by death, by
epidemic disease and impoverishment, the result of
war, is certainly not deliberately planned to protect the future from possible starvation and suffering. If human means were necessary to obstruct for
the general welfare a too rapid increase of population, a more direct measure might be conceived than
war. The argument is but a trick which meets
with success, because for the moment it puzzles us.
It sounds so monstrously learned and so humane.
For think upon it; we ought to leave elbow room
for our descendants a thousand years from now.
But few people are conversant with such matters
of social economy and natural law; but few are
aware that the relative rate of deaths and births
remains about the same, that the danger to existence, developed by unusual vicissitudes, does not
reduce population, but rather tends to increase it.

After a war the number of births increases and the loss is soon made good; after a long peace population decreases, and so this phantom of surplus population disappears. All this we do not keep clearly in view; we only feel instinctively that this famous number three is not quite right, and is not honestly believed by the opponent. One is generally satisfied to quote the old proverb: "It is already provided that trees shall not grow into the heavens," and to add that the powers that be do not have this result in mind.

The contention will never end. The military mind reasons in a circle, where we may continually pursue but never come up with it.

New Year's Eve, 1866. We sat together around my father's table when the first hour struck of this momentous year. When the hand of the clock pointed at twelve and shots were fired on the street below, our enterprising cousin Conrad drew Lilli to him and—to our surprise—pressing his lips to hers, boldly asked:

"Will you have me in '66?"

"Yes, I will," she roguishly replied, and congratulations were showered upon them.

My father brought the tumult to an end by striking his seal ring upon his glass as he rose to offer his New Year's toast:

"My dear children and friends, the new year begins well, with the prospect of the fulfillment of my dearest wish, for I have long wanted Conrad as a son-in-law. It is to be hoped that during this year Rosa may find her ideal and that you—Martha and Tilling—may have a visit from the stork. For you, Doctor Bresser, I wish swarms of patients —a wish not quite consistent with the good wishes we have all exchanged; and for you, dear Marie, who are so fatalistically inclined, a grand prize or a full indulgence, or whatever else you desire. For you, my Otto, I could wish all manly and heroic virtues, that you may become the ornament of the

army and the pride of your old father's heart.
I must hope something for myself, and since I
have no greater desire than the welfare and fame
of Austria, may the coming year bring Lombardy
back to us—or, who knows?—Silesia also.   It is
possible that we may re-conquer from the arrogant Prussian this province stolen from the great
Maria Theresa."

I remember that the termination of my father's
oration fell like a cold chill upon the company.

"No, dear Father," I replied; "in Italy and Prussia it is also the New Year; we will not wish them
any evil.   May this year '66 make all mankind
better, more harmonious, and happier."

My father shrugged his shoulders.

"O, you fantastic dreamer," he said compassion-
ately.

"No," replied Frederick, coming to my relief,
"Martha's wish is not that of a dreamer, but its
fulfillment is pledged to us.   Mankind has grown
better, happier, and more united from primeval
ages to the present, but so slowly, that a little span
of time like a year can mark no perceptible progress."

"If you are so sure of perpetual progress," exclaimed my father, "why are you continually complaining of the re-action, of the relapse into barbarism?"

"Because"—and Frederick pulled a pencil from
his pocket and drew on a piece of paper a spiral—
"because the progress of civilization goes on just
like this.   Does not this line continually ascend,
though it appears to be tending backward.   This
coming year may be represented by one of these
curves, particularly if, as seems only too probable,
a war is forced upon us.   Such an event hurls civilization in material as well as moral things a long
way backward."

"You are not talking like a soldier, Tilling."

"I am talking of a matter of universal interest.
Whether my views are right or wrong, those of a

soldier or a civilian, is of no consequence. The truth is always the same. If a thing is red should one obstinately maintain that it is blue?"

"A what?" said my father. When a discussion was disagreeable, he was very apt to be seized by spasms of deafness. Few people had the patience to repeat, and most of them preferred to give up the battle.

When we had returned to our own home, I asked my husband:

"What did you say, that there is prospect of war? I will not allow you to go into another campaign— I will not."

"How can this passionate 'I will not' help us, Martha. The nearer the war is to our door the more impossible it will be for me to resign. Immediately after Schleswig-Holstein it was possible, but not now."

To arms! to arms! was now the general cry For defensive purposes it was necessary that we should arm ourselves. Prussia maintained that we were secretly arming, therefore she proceeded to arm herself. What is the use of all this clash of arms if neither intends to attack? Whereupon my father quoted the old proverb: *Si vis pacem, para bellum.* Each keeps an eye upon the other; each accuses the other of malice aforethought.

Again this endless circle.

On the twelfth of March my father rushed, beaming with joy, into my house.

"Hurrah!" he cried; "good news!"

"Disarmament?" I questioned eagerly.

"On the contrary, yesterday a great council of war was held, and our military condition is really magnificent. We are ready at an hour's notice to march out with eight hundred thousand men. Benedek, our ablest strategist, is general-in-chief with absolute powers. I tell you in confidence, child, Silesia is ours if we desire it."

For days uncertainty was all we knew. On the

twenty-fourth of March Prussia issued a proclamation complaining of the armament of Austria. On
the twenty-eighth it was announced in Berlin that
the fortresses in Silesia had been re-enforced by
Prussian troops, and that two army corps were in
readiness to protect the country. The thirty-first
of March Austria disclaimed any intention of at-
tacking Prussia, and demanded that the latter disarm. Prussia also declared herself as innocent of
any belligerent intention toward Austria, but, in
view of the threatening aspect of the standing army
of the latter, felt compelled to continue her own
preparations. So the duet continued. Italy organized and armed as fast as possible, and the duet
became a trio. Austria declared herself for the
rights of Augustenburg, and Prussia complained
that this was a breach of the Treaty of Gastein.

The most thoroughly hated man in Europe was
Bismarck. An attempt was made upon his life.
I received a letter from Aunt Cornelia who wrote
that in Prussia the approach of war was regarded
with intense dissatisfaction, while with us there
was general enthusiasm in its favor. She added
that Bismarck was almost as much hated and feared
in Berlin as in Vienna. Loud protests were heard
against this "fratricidal war," and it was said
Queen Augusta had implored her husband to insist upon peace. If our beautiful Empress had
done the same, and every other woman whose
right to the life of husband and son is greater than
that of the state, would it have helped the cause
of peace and humanity?

On the first of June Prussia announced that she
would disarm when Austria and Saxony did so;
Austria excused herself so long as Italy's full equip-
ment was a menace to her borders, and demanded
that the German Alliance undertake the settlement of the question of the duchies. Prussia protested, claiming rights granted by the Gastein
treaty; the Treaty of Vienna was appealed to as
insuring mutual occupation; Prussia therefore pro-

ceeded to invest Holstein and made no pretense to any right to obstruct Austria's possession of Schleswig. As Prussian troops marched into Holstein Gablenz retreated without drawing sword, but under protest.

Bismarck had said, in a diplomatic circular just before this event, that Austria had not met the advances of Prussia, and that from the most authentic sources the King had been informed of expressions used by the Emperor's cabinet ministers and advisers (tittle-tattle), which indicated that these men were determined to force war upon the country, partly in the hope of aggrandizement by success in the field, and partly with the expectation of improving Austria's bankrupt financial condition through Prussian tribute.

On the ninth of June Prussia again declared that Parliament had no authority to settle the Schleswig-Holstein question. The press now grew more defiant in tone, and, as is the patriotic custom, it was certain of victory. The possibility of defeat must never be suggested to the loyal subject whose monarch calls him into the battlefield. Brilliant editorials pictured the prospective march of Benedek into Berlin, as well as the probable plundering of the city by the Croats. Some journals demanded that Prussia's capital should be leveled with the ground. "To pillage," "Level with the ground," "Put to the sword"—these expressions do not represent the opinions or the conscience of the time, but stick to people who learned them at school— from the histories of wars and conquests. Having been copied in exercise books at school and learned by rote, they naturally fly to the point of the pen so soon as one sits down to discuss the theme of war. Contempt for the enemy cannot be expressed too fiercely; the Vienna press no longer spoke of Prussian troops otherwise than as tailors' apprentices. Adjutant-General Count Grünne contemptuously declared that we would chase these Prussians with wet rags. Such are the conventional methods of making a war "popular." Such things nourish national self-conceit.

On the eleventh of June Austria appealed to the Imperial Council of the German Confederation that it should take issue with Prussia's investment of Holstein, and call out all the troops subject to the German Alliance.

On the fourteenth of June this appeal came up and was approved by a vote of nine to six.

All is over. The embassadors have received their passports. On the sixteenth the Imperial Council called upon Austria and Bavaria to come to the help of Saxony and Hanover, already attacked by Prussia.

On the eighteenth Prussia's war manifesto was published. On the same date the manifesto of the Emperor of Austria and Benedek's proclamation to his troops were announced. On the twenty-second Prince Frederick Charles issued his first army order, and the war was begun. I have preserved these four documents.

King William said:

"Austria never forgets that her princes once ruled Germany, and is not willing to recognize in Prussia simply a member of the Confederation, but always regards her as a rival. Prussia, she insists, must be antagonized in all her undertakings, because what benefits Prussia injures Austria. An old, unjust jealousy has again burst out into fierce flames; Prussia must be crushed, destroyed and dishonored. Treaties can no longer be observed with her. Wherever we turn in Germany, we find ourselves surrounded by enemies whose battle-cry is the humiliation of Prussia. To the very last moment I have sought the road of reconciliation—but Austria would not agree to it."

On the other hand the Emperor Francis Joseph announces:

" The latest events indicate the incontestible intention of Prussia to set might in the place of right. So that this most unholy of wars—a war of German against German —has become unavoidable. To answer for all the misery to be brought upon individuals, families, and country, I summon him, who has precipitated this war, before the judgment seat of history and of the eternal, almighty God."

Always the other side that wishes war! Always the other one who is accused of resolving that might shall overcome justice. An "unholy war," because it was "German against German." Quite right; it is a step forward when above Prussia and Austria the appeal to Germany is made. But a much higher plane would be reached if every war were recognized as a war of mankind against mankind, that is, civilized man against civilized man, and were regarded as an unholy fratricidal contest.

And of what use to summon before the judgment seat of history? History as hitherto written gives judgment to the victor. Around the conqueror falls the golden halo of history, and he becomes the great promoter of civilization.

And before the judgment seat of God, the Almighty? Is he not the same who is always represented as the Lord of Hosts, and is the outbreak as well as the termination of every war other than the result of the immutable will of this same Almighty? Oh, contradiction upon contradiction! Where shall we find truth under all these conventional phrases, where two antagonistic principles—war and justice, international hatred and love of humanity, the God of Love and the God of Battles—are set against each other as equally holy.

And Benedek said:

" We find opposed to us an armed force composed of two distinct parts: militia and troops of the line. The first is composed of young men unaccustomed to fatigue or privation, who have never engaged in an important campaign. The last consists of an untrustworthy, dissatisfied element, which had much rather attack its own unpopular government than fight against us. In consequence of long years of peace the enemy does not possess one single general who has had the opportunity to perfect himself upon the battlefield. Veterans of Mincio and Palestro, I hope under your old experienced leaders you will not give such opponents the slightest advantage.

For some time the enemy has boasted of his new rapid-firing rifles; but, my men, I think we will not allow him to put these into use. We will charge upon him with bayonets and clubs. With God's help the enemy will be beaten and forced to retreat; we will follow close upon his heels, and in the enemy's country you will find rest and compensation in the richest measure, to which such a victorious army has the fullest right."

Prince Frederick Charles finally spoke:

"Soldiers! Faithless and treacherous Austria has without declaration of war long since ceased to respect the Prussian boundaries of Upper Silesia. I should have been justified, even before a declaration of war, in crossing the Bohemian frontier. I have not done it. To-day I issue this general order, and to-day we will enter the territory of the enemy in order to spare our own country. Our beginning is with God. (Is this the same God with whose help Benedek has promised to drive back the enemy with bayonets and clubs?) In his hands we rest our cause who guides the hearts of men, who decides the fate of nations and the outcome of battles. As it is written in Holy Scripture: 'Lift up your hearts to the Lord and your hands against the enemy.'

"On the issue of this war depends, as you know, Prussia's holiest interests and the existence of our beloved country. The enemy is determined upon its partition and humiliation. Shall the streams of blood shed by our fathers under Frederick the Great, and by ourselves at Düppel and Alsen, have been shed in vain? Never! We will not only maintain Prussia as she is, but make her, through victory, mightier and more glorious than ever. We will be worthy of our fathers. We depend upon the God of our fathers that he will be gracious to us and bless Prussia's arms. And now, forward with our old battle-cry: 'With God for king and country. Long live the king!'"

FOURTH BOOK.

1866.

SO it was here again, that greatest of all conceivable miseries, and was hailed by the populace with the usual jubilant shout. The regiments marched out (would they ever return?) with blessings and cheers, followed by the wild plaudits of the youngsters of the streets and alleys.

Frederick had already been ordered to Bohemia before the declaration of war. This time I was spared the heart-rending parting which followed the direct order into the field. When my father brought me the triumphant assurance, " now it has begun," I had already been alone fourteen days, during which I had lived like the criminal in hourly expectation of sentence of death.

I bowed my head and said nothing.

" Be of good courage, child. The war will not last long—day after to-morrow we may be in Berlin. Your husband returned from Schleswig-Holstein in safety, so he will probably get back from this campaign with brighter laurels than ever. Unpleasant as it must be to him, being of Prussian origin, to fight against Prussia, still he is Austrian to the core. Those Prussians! We will drive them out of the German Confederation—the arrogant wind-bags! They will have reason to repent when Silesia is again ours and when the Hapsburgs—— "

I stretched out my hands:

"Father, I implore you, let me alone."

He may have suspected an outbreak of tears, and as he was an enemy of all pathetic scenes he hastily retired. But I had no place for tears. It was as if a crushing blow had fallen upon my head. Breathing with difficulty, staring at vacancy, I sat motionless. Finally I rose and going to my desk wrote in my red journal:

"The sentence of death has been passed. A hundred thousand human beings will be executed. Will Frederick be among them? And I among them—for what am I that I should escape destruction with the other hundred thousand? I wish I were already dead."

On the same day I received from Frederick a few hastily written lines.

"My wife! Be brave, keep up your heart. We have been happy; the past no mortal can take from us, even if for us, as for many others, the decree is issued. To-day we advance upon the enemy. Perhaps I shall recognize among them a few old comrades of Düppel and Alsen— possibly my cousin Gottfried. We march upon Liebenau with the advance guard of Count Clam-Gallas. From this time expect no letters, or at the most a line, should I have the opportunity to assure you of my safety. I can think of but one word which expresses my whole love for you—Martha! You know all that means to me."

Conrad Althaus had also been ordered into the field. He was full of fire and martial ardor and infused with the necessary hatred of Prussia to enable him to go cheerfully; but the parting was hard. The official permission to marry had arrived but two days before marching orders.

"Oh Lilli, Lilli," he exclaimed, "why have you hesitated so long? Who knows whether I shall ever return?"

My poor sister was filled with remorse. Passionate love now awoke and she wept bitterly in my arms.

"Why have I been so foolish! If I were only his wife!"

"That would have made the parting much harder my poor Lilli."

I joined the family at Grumitz. I was oppressed with the idea of widowhood. Occasionally the cheerful thought of the possibility of Frederick's return restored me to a more temperate frame of mind, but it was not for long. I constantly saw him wounded, suffering untold agony, perishing for a drop of water, heavy wagons rolling over his mutilated limbs, gnats and stinging insects tormenting his open wounds, or the people employed to bury the dead carrying him yet living to be thrown into the trench.

With a shriek I sprang up at this thought and my father scolded angrily.

"What is the matter with you, Martha? You will become insane if you brood in this way. Drive all such thoughts from your mind. It is wicked."

I had several times given utterance to these fears, which exasperated my father to the highest degree.

"Wicked," he continued, "and improper and foolish. Such things occur once in a thousand times among private soldiers, but they would not neglect a staff officer like your husband. One should not think about such horrible things. It is a species of frivolity, of desecration of war, if one allows the misery of the individual to keep out of view the grandeur of the result."

"Yes, yes, do not think of it," I answered. "That is the proper attitude in regard to all human misery. Not think! and barbarism rests upon it."

The Red Cross organization had been created a little time before. I had read the pamphlet of Dunant which had suggested its necessity. The little book was a heart-breaking cry of anguish. The noble author, a patrician of Geneva, had hastened to the field of Solferino; and what he saw there he told to all the world. Countless wounded had lain five, some even six, days without assistance. He had done all in his power, but what could he, a single man, do to alleviate this mass of misery? He saw many who could have been saved by a bit of bread or a drop of water; he saw others, still breathing, buried with frightful haste. Then he spoke out what had often before been realized, which now first received attention, that the field

hospital organization of an army could no longer
meet the necessities of a modern battlefield. And
the Red Cross was organized.

Austria had not sent delegates to the Geneva
convention. Why? Why is everything which is
new, no matter how simple and beneficent, met with
opposition? The law of indolence—the power of
sanctified precedent. "The idea is very fine, but
impracticable," I heard my father several times
repeat in the year 1863, when different delegates
had argued with him. "Impracticable, and, even
if practicable, in many respects undesirable. The
military service could not tolerate the presence
of private individuals on the battlefield. In war
tactics must take precedence of humanity. How
could this private undertaking prevent its abuse
by spies? And the expense. Does not war cost
enough already? The volunteer system of nurses
would become burdensome through their unavoidable additional cost; or if they provided for themselves in the occupied country, would not this
cause greater expense to the commissary department, by consequent rise in prices?"

Oh, this magisterial sagacity!—so dry, so learned,
so neutral, so dripping with wisdom, and—oh, bot-
tomless stupidity!

The first engagement in Bohemia took place on
the twenty-fifth of June at Liebenau. The report
was brought by my father with his usual triumphant manner.

"It is a magnificent beginning! We see that
Heaven is with us. It is significant that the first
with whom these wind-bags have had to deal are
our men of the famous 'Iron Brigade.' You remember the brigade of Poschacher, which so nobly defended Königsberg in Silesia. They must have
punished those fellows well!" (The next report
from the seat of war was that, after five hours combat this advance guard of Clam-Gallas retreated to
Podol. Later I knew that Frederick was in this en-

gagement, and that the same night the barricaded Podol had been attacked by General Horn, and the battle continued by bright moonlight.' "But better news than that from the north," continued my father, "is the beginning in the south. At Custozza a victory has been won—a brilliant one. I told you Lombardy would be ours yet. I regard the war as decided. If we so soon finish off the Italians, a regular, disciplined army, we shall not have much trouble with the tailors' apprentices. This militia—it is pure impudence, and of a piece with everything Prussian, to consider itself fit to engage regular soldiers. Fellows from the shops, from the bench, and such rubbish, cannot possibly stand against such blood and iron soldiers as ours. See here what a special correspondent of the Vienna Press writes, under date twenty-fourth June. It is good news: "

" The cattle plague in its most serious form has broken out in Prussian Silesia."

"'Cattle plague,' 'serious!' Is this your good news?" said I, shaking my head. "Fine things we are asked to rejoice over in war times. It is lucky that black and gold turnpike gates stand on the frontier—perhaps they will keep the plague on that side."

But my father paid no attention, and read on with increasing pleasure:

" Among the Prussian troops fever is raging. The unwholesome swamp lands, bad subsistence, and miserable quarters in the crowded villages of the surrounding country could not but produce such results. The Austrians have no idea of the character of the subsistence of the Prussian soldiers. The nobility believe they can ask any sacrifice of the common people. Three ounces only of salt pork are issued to each man. These men are unaccustomed to forced marches, or to any other hardships, and find such short rations next door to starvation."

"The papers are full of stirring news. You ought to save the papers, Martha."

I have saved them. We ought always to do that;

then, when a new struggle is in prospect, we should
not need to read the latest news, but could refer to
the accounts of the preceding war.   We could thus
judge of the amount of truth in all the prophecies,
army orders, and reports.   It is instructive.

From the seat of war in the north:

" From the latest reports the Prussian army has moved
its head-quarters to Eastern Silesia. (Here follows in the
usual tactician's style a lengthy account of the evolutions
and position of the enemy, of which the gentlemanly correspondent evidently has a much clearer conception in his
mind's eye than either Moltke or Roon.)   It appears to
be the object of the Prussians to prevent the march of our
army upon Berlin, which, however, in view of the preparations to this end (which our special correspondent
knows more about than Benedek), they will scarcely succeed in doing.   With the fullest confidence the public
may await important movements on the part of the northern army, which though not so speedily forthcoming as
perhaps anticipated, will be all the more fraught with far-
reaching consequences.

.   .   .   " The New Frankfort Journal reports an interesting occurrence which took place at München when
the Austrian troops of Italian nativity marched through.
They consisted of several battalions of infantry recruited
in Venice, and they were marched from the railway
station to a neighboring beer garden and restaurant.   All
were convinced of the enthusiasm with which these Venetians served against the enemies of Austria. (Perhaps
everybody realized how easily drunken soldiers can be
made to shout for anything.)   At Würzburg these troops
found the railway station filled with an Austrian regiment of infantry on their way to the seat of war; these
were also Venetians, and the rejoicing was universal (all
being equally drunk) over the opportunity of meeting and
punishing these dangerous enemies of peace. (It is always
the other side which breaks the peace.   Those who were
so gratified by these *vivas* of drunken soldiers should remember there is nothing so deceptive as such accla-
mations.   A thousand roaring voices are not the expression of a thousand minds, but simply indicate the
imitative instinct of mankind.)"

Field Marshal Benedek sent out from Trübau, in
Bohemia, three bulletins announcing to the army

of the north the victories of the south. Attached to them was the following order for the day.

" In the name of the northern army I have sent the following to the commander of the army of the south: ' Field Marshal Benedek and the entire northern army congratulate the glorious commander and the brave army of the south upon their great victory at Custozza. With a magnificent victory the campaign has been opened in the south. Glorious Custozza adorns the shield of honor of the imperial army.' Soldiers of the army of the north, with shouts you will receive this news, which will inflame your zeal for battle, when we also can decorate our shield with the name of a famous victory, and report to the Emperor a no less notable triumph, for which your martial enthusiasm burns, and which will be won by your bravery and self sacrifice with the shout: Long live the Emperor. BENEDEK."

A telegraphic report of the reply was received at Trübau:

" The army of the south and its commander send heartfelt thanks to their beloved former field marshal and his brave soldiers, convinced that shortly congratulations for a similar victory on their part will be exchanged."

" Does not your very heart laugh, child, when you read such news as this?" cried my father. " Can you not rise to such a pitch of patriotic enthusiasm as to forget for a moment your private affairs— that your Frederick, Martha, and your Conrad, Lilli, are exposed to danger, danger from which they will probably escape, and to endure which—a lot they share with the noblest sons of the nation —is both fame and honor? There are no soldiers who would not willingly die for their country."

" If after a defeat they are left with shattered limbs upon the field," I said, " and are there neglected for four or five days and nights to suffer from hunger, thirst, and inconceivable anguish, decaying while still alive, slowly dying, knowing all the time that through their death their country gains nothing, though family and loved ones are brought to the verge of despair; I should like to know if these men will spend their time crying that they die willingly."

"You are outrageous! You use such coarse language; for a woman it is not decent."

"Yes, yes, that is the truth; the actual circumstance is outrageous, infamous," I cried. "Only the phrases sanctioned by a thousand-fold repetition are respectable."

Among Frederick's papers—many days later—I found a letter, which I wrote at that time and sent to him at the seat of war. This letter shows most clearly the sentiments with which I was then oppressed.

GRUMITZ, 28 June, 1866.

DEAREST:

I do not live . . . Picture to yourself that in the next room people are discussing whether you shall be executed within a few days or not, while I outside must abide by their decision. During this period of uncertainty I breathe, it is true, but can I call that living? The next room, in which this question is to be decided, is Bohemia. But after all, my love, the comparison is not apt. For if the question were as to my own life or death the terror would not be so great. My anxiety concerns a much dearer life than my own,—and, even more than your death, it tortures me with fears of your possible mortal agony. Oh, if it were only over! If our victory would only follow swiftly—not because of the victory, but because the end would be reached!

Will you receive these lines? And where and when? Will it be after a fierce day of battle, or in camp, or possibly in the hospital?—in any event it will be grateful to you to receive news from your Martha. Even if I cannot write otherwise than sadly—how can anything but sadness be felt at a time when the sun is obscured by the great, black funeral pall which has been suspended above our country, to be dropped over her children! Even then these lines must bring you pleasure, for you love me, Frederick—I know how dearly—and these written words rejoice and move you as the soft stroke of my hand.

I am with you, Frederick, you must know, in every thought, in every breath you draw, by day and night. Here at home I live and move and speak and act mechanically; my own self—that which belongs to you—does not leave you an instant.

My boy alone reminds me that the world contains some other being which is not yourself. The good little fellow! If you only knew how often he asks after you and how anxious he is about you. We two talk of nothing else than of " Papa." He knows very well, the sympathetic child! that this is the one thing of which my heart is full, and small as he is, he is already, in his fashion, the friend of his mother. I talk to him as if he were grown and he shows his gratitude. On my side, I am grateful to him for the love which he dedicates to you. It is rarely that children love their stepfather—certainly there has never been anything of the traditional stepfather in you. You could not be more tender, more gentle with your own son, my dear, faithful lover. Yes, goodness, gentle, great, and generous, is the foundation of your character; and what does the poet say? " As the heavens mould themselves into one great sapphire vault, so the whole greatness of a noble human being is embraced in goodness." In other words: I love you, Frederick! That is the refrain of all when I reflect upon your character. So confidently, so securely I rest in you, Frederick, when I am with you, understand. Now that you are torn from me I have no rest or peace. If the storm were only over, or if it had reached Berlin! My father is convinced that this will certainly be the result of the campaign, and according to all that we hear and see, we are led to believe it.

" So soon as with God's help the enemy is defeated," says Benedek's proclamation, " we will follow close upon his heels, and in the enemy's country we will rest and compensate ourselves," etc. What sort of compensation does he mean? Nowadays no general dares say aloud: " Come, you may plunder, burn, and ravish," as was the custom in the Middle Ages, in order to incite the hordes. Now one can only promise at the most a slice of territorial sausage, but as that is somewhat uncertain, they decorate it in flowery style as " those compensations," etc. You can understand it as you please. The principle of compensation from the resources of the enemy's country still lives in the style of soldierly ethics. And how could you compensate yourself in the enemy's country, which with you is your land by inheritance, where your friends and your cousins still live? Will it be to you a compensation to level with the ground the pretty villa where your Aunt Cornelia lives? " The enemy's country!" That is one of those fossil ideas of a time when war was unreservedly a robber's raid, and when the enemy's country was simply the booty to entice the vassal recruit.

I write to you as we talk in those lovely hours when you are at my side, when we have finished one of those works of progress, over which we philosophize upon the contradictions of our times, and when we so tenderly, so sympathetically understand each other. Around me now there are none to whom I can speak of these things. Doctor Bresser was the only one with whom I could exchange sentiments in condemnation of war, and he is now gone, drawn into the service to heal wounds, not make them. What a contradiction is this humanity in war! It is much like reason and faith. One or the other; but humanity and war, reason and dogma—they do not go together. An outright, burning detestation of the enemy, coupled with a complete contempt for human life—that is the inspiring soul of war, just as the unquestioning stifling of the reason is the fundamental condition of faith. But we live in a period of accommodation where old institutions and new ideas are equally powerful. People cannot quite break with the old, and cannot quite comprehend the new, and so they try to mould the two together, and hence results this inconsequent, contradictory, deceitful, half-hearted confusion under which the soul, thirsting for truth, justice, and consistency, groans and suffers.

Ah, see what I have written! You will scarcely be in the mood—as in our quiet hours of musing—to listen to such generalizations. You are surrounded by a terrible reality to which you are compelled to succumb. How much better it would be for you, if you could accept it with the simple sentiment of the old times, when a martial life was actually the soldier's delight. And it would be better if I could write, like other women, letters full of prophecies of victory, spurring you with promises of blessings. The girls are trained to patriotism, so that at the proper moment they can urge men to die for their country, as the noblest death, or promise: "When you return crowned with victory, we will reward you with our love. In the meantime we will pray for you. The God of Battles, who protects our armies, will hearken unto our prayers. Day and night our petitions will mount to Heaven and we will obtain its favor. You will return crowned with fame and victory! We do not tremble, for we are the worthy mates of brave men. No, no!—the mothers of your sons dare not be cowardly, if they would bring into the world a new race of heroes; and we must give up our dearest. For king and country no sacrifice is too great!"

That would be the right sort of a letter to a soldier, would it not? but not the letter which you would wish to receive from your wife, from the partner of your thoughts, who shares with you the detestation of blind and antiquated human madness—oh! a detestation, so bitter, so painful that I cannot express it. When I picture to myself these two armies, composed in the main of reasonable, good, and gentle human beings, who dash upon each other for mutual destruction, devastating the unhappy country and like chess players capturing and recapturing defenseless villages; when I think upon all this, I feel like crying out: " Reflect a moment—stop for an instant!" and of a hundred thousand ninety thousand, as individuals, would willingly stop; but as a mass they rage onward. But enough of this. You had rather hear the gossip and news from home. To begin: we are all well. Father is in a continual ferment over the present complications. The victory of Custozza filled him with most radiant pride. He acts as if he had won it himself. In addition, he regards the event as so brilliant that a portion of its glory he shares as an Austrian and as a general. And Lori, whose husband, as you know, is with the army of the south, has written me a letter of triumph over Custozza. Frederick, do you remember how jealous I was of the good Lori for a quarter of an hour, and how from this little circumstance has grown a still stronger love and confidence? Oh, if you had ever deceived me or even treated me a little shabbily, I could bear this separation more easily; but to know that such a husband is in the range of bullets! But to go on with the news: Lori has informed me that she with her little Beatrice will spend the rest of her straw widowhood in Grumitz. I cannot decline the visit; but just now her presence will be a burden to me. I should prefer to be alone, alone with my longing for you, which no other being can realize. Next week Otto begins his vacation. He laments in every letter that the war broke out before instead of after his officer's commission. He hopes to God that peace will not " break out " before his release from the academy. The words, " break out," he did not actually use, but it expresses his state of mind, for he regards peace as a genuine calamity. Well, certainly, that is the way they are all trained. So long as wars exist, war-loving soldiers must be found, and so long as war-loving soldiers exist- so long will wars endure. Is that to be the eternal, hope-

less circle? No, thank God! For human love, spite of
all this drilling of the schools, grows apace. We found
in Buckle, you remember, the evidence of this development. But I do not need a printed book as proof. I
only need to look into your noble, human heart, Frederick, to convince me of this truth.

But to return: from our relatives in Bohemia, we receive on all sides the most piteous letters. The march
of an army through a country—even when on the road to
victory—desolates and devastates the land; how will it
be when the enemy penetrates the region, when the
battle ground is chosen in their neighborhood and their
castles and fields are at stake. Everything is prepared
for flight, their goods are packed, their valuables are
buried. Good-by to the pleasant visits to Bohemian
watering places; good-by to brilliant autumn hunting
parties; and most of all, good-by to the accustomed reve-
nues from harvest and manufactures. The crops are
destroyed, the factories which have not been burned
down have been robbed of their workmen. "It is a
genuine misfortune," they write, "that we live in the
border lands, and a second misfortune that Benedek has
not more promptly adopted the offensive and carried the
war into Prussia." Perhaps one might consider it a misfortune that the whole political squabble could not be
decided by a court of justice, instead of by murderous
onslaughts either upon Bohemian or Silesian soil. According to trustworthy reports of travelers, human beings,
green fields, and factories are also to be found in Silesia.
But no one thinks of such a thing as that.

My little Rudolph sits at my feet while I write. He
sends his embraces and his love to our little Puxl. We
both miss the funny little creature, but on the other hand
he would have missed his master, and he is a pleasure to
you. So we both send our regards to Puxl. I shake
his honorable paw and Rudi kisses his good, black nose.

And now, for to-day, good-by, my all!

" It is extraordinary! Defeat after defeat! First
the capture by moonlight of the village of Podol,
where the brigade of Clam-Gallas had thrown up
breastworks; then the taking of Gitchin. The
needle gun, the damned needle gun, mowed down
our men by windrows. The enemy's two great
army corps, under the Crown Prince and Prince

Frederick Charles, have united and are marching upon Münchengratz."

Such was the terrible report brought by my father, though he would not acknowledge the possibility of further disaster.

"They ought to enter Bohemia—all together—and there meet destruction to the last man. A retreat would not be possible for them, we would surround them and the outraged population would turn upon them. It is not very easy to operate in the enemy's country, for you have not only the army, but the people, against you. At Trautenau the people poured boiling water and oil from the windows upon the Prussians."

I uttered a cry of horror and disgust.

"What would you have?" said my father shrugging his shoulders. "It is certainly horrible, but it is war."

"Then do not dare assert that war ennobles a people! Acknowledge that it debases, brutalizes, is devilish!"

"Justifiable self-defense and a fair revenge, Martha. Do you think their needle guns are pleasant weapons against our side? Our brave fellows are mowed down by those murderous weapons like slaughtered beeves. But we are too well disciplined, too numerous, not to beat the 'tailors' apprentices.' In the beginning a few mistakes were made, that I will acknowledge. Benedek ought to have crossed the Prussian frontier at once. I am a little doubtful whether our choice of a field marshal was wise. It might have been better to have sent the Archduke Albrecht north and Benedek to the army of the south. But I will not find fault so soon—the decisive battle is yet to come. We are now concentrating our forces at Königgrätz; there—over a hundred thousand strong—we will await the enemy; there we will win our northern Custozza."

There Frederick would also be engaged. His last letter, which had arrived this very morning

(I had heard regularly from him), reported: "We
are on the march to Königgrätz."

I have in my possession all of these notes, written on horseback, in his tent, with pencil, on sheets
torn from a note-book. There is no carefully written army report style about them; none of the ef-
fusive strategic wisdom of the special correspondent; no rhetorical display of battlefield landscape;
but such as they are I give them:

"It is a warm, lovely summer night—the broad, indifferent heavens are full of glittering stars. The men lie
upon the ground, exhausted by the long forced march. A
few tents have been pitched for us staff officers. In mine
there are three camp beds. My two comrades are asleep,
while I sit at a table with a candle and a lot of empty
glasses. By the feeble, flickering light I am writing to
you, my beloved wife.

"I have laid Puxl on my bed. How tired the poor rascal is! I almost regret that I brought him; he, also, as
some of our side are repeatedly saying of the Prussians,
is not accustomed to the fatigues and privations of a campaign. He is sleeping and snoring, possibly dreaming of
his friend and patron, Rudolph, Count Dotzky. And I
am dreaming of you, Martha. True, I am awake; but as
deceptively as in a dream I see your figure in a dusky
corner of the tent, sitting on a camp stool. What a longing possesses me to go over there and lay my head in
your lap. But I dare not move else the image will disappear."

"I stepped out a moment. The stars shine with greater
apathy than ever. Here and there shadowy forms flit
over the ground; they are the stragglers, who, guided by
the camp fires, have made their way to us. But not all—
many lie far behind in ditches and cornfields. The heat
was fearful during this march. The sun was as brass and
burned into the very brain, the knapsacks were heavy,
and the guns rested on sorely bruised shoulders; yet no
one complained. Many have fallen and could not rise
again. Some died instantly from sunstroke. Their
bodies were loaded upon an ambulance.

"This night of June, so clear and warm, is enchanting.
We do not hear the nightingales nor does the odor of
roses and jasmines reach us. All sweet sounds are over-

powered by the stamping and neighing of horses, the voices of restless men, and the even tramp of the guard. But more is to come; we do not yet hear the croak of the raven nor smell powder, blood, and corruption. All this hereafter, *ad majorem patriae gloriam.* Astonishing how blind mankind are! They will break out in curses upon the fearful fanaticism which lit martyr fires 'to the greater honor of God'; and yet for the corpse-strewn battlefields of the present they have nothing but admiration. The torture chambers of the dark Middle Ages fill them with abhorrence, but they are proud of their arsenals.

"From the esthetic standpoint the most desirable situation to obtain a view of the battlefield is to be upon a hill surrounded by a group of generals and distinguished officers. You hold a field-glass to the eye. The painters of battle scenes and the illustrated papers, recognize the due value of the position. They frequently picture another view of a field marshal on a rise of ground, dictating orders to his staff, or the same figure on a white, high-stepping horse, with one arm stretched toward a smoke covered part of the plain, and the head turned as if calling to those behind: 'Follow me, my children.'
"From these commanding situations we really do get an idea of the poetry of war. The picture is magnificent and at a sufficient distance to give all the scenic effect, without its horrors and disgusting realities: no flowing blood, no death rattle, nothing but superb effects of line and color. On the roads, perhaps, long serpentine marching columns, far as the eye can reach, upon the plain regiment after regiment of infantry, detachments of cavalry, and batteries; then the ammunition train, farm wagons pressed into service, pack horses, and, behind all, the baggage.
"Still more forcible is the picture, when on the plain below we watch the onslaught and encounter of two hostile forces. The glitter of arms, the floating banners, the uniforms of all sorts, excited, prancing horses, all in one mad whirl of action; over these clouds of smoke, so thick in many places that it veils all within it; at times it rises and we catch a glimpse of struggling, fighting masses. Then as accompaniment, echoing through the hills, the roar of artillery whose every shot means death —death. Yes, this is something to inspire a battle song. It is something also for the writer of the history of his

times, which must be published after the campaign is
over, to have been upon this hilly outlook. With some
show of truth he can relate how Division X attacked the
enemy, drove them back, and reached the critical position; how strong re-enforcements marched up and were
seen on the left flank, etc., etc. But he who has taken
active part on the field and has had no such point of
observation can have no idea of the progress of a battle.
He sees, thinks, and feels only what is nearest him; what
he afterwards reports is mainly conjecture or the result
of later reading.

" The village is ours—no, the enemy has it—it is again
ours—and again the enemy has it, but a village no longer
exists; nothing but a heap of flames and ashes. The
inhabitants (was it not really their village?) had, fortunately, early abandoned it; for a skirmish in inhabited
places is horrible; shells and balls strike all alike, women
and children. One family had remained behind, an old
couple and a married daughter in childbed. Her husband served in my regiment. He said to me as we
approached the village. 'Over there, Lieutenant-Colonel,
in the house with the red roof, my wife lives with her old
father and mother. They could not get away. For
God's sake order me to go there.' Poor devil! he arrived
in time to see his wife and child killed by a shell and the
walls falling about the old people; he never saw them
again. I once saw an attack upon a village where a
breastwork had been made of the dead bodies of the
fallen—not all dead—I saw one move his arm from out
the hideous pile.
"Living still! That is the most awful, too frequent
condition of many hopelessly wounded. Is there no
angel of compassion to hover over battlefields and touch
with the tender hand of death all these poor wretches.
"To-day we had a little cavalry engagement in the
open field. A Prussian regiment of dragoons came
trotting up and deployed into line; then, with horses well
in hand and sabers above their heads, they rode on to us
at a sharp gallop. We did not wait for the attack but
sprang to meet them. Not a shot was exchanged. A
few steps from each other both ranks broke out into a
thundering cheer (maddened by sound! that the Indians
and Zulus understand better than we), and we sprang
upon one another, horse to horse, knee to knee, sabers
swinging in the air and crashing down upon the heads.

We were soon so mixed up that weapons could not be used; pressed breast to breast the horses became mad with fright and pranced and reared, striking out with their hoofs. Once I fell upon the ground and saw—what is not a pleasant thing—struggling and striking hoofs within an inch of my head.

"We are again upon the march, skirmishing on the way. I have had a great grief. It pursues me like a tragic picture. Amidst the many scenes of misery surrounding me, it ought not to cause me such keen regret. But I cannot help it; it touches me nearly, and I cannot shake it off. Puxl—our poor, lively, warm-hearted dog—I ought to have left him at home with his little master Rudolph! He ran after us, as usual. Suddenly he uttered a mournful howl—a grenade had shattered his front legs. He could no longer follow us and I was obliged to leave him, living still. Twenty-four, forty-eight, hours may pass before he dies. He whined after his master: 'Dear, good master, do not leave your poor Puxl and break his heart!' What torments me most is that the poor creature cannot know my regrets—that I heard his cry for help and yet so cruelly passed him by. He does not know that a marching regiment, from whose ranks comrades fall and are abandoned, cannot halt for a poor, wounded dog. Of my higher duty he knows nothing, and the poor, faithful heart mourns over my lack of sympathy.

"The knowledge that a man in the midst of such important events and such gigantic misfortunes, which fill the present, can allow such small affairs to trouble him, would cause many to shrug their shoulders—but not you, Martha, not you. I know you will shed a tear for our poor Puxl."

"What is the matter there? Has a spy been caught? One? Seventeen. There they come in four rows, four in a row, marching with bowed heads, surrounded by a guard. Behind them, in a wagon, a corpse is lying, and bound to the corpse, sitting on it, the son of the dead man, a twelve-year-old boy—also to be shot. I cannot witness the execution. I turn away but hear the firing. Behind the wall a smoke rises, all are gone. The boy with them!

"At last we find comfortable quarters for the night in a little town. (A miserable hole!) Supplies, which the inhabitants have taken months to hoard, we have coolly taken on a requisition. 'Requisition!' it is always fine to be able to give a right, melodious, diplomatically sanctioned name to a thing.

"I was very glad, however, that good quarters and a comfortable meal were to be had. And—I have something to tell you.

"I was ready for bed, when my orderly announced that a man of our regiment was without and had something for me. He came in. When he left I had rewarded him richly and shaken both hands, and promised him to care for his wife and child, should anything befall him, for what the good fellow brought me gave me great delight and relieved me from the pain I had suffered for thirty-six hours—it was our little Puxl. He was badly mangled but still living, and so happy to see his master, who in turn so rejoiced over him that he could no longer feel that he had been willingly abandoned. Yes, that was a happy meeting! but first a drink of water. How good it was! he stopped now and then to bark his joy. Afterwards I bound up his stumps of legs, gave him a supper of meat and cheese, and carefully put him to bed. We both slept well. In the morning, when I awoke, he licked my hand, then stretched out his legs, breathed heavily and ceased to be. Poor Puxl, it was better so!"

"What have I seen to-day? If I shut my eyes it all comes before me with frightful clearness. Nothing but scenes of horror and agony! Why do others bring back from war such fresh, joyful experiences? They do not attempt, in their accounts, to stick to truth and nature, but paint the scenes, story-book fashion, as is deemed heroic—the more horrible, the more indifferently; the more shocking, the more dispassionately. Of disapprobation, indignation, rebellion, not a word. Possibly they heave a few sentimental sighs of sympathy. But up with the head again—'Lift up your hearts to God and your hand against the enemy.' Hurrah!

"Here are two of the scenes imprinted on my memory.

"There were steep, stony heights in the foreground, with jägers climbing up them like cats. The order was to take the position. From above the enemy kept up a fierce fire. What I saw were the figures of the struggling men leading the attack. One was struck by the shot of those above. He threw up his arms, his gun fell, and head backwards he rolled over and over down the cliff, breaking bones and crashing to the bottom.

" Or this other scene: A rider a short distance from me was struck by a shell. His horse sprang to one side, touched the flank of mine, and shot forward. The rider still sat in the saddle, though the shell had torn away the lower part of the body; an instant later he fell, and with foot hanging in the stirrup was dragged by his horse along the stony ground.

" Upon a steep and overflowed roadway stood a section of artillery with wheels sunk deep in the mire. Only by most extreme efforts, dripping with sweat and urged by cruel blows which were rained upon them, could the horses drag the guns through; one, overcome with fatigue, dropped in its tracks. Blows were of no service; it could not move. Does not the man, whose blows are falling upon the head of the poor beast, see this? If the rough rascal were the driver of a wagon loaded with stone upon the highway, any policeman—or I myself—would have arrested him. But this cannoneer, who was responsible for his gun, only fulfilled the duty of his position. This the horse could not know; the tormented, willing, faithful creature, who made the most desperate exertions to do his duty—what must it think of such cruelty and such misunderstanding of its efforts—think, as animals think, not with words and ideas, but with sensations—sensations the more powerful because of their impossibility of expression? Only one audible sign can it give: a shriek of agony. And it did shriek as it fell—the poor creature!— a cry so long-drawn and agonizing that it sounded in my ears for hours after, and pursued me in dreams. It was a frightful dream. It seemed to me—how can I tell it? dreams are so irrational that they are difficult to render into reasonable speech—it seemed as if I heard the shrieks not of one but one hundred thousand artillery horses, for in the dream I rapidly calculated the numbers perishing on the field. ' Mankind, which causes this frightful danger to life, knows the why and wherefore; but we unhappy creatures can see no cause for all this suffering and misery. Mankind marches upon the enemy, but we are surrounded by enemies—our own masters, whom we love and serve, to whom our best powers are offered, hew us down and let us lie helpless in our agony. And what anguish we endure; terror so great that sweat drenches our bodies; thirst—for we, too, have fever—oh, this thirst—this thirst suffered by us miserable, abused one hundred thousand horses!' Here I awoke and grasped for my water flask—I was parched with fever.

"There was a running fight going on in the streets of a town. To the shouts of the combatants were added the crash of falling timbers, the tumbling of walls. Fighting along the narrow streets, we reached the open market square. In the middle stood a stone image of the Madonna. The mother of God held her child on one arm, the other she stretched out in blessing. Here the struggle was demoniac, man to man. A Prussian dragoon, strong as Goliath, seized one of our officers (a smooth, elegant lieutenant, the darling of the ladies), dragged him from the saddle, and beat his brains out at the foot of the statue of the Madonna, who looked on indifferently. Another, also a giant in stature, seized my neighbor and bent him backward until I heard the backbone crack, and then threw him under the outstretched hand of blessing."

"From the hills the staff officers had again to-day a diversified view of the spectacle of battle. For instance, there was the falling of a bridge while a train of wagons was crossing it. Were the wagons filled with wounded men? I do not know, I could not see, I only saw that horses, wagons and human beings sunk and disappeared in the deep and rapid stream. The circumstance was regarded as rather lucky, for the wagons belonged to 'the Blacks.' I always mentally call our side the white, the other the black party. The bridge had not fallen accidentally. The white party, knowing that the enemy would pass over it, had sawed the timber supports—so that it was a successful strategy.

"A second glance which one had from the same eminence disclosed a misfortune for 'the Whites': Khevenhüller's regiment was inveigled into a swamp, where it sunk and was almost entirely destroyed by the shells of the enemy. They sunk in the mire, mouth, nose and eyes filled with the slime; they could not utter a sound. Of course it was a tactical mistake, but 'to err is human,' and the loss of a few peasants more or less is not worth consideration. The slime remains in the eyes and mouths of the fallen; but that is of no special consequence, and the mistake of the tactician can be made good by some lucky later combination, for which the leader will receive a few fine orders and decorations. That lately, in a night attack, our Eighteenth jäger battalion fired for several hours upon another of our regiments, only discovering the mistake when day broke; and that a portion of the regiment of Gyulai was led into a pond: all these are small affairs which in the heat of conflict can happen to the best regulated commands."

"It is decided; when I return from this campaign I shall leave the army. Without any other consideration, when a man has learned to abhor a thing so thoroughly as I now detest war, it is a living lie to remain in the service. I have always, as you know, gone into the field with repugnance, but this detestation is so increased, my judgment so sharpened, that all grounds formerly held by me as reasons for remaining in my profession are now abandoned. The views of war instilled into me during my youth have not outlived the horrors of the reality. I do not know how much I owe to our mutual study of the subject for this new conception, which is shared by the noblest spirits of the time. However it may be, my determination is unalterable at the end of the campaign to cease to do homage to the God of War. It is a change brought about in somewhat the same way that many people experience a gradual change of faith. At first they are a little doubtful and indifferent, but they attend divine services with a certain reverence. When, however, they get beyond the influence of mysticism, when to them the ceremonies which they attend become absurdest folly, they will no longer kneel with the other deluded beings, will no longer deceive themselves and the world, and will cease to enter the no longer reverenced temple. "This is my experience in the service of Mars. The mysterious, supernatural influence which this god has exercised over mankind, and which in my earlier days darkened my judgment, has now entirely ceased. The liturgy of army proclamations, and the ritualistic, heroic phrases have no longer for me the air of an inspired text; the powerful organ tone of the cannon, the consecrated smoke of powder no longer entrances me. Without respect or faith I now stand by, viewing the frightful results of this aspect of civilization, but can see nothing save the anguish of the sacrifice, hear nothing save the melancholy cry of death. This is the reason why these sheets which I fill with my impressions of war convey but one idea of heart-breaking pain."

The Battle of Königgrätz had been fought. Again it was a defeat. This time it seemed a decisive one. No letter, no telegraphic despatch came from Frederick. Was he wounded—dead? Conrad reported his safety to Lilli.

The list of fatalities had not yet arrived; it was said that the loss in killed and wounded would reach forty thousand. On the third day there was still no sign. I wept and wept, hours at a time. Because my anxiety was not yet hopeless certainty I could weep; if I knew the worst I could shed no more tears. My father was profoundly depressed, and Otto, my brother, full of revenge. A volunteer corps was to be recruited in Vienna, and he talked of joining it.

Benedek was to be removed, it was rumored, and the victorious Archduke Albrecht ordered to the command in the north.

After a few days a letter arrived from Doctor Bresser. He was serving in the neighborhood of the battlefield, and he wrote that the misery was infinite, defying all powers of description. He had joined a Saxon surgeon, Doctor Brauer, who had been sent by his government to report the situation. Two days later a Saxon lady was expected, Frau Simon, who had been active, since the war, in the Dresden hospitals, and who had offered to visit the Bohemian battlefields and give such aid as lay in her power. The surgeons were to meet her upon a certain date at Königinhof, the last station touched by the railroad nearest Königgrätz. Bresser begged us to send bandages, and anything else that would be useful, to this station, where he would receive them. I at once determined to take the box myself, though I did not dare to inform my family of my intention.

I announced that I would prepare the box, and without difficulty left Grumitz. From Vienna I determined to telegraph to my father that I was on my way to the battlefield. True, I had doubts as to my capacity for usefulness, and my inexperience troubled me; in addition, my profound disgust for wounds, blood, and death hampered me. But I was oppressed by a continual presentiment that

Frederick was in danger, and heard in imagination his piteous appeals for help; from his bed of pain he seemed to stretch out his hands to me, and "I come, I come," was the only thought of which I was capable.

In a few hours I was on the way. I found Vienna in the wildest excitement, and drove to the Northern Station under continual stress of fear. Around and within the station were crowds of wounded and dying men, who were hurried to hospitals as fast as possible on their arrival. The most intense life— or should I not say death?—raged about us. The corridors, the waiting-rooms, the ante-rooms, were filled with wounded in the agonies of death. Swarms of citizens brought presents for the suffering, and anxiously searched for their own relatives, while nurses, the sanitary police, Sisters of Charity, surgeons—formed a mass of eager, surging humanity. In vain the officials endeavored to drive back the crowd.

"What do you want? Make way there! The distribution of food and liquors is forbidden. Hand everything over to the committee—they will receive your presents."

"No, no," I replied, "I want to take the train; at what hour can I go?"

It was with difficulty that I got any information as to departing trains. Passenger trains were no longer going out. I caught sight of Baron S——, president of the Patriotic Relief Corps, and implored his aid.

"Could I not go with the next supply train?"

"Impossible."

I seemed to hear Frederick's voice, pleading more and more piteously for me to come. I was driven to the brink of despair.

"For God's sake help me, Baron S——. You surely recognize me?"

"Baroness Tilling, daughter of General Althaus, certainly I have the honor."

"You are about to send a train to Bohemia. My

dying husband needs me. If you have a heart—and you show by your activity how good and noble your heart is—do not refuse my request."

With many doubts he finally consigned me to the care of a surgeon who was to accompany a train carrying hospital and sanitary supplies. The train would not be ready for an hour. Not a corner was to be found not already occupied by the wretched sufferers. A long train came in filled with more wounded. The less seriously injured stepped down unaided; for the worst cases cots were provided, upon which they were carried under shelter. At my feet they laid a man who gasped unceasingly. I stooped over him to say some sympathetic word, but sprang back in horror, covering my face with my hands. His features no longer bore the semblance of a human countenance; the under jaw was shot away, one eye was hanging out, and there was a suffocating odor of blood and corruption. The idea came into my head that this might be Frederick, and I compelled myself to look again. No—it was not my husband.

The poor wretch was carried away.

"Lay him on the bench there," I heard the regimental surgeon order. "No use in sending him to the hospital. He's already three-fourths dead."

He was three-fourths dead! And yet he must have understood these words, for with a gesture of despair he raised his arms to heaven.

The hour passed, and with four Sisters of Charity and several surgeons I sat in the car. It was suffocatingly warm, and the odor of carbolic acid and medicinal supplies was nauseating. How grateful I felt to these people for their self-sacrificing spirit in hastening to the aid of the sufferers. These brave women, who cherished for all mankind a love which I felt only for my husband, by its power were enabled to master that repugnance natural at the sight of such horrors, through the greater love they bore their bridegroom, Christ. But what a small measure of love to conquer the result of a thousand-fold of hate.

The train was set in motion. That is always the moment when every traveler feels as if on the road to his goal. I had often gone over this route and every moment I was reminded of hospitable visits in castles which we passed, of the charming watering places I had seen, and most of all of my wedding journey, when on our way to a warm welcome in the capital of Prussia (what a different meaning this last word had for us now!). And to-day? What was our aim to-day? To reach a battlefield and a hospital—death and suffering. I shuddered.

"You are unwell, Madam?" asked a young and sympathetic surgeon. "I have been told you go to join your husband, wounded at Königgrätz?"

"No, Doctor," I answered, "I am not ill, only weary."

"Baron S—— informed me that your husband is wounded at Königgrätz," said the staff-surgeon joining in the conversation. "Do you know in what locality to look for him?"

"I do not know where to find him. I expect to meet Doctor Bresser."

"I know him. He was with me when I visited the battlefield three days ago."

"Visited the battlefield!" I repeated, shuddering; "tell me——"

"Yes, tell us about it, Doctor," said one of the Sisters, "it may aid us in our work."

The surgeon told his story. The exact wording I no longer remember, but it all made so deep an impression that I afterwards wrote it in my journal, from which I now copy it.

Under ordinary circumstances I might have found it difficult to remember it so accurately; but the impression that Frederick was wounded and calling for me had become a fixed idea. Hence I imagined him figuring in every scene, and consequently the narration became intensely real.

"The ambulance corps had established its quarters just below some protecting hillocks, not far from where the

engagement had already begun. The earth and the very
air trembled with the shock of battle. Clouds of smoke
rose to the heavens; the guns roared unceasingly.

"Orders came to send out the relief patrol to bring in
the wounded.

"It is heroism to march steadfastly in the midst of
showers of bullets, shot and shell, to witness all the
horrors and all the dangers of the struggle, and be sus-
tained by none of the wild passion of the conflict? According to all the accepted theories of war, no fame may
be accorded to such courage as this. With the Sanitary
Commission there serves no dashing, gallant, swaggering
youngster; for them no enthusiastic girls turn for an after
glance, nor can regimental surgeons measure attractions
with a cavalry lieutenant.

"The corporal having charge of the relief corps ordered
his men to a point on the field upon which one of the
batteries of the enemy had opened fire. They marched
through the grey veil of powder, smoke, and dust, balls
falling in front and around them. They had scarcely
crossed the open ground when they met straggling
groups of wounded—these only the slightly wounded,
able to help themselves and each other. One fell insensible. It was not because of his wound, though that
was serious; it was exhaustion. 'We have eaten nothing
for two days,' they said; 'we made a forced march of
twelve hours, went into camp, and two hours later came
the long roll and the battle.'

"The relief moved forward. These men must help their
comrade. On the stony side of a rise of ground lay a
bleeding mass—a dozen or more men. The surgeons
bound up the most urgent and desperate wounds, but
neither can these victims be taken back; perhaps later
they may be helped, after those now lying in the thick
of the battle have been looked after. 'Forward relief!'
As they approach the point of attack, the groups of
staggering wounded increased and surrounded them.
Water and spirits were measured out, bandages hastily
applied, a word of encouragement was spoken, and the
way to the ambulance was pointed out. On again they
went, past the dead,—the piles of dead. All these creatures, horse and human being, showed in feature and attitude the extreme of suffering. Staring, agonized eyes,
hands ground into the earth, the hair of the beard stiff-
ened, teeth clinched together under tortured, half-open
lips, legs and arms rigid in the awful convulsions of death
—there they lay.

" Now the relief patrol entered a ravine. Here the men lay as in a slaughter house, dead and wounded mixed together. The wounded greeted them as rescuing angels, and with broken voices, weeping, whispering, implored piteously a little help—only a little water. In vain! Supplies were almost exhausted, and the little served so few. One needed a hundred hands. Suddenly there arose above the roar of battle the long drawn notes of the sanitary call. The corporal started, waiting for the second signal, while the broken and mangled wretches piteously begged not to be left upon the field. Again and again the bugle shrilly called, and an adjutant rode furiously up. ' Sanitary Corps!' he sharply called, and they followed his command.

" Evidently it was a wounded general. Orders must be obeyed and these men must be abandoned. 'Courage and patience, comrades; we will be back again.' Those who spoke and those who heard knew this was not true.

" They rushed forward after the adjutant. They could not stop a moment, though right and left rose cries for help and groans of agony. One or two fell on the field, struck by a passing ball, but they too were left. They swung round heaps of human beings mangled by the feet of cavalry and crushed by the wheels of cannon, but even here were remnants of desperate life struggling to rise at sight of the rescuing party."

So it goes on, page after page, in my red notebook. There is an account of the moment when, in the midst of the binding up of wounds, shells burst over the group and new wounds were torn open; or, when the chance of battle brought the conflict around the ambulances, and surgeons, wounded, and dying were swept down by the fleeing and pursuing troops; or when terrified horses, mad with agony, rushed over the stretchers on which the desperately wounded were being carried, who were thus thrown crushed and lifeless on the ground. Or this is described—the most frightful scene of all. A hundred helpless men had been carried into a farmhouse; their wounds had been dressed and they had been made as easy as possible. The poor creatures were cheerful and grateful for their rescue. A shell set the place in a blaze. A moment later and the shrieks of despair were heard even above the ceaseless roar—such wild and desperate despair as will be remembered to their dying day by those who heard it. Ah, me! Though I did not hear it, save through the surgeon's account, it remained hideously unforgotten. For while he told it I seemed to hear Frederick's voice rising from the raging flames where these poor martyrs died.

" You are unwell, dear Madam," the surgeon said hastily. " I have tried your nerves too much."

But I had not heard enough. I assured him that my faintness was merely the result of the heat and a preceding bad night. I begged him to continue. It seemed to me as if of all these pictures of demoniac passion the last and the most terrible remained.

"There is one thing still more frightful than the battlefield; that is, the field after the battle. We hear no thunder of cannon, no roar of musketry, no roll of drums nor blast of trumpets; we see no flutter of flags, no regimental guidons; we only catch low, shuddering groans and dying gasps. The trampled earth reeks with damp, shimmering puddles. All the fruits of the field are destroyed save here and there some straw-covered remnant of grain. Smiling villages are laid in ruins and ashes. The trees of the forest are charred and destroyed; the hedges are torn up by shells; and upon this desolated spot lie thousands and thousands of dead and dying—hopeless, helpless, dying. Not a blossom or a blade of grass is to be seen, nothing but sabers, bayonets, knapsacks, clothing, abandoned caissons, spiked cannon. Near the cannon the ground is the bloodiest; there lies the greatest number of dead or half-dead bodies, literally torn to pieces by shot. And the mangled horses—such of them as have any legs left—make efforts to rise, fall again, and again struggle up, until at last, throwing up their heads, they announce in agonized, dying shrieks nature's utter overthrow. A gully was filled with mangled bodies. The unfortunate men, severely wounded, had crept into it, hoping to be hid; but a battery had run over them; horses' hoofs and wheels had crushed them. Many were still living, hopelessly living.

" There is something more devilish than all this, the appearance of the vilest scum following in the wake of war-waging humanity—the battlefield hyena. Scenting the booty on the bodies of the fallen, these monsters in human shape stoop over dead and living and tear the clothing from their bodies. Merciless! Boots are jerked off bleeding limbs, rings are drawn from wounded hands, or if the ring does not slip easily, the finger is cut off with it. If the living victim faintly protests the hyena quickly puts a knife into his throat, or, for fear of after recognition, tears out his eyes."

I screamed aloud as the doctor paused. I had followed his story with absorbed attention, and the eyes he described became to me for the moment the clear, blue, loving eyes of Frederick.

" Forgive me, Madam," he said gently. " But you would hear it."

" Yes, yes, I wish to hear it all. What you have described was the night which immediately followed the battle. Was it starlight when these things happened?"

" Yes, and torches were seen all over the field. The details sent out by the victors to search for and bring in the wounded carried torches and lanterns, and red lanterns were hung on poles to indicate the position of field hospital work."

" And the next morning—how did the place then look?"

" Even more fearful. The contrast afforded by the clear, glorious light of day made the fiendish work of man seem doubly horrible. Night had given a ghostly, fantastic aspect, which by day became simply hopeless. One then first realized the astonishing numbers of the dead; upon the streets, in the fields, in the ravines, behind crum-

bling walls, everywhere was death.   Plundered and
naked, the dead and wounded were in the same
condition.

"Notwithstanding the untiring work of the Sanitary Corps, numbers of these poor wretches still lay
uncared for, either benumbed and half-unconscious,
or calling upon all who passed to shoot or stab
them to put an end to their misery.   Swarms of
carrion crows settled on the boughs of the trees,
croaking their satisfaction at the approaching
meal.   Starved dogs from the villages licked the
wounds.   A few of the human hyenas still stealthily
plied their trade.   And then after all this came the
great burial."

"Who does that, the Sanitary Corps?"

"How could they undertake such a gigantic
task?   They have enough to do to care for the
wounded?"

"Details of soldiers?"

"No; whoever can be picked up, generally camp
followers or laborers from the farms around about.
But they manage it easily enough.   They sometimes dig long trenches and throw the bodies in
head over heels, just as it happens; or they make
a mound of corpses and throw about two feet of
earth over them.   In a few days a heavy rain will
come and wash the earth all away; but what do
these fellows care.   They were a cheerful set, I
can tell you; they sang and whistled at their work,
and made all manner of bad puns.   They did not
trouble themselves to examine very carefully
whether there was still any life in these bodies.
Some of those who made the narrow escape of being buried alive have told me by what a mere
chance they escaped.   That is a picture of the
next morning," concluded the surgeon.   "Shall I
tell you what happened the next evening?"

"I can tell you that," I said.   "In one of the
capitals of the belligerent powers the telegraphic
reports of victory have arrived.   In the forenoon,
while they are dancing this hyena rondo around the

trenches of the dead out on the battlefield, the people in the city are collected in the churches singing 'Praise God from whom all blessings flow,' and in the evening the mothers or the wives of some of these poor fellows who are buried alive, fasten a few wax candles in the window, for the town is being illuminated."

"Yes, dear Madam, this comedy is usually played. In the meantime, upon the battlefield itself, the curtain has not been rung down upon the last scenes of the tragedy. Besides those buried or in the hospitals, there yet remain the missing. Behind dense thickets, or in the cornfields, or hid beneath the fallen branches of some shattered trees, they have escaped the search of the Sanitary Corps and the grave digger. A martyrdom of several days and nights of agony is the fate of these; they lie in the sweltering heat of midday, the damp chill and horror of the night, bedded on stones and thistles, within reach of the stench of decaying corpses, and dreading the descent of the carrion birds upon their own festering wounds."

It was a wearisome journey. The surgeon had long since ceased to speak, and we all sat absorbed in thought, aroused by an occasional glimpse, from the windows, of the effects of war. True, there were no smouldering ruins of deserted villages; the enemy had not yet marched through the country, but everywhere were evidences of the universal terror at the prospect of their approach. The roads were filled with people following farm wagons loaded with all their household effects. Everything indicated the haste of departure, and they fled knowing but vaguely where they were to find refuge. "The Prussians are coming!" had been the cry filling them with wild unreasoning terror.

Occasionally a train passed us, carrying the wounded to inland hospitals. All showed the same ashen faces and bandaged heads and limbs. We

passed stations filled with such men waiting for
transportation further south. They had all been
brought so far on cots, or, when able to sit up, by
the best available conveyances from the field or
the temporary hospitals, and were obliged to wait
until room could be found in the crowded trains
for transfer to Vienna, there to enter the hospital
or the cemetery.

Whenever we stopped the Sisters of Charity
moved rapidly and sympathetically among these
sufferers, supplying them with water or wine, and
bestowing a little care through deft adjustment of
a tired shoulder or a weary head. I was useless,
unable to control my emotion or repress my physical repulsion. The doctor usually led me hastily
into a quiet corner and gave me a biscuit and a
little wine.

This rush and uproar about the stations bewildered me; it all seemed a frightful dream—the running hither and thither, the departing troops, the
fugitives, the bearers of the wounded who lay on
stretchers, the swarm of bleeding, moaning soldiers, the women crying and wringing their hands;
the harsh words of command, the pressure everywhere—not a foot of space to pass through—the
rumbling of passing cannon, the baggage wagons,
the neighing horses, and now and then the announcement of approaching trains of reserves from
Vienna—I was helpless indeed. And yet I suffered
the very anguish of sympathy. Loaded trains from
Vienna filled with reserve troops met us, and sometimes stopped at these stations. I could not even
glance at these sound, bright young fellows without
heart-sickening regrets. With the speed of the
wind they were going to meet a similar fate, or perhaps death, and not of their own volition, cheerfully
as they might march out.

However the individual may console himself
with the uncertainty of his fate, there is always a
certain per cent of the whole which must and does
fall. The march into the field, whether of foot or

horse, has a certain antique poetry attached to it; but the modern mode of transit, the railroad, the symbol of the unity of civilization, is a hideous contradiction. How false sounds the click of the telegraphic instrument—this superb result of human intellect, which conveys the thought of nations with lightning-like rapidity—all these discoveries to advance the general interests of peoples, to relieve the cares of life, to beautify and enrich it; they are all abused to maintain a relic of an old-world principle which divides nations and destroys life.

"Look at our railroads! see our telegraph lines! we are civilized!" we boast, in order to confute barbarians, and then abuse these results of culture that we may develop our own barbarism.

Such thoughts embittered and deepened my· suffering. I almost envied those who found comfort in simply weeping and wringing their hands. They could not realize my rage against the whole terrible comedy.

It was late in the evening when I arrived in Königinhof. My traveling companions had left me at another station. I dreaded lest Doctor Bresser should fail to meet me. I was completely unnerved by the experiences of the night, and nothing except the intolerable anxiety about Frederick enabled me to retain my senses.

I carried a hand-satchel with a change of clothing and toilet articles. Custom rendered it impossible to conceive of existence without the dainty combs and brushes, the pure soap and water, the silver boxes and fine towels. Cleanliness, that virtue of the body which corresponds to purity of the soul, the second nature of the cultivated human being, I was soon to learn must at such times be entirely renounced. Is it not the natural result? War is the antagonist of civilization, and all the sweet courtesies of culture meet with destruction through it; it is a return to barbarism, and all barbaric evils follow in its train, among them that most loathed by the cultivated soul—filth and all uncleanness.

Königinhof was filled with the wounded and the station was densely packed; upon the ground, upon the stones, every nook and corner was filled. It was a dark night; the moon had not yet risen and the sky was almost without a star. Two or three lanterns lighted but imperfectly the little station where I left the train. I now began to realize the madness of my mission. Who could tell? perhaps Frederick was on his way home, or perhaps dead and buried; how could I find him here? With the thought of my child and the fear of missing Doctor Bresser I searched for my pocket-book well supplied with bank-notes. It was gone!

The surgeon-in-chief was pointed out and I was about to hasten to him when I caught sight of Doctor Bresser. In my excitement and relief I threw myself into his arms.

"Baroness Tilling!" he exclaimed, "what are you doing here?"

"I have come to help. Is Frederick in your hospital?"

"I have not seen him."

The reply was both a relief and a disappointment. It was evident I must search for him.

"And Frau Simon?" I asked.

"She has arrived—a magnificent woman! Quick to decide, and prudent; she is just now engaged in having the wounded carried into empty railway cars. She has discovered that the suffering is greatest at Horonewos, and we are going there at once."

"Let me go with you, Doctor."

"You—so spoilt and unaccustomed to exertion; why, it is hard, repulsive work."

"What can I do here, Doctor? If you are my friend, grant my wish. Introduce me to Frau Simon as a volunteer nurse and I will do all I can."

"Very well, yonder is the noble woman; come."

When I was introduced to Frau Simon as a volunteer nurse she nodded, but turned at once to order that attention be given to something just brought to her notice. I could not clearly distinguish her features in the uncertain light. Five minutes later we were on our way. A hay wagon which had brought some wounded men to the station had been impressed into the service. We sat upon the straw, possibly still wet from the wounds of its previous occupants. The soldier who sat near the driver held a lantern, which threw uncertain shadows upon the street. "Bad dreams, bad dreams," was the continual impression made upon me by all around me. The only thing which forced upon me the reality of the situation was the presence of Doctor Bresser. I had laid my hand on his and his arm supported me.

"Lean on me, Baroness Martha—poor child," he said softly.

But what an uncomfortable ride. When one has been accustomed all one's life to rest upon soft beds and ride upon spring cushions, a rickety hay-wagon with a little straw over the rough boards is torture. And I was sound and well. What must it have been to the mangled limbs, the shattered bones, to be driven over the rough stones in such a conveyance! My eyelids felt heavy as lead and finally closed, but sleep seemed impossible to me. The discomfort of my position, the excitement of my nerves prevented it, while thoughts and images of the disaster through which we were passing, all pressed in disordered array upon my brain. Leaning on Doctor Bresser's shoulder, half waking, half dreaming, I caught occasional snatches of the conversation.

"A portion of the defeated army fled to Königgrätz. The fortress gates were locked and the fugitives were fired upon from the walls; particularly was this the case with the Saxons, who were mistaken in the darkness for Prussians. Hundreds threw themselves into the moat and were drowned. On the Elbe the alarm and confusion reached the highest pitch. The bridges were so crowded with horses and cannon that the infantry could make no

use of them. Thousands threw themselves into the
river, the wounded men especially."

"It is said to be frightful at Horonewos," said
Frau Simon. "The inhabitants have left the village and the castle. The ruins are filled with helpless, wounded men. How thankful they will be for
our help! But it is so little that we can do."

"And our surgical aid is so inadequate," said
Doctor Bresser. "Hundreds of us could be constantly employed. We lack instruments and medicine. The over-crowding of all these places threatens the outbreak of dangerous epidemic diseases.
The first care must be to send away as many as
possible, but the condition of the majority is so de-
plorable that we cannot conscientiously move them;
to send them away means to kill them, to keep
them means an outbreak of hospital fever—a hard
alternative! What I have seen of misery and suffering since the Battle of Königgrätz passes comprehension. You must prepare yourself for the
worst, Frau Simon."

"I have courage and years of experience. The
greater the misery the greater my powers of endurance."

"I know that is your reputation. I, on the contrary, in the midst of so much misery, lose my
courage and my heart fails me. To hear hundreds,
nay thousands, pleading for help, when we cannot help, is horrible! Not one of our ambulances
has had a sufficient supply of stimulants, and we
have, also, particularly lacked water. The inhabitants, before they fled, rendered the springs useless; far and near not a piece of bread is to be had.
Every roof-covered space—churches, houses, barns,
granaries—is filled with sick men. The streets
are jammed with everything which goes upon
wheels, crowded with wounded men. They are
lying there, officers and men, disfigured with blood,
dust, and dirt, and dying of incurable wounds."

"Many die on the way?"

"Certainly. Many turn over quietly when laid

upon a bundle of straw, and breathe their last; others suffer such excruciating agony that they give utterance, in their ravings, to the most fearful curses. Mr. Twining of London must have heard such curses, which prompted, perhaps, the suggestion made by him to the Geneva Red Cross Conference. He says: 'When the condition of the wounded does not offer the slightest hope of recovery, would it not be justifiable, after offering them the consolations of religion, so far as circumstances would admit, to give them a moment of reflection and then put an end to their agony in the least painful manner. We should thus preserve them from the torments of fever which madden the brain, and perhaps prevent their dying with curses of God upon their lips'."

"How unchristian," cried Frau Simon.

"What? The gracious method of relief?"

"No; but the idea that such martyrs can commit sin through the curses of a maddened brain. The God of the Christians is not so unjust, and surely takes every fallen soldier unto himself."

"Mohammed's paradise is promised to every Turk who slays a Christian," replied Bresser. "Believe me, Frau Simon, all these gods represented as inciting to war, whose blessing and assistance the priests and commander-in-chief promise to the soldier as the reward of murder, are alike deaf to curses and to prayers. Look up there at that star of the first magnitude with a red light; every two years it shines directly above our heads. That is the planet Mars, the star consecrated to the God of War; that god in ancient times was so feared and honored that far more temples were dedicated to him than to the Goddess of Love. At the Battle of Marathon, in the pass of Thermopylæ, that blood-red star shone down upon men, and the curses of the dying mounted up to it; they accused it of being the cause of their misfortune, while it apathetically and peacefully, just as to-day, moved round the sun. Unfriendly stars? There are none.

Mankind has no other enemy than man—and no other friend."

"O Doctor! look there at the flames on the horizon; surely it is a burning village."

I opened my eyes and saw the red light.

"No," said Doctor Bresser, "it is the moon rising."

I endeavored to obtain a more comfortable position and sat up. I determined that I would not again close my eyes; this half-waking, half-dreaming condition, in which the most frightful and fantastic images filled my brain, was unendurable. It was far better to take part in the conversation and break loose from my own thoughts.

But the Doctor and Frau Simon were silent. They watched the spot where the moon was slowly rising. At length sleep really closed my eyes.

After a lapse of time which I could not measure, I was roused from my fitful slumber by an unendurable, pestilential odor.

"What is that?"

The wagon turned a corner and the cause was apparent.

By the clear light of the moon there rose a high, white wall, probably that of a churchyard. It had served as a breastwork and at its base lay piled up countless corpses. The odor of corruption which rose from these bodies had aroused us all. As we drove by swarms of ravens and crows arose croaking from the pile, fluttered about, and again settled down upon their feast.

" Frederick, my Frederick!"

"Be still, Baroness Martha," said the Doctor sharply. "Your husband could not be among them."

Why not? The husbands of other women were there.

The soldier who was driving whipped up his horses to escape the sickening odor. The wagon creaked and rocked as if we were in wildest flight. I thought the horses were running away. With fright I held on with both hands to Bresser's arm, but I could not help turning my head to see that dreadful wall and—was it the deceptive light of the moon, was it the motion of the wings of the carrion birds? It seemed to me as if all these bodies stretched their arms, as if they raised themselves to follow us.

I would have shrieked, but terror held my throat as in a vice.

We again turned a corner.

"Here we are, this is Horonewos," I heard the Doctor say.

"What shall we do with the woman?" complained Frau Simon. "She will be more of a burden than a help."

I roused myself.

"No, no," I begged, "I am better now. I will help all I can."

In the middle of the village we found ourselves at the door of an old castle.

"We will see here first what we have to do," said the Doctor. "The building, now abandoned by its owner, is said to be filled from cellar to attic?"

We got out of the wagon. I could scarcely stand, but made the greatest exertions to prevent this being observed.

"Forward!" said Frau Simon. "Have we all of our bundles? What I carry will bring comfort to these poor fellows."

"And in my bag I have bandages and liquors," I answered.

"And my bag contains instruments and medicines," added Bresser, who then ordered two of the soldiers to accompany us and the other two to remain with the horses.

Loaded down with our satchels of bandages, medicine, and wines, we entered the great door. Low sighs and groans were heard on all sides.

"Light! Give us a light," cried Frau Simon.

Alas! we had brought much, but not the most necessary thing. There was not a possibility of penetrating the darkness. A small box of matches

which the Doctor chanced to have in his pocket
served for a few seconds to show us the scene of
misery which filled the hall we had entered. The
foot slid along the floor slippery with blood. What
was to be done?

"I will hunt up the house of the village priest,"
said Frau Simon. "Come, Doctor, to the door with
your matches. Frau Martha, you stay here until
he returns."

I shuddered in every limb. Stay here in this
terrible stench, surrounded by these groaning men!

" No," said the Doctor, " come with us. You can
not stay in this purgatorial fire."

Thankfully I seized his arm. Alas! I was the
average woman, helpful and faithful in the ordinary walks of life, but in unusual emergencies un-
fit to cope with circumstances. As we made our
way back I repeatedly called " Frederick," but
there was no response. I climbed into the wagon
at the door to wait for the return of the Doctor and
Frau Simon. Two soldiers stood near me, the others
accompanied the Doctor. In a short time they
returned from the unsuccessful expedition. They
had found the pastor's house in ruins and nowhere
was a light to be had; there was nothing to do
but to await the morning. How many of the unhappy wretches, in whose hearts hope had been
awakened by our coming, would die before the
light of day?

Morning dawned. Now to work. Frau Simon
and Doctor Bresser went about to hunt up the inhabitants of the village. They succeeded in finding a few frightened peasants hid among the ruins
of their former homes. At first they were obstinate and suspicious. A little earnest talk in their
own dialect from Doctor Bresser, and a few sympathetic words in the soft voice of Frau Simon
reassured them. They disappeared and brought
others, who at once went to work assisting in the
manifold duties before us all. Some buried the
dead, others cleared out the choked-up springs in

order that an abundance of water might be obtained; mess chests and knapsacks were collected to furnish table ware and clothing; a Prussian surgeon with a staff of assistants arrived, and before long marked progress was made in relieving the general distress.

Frau Simon joined the Prussian surgeon at the castle where the majority of the wounded were lying. Doctor Bresser undertook to visit other localities in the village and I joined him to pursue my search. The Doctor had discovered that Frederick was not at the castle.

We had scarce gone a hundred rods when a loud cry of distress fell upon our ears. We pressed forward into the open door of the little church from which the sound seemed to come. About a hundred men lay upon the hard stone pavement— severely wounded and mangled. With feverish and wandering eyes they cried and begged for water. Almost fainting with terror I sought through the rows for Frederick—he was not there. Bresser and his attendants went to work among them; I leaned on a side altar and looked with inexpressible horror upon this scene of suffering.

And this was the temple of the God of eternal Love, these were the wonder-working saints whose images around the walls and in the niches piously folded their hands and lifted their heads under their halo of glory?

"O Mother of God, dear Mother of God, a drop of water! Have mercy!" I heard a poor soldier cry. He might have vainly called upon the painted image to all eternity. O miserable men, until you obey the law of love which God has stamped upon your hearts, you vainly petition for the love of God. So long as cruelty among you is unsubdued, you have little to hope from Heaven's compassion.

What did I not experience through that dreadful day!

Do not repeat it; that would certainly be the

pleasantest and simplest way. We shut our eyes
and turn away our heads when things unpleasant or
harassing are in view; it is convenient also to lock
the door upon memory. And we cry: "How can
we help it; how can we amend the past; why torment ourselves and others with the repetition of
the horrible."

Why? I will tell you later. This much I say, I
must say now; it is drawn, not from my own experience alone, but from that of Doctor Bresser,
Frau Simon, and the Saxon surgeon-in-chief, Doctor Naundorff. Compare my story with a recent
and most touching report called "Under the Red
Cross."

As in Horonewos, so in many other neighboring
localities Hell had held high carnival. In Pardu-
bitz, first occupied by the Prussians, "there were
over a thousand wounded men with amputated
limbs, or otherwise suffering from the experiments
of desperate science, the last chance for life, in
unusual cases, being risked on a surgical venture.
Nature's rough nursing was all they had; some
were dying, some already dead, some lying next
the dead and envying their release. Many with
no covering save a bloody shirt, so that it was
impossible, through lack of uniform, to tell from
what part of Germany they came. All who had a
spark of intelligence left begged piteously for
water and for bread, writhing under the agony of
their wounds, and imploring Heaven for the release
of death."

"Rossnitz," wrote Doctor Bresser afterwards,
"Rossnitz is the place which will be stamped upon
my memory until my dying hour. I was sent there
the sixth day after the battle, and there found the
greatest physical misery possible for the human
imagination to picture. I found our R. with six
hundred and fifty wounded, surrounded by the
dead and dying, who had lain all these days, without succor, in the most miserable, most filthy stables
and cattle pens. It was here that after burying

Lieut.-Col. F—— I was so overwhelmed with the hopeless magnitude of the suffering, that for an hour I shed the bitterest tears. Although as a surgeon I was accustomed to witness the extreme of human misery, and in the practice of my profession had learned to exercise self-control, in this place it required all my manhood to recover self-possession."

"It is impossible," wrote Doctor Naundorff, "to picture truthfully the condition of these six hundred men. The undressed, open wounds were tormented by swarms of flies; the delirious patients vainly pled for water, bread, and help, their clothing saturated with blood and stiff with the corruption of mangled flesh, covered in many cases with living worms generated in this decay. A terrible stench filled every place. All these soldiers lay upon the bare ground, with the exception of a very few who had secured a little straw upon which to stretch their wretched bodies. Under some the filthy soil was so soft that they had sunk in it and were unable to raise themselves."

"In Masloved," Frau Simon tells us, "eight days after the battle, we found seven hundred wounded men. The hopelessness of their condition as well as their suffering cried to Heaven. In one stable there were sixty crowded together. The character of their injuries was desperate under the best circumstances: here, from lack of every surgical attention, and with no other care, their condition had become hopeless; among all gangreen had set in. Shattered limbs had become a mass of corruption; swollen faces, covered with dirt or encrusted with blood, seemed to have but one black opening to indicate the mouth from which issued ceaseless groans. There had been no one to remove the dead bodies, and we hesitated as to which were the living and which the dead. It is astonishing what human nature can endure."

What is more marvelous to my notion is that human beings will subject themselves to such possibility of agony; that men will not swear before

high heaven that war shall not be; if they are
princes, that they do not break their swords; if
they have no other power, that they do not devote themselves by thought and word, by writing,
by preaching, and by acting to one common cry:
"GROUND ARMS!"

Frau Simon was a heroine, the "Hospital Mother,"
they called her.   Through her efforts and her wise
superintendence hundreds were saved.   One moment she performed the humblest service, the next
she was superintending the transportation of supplies.   She hastened from one place to another and
overcame, by her tremendous energy, the most discouraging obstacles.
And I? Terror-stricken, despairing, overcome
with anxiety and repulsion, I fainted on the steps
of the altar of the little church we had entered,
and when I again fully realized my situation, I
found myself in a railway car, surrounded by numbers of slightly wounded officers, and seated by
Doctor Bresser. We were on our way to Vienna
leaving Frau Simon delighted to be rid of me. I
had not found Frederick, and I had not abandoned
hope. I might find some news of him at home.
But the gigantic misery I had witnessed had
sunk so deep into my heart that it seemed to me
I could never recover from it. Even if I found
Frederick, and a long future of happiness and love
was granted us, I could never forget that so many
of my poor human brothers and sisters had borne
such indescribable agony.
I slept during nearly the whole journey. Doctor
Bresser had given me a light narcotic in order that
a long and sound sleep might quiet my nerves.
When we arrived at Vienna I found my father
waiting for me. He embraced me silently and
then turned to Doctor Bresser.
"How shall I thank you? If you had not taken
this crazy woman under your protection——"
But the Doctor hastily shook hands.

"I cannot stop. The young woman needs care; no complaints, no reproofs; put her to bed, give her orange-flower water, rest—good-by."

"Have you heard from Frederick?" came to my lips, but I had not the courage to utter the words. At last hope desperately mastered fear.

"Up to last night not a word," he replied. "But possibly we may find news at home. I left there last night, as soon as Doctor Bresser's despatch came. How anxious you have made us, you silly thing. To venture upon the battlefield in the neighborhood of the enemy—those fellows are savages. They have become insane about their needle guns. They are not disciplined soldiers either, and all manner of outrages are to be expected from them. And you, a woman, must run right into the midst of them. Well, well, the Doctor said I must not scold——"

"How is Rudolph?"

"He cries and howls because he cannot find you in the house; he will not believe you have gone away, because you did not kiss him good-by. Why do you not ask after the others—Lilli, Rosa, Otto, Aunt Marie? You act so strangely indifferent."

"How are they all? Has Conrad written?"

"All are well. A letter came from Conrad yesterday, and Lilli is happy. You will see Tilling will come out sound and well. Unfortunately there is nothing good to report in the political horizon. You have heard of the great disaster?"

"I have heard nothing, I have seen nothing but disaster and misery."

"Our beautiful Venice is handed over on a plate to Louis Napoleon, and that after such a brilliant victory as we won at Custozza. Instead of recovering Lombardy we have given up Venice. By this arrangement we have peace in the south, have got Louis Napoleon on our side, and can revenge ourselves for Sadowa, drive the Prussians out of the country, pursue them and conquer Silesia. Benedek has made dreadful mistakes, but the command

is turned over to the glorious general of the army
of the south. Why do you not answer? Well, I
will obey Bresser's order and leave you alone in
peace."

After a two-hour's drive we arrived at Grumitz.

My two sisters rushed to meet us as the carriage
stopped.

"Martha, Martha," they cried, "he is here."

"Who?"

"Frederick."

Yes, it was true. He had arrived the evening
before. A bullet had gone through his leg inca-
pacitating him at once. He had been carried from
the field to the nearest station, and as soon as possible had been sent to Vienna.

But even joy is hard to bear. The report that
Frederick was there had the same effect as the terrors of the preceding day—it robbed me of my
senses. I was carried from the carriage and put to
bed. Here, thanks to the after effects of the narcotic, or to the shock of relief caused by joy, I
spent several hours, half sleeping, in half delirious
unconsciousness. When I awoke and looked about
me, I believed that I had wakened from some awful
dream and that I had never left Grumitz. The
letter from Bresser, my determination to go to
Bohemia, my experiences there, the journey back,
the report of Frederick's return—all seemed but a
dream.

I looked up. At the foot of the bed stood my
maid. "Is my bath ready?" I asked, "I would like
to get up."

Aunt Marie started up from a corner of the room.

"Ah, Martha, my treasure, are you really awake
and in your senses. Thank God! Yes, yes, get
up; yes, yes, take your bath, it will do you good,
covered as you are with dust and dirt from the
cars——"

"Dust from the cars—what do you mean?"

"Quick, get up. Netti, get everything ready.
Frederick is dying of impatience to see you."

"Frederick, my Frederick!"

How often during the preceding days I had with agony called this name, but now it was a cry of joy. It was not a dream; I had returned and should see my husband.

A quarter of an hour later I went to him. Alone —I had begged that no one should follow me. I wished no one to witness our meeting.

"Frederick!" "Martha!" I sunk upon his bed and sobbed upon his breast.

This was the second time in my life that my husband had returned to me in safety, for his wound was not of a dangerous character. What was I that I had reached the shore of happiness, when so many thousands had sunk beneath the waves of this flood of misery.

Happy are they who in such a case can lift a glance to heaven and express their deep gratitude to the Almighty Guide; through such thankfulness, when humbly uttered and humbly felt, but which they do not realize to be founded in presumption and self-conceit, they feel that they are absolved, and that for this peculiar advantage, which they call special grace and favor of Providence, they have, according to their standard, balanced their account with Heaven. This was not possible to me.. When I thought of the misery which I had seen, and of the despairing wives and mothers whose husbands and sons, by the same fate which favored me, had been plunged into the abyss of torment and destruction, it became to me impossible to accept my happy lot as a decree of Providence for which my thanks were due. I remembered how I had one day seen our housekeeper sweep out a closet where swarms of ants had congregated; fate had in just such a fashion swept over the Bohemian battlefields, and the poor industrious workers had been as mercilessly crushed, scattered, and destroyed. Only a small remnant remained unhurt. Would it have been reasonable and just if those few ants had sent up their prayers of gratitude to Frau Walter?

No; however great the joy of re-union, this could
not drive from my heart the sorrow and suffering
I had seen. I had an account to settle with the
world. I had not been able to do efficient service
like the Sisters of Mercy or Frau Simon. But the
compassion which springs from inmost sympathy
I felt for all these, my fellow men, and I dared not
forget them in egotistical self-enjoyment.

" O Frederick, Frederick!" I exclaimed one day
with tears and kisses, "have I really found you
again?"

"And you rushed out to find and nurse me,
Martha?   That was heroic and—foolish."

"Foolish—I know it. I imagined I heard your
voice calling me; I had a presentiment, which was
imagination and superstition, that you were lost
to me. But heroic—no. If you only knew how
cowardly I was in the presence of all that misery.
You I could have nursed, only you. Oh, our beautiful world! how can man make it so terrible? A
world in which two human beings can love each
other as you and I love, in which such fiery happiness as ours can blaze—how can one be so mad
as to light the flame of death and misery-laden
hate?"

"I have seen things horrible enough, Martha—
something I shall never forget. One day, whom do
you think I saw spring upon me with uplifted
saber, during a cavalry engagement at Sadowa?
Gottfried von Tessow."

"Aunt Cornelia's son?"

"Yes; he recognized me in time and dropped
his sword."

"Which he was not justified in doing. What!
spare an enemy of king and country, under the
unworthy pretense that he was a dear friend and
cousin!"

"The poor young fellow! He had scarcely
dropped his arm when a saber fell on his own
head. It was done by my neighbor, a young lieu-

tenant, who saw his colonel in danger and wanted to save him."

Frederick covered his face with his hands.

"Killed?" I asked shuddering.

He nodded.

"Mamma, Mamma!" came from the adjoining room, and the door was thrown open. It was my little Rudolph with Lilli.

I hurried to meet the child and clasped him passionately to my heart. "Ah, poor, poor Aunt Cornelia!"

The war was drawing to a close. The abandonment of Austria's claim to Venice ended the conflict with Italy and France, and we were in a position to make favorable terms with Prussia. Our emperor was anxious to end the unhappy campaign before subjecting his capital to a siege. The Prussian victories in other parts of Germany, as well as the triumphant entry into Frankfurt on the sixteenth of July, lent the enemy a certain nimbus, which like all success excited the admiration of Austria and imbued the popular mind with a belief that Prussia must have a certain historical mission, to be accomplished only through the recent victories. "Truce" and "peace" were words frequently uttered, and we could as securely count upon their realization as in times when war is threatened we can depend upon its outbreak. Even my father acknowledged that under existing circumstances peace was desirable. The army was exhausted, the superiority of the needle gun recognized, and a march of the enemy upon Vienna—the destruction of Grumitz upon the way being probable—all were events which even his martial mind could not contemplate with equanimity. His confidence in the invincibility of the Austrian troops had been rudely shaken, and as it is a peculiarity of human nature to regard current events as being alternative in character—that is, that success follows success, misfortune again succeeds misfortune

—it was better to halt during the unlucky period. With time we might obtain compensation, and probably, also, the opportunity for revenge.

Revenge, and again revenge! Every war must leave one side vanquished, and if the defeated seek for satisfaction through another war, and those who lose struggle again through another, where will it end? How can justice be attained, when, in the expiation of an old wrong, another wrong is to be committed? No reasonable creature would conceive of the idea of obliterating ink stains with ink, or spots of oil with oil. Only blood must be washed out with blood.

The prevailing sentiment in Grumitz was of the gloomiest character. In the village the inhabitants buried or hid away their valuables, under the impression that the Prussians were approaching; even at the castle Aunt Marie and Frau Walter had secreted the family silver. We read nothing, we talked of nothing save the war and our own experiences. Lilli suffered the most intense anxiety in regard to Conrad, of whom she had heard nothing for days. My brother Otto had been charmed by the report from his military academy, that in the event of the prolongation of war the Senior and Junior classes might be called into service. Like the boarding-school miss looking forward to her introduction to society, he longed for his gay uniform and the great cannon cotillion. I had ceased by Frederick's advice my incessant attacks upon the principle of war, as its discussion caused unpleasant feeling. But we were both decided that at the announcement of peace, Frederick should send in his resignation, and I inwardly determined that under no circumstances should my son Rudolph be educated at any school where the whole bent of education was to awake in youth the desire for military glory. I examined Otto as to the method which was employed to this end. The boys were taught that war is a necessary evil (at least an evil—in that an acknowledgment of the spirit of the age), but at the same time the supreme incentive to the noblest manly virtues, which are courage, endurance, and self-sacrifice; through it the greatest earthly glory can be obtained; and, lastly, it is the most important factor in the progress of civilization. The mighty conquerors and founders of the so-called empires of the world, as Alexander, Cæsar, Napoleon, were commended as the most notable examples of human greatness; the benefits and successes of war were set forth in most laudatory fashion, while the evils resulting therefrom were piously ignored— such as the moral and physical degeneration, the poverty and the barbarism. Yes, it was the same system as that pursued in my education as a girl, and which then filled me with enthusiasm for war. Could I blame a boy that the possibility of being ordered into the field filled him with delight and impatience?

So I made no comment when one day Otto complained of the present inaction. I held a paper in my hand from which I had been reading.

"Here is a letter from a surgeon who accompanied the retreat of our army; shall I read it?" I asked.

"The retreat?" cried Otto; "I had rather not hear it. If it were the story of the retreat of the enemy, it would be a different thing."

"It is an episode of war that we are accustomed to pass over in silence," remarked Frederick.

"A well ordered retreat is not a flight," my father hastily added. "Why, in '49——"

But I knew the story of '49 and headed it off by beginning to read:

"About four o'clock our troops began to retire. We surgeons were absorbed in the care of the wounded— numbering several hundred—who were each patiently waiting their turn. Suddenly the cavalry sprang upon us from all sides, rushing over the hill and across the field, and at the same moment the artillery and baggage-wagons joined in the flight, all making their way toward König-grätz. In the mad rush many of the cavalry stumbled, and those riders who fell were crushed under the feet of the horses. Wagons were overturned, and obstructed the way of the crowds of disordered infantry. We were swept from our temporary field of work. We were told, at the first onslaught, to look out for ourselves; but the warning was drowned by the roar of cannon and the bursting of shells right in our midst. We were carried forward by the surging mass without knowing where. Suddenly we came to water; to the right was a railway embankment, to the left a ravine filled with wagons and ambulances; behind, as far as the eye could reach, were the ranks of cavalry. We waded through the water, and a moment later were ordered to cut the traces and abandon the wagons, saving the horses, but leaving the wounded to their fate. We on foot were on the verge of despair; we crossed other streams with the expectation of being ridden down and drowned at any moment. Finally we reached a railway station which we found barricaded. We broke through the barricade, and with thousands of infantrymen we hurried on in the wildest panic. At last, at one o'clock at night, we reached a little wood, where we sank on the ground at the verge of utter exhaustion. At three, wet and cold, we pressed forward, leaving a portion of our number to die without possibility of rescue. The villages were abandoned, not a human being was left in them; there was no food, no water; the air was loaded with pestilential odors from decaying corpses lying on the trampled wheatfields—bodies with blackened faces, eyes protruding from the sockets——"

"Enough, enough!" cried the two girls.

"The censor of the press should not allow the publication of such stuff," exclaimed my father angrily. "It takes away all pride in the profession of arms."

"And especially all joy in war itself! That is really a pity," I murmured half-aloud.

"In fact, those who take part in a flight should have enough self-respect to keep quiet about it," scolded my father, "for it is certainly no honor to join in a general 'save who can.' The rascal who cries, 'Look out for yourself,' gives the first signal for a rout and ought to be shot. A coward yells and thousands of brave men become demoralized and run with him."

"Exactly so," responded Frederick; "just as when a brave fellow shouts, 'Forward!' a thousand cowards sweep after him and for the moment are actually inspired with courage. You cannot classify men arbitrarily as courageous or cowardly; every one of them has his moments of more or less courage, of more or less cowardice. Among masses of men each one is in a measure dependent upon the state of mind of his fellows. We are creatures who herd together and are ruled by the feelings of the herd. One shouts, 'Hurrah!' and all the others follow suit; one man throws down his rifle to run, others imitate his example. We applaud the brave fellow who shouts, 'Hurrah!' and then preserve silence about the one who runs; they are one and the same man. Courage and cowardice are not to be considered personal attributes, but as conditions of nature, just as joy and sorrow mark two phases of sensibility. During my first campaign I was drawn into the confusion of just such a wild, unreasoning flight. In the official reports the affair appears as a well-ordered retreat, but it was in truth a complete rout. Guns, knapsacks, cloaks, side arms—everything was thrown away in the wildest confusion by a raging, rolling, insane mass; not a word of command could be heard, and the battalions, driven by despair, tore along pursued by the equally maddened enemy. Of all the horrible phases of war, this is the worst—it has the most of beastliness about it. No longer as gallant soldiers, but as huntsmen and prey, both sides assume these most barbaric of *rôles*. All the elements of the savage hunter are developed in the pursuer, all the delirium of terror of the hunted wild beast are seen in the pursued. Patriotism, ambition, thirst for glory, all are lost in the most powerful impulse which can possess the living animal, the instinct of self-preservation."

Frederick improved rapidly. The feverish outer world also seemed to be in a sounder condition; daily we heard more and more of peace. The ad-

vance corps of the Prussians, which no longer found
any obstacle on their route, and which slowly and
surely approached Vienna, had passed through
Brünn—whose keys had been handed over to King
William by the civil authorities. This march assumed more the air of a military promenade than
an offensive campaign, and on the twenty-sixth
of July a truce was announced, and the prelim-
inaries of peace were announced at Nikolsburg.

The only comfort my father found in the general
disaster was the report of Admiral Tegethoff's victory at Lissa. Italian vessels were blown into the
air, the "Affundatore" was destroyed; what a satisfaction! I could not join in the general rejoicing.
Neither could I understand the necessity for this
naval engagement, as Venice had already been surrendered. But there was a great clamor of joy in
the Vienna press. The glory of a martial victory
has through the traditions of centuries been exalted
to such magnitude that intense national pride is
roused by it. If in any case a general, commanding
our own countrymen, defeats another general at
the head of the enemy, all our fellow-citizens congratulate one another, and as each one rejoices the
community at large take fire—the herd sentiment,
as Frederick would say.

Another political event of those days was that
Austria joined the Geneva alliance of the Red
Cross.

"Now, are you satisfied?" asked my father as he
read the news aloud. "Do you not see that war,
which you insist is barbarism, with advancing civilization becomes more humane. I am in favor of
all these humane efforts for the relief of the
wounded; even from the standpoint of the statesman it is wiser. By greater care of the wounded
and sick, more men are able to return speedily to
the field."

"You are right, Papa, as useful material for
future wars. But the things which I have seen no

Red Cross Legion can do more than alleviate.
Were they ten times the number, with a hundred
times the means, they could not parry the misery
which one battle calls into being."

Day by day it became a fixed idea with me that
war must cease, that every human being should do
what he could to educate mankind to the attainment of this end. It was impossible to rid myself
of the scenes I had witnessed in Bohemia. Particularly in the stillness of night, I would wake with
this anguish oppressing my heart and this feeling
of duty pricking my conscience.

Only when I was entirely awake did I begin to
realize my own incapacity to stem the tide. I
could as easily still the tides and hush the roar of
the tempest-tossed waters. But we must not endure it! It must be stamped out! And my second
thought was—especially when I heard the sound of
his even breathing—" But I am happy; Frederick is
my own again," and I lost myself in this assurance,
often laying my arm across his breast and softly
kissing him on the lips.

My son Rudolph was justified in being intensely
jealous of his stepfather. This sentiment had been
awakened about this time in the breast of the
affectionate child. That I had left Grumitz without
any leave-taking, and that upon my return he was
not the first to embrace me—that in fact I shut myself up the entire day with my husband—all this
together had deeply wounded him. One morning
he threw himself into my arms exclaiming:

"Mamma, Mamma, you do not love me any
more!"

"What nonsense, my child; what do you mean?"

"Yes—now—only Papa. I—will not—will not
grow up if you do not love me any more——"

"Not love you any more? You, my jewel!" I
petted and kissed the weeping child. "You, my
only son, my pride, the hope of my future! I love
you more—no, not above everyone, but devotedly."

After this occurrence my love for my child was

more often demonstrated to his satisfaction. In
the terror of my anxiety for Frederick I had in
truth allowed the child's interest to retreat to the
background.

We had well considered our plans for the future.
At the close of the war Frederick was to resign,
and we would retire to some small country place
where his pension and my allowance would enable
us to live in a simple way. Frederick determined
to take up the study of international law, and aside
from sentimental theories and utopian ideas, to
master from the practical standpoint the question
of the possibility of attaining the universal peace
of nations.

The work of Buckle had first suggested a new
field of ideas. Then an acquaintance, through
such writers as Darwin and Büchner, with the
latest scientific theories, had convinced him that
the world stood on the threshold of a new phase
of knowledge. To master this fresh view of life
and matter he deemed enough to fill out not un-
worthily, when added to the happiness of his home,
the remainder of his life. Our little Rudolph was
not shut out from our plans; in truth, to educate
this plastic mind was to become the main duty of
our lives. We had learned through recent events
how sympathetically we regarded the interests of
the world at large, and we rejoiced over the prospect of our united future like any pair of youthful
lovers.

In the meantime my father, to whom we had
not confided our plans, expressed himself one day
quite differently.

"You will be a young colonel, Tilling, and in
ten years you will certainly be a general. Before
that time another war will break out and you may
command an army corps or—who knows?—reach
the rank of general-in-chief. Perhaps you may
have the fortune to restore the ancient splendor
of Austria's fame, now for the moment tarnished.
When we have adopted the needle gun, or perhaps

introduced a still more effective weapon, Prussia must lower her colors."

"Who knows?" I suggested, "we may close an alliance with Prussia."

My father shrugged his shoulders.

"If women would only let politics alone!" he said contemptuously. "Our honor and the interests of Europe demand that we should humble these braggarts and help those recently annexed states to attain their old independence. Friendship! alliance with these wanton offenders! Never, unless they humbly petition for it."

"In which case," replied Frederick, "we would set foot upon their necks. Alliances are concluded only with those of whom we are afraid, or when we want to humble a common foe. In statecraft, egoism is the main principle."

"Well, yes," my father acknowledged; "when the ego represents our country, all other interests must be subordinated to it."

"We can but wish," replied Frederick, "that in the consideration of the common weal the same spirit might prevail which, in the habits of the refined, has taken the place of the rude club-law egoism of the individual. We might hope that the idea might replace it, that our own interests are advanced not in antagonisms, but in a union with the interests of others."

"What's that?" said my father, with his hand on his ear.

Frederick had no courage to repeat his long sentence, and the discussion came to an end.

I will be in Grumitz at one o'clock to-morrow.

CONRAD.

The welcome which this despatch received from Lilli can be imagined. No other guest is received with such gracious and loving welcome as he who returns from war. In this case certainly it would not be in the style which confronts us in ballads and engravings entitled, "The return of the vic-

tors." The natural sentiment of the affectionate
girl was not biased by patriotism, and Conrad's
greeting would not have been warmer had he personally captured Berlin.

Naturally he would have preferred to return home
with victorious troops, if he had aided in conquer-
ing Silesia for his emperor; but to have fought at
all is an honor for a soldier, even though he is the
vanquished—or may be numbered among the fallen,
for the latter fate is particularly glorious. Otto
said that in the Vienna Academy the names of all
graduates who have been so fortunate as to remain
upon the field are inscribed upon a roll of honor.
Tué à l'ennemi, as they say in France, was in the
time of our ancestors, and is even at the present day,
especially praiseworthy. The greater the number
of our forefathers who fell in battle—no matter
whether the cause was won or lost—the prouder
becomes their descendant; the more honorable their
record in this respect, the less value should their
living representative place upon his own life. To
prove oneself worthy of ancestors thus killed one
must both actively and passively rejoice in this species of massacre itself.

Well, so much the better, that so long as wars
endure those people should be forthcoming who
actually find in it matter for emulation, inspiration,
even for enjoyment. The number of this class will
grow daily less and less, while the number of soldiers continually increases. To what must this
finally lead? The situation will simply become intolerable.

And to what will this intolerable condition lead?

Conrad did not pursue the idea thus far. His
comprehension of the matter was quite in harmony
with the well-known song of the lieutenant in the
"White Lady": "Ha! what joy to be a soldier, ha!
what joy!" To listen to him was enough to make
one fairly envy him the delight of the expedition.
My brother Otto was completely absorbed in admiration of the heroic halo encircling this warrior.

Baptized in blood and fire (he was always a soldierly figure in his hussar uniform), and having
passed through a rain of bullets, and doubtless having laid many an adversary low, he was especially
adorable, particularly with the addition of his honorable scar across the chin.

"It was not a very fortunate campaign, I will
admit," said Conrad, "but I brought back a few
memorable experiences."

"Tell us about it!" cried Lilli and Otto.

"I cannot say much about particular incidents,
the whole lies behind me in wild confusion. The
powder fairly mounts into your head. In truth,
this intoxication, or this fever—this martial fire,
in a word—begins with the order to march. The
parting from your sweetheart is hard—softens the
heart a bit—but when you are once on the march,
surrounded by your comrades, you are filled with
the idea of the highest duty which life can demand
of man, the defense of your native land. When
the bands played the "Radetzky March," and the
silken folds of our flags fluttered in the breeze, I
would not have turned back even to the arms of
my sweetheart. I felt as if I were not worthy of
this love if I did not do my duty by the side of my
brothers. That we were marching to victory I did
not doubt. What did we know of those horrible
needle guns! They alone were the cause of our
defeat. I tell you, the bullets fell upon our ranks
like hail. And we suffered from bad generalship;
you will see they will court-martial Benedek yet.
We ought to have begun the attack. If I had been
Field-marshal my tactics would have been to attack,
drive, and attack, and fall upon the country of the
enemy. Defense is of course an art and a difficult
one. But as the Emperor did not appoint me to
the command, I am innocent of the failure of the
tacticians. The generals have to settle it with
their superiors and their conscience. We subordinate officers and soldiers have done our duty; we
were ordered to fight and we have fought. That of

itself is a peculiar sensation. To stand in expectation and suspense as to when we are to attack the
enemy, waiting for the order to begin; this consciousness that in a moment a scene in the world's
history is to be played; and then, the pride, the
joy in one's own courage—death to the right and
left of you, the great, the mysterious unknowable,
which you manfully defy——"

"Just like poor Gottfried Tessow," murmured
Frederick to me; "it is to be expected, it is the
same school."

Conrad continued with enthusiasm:

"The heart beats higher, the pulse rises, and then
comes the peculiar ecstasy,—the love of battle
wakes, the ferocity of hatred of the enemy, and
the burning love of our outraged country,—and
the attack and hewing down become a delight.
You feel as if you had been transported to another
world, where all the usual sentiments and feelings
had been metamorphosed. Life itself becomes the
prey; to kill, a duty. Honor, heroism, magnificent
self-sacrifice alone remain, all other sentiments
are lost in the confusion. Add to that the smoke
of powder, the cries of conflict,—I tell you it is a
situation to be compared with nothing else. The
nearest to it is when one is fired by the hunt of the
tiger or lion and faces the maddened beast."

"Yes," said Frederick. "When man was in continual danger from the attacks of two- and four-
legged enemies, and could enjoy life only through
their destruction, such strife was a delight. When
with us civilized men this same fierce joy riots in
our blood, it is but an inherited reminiscence. And
as we in Europe have now neither wild beast nor
barbarians, we create artificial aggressors. So we
say: 'Look here, you here have blue coats and you
on the other side, red coats.' Clap your hands three
times, presto! change the red coats into tigers and
the blue coats into wild beasts. Again, attention!
one, two, three. Trumpets, blow; drums, beat; now,
begin; eat each other up. Should there be ten thou-

sand, possibly in these times a hundred thousand of these artificial tigers devoured amidst universal howls of combative delight, at X——, then we have in history the famous X—— battle. The magicians who have clapped their hands assemble round a green table in X——, lay down their maps, re-arrange boundaries, pushing them here and there, squabble over who shall pay the costs, sign a paper which is known in history as the X——treaty; they clap their hands three times more and order the blue and the red coats: 'Now, my children, embrace as men and brothers.'"

Prussian troops were quartered in the neighborhood, and Grumitz might any day expect the common fate. The greatest terror of the hated Prussians possessed the minds of the villagers. The very name of the enemy becomes in time of war the synonym of everything evil, so that the people trembled as if these men were wolves personified, when the Prussian quartermaster rode down the street to arrange quarters for his soldiers. It had occasionally happened that a Prussian soldier had been shot down by some hidden cowardly assailant, who for this had been dragged out and summarily executed. Of course, the result was that the allotment was quietly accepted, and the unwilling hosts soon discovered that these hated Prussians were pretty generally a good-natured, friendly lot, who punctually paid their bills.

I was sitting in the library one morning, near a window which commanded a wide prospect. Looking up suddenly, I saw in the distance a troop of horse evidently coming in our direction. I seized a field-glass and saw a detachment of possibly ten horsemen surrounding a figure on foot in hunting dress. Who could this be? some prisoner who had fired upon them? There was small hope for him if this was the case.

I ran down into the drawing-room to report their approach to my father and aunt. The latter calmly

remarked that she must see the housekeeper on
some final matters—they had for days anticipated
the arrival of the enemy, and had a well-filled lar-
der and numerous beds in order.

"The Prussians, the Prussians are coming," I
exclaimed breathlessly. We are always delighted
to be the first to make an important announcement.

"The devil take them," was my father's inhospi-
table exclamation.

"Where is Otto?" I asked. "He must know of
it and be warned to restrain the expression of his
hatred of Prussia. He must treat guests with
courtesy."

"Otto is not at home," answered my father, "he
went out early to hunt birds. You ought to have
seen how becoming his hunting suit is to him—he
is going to be a handsome fellow; I will have a
deal of pride in him."

In the meantime there seemed some disturbance
in the house; we heard excited voices and hasty
steps.

"They have come, the wind-bags," sighed my
father.

Franz, the footman, white with terror, forgetting
all discipline, flew into the room shouting: "The
Prussians!" in the same tone in which he might
announce that the house was on fire.

"They will not eat us up," responded my father
snappishly.

"But, your Excellency," gasped Franz, "they
have a prisoner, your son, who is said to have fired
on them."

My father, with an exclamation of alarm, hastily
left the room. In a few moments he returned with
Otto. It appeared that in crossing a field he had
stumbled over a furrow and his gun had gone off.
The approaching party had immediately seized
him, but having learned on their arrival at the castle
that he was the son of the house, and a cadet from
the military academy, they immediately released
him.

"It would be impossible to suspect an honorable soldier of intention to commit a cowardly murder," they honestly remarked.

I asked Otto if he was really innocent, and wondered if his hatred of the Prussians might not have carried him so far. He shook his head:

"I will have opportunity enough in my life to shoot a few of them, but not without offering my own breast to their bullets."

"Bravely said, my boy!" cried my father.

I could not share this delight. All these phrases in which human life is treated as so insignificant and is so boastfully thrown away, had to me an offensive sound.

Two colonels and six subordinate officers, with two privates as guard, were quartered upon us, and were speedily, with all due courtesy, directed to their rooms.

I can remember to this day the singular impression made upon me as I entered the drawing-room that evening. Lori, the coquette Lori, had arrived on a visit from Vienna, and the opportunity to turn the heads of a few of even the hated enemy was not to be despised. She had made herself as captivating as possible. Lilli would naturally, in Conrad's presence, omit no artificial addition to her attractions, and Rosa, heartily glad to see a few cavaliers once more, had on a light colored dress which did not lessen her capacity to do mischief. I alone, regarding the time of war as a time of mourning, wore a black gown.

What a contrast all this was—these beautifully dressed women, these brilliant uniforms—to the scenes of sorrow, anguish, and terror witnessed so short a time before. It is always the brilliant, the merry, and the high in social rank who bring about all this trouble; it is they who use it as a means of self-glorification, and by their decorations and glittering orders distinguish themselves as the supporters of the whole miserable system.

My entrance broke up the various groups into which the company had gathered, and the Prussian guests were severally introduced to me. Distinguished names they bore, ending in "ow" and "witz"; also many a "von" and even a prince— Prince Henry, of the house of Reuss.

So these were our enemies! courtly gentlemen with the most approved conventional society manners. It is true that in these days we do not war with Huns and Vandals, but it is a little hard to remember that the other side represents the same civilization as our own.

"God, who art the support of those who trust in Thee, hear us who appeal to Thy compassion, and through the might of Thy protection defend us from the rage of the enemy that we may praise Thee to all eternity."

That was the way the Grumitz pastor prayed every Sunday. How was it possible for his congregation to picture to themselves this wrathful enemy? Certainly not with the manners of these elegant gentlemen who led these ladies out to dinner in such graceful fashion. Then it was to be remembered that God this time had heard the prayers of the other side, and suppressed our wrath; we were the murderous, raging enemy who through the might of Divine protection (we thought it was the needle gun which had done it) had been hurled down, and *they* would offer thanks to all eternity—what a saintly contradiction!

These were my thoughts as I looked across the table decorated with fruit and flowers, and observed the conversation and manners of all about me. I sat between a stately colonel and a slender lieutenant. Lilli, naturally, was next to Conrad, and Rosa had as attendant Prince Henry; the malicious Lori had captured Frederick. All mention of the war was carefully avoided, and the strangers acted as if they were guests traveling for pleasure. My young lieutenant paid assiduous court to me; he assured me that Austria was the most delightful country in the world, and its women the most charming. I do not deny that I flirted a little; it was just as well to let Lori Griesbach and her neighbor understand that I knew how to revenge myself. It would have been more to the purpose, however, if my lieutenant had directed his killing glances in Lori's direction, where they would have been better appreciated. Conrad and Lilli in their province as acknowledged lovers (such people ought to be caged) whispered and went through all the conventional turtle-dove maneuvers. I began soon to suspect a third flirtation, for Prince Henry's countenance expressed unalloyed admiration of my sister Rosa.

After dinner we returned to the drawing-room, now brilliantly illuminated. The door leading to the terrace stood open. The soft summer night was flooded with mellow moonlight. The queen of night threw her beams over the hay-scented sward of the park and mirrored herself, sparkling like silver, in the lake beyond.

Was that really the same moon by whose light I had so lately seen the mouldering corpses piled up against the churchyard wall? Were these the same men—one of the Prussian officers opened the piano at this moment to play one of Mendelssohn's Songs Without Words—were these the same who so lately, saber in hand, cut open the heads of those other men?

After a while Prince Henry and Rosa came out. They did not notice me in my dark corner as they passed near me. It seemed to me the young Prussian—our enemy—held Rosa's hand in his own. They spoke softly, and I could only now and then catch a word. "It is fate——do not say no——do you detest me?" Rosa shook her head. He lifted her hand to his lips and endeavored to draw her to him. She, the well-bred young woman, drew back quickly.

Oh, I had been much better pleased if the soft moonlight had witnessed a lover's kiss. After all

the evidences of hate and bitterest misery, which I
had lately seen, such a scene of love and pure delight would have seemed some compensation.

"Ah! is that you, Martha?" exclaimed Rosa,
suddenly aware of my presence.

The Prince was much embarrassed. He stepped
up to me.

"I have offered my hand to your sister, dear
Madame. I hope you will say a good word for me.
My conduct may seem rash and bold. At another
time I might have been more modest and considerate—but in the last few weeks I have accustomed
myself to quick and decisive measures—no dally-
ing or hesitation was allowed—and what I have
learned in war I have involuntarily applied in love.
Forgive me and be my friend. You are silent,
Countess. Do you refuse my hand?"

"My sister cannot so rashly decide her fate," I
said, coming to Rosa's aid. "Whether our father
will give his consent to a marriage with an enemy
or whether Rosa can return an attachment so suddenly announced, who can tell to-day?"

"I know I can," she answered, holding out both
hands to the young man!

He caught her in his arms.

"O, you foolish children!" I said, and softly
moved away to the door in order to watch that—
at least just at this moment—no one should come
out.

On the following morning the engagement was
announced.

My father made no objection. I had believed
that his hatred of Prussia would make it impossible for him to admit to his family one of the victorious enemy; but it seemed that he separated
the individual from the national question. This is
a popular custom. "I hate them as a nation, not as
individuals," one hears repeatedly, although the
remark is no more sensible than if we were to say:
"I hate wine as a drink, but swallow every drop
willingly." But it is not necessary that such cur-

rent phrases should be sensible, quite the contrary. Perhaps gratified pride got the upper hand, for a connection with the princely house of Reuss was in every way desirable; possibly the romantic suddenness of the love of the young people touched him. At any rate, he gave a willing consent. Aunt Marie was not so easily reconciled.

"Impossible," she exclaimed, "the Prince is a Lutheran."

She finally consoled herself with the reflection that Rosa would probably convert him.

Otto rebelled the most. "How would it be if, when war breaks out again, I am obliged to drive my brother-in-law out of the country?"

But at last the famous theory of the difference between nation and individual was explained to him, and, to my astonishment, for I never could grasp it, he understood it.

How quickly and easily one forgets past sorrow in happy surroundings. Gradually the fearful scenes of the past few weeks passed from my mind. I realized, not without a twinge of conscience occasionally, that my passionate sympathy had somewhat melted away. From the outside world one heard many a sorrowful echo: the lamentations of people who had lost in the war all their fortune and all their friends; reports of probable financial catastrophe; or rumors of an outbreak of the cholera, which had made its appearance among the Prussian troops. One case had occurred in our village. "It is probably nothing serious," we comfort ourselves by saying, when disagreeable probabilities are suggested. To drive everything unpleasant from our thoughts, by "It is of no consequence," or "That is all over," or "There is nothing in it," is all so easy, and we utter the words with a toss of the head.

"Do you know, Martha," said Rosa one day, "this war was certainly something terrible, but I could bless it. Without it I should never have been

so happy as I am now.   Should I ever have known
Henry? and he—would he have found such a loving
wife?"

"Really, Rosa, I will make this suggestion: it is
possible your two happy hearts may weigh in the
balance against the many thousand broken ones."

"One must not think of the fate of individuals.
In the case of the nation, war brings to the victors a
great gain.   You ought to hear Henry talk about
it.   He says, Prussia has won a grand position; in
the army general enthusiasm prevails, and a sentiment of universal gratitude and love for the field-
marshals who have led it to victory and thereby
improved the general condition of trade—and the
historical mission— oh, I can't tell you exactly all
he says.   You ought to hear him."

"Why does not Prince Henry talk rather of your
love than of political and military affairs?"

"Oh, we talk about everything—and all he says
is music in my ears.   I can sympathize with his
feeling that he is proud and happy to have had a
part in this war for his country."   ·

"And as booty means to carry back such a pretty
wife," I replied.

My father was well pleased with his future son-
in-law (who would not be pleased with the fine
young fellow?)   He dispensed his blessing and his
sympathy with certain qualifications and conditions.

"You are worthy of all esteem as a man, soldier,
and prince," he would expound to him repeatedly,
"but as a Prussian officer I cannot endure you, and
I retain the right, notwithstanding future family
relationship, to wish nothing so earnestly as a war
in which Austria may amply revenge herself for
this late humiliation.   Political questions are entirely distinct from personal ones.   My son Otto
will sometime—I pray God that I may live to see
it!—go into the field against Prussia.   Old as I am,
if my emperor desired, I would also accept a command to humble William I. and your arrogant
Bismarck.   I acknowledge the military virtues of

the Prussian army and the strategic skill of its
leaders, and I should consider it perfectly natural
if you, in the next campaign, were compelled, at
the head of your battalion, to storm our capital and
set fire to the house in which your father-in-law
lives; in short——"

"In short the confusion of sentiments is frightful," I interrupted him upon one occasion. "Contradictions of all sorts are inextricably mixed, like
the infusoria in a drop of foul water. To hate the
whole and love a part, to consider one first as a
man and next as a representative of his country—
it will not do. I prefer the custom of the savage
Indian who never heard of anybody as an 'individual.' He only wants to scalp every man of the
other tribe."

"But Martha, my child, such savage sentiments
are unworthy the refined and humane condition of
our civilization."

"Say rather, the character of our civilization is
not consistent with the inherited barbarism of ancient times. So long as the spirit of war is not
shaken off, our much vaunted humanity has no
common sense standpoint. You will scarcely call
your last assertions sensible, when you assure
Prince Henry in one breath that you love him as a
son-in-law and hate him as a Prussian, value him
as a man and abominate him as lieutenant-colonel;
that you will gladly give him your blessing as a
father and at the same moment grant his right to
shoot you down if convenient. Forgive me, Father,
you will scarcely call such talk common sense."

"What do you say? I do not understand a
word."

The convenient deafness had come upon him
again.

After a few days it was again quiet in Grumitz.
Our guests departed. It was decided that the
marriage of my sister should take place in October.
Prince Henry expected to retire from the service,

which he could honorably do after so glorious a campaign, in which he had taken an active part. The four parted secure of future happiness.

How can one be confident of happiness, in times of war least of all? Misfortune then hovers over us dense as swarms of gnats buzzing in the sun, and the chance of standing aside beyond the reach of the impending scourge is but small.

Certainly the war was over. That is, peace had been declared. A word had been enough to let loose all war's terrors, and it was believed a word would again be enough to relieve us from its results. Hostilities were suspended but malign influences continued. The seeds of future wars were scattered and the fruits of the war just ended rapidly ripened in want, demoralization, and pestilence. One might protest in vain and decline to think; it was useless, the cholera raged throughout the country.

On the morning of the eighth of August when I opened the paper at breakfast, the first thing my eye fell upon was the report from Vienna:

"Cases of cholera increase rapidly; the civil as well as military hospitals have reported many cases of the genuine Asiatic type, and most energetic measures have been taken to prevent the disease becoming epidemic."

I was about to read the despatch aloud when Aunt Marie exclaimed, holding up a letter written by a friend on a neighboring estate:

"Dreadful! Betty writes that two people have died of cholera in her house and that her husband is very ill."

"Excellence, the school teacher wishes to speak to you," the servant announced.

The teacher came in close upon the heels of the speaker.

"Count Althaus, I come to report that I have closed the village school. Yesterday two children were taken with the cholera, and to-day they are dead."

"The cholera?" we exclaimed.

"There is no doubt of it. The doctor who has been sent from the city says that it has become epidemic."

We looked at each other in dismay. Here it was again, our frightful enemy, death, and each of us saw his skeleton hand stretched over the head of some one we loved.

"We must go away!" said Aunt Marie.

"Where?" replied the teacher. "Everywhere the disease is spreading."

"Across the frontier."

"Quarantine will be established. That will not be possible."

"That would be horrible. They will not prevent people flying from the region of pestilence?"

"Certainly. Healthy communities will not tolerate the spread of the disease within their borders."

"Then God's will be done," exclaimed my father with a deep sigh. "You are usually so firm a believer in destiny, Marie, I cannot understand your wish to run away. The fate of every one will reach him wherever he is, you say. But still I would much rather you and the children should go away—and Otto, you must eat no more fruit."

"I will despatch to Bresser," said Frederick, "to send us the means for disinfection."

Later events I cannot minutely describe, for the episode at breakfast was the only one I transferred to my note-book. I can only report from memory the incidents of the days immediately following. Terror and dread oppressed us all. Who does not tremble in times of epidemic, when all we love are in danger? Above every loved head hangs a sword of Damocles, and one does not willingly die—so needlessly and fearfully. Courage consists alone in the ability to desist from thought.

Flee? This idea took possession of me on account of my little Rudolph. My father insisted upon the family leaving the castle. On the following day he decided that the family must depart. He meant to remain himself, not being willing to

leave his servants and the villagers to face the
danger alone. Frederick declared he would remain
also, and I would not leave his side.

Aunt Marie was to go with the two girls, and
Otto and Rudolph. Where? that was not yet determined; at the outset to Hungary. The young
women busied themselves anxiously and hurriedly
with the preparations. Die! just when happiness
was promised in the near future—that would be a
tenfold death.

The boxes were brought into the dining-room
to hasten the work of packing. I brought a bundle
of Rudolph's clothes upon my arm.

"Why does not your maid do that?" asked my
father.

"I do not know where Netti is hiding; I rang
several times and she does not come. I thought it
was better to bring them myself."

"You spoil all your servants," said my father
angrily, and he ordered a servant standing near to
hunt up the girl.

In a short time he returned with an anxious
countenance.

"The—Netti is in bed in her room. She is—
she has—she is——"

"Why do you not speak?" scolded my father.
"What is she?"

"She is already quite black."

A shriek came from all lips. So it was among
us—this horrible plague—in our own house.

What was to be done? The unfortunate girl
must not be left to die alone. But whoever approached her sought certain death, not only for
himself, but for all others whom he might afterwards approach. A house in such a strait is as if
surrounded by bandits, or as if in flames, with no
means of escape for the inmates. Everywhere,
from every nook and corner—following upon every
step and act—death stared upon us.

"Bring the doctor at once," my father ordered.
"And you children hasten your departure."

"The doctor returned to town an hour ago," answered the servant.

"Oh, I am so ill!" exclaimed Lilli, who had grown deathly pale as she sank upon the sofa.

We sprang to her aid.

"What ails you? You are silly, it is nothing but anxiety."

But it was not anxiety, it was—no doubt—we dared not think, but hurried her to her room, where she was at once seized with all the most aggravated symptoms of the dread disease. This was the second case of cholera in one day at the castle.

It was frightful to see what the poor sister suffered—and no doctor to be found. Frederick was the best adapted to supply his place, and he ordered all the well-known remedies, warm flannels, broken ice, champagne. Nothing was of any avail. These means, well adapted to light cases, were of no service here. Cramps of the whole body set in which seemed to make even the bones crack. The unhappy girl could not utter a sound, her voice failed, the skin became blue and cold, the breathing grew difficult.

My father walked up and down wringing his hands. Once I stopped him and said gloomily:

"This is the result of war, Father! Will you not curse war now?"

He shook me off without a reply.

After ten hours of suffering Lilli was dead. Netti, my maid, had died alone in her room; we were all busied with Lilli, and none of the servants would go near her.

In the meantime Doctor Bresser arrived and assumed control of the house. He brought all new means of relief. I could have kissed his hand when the old friend stood so unexpectedly in our midst, ready to sacrifice himself to our welfare. The two bodies were carried to a distant chamber, the rooms lately occupied by them were locked, and the strictest measures were taken for the safety of the other members of the family. An intense odor

of carbolic acid filled the house, and to this day
this smell brings back to memory all the events of
that terrible time.

The flight was attempted a second time. The
day after Lilli's death the carriage stood at the
door which was to carry Aunt Marie, Rosa, Otto,
and my little one, when the coachman dismounted
from the box and declared himself unable to drive.

"I will drive you myself," said my father. "Quick
—is everything ready?"

Rosa stepped back.

"Go on," she said, "I must remain; I shall follow
Lilli."

And she was right. By daybreak of the second
day her body was carried to the vault.

Of course flight was no longer thought of for a
moment.

Even in my agony I was seized with the deepest
scorn of the gigantic folly which had voluntarily
brought about all this misery. As Rosa's body
was carried from her chamber my father sank on
his knees, his head against the wall.

I seized him fiercely by the arm. "Father," I
cried, "that is war!"

No answer.

"Father, do you hear? Now will you not curse
war?"

He sprang to his feet.

"You remind me of my duty; this misfortune
must be endured with a soldier's courage. Not I
alone; the whole country brings its offering of
tears and blood."

"What advantage has your suffering and that of
your brothers been to our country? What gain to
it the lost battles, the shortened lives of your two
children? Father, I implore you, if you love me,
curse war. See there," I drew him to the window
where a hearse had rolled into the court; "see, that
is for our Lilli, and to-morrow it will come for
Rosa, and day after to-morrow perhaps for a third,
and why, why?"

"Because God wills it, my child."

"God—always God? All folly, all barbarity, all the mad violence of the human being hides behind this shield: 'God wills it.'"

"Do not blaspheme, Martha, not now when God's reproving hand is so clearly seen."

I had written to Conrad: "Lilli is sick."
Four days later he entered the house.
"Lilli," he cried, "is it true?"
We nodded.

He remained profoundly quiet, without shedding a tear. "I have loved her many years," he said softly to himself.

"Where is she—in the churchyard? I will go there. Farewell, she must expect me."

"Shall I go with you?" some one asked.

"No, I had rather be alone."

He went out—we never saw him again. He shot himself on Lilli's grave.

At any other time the full realization of this tragedy would have been more overpowering. But at the moment it was announced the hope and pride of my father's heart, my brother Otto, was attacked with the dread disease. No efforts could save him, and at seven o'clock of the following evening all was over.

My father threw himself down by the body with a heart-breaking cry which resounded through the house. With difficulty we dragged him away, and for hours his despair was terrible to witness. Upon this outbreak followed stolid apathy, and he lay upon a couch motionless and almost unconscious. Doctor Bresser ordered that he be carried to his bed.

After an hour he seemed to rouse himself. Aunt Marie, Frederick, and I were at his side. He glanced about, then sat up and tried to speak. He could not utter a word and struggled for breath. Finally he murmured "Martha."

I fell on my knees at the side of the bed.

" Father, my poor, dear father! "

He lifted his hand over my head. " Your wish," he gasped painfully. "I curse—I curse——"

He could not finish, and fell back upon the pillows.

Doctor Bresser anxiously leaned over him. He was dead.

" The most dreadful thing about it is," said Aunt Marie, after we had buried him, "that he died with a curse upon his lips."

"Be comforted," I said to her. "If this curse fell from the lips of all mankind it would be the greatest blessing to humanity."

Such was the cholera week in Grumitz. In seven days ten of the inhabitants of the castle had been carried away: my father, Lilli, Rosa, Otto, my maid Netti, the cook, the coachman, and two of the stablemen. In the village they had buried eighty persons.

When one speaks of it in this cold way it sounds like a statistical report; when it is written in a book it looks like an extravagant phantasy of the author. But it is neither so dry a fact as the one nor so sentimentally terrible as the other; it is cold, frightful, heart-breaking reality. The annals of the time show a similar condition in all those localities where the Prussians had been quartered.

We spent the remainder of the summer in Geneva.

It was through Doctor Bresser's urging that we fled from the scene of so much sorrow. At first I apathetically refused to leave the place where all my dead lay buried, but Bresser appealed to my mother love for my little Rudolph, who must be removed as much as possible from the danger of contagion.

We chose Switzerland as a place of refuge by Frederick's special wish, as he desired to make the acquaintance of the men who had organized the " Red Cross," and to be better informed as to the object of the association.

Frederick had sent in the resignation of his commission and now only awaited its acceptance. His leave of absence would cover our six months' visit. I was now rich—very rich. The death of my father, brother, and sisters left me the entire family estate.

"See here," I said to Frederick, as the notary transferred the deeds to me. "What would you say if I should regard war as a benefit because of the advantage its results have brought to me?"

"You would not be my Martha! But I understand what you mean; you are thinking of the heartless egotism which will rejoice over material prosperity won by the destruction of others; those who feel it are careful to conceal it, while nations and dynasties openly and proudly acknowledge it. Thousands have gone down in irretrievable ruin, but we have won territory and power, therefore Heaven be praised for fortunate war."

We lived in absolute retirement in a little villa on the shore of the lake. I was so overwhelmed by the experiences of preceding events that I could not endure the society of strangers. I owed it to my Grumitz graves—that my tender-hearted husband realized—to be allowed to weep out my sorrow in quietude. Those torn so mercilessly from the beautiful world should have some little time allotted them in the memory of one whose sorrowful heart had been so suddenly and coldly robbed of them.

Frederick himself went often into the city to pursue the object of his sojourn—the study of the system of the Red Cross.

Of the result of this study I have now no report, as at that time I dropped the notes in my diary. Only one impression remained as produced by my entire environment: the quiet, the content, the cheerful temper of all whom I met—as if we all lived in the happiest of times. Scarce an echo was heard of the recent war, and each allusion to it took the form of anecdote or some pleasant, interesting experience—as if the terrific thunder of the cannon from the Bohemian battlefield were nothing more than one of Wagner's operas. The whole thing was now relegated to history, and to the maps marking certain changes in boundaries, but all its misery was thrust out of sight; it had never been a part of the life of those not engaged in the war and was forgotten, its agony outlived and wiped out. The newspapers—I read French ones mostly —were all full of the preparations for the World's Exposition at Paris, the festivities at Compiègne, the latest literary events (much was said of Zola and Flaubert), the newest plays; the last opera by Gounod—one by Offenbach, in which Hortense Schneider played a brilliant *rôle*. The piquant duel between the Prussians and Austrians was an old, worn-out story. O, all that lies three months behind us, or is thirty miles away—all that is not in our immediate present—cannot be expected to be part of the overfull human heart or retain a place in human memory.

In October we returned to Vienna, intending after the settlement of my affairs to go to Paris for a prolonged residence. Frederick had in mind the organization of a league of peace, and thought the approaching World's Exposition the best opportunity to call an international congress together, and Paris the most suitable location for the purpose.

"I have laid down the profession of arms," he said, "and have done that because of the convictions gained through my experience of war. I enlist now in the army of peace. Truly, small in numbers, armed by no weapon save a love of justice and humanity. But all that becomes great had but a small beginning."

"Ah," I sighed, "it is a hopeless task. What can you—one man—do against the mighty barricade defended for centuries by millions of men?"

"What can I do—I? In truth I am not so foolish as to hope that I personally can lead to this revolution. I say only that I enter the ranks of the army of peace. Did I ever, when in the army of war, hope to rescue my country or to conquer a province? No, the individual can only serve. More yet—he must serve. He who is inspired by a cause can do no other than work for it, he can set his life upon it, even if he knows how little this life in itself can contribute to victory. He serves because he must; it is not alone the State, but private conviction which demands this duty of him."

Before our departure for Paris we intended going to Berlin to visit poor Aunt Cornelia. I left Rudolph with Aunt Marie, who, since the deaths in our family, devoted herself to him; around the child centered all her interest in life.

On the eve of the first of November we arrived in Prague. We remained over night, and the next morning made a new pilgrimage.

"All Saints' Day!" I said as I glanced at the date of the newspaper brought to our room with our breakfast.

"All Saints' Day," repeated Frederick. "How many of our dead on these new battlefields cannot be honored because one knows not where they lie! Who will visit them?"

I looked up at him a moment silently, then said softly: "Will you?"

He nodded. An hour later we were on the way to Chlum and Königgrätz.

"Lo! what a sight!"
An elegy of Tiedge occurred to my mind: *

" Lo! what a sight! stand here in thy lordly pride,
  By these mouldering bones, thou ruler ' by right divine,'
And swear that the tyrant of men shall become their
      guide—
  That as ' prince of peace ' thou wilt rule with a sway
      benign.

---

*The metrical translations in "Ground Arms!" are by Mr. Thomas C. Roney.—A.

Gaze round about thee when thirsting for glory and fame,
  O tender shepherd, who guardest thy flock from the
      foe;
Number these skulls—their ravager's hand is the same
  As his at whose stroke thy head shall forever lie low.

If in thy dreams thou shudderest, hearing the groan
  Of a wretch whose life thou in grewsome horrors hast
      ended;
How shalt thou dream as thou sittest upon thy throne:
  'My name is secure—with the great world-history
      blended'?"

So long as this world-history is written by those
who set up for its heroes pictorial monuments built
from the ruins made by war, just so long will the
Titans among the murderers of peoples be crowned
with laurels.   "To refuse the laurel wreath, to sacrifice fame would be noble," does the poet say?
Rob of its ancient nimbus the thing which it seems
meritorious to refuse, and no ambitious man will
strive to grasp it.

It was twilight when we arrived in Chlum, and
from there, arm in arm, in silent, deep depression,
approached the dread battlefield of Sadowa. Small
flakes of snow fell softly through a light mist, and
the bare branches of the trees were swayed about
by a cold November wind. Rows upon rows of
graves and masses of graves were all about us.
But was it the quiet churchyard? No. Not one of
life's tired pilgrims had been laid here to peaceful
rest, but in the flush of youthful fire, in the full-
ness of manhood's prime, most defiant expectants
of the future, they had been violently hurled down
and the earth of the grave shoveled over them.
All the breaking hearts, the bloody, mangled limbs,
the bitterly weeping eyes, the despairing cries, the
fruitless prayers, were engulfed in eternal silence.

It was not lonely on this burialfield. All Saints'
Day had brought many here—friends and foes of
those who had fallen. The train had been filled
with mourners, and for several hours I had heard
sobs and murmurs of lament.

"I lost three sons—each nobler than the other—
on the field of Sadowa," I heard one old, heart-
broken man say. There were mourners for brothers, husbands, and fathers, but none of them so
impressed me as the hopelessness of the tearless
sorrow of this father for his three sons.

In the fields we saw upon all sides black-robed
figures kneeling, or rising and going with sobs from
the spot. Few single graves were to be seen, and
few marked by cross or stone. We stooped and
deciphered, as well as the twilight permitted, a few
names.

Major von Reuss, of the Second Prussian Regiment of the Guards.

"Possibly he was a relative of the betrothed of
our poor Rosa," I remarked.

Count Grünne—wounded the third of July—
died the fifth of July.

What must he have suffered in those three days!
I wondered if he were the son of that Count
Grünne, who before the war had uttered the well-
known sentence: "We will drive out the Prussians
with wet rags." How absurd and offensively silly
such expressions sound, when repeated in such a
place. Words, words—nothing more—contemptu-
ous words, bombastic words, threatening words—
spoken, written and printed—these have caused this
field to be filled with dead.

We walked on. Everywhere there were hillocks
of greater or less height, greater or less breadth,
and spots without any elevation, which covered soldiers' mouldering bodies.

The mist grew denser.

"Frederick, put on your hat. You will take
cold."

But Frederick remained uncovered—and I did
not repeat my admonition.

Among the mourners who wandered about were
many officers and soldiers, apparently those who
had taken part in the battle and had made this
pilgrimage in honor of fallen comrades.

We approached that part of the field where the
greatest number—friend and foe—had been buried
together. The place had been inclosed. Toward
this streamed the greatest number of pilgrims, for
on this spot in all probability they might find their
dead. All around the inclosure they knelt to pray
and hung their funeral wreaths upon the palings.

A tall and slender man of noble presence,
wrapped in a general's cloak, came up to this cen-
tral point. All drew back respectfully and I heard
the whisper:

"The Emperor."

Yes, it was Francis Joseph, the country's ruler,
the Commander-in-chief of the army, who had
come on All Saints' Day to offer a silent prayer for
the dead children of the nation. He stood uncovered with bowed head, in painful, reverential homage before the majesty of death.

He remained for a time sunk in profound medi-
tation. I could not take my eyes from his face.
What memories must have oppressed his soul,
what sentiments overwhelmed his heart? For he
had a gentle, tender heart, I knew. I felt imbued
with a clairvoyant sense as if I could read his
thoughts as he stood there with his bowed head.

"My poor, brave souls who died—for what? We
have not conquered; my Venice is lost—so much
is lost and all your young lives! I have not wished
the sacrifice—it was for yourselves, your country,
that you were led into this war. Not through me
—though it came at my command. I have been
compelled to fight. Not for me have my subjects
fallen—no; on their account I was called to the
throne, and every hour I have been ready to die
for my people's good. Had I but followed the
impulses of my heart and never murmured 'yes'
when all about cried 'war! war!' But could I have
withstood the clamor? As God is my witness—no!
The pressure was from you, yourselves, my dead
soldiers. O how miserable, most miserable—what
have you not suffered; and now to lie here, slain

by shot and shell, saber cuts, cholera, and typhus!
Could I have said 'no'? The thought is unendurable."

While I watched him, following his train of
thought, he covered his face with his hands and
broke into a passion of tears.

FIFTH BOOK.

TIME OF PEACE.

WE found Berlin in evident jubilation. Every petty clerk and every porter had an air of conscious victory. " We have beaten the other side," seemed a reflection which had a very exhilarating effect upon the whole population. Nevertheless, we found a melancholy tone pervading all the families we visited, for there were none which had not one unforgotten dead lying on the battlefields of Germany or Bohemia.

We dreaded our first visit to Aunt Cornelia. I knew that Gottfried had been the idol of her heart, and I could not measure the sorrow of the bereaved mother. I could only reflect upon what I might suffer should I lose Rudolph—no, I would not even think of that.

We announced our visit, and with beating heart I entered Frau von Tessow's home. Even in the entrance hall we realized that this was a house of mourning. The servant who admitted us wore black livery; in the great reception room the furniture was all covered and there was no fire. We were led into Aunt Cornelia's bedroom, where she awaited us. This was a large apartment divided by curtains hiding the bed, and which now served also as a sitting-room. She never left the house except to go to church on Sunday, and very rarely went out of her room, with the exception of one hour daily, which she spent in Gottfried's little study.

During our visit she took us into this little room and showed us a letter which he had laid on his desk.

My Precious, Darling Mother:

I know, dear Heart, that you will come here after my departure—and you shall find this letter. Our personal parting is over. So much the more will you be pleased and surprised to read these last words and these cheerful, hopeful ones. Be of good courage; I am coming back. Fate cannot divide two hearts which so depend upon each other. My presentiment is that I shall make a fortunate campaign, win stars and crosses, and then come back to present you with six grandchildren. I kiss your hand, your soft, tender forehead, my most worshiped of mothers.   Yours,   Gottfried.

We found that Aunt Cornelia was not alone. A gentleman in a long, black coat, whom we recognized at a glance as a clergyman, sat near her. We embraced with tears, and for several moments it was not possible to speak.

As she led us back and offered us chairs she introduced her guest as Mr. Mölser, an army chaplain and a counselor of the consistory.

"My friend and spiritual adviser," she added, "who takes an interest in offering such consolation as he can in my sorrow."

"Who unfortunately, my dear friend, has not yet succeeded in teaching you proper resignation or how to bear this cross with the right, cheerful spirit," the gentleman replied. "Why do I see you still yield to these weak outbursts of tears, as you did just now?"

"Forgive me. When I saw my nephew and his young wife last my Gottfried was with me," she could scarcely reply.

"Yes, your son was then in this sinful world, exposed to all its dangers and temptations, while he is now in the bosom of the Father, after he has lost his life in the noblest, most blessed way for king and country. You, Colonel, can help me comfort this afflicted mother, for as a soldier you know that the fate of her son is an enviable one. You must know how joyfully the brave soldier meets death, how the decision to lay his life upon the altar of his country transfigures the agonies of

death, and how, when he falls in battle, in the
midst of the thunder of cannon, he fully expects
to be transferred to that greater army above, there
to remain until the Lord of Hosts holds his grand
review. You, Colonel, are among those who, by
the divine blessing, have helped win the righteous
victory——"

"Pardon me, Mr. Mölser," said Frederick, "I
was in the Austrian service."

"Ah, I thought——," stammered the reverend
gentleman, much embarrassed. "It was a fine—a
brave army also. But I will not disturb you further. You have family matters to talk about, no
doubt. Good day, dear Madam, I will see you
again in a few days. Until then lift up your hearts
to the All Merciful, who does not permit a hair to
fall from our heads without his knowledge, and
who does all things for the best, whether he suffers
us to endure sorrow and suffering, or death itself."

My aunt shook hands with him gratefully.

Frederick detained Mr. Mölser a moment.

"I have a favor to ask of you," he said. "I
should judge from your conversation that you are
thoroughly imbued with the religious and military
spirit. Now, my wife here is much troubled by
certain doubts and scruples. She maintains that
from the Christian standpoint war cannot be excused. I know quite the contrary, for the priest-
hood and the military class stand shoulder to
shoulder, but I lack the facility of language to
make this clear to her. Would you kindly appoint
an hour when we might hope for an interview to
discuss this subject?"

"Certainly," replied the clergyman, and a day
and hour were at once appointed.

"Can the conversation of this friend afford you
any consolation?" said Frederick to his aunt when
we were alone.

"Consolation? I do not expect that in this
world. But he speaks so earnestly of the things of
which I now love most to hear, of death and sorrow,

of the cross and sacrifice and renunciation. He pictures the world, which my poor Gottfried has left and which I long to leave, as a vale of tears, of corruption, of wickedness, of total depravity; and then it seems to me not so great a sorrow that my child has been taken away. He is in heaven and here on earth——"

"The powers of hell prevail; that is true, as I have very recently seen," replied Frederick reflectively.

Our visit was a long and sorrowful one and our conversation mainly of the recent campaign. Frederick was able to give the poor mother the same comfort he had once brought me, in the assurance of the instantaneous, painless death of her son.

"Now tell me," I said to Frederick, as we left the house. "What did you mean by asking that clergyman to meet us?"

"To furnish material for study. I really want to hear how the clergy excuse this murder of a people. I used your convictions as an excuse because it is more reasonable that a woman should, from the Christian standpoint, doubt its justification of war than that a lieutenant-colonel should have those views."

"But you know very well we have doubts of its justification from the humane, not from the religious point of view alone," I replied.

"You must not acknowledge that to the clergyman, or the question will be transferred to another field. There is no inherent contradiction in the position of the freethinker when he strives for the maintenance of peace, but the contradiction between the Christian principle of love and those theories claimed to be of divine origin justifying war, which these same Christian clergymen so curiously defend, is just what I want to hear from the lips of one of them."

The chaplain made his appearance punctually. It was evident that the opportunity for a contro-

versial discourse was enticing, especially with the
prospect, which he did not doubt, of my conver-
sion to his side of a disputed question. I, on the
contrary, had looked forward to the interview with
very uncomfortable feelings, for I felt as if occupy-
ing an insincere position. But for the good of the
cause to which Frederick had devoted himself I
surrendered my objections, comforting myself with
the reflection that the end justified the means.

"Allow me, dear Madam, to proceed at once to
the discussion of the object of my visit," said the
gentleman a day or two later, having made himself comfortable in an arm-chair near the fire.
"Your mind is troubled by certain scruples, which
are apparently just, but which can be proved to
be mere sophistry. You believe that the command
of Christ to love our enemies, and the warning,
'He who takes the sword shall perish by the
sword,' to be a contradiction of the duties of the
soldier, who is required by his position to injure
the enemy even to the destruction of life, if necessary?"

"Certainly, Mr. Mölser, this contradiction appears
to me irreconcilable. We have also the express
command of the decalogue 'Thou shalt not kill.'"

"Well, yes, superficially considered, that is an apparently insurmountable difficulty; but when one
gets below the surface all doubts disappear. The
proper translation of that command, however, is
'thou shalt not murder.' To kill through necessity
is not murder—no courts hold it so—and war is a
necessity, therefore, no murder. We can and must,
according to the gentle command of our Saviour,
love our enemies; but that does not mean that we
shall endure injustice and acts of violence."

"Then it simply amounts to this, that defensive
wars are alone justifiable, and the sword should be
drawn only when the enemy crosses the frontier.
Suppose the opposing power were actuated by
the same principle, how in the world is war going
to be begun? In the last war it was your army,

Mr. Mölser, which first marched over the border and——"

"When it is necessary to avert catastrophe, dear Madam," replied the theologian quickly, "and we certainly have a sacred right to do so; it would be inexcusable for us to neglect the favorable time for action; neither is it necessary to wait until the enemy falls upon us, and the ruling authority must be at liberty to forestall violence and injustice. That is the meaning of the warning, 'He that taketh the sword shall perish by the sword.' The ruler stands as the servant and avenger of God against the enemy who have drawn the sword against him, and who therefore must perish by it."

"There is a fallacy here somewhere," said I, shaking my head; "it is impossible to make these grounds answer for both sides."

"In regard to other scruples of conscience," continued the clergyman, without noticing my remarks, "for instance, that war in itself must be displeasing to God, every Bible-reading Christian knows that the God of Israel himself commanded his peculiar people to conquer the promised land, assuring them of victory and his blessing. In the twenty-first chapter and fourteenth verse of Numbers there is an allusion to the book of the wars of the Lord. Often we find praises to the Lord in the Psalms for the help which Jehovah has given his people in war. Do you not remember, in Solomon's proverbs, twenty-first chapter, thirty-first verse, we find: 'The horse is prepared against the day of battle, but safety is of the Lord.' In Psalms we find David thanking God, 'who teacheth my hands to war and my fingers to fight.'"

"There appears to be a material difference in the teaching of the Old and New Testaments. The God of the Hebrews and of the old dispensation was a warlike Jehovah, but the mild and gentle Jesus proclaimed the mission of peace and taught love of our neighbor and our enemy," I ventured to assert.

" Even in the New Testament, in the Gospel of St. Luke, Jesus speaks without condemnation of a king going to make war upon another king. Paul often uses metaphors borrowed from a condition of war, as where in Romans he speaks of the ruler who beareth not the sword in vain, but is God's servant and avenger against those who do evil."

"But, Mr. Mölser, you cannot overcome my scruples by proving the existence of contradictions in the Bible itself," I exclaimed.

" There you exhibit the superficial reasoning of those who rely upon feeble private judgment. A contradiction indicates something incomplete and ungodly; when I show that a thing is to be found in the Bible—no matter if it is apparently incomprehensible to human understanding—that fact alone is proof of there being no contradiction, only a misconception."

"I should think it complete evidence that the matter in dispute could not possibly be of divine origin," I muttered, but only half aloud, as the utterance would completely upset our discussion.

"I have evidence here which may interest you, Mr. Mölser," said Frederick, " of the position assumed by an army officer of the seventeenth century, as justification of the view that war is derived from the Bible. You can judge of the advance you have made. It appears to me somewhat extravagant." .

He opened his desk and drew out a paper from which he read:

" War was the invention of God and by him taught to men. God set the first soldier with a flaming, two-edged sword at the gate of the Garden of Eden in order to punish the first rebel, Adam. In Deuteronomy we read that God, through Moses, encouraged his people to victory and gave them his priests as an advance guard.

" The first stratagem was against the city of Hai, and during this war the sun stood still in the heavens in order that victory might be assured and many thousands slaughtered.

"All the horrors of war are tolerated by God, for the Holy Scripture is full of the account of them, and this also indicates that as wars were approved by him every honest man can with a good conscience take part in them.

"The story of Deborah and Sisera; of Gibeon and of David, who invented the most horrible tortures for the children of Ammon and——"

"But this is outrageous," exclaimed the clergyman. "No one but a rough mercenary soldier of the Thirty Years' War could so malevolently distort examples given in the Bible for the purpose of excusing the fiendishness of his own era. We now proclaim a far different doctrine. In war we can now only do enough to render the enemy harmless. We pursue him to the death with no malicious sentiment against the individual. Against the defenseless all outrage to property or injury to life becomes as immoral and inexcusable in war as in peace. Yes, such arguments as you have read would be used in past centuries when robber adventurers at the head of hirelings roamed the land, with their hand against every man who ventured to defy them, but not to-day when soldiers are not recruited for pay and booty, and without knowing whom they are to fight against, but are enrolled for the highest ideals of humanity, for freedom, independence, national life, for right, honor, discipline, and morality."

"The times are changed, Mr. Mölser," I suggested, "and you are more humane than the captain of the seventeenth century. But is it not the same book and the same Jehovah to whom both sides now appeal, whom you do not consider to have altered even if the times have changed?"

Indignantly I was called to account for a lack of reverence for the Word of God, and also for a lack of common sense. I allowed the reverend gentleman to finish his argument without further protest, and he entered upon a long harangue in which he spoke of the connection between the military and the Christian spirit; how elevating to the heart it was to see the new standards carried to the altar to be consecrated, dedicated to the cause of justice and the cause of God. Or, if battleworn and brought for re-consecration, accompanied by martial music and guarded on both sides by officers with drawn swords, this flag, torn as it may be and decorated with the names of battles won, is a grand incentive to the raw recruit, who first sees it in such holy surroundings. He repeated the prayer used on Sunday in all churches: "Protect, O Lord, the royal army and all faithful servants of the king and country. Teach them as Christians to consider their end and to consecrate their lives to Thy honor and the good of their native land."

"God with us," he continued, "is the motto upon the belt-buckle worn by the infantry, and this inscription should give each man courage. Is God with us—who can prevail against us? The church appoints fast days and periods of prayer at the beginning of war, in order that the people may appeal to God, certain that through the power of earnest prayer the assistance of the Almighty may be secured, and through this mediation victory be assured. How powerfully the soldier marching into the field is aided by this consecration to duty. When called upon by his king to step into the ranks, how securely he can reckon upon victory and blessing for a righteous cause! God, the Lord of all, will lead his people, as he once led his people Israel, if we prayerfully commit the battle to him. The intimate connection between prayer and victory, between piety and bravery is easily understood; for what can afford greater security in the face of death than the assurance that, if in the turmoil of battle the last hour strikes, the soldier will then find himself in the presence of a gracious and well pleased Judge? Faith and loyalty in connection with valor and capacity for war belong to the old traditions of our people."

In this style he continued for some time: one moment with bowed head and softest tone he spoke of love, heaven, humility, salvation, and sacred things; the next, with military precision, sonorous voice, and sharp and cutting emphasis, he discoursed of strictest morals and sternest discipline of sword and gun. The word *joy* was not otherwise used than in connection with death and battle. From the standpoint of the army chaplain, to kill and to be killed seemed the chief joy of life. Verses were declaimed, battle songs recited. First that one by Körner:

> " My Father, lead Thou me,
>   Or to the victor's crown, or to death's altar!
>   At Thy divine command ne'er will I falter.
> Lord, as Thou wilt, oh, lead Thou me.
> My God, I bow to Thee."

Then the old folk song of the Thirty Years' War:

> " Brave men no holier death can die,
>   No fate more fondly cherish,
> Than here, beneath the open sky,
>   By the foe's good sword to perish.
>
> In peace the grassy hillocks swell
>   Above each lonely sleeper;
> But soldiers true lie as they fell,
>   Like grain beside the reaper."

Again, Lenau's War Song of the Merry Armorer:

> " Peace destroys the life of nations,
>   Saps the soldier's strength, defaces
>   Martial pride, with cobwebs traces
> All his hard-won decorations.
>
> Ha! war's ringing call elates him.
>   Blood is flowing; wounds are gaping,—
>   Into living mouths seem shaping.
> Deadly strife rejuvenates him."

He closed with this quotation from Luther: "When I consider that war is the protection of wife, child, home, country, goodness, and honor, how can I refrain from regarding it as a most valuable means to a noble end."

"Well, yes—when I look upon the panther as a dove, certainly I must consider him as a harmless creature," I murmured to myself. How gladly would I have replied to his rhythmical flood by a poem from Bodenstedt:

> Of battles and heroic deeds
>   Discourse in pompous declamation;
> But tell me naught of Christian creeds
>   That need the cannon's punctuation.
>
> If, to proclaim your valor good,
>   You indulge such heathenish behavior;
> Spill without stint your victim's blood,
>   But talk not then to me of 'Saviour.'
>
> The Turk, devout and credulous,
>   Fights for the honor of his Allah;
> But Odin lives no more for us—
>   Dead are the gods of the Walhalla.
>
> Be what you will, unfettered, free
>   To slay on this side or the other;
> Abhorred be that hypocrisy
>   Which calls the Nazarene your brother."

But our "Martial Nazarene" could not know our thoughts, and with evident pleasure in what he considered a triumphant ending to a most instructive discourse, he rose and departed, after congratulating Frederick upon having silenced the scruples of his wife, whose previous point of view must have been very annoying to a soldier.

"Ah!" I sighed, "what a torment!"

"Yes, it was, and was increased by the consciousness that we were not acting fairly. I was sometimes almost driven to say to him that I shared the convictions of my wife, and that what he had said only showed the weakness of his own position and would invite me to prove further how untenable it was. But I was silent. Why should I outrage the convictions of an honest man, convictions which must necessarily lie at the foundation of his profession?"

" Honest convictions?   Are you sure of that?
Does he reason at all?   Does he actually believe he
is speaking the truth, or does he not consciously
deceive his soldier congregation when he promises them victory through the help of a God who he
knows is appealed to in the same manner by the
other side?   This appeal for 'our nation' and 'our
cause,' as if it were the only righteous one, and at
the same time the cause of God, belongs to a period when one tribe, shut out from all other peoples, considered itself the special favorite of heaven.
And then these consolatory pictures of heavenly
bliss, in order to reconcile one to the sacrifice of
this life on earth—these ceremonies and consecra-
tions, sacred oaths and anthems, manipulated with
the object of arousing in the breast of those ordered into active service a contempt for death—are
all too horrible."

" There are two sides to every question, Martha,"
said Frederick.   " Because we hate war, everything
used to excuse it seems horrible."

" Certainly, because through all these artificial
means the atrocity is maintained."

" Not entirely.   Old customs are embedded with
a thousand roots, and so long as they endure it is
as well that all mitigating sentiments and notions
should live with them.   How many poor devils
have been helped in the hour of death by these
careful instructions as to the glory of life's surrender in such a cause; how many pious souls have
confidently relied upon the promises of divine help
made by the clergy; now much innocent vanity
and what lofty sentiments of honor have been
awakened and satisfied by these religious ceremonies; how many hearts have beat higher under the
inspiration of this noble music!   Among all the
sorrows which war has brought upon mankind we
must leave out that anguish which the bards of
battle-hymns, and the preachers have through their
chants and sermons sung and lied away."

We were suddenly called from Berlin by the dangerous illness of Aunt Marie.

I found our old friend at the point of death.

"I am glad to go," she said; "since my poor brother and his three children were taken away I find no comfort in life. Conrad and Lilli are also united up there. They were not destined to union on earth. It is a comfort to me that you are happy, Martha, and the fact that your husband has escaped the dangers of two campaigns proves that you are ordained to grow old together. Be careful to educate Rudolph as a good Christian and a good soldier, in order that his grandfather may rejoice over him. I will pray incessantly that you may live long and happily."

I could not at such a time comment on the contradiction of foreordination to live and the necessity of incessant prayer to that end. After three days of suffering the last of the friends of my childhood quietly passed away after receiving the consolatory last sacraments of the church. She left her small fortune to Rudolph and appointed her old friend, the Minister of Finance, as trustee. We remained some months in Vienna, as a long residence in Paris would not be possible until our business affairs were in order.

Twice a week our old friend dined with us, and Frederick took great pleasure in turning the conversation upon the study of human rights. For the old gentleman, who was a born and trained diplomat and bureaucrat, the position of Frederick was difficult to grasp. He was acquainted with practical politics, which, as it simply considers expediency as a rule of action, does not even know the theoretical questions of social science.

I sat near at hand, busied with needlework, and did not join in the conversation. This was quite proper according to the standpoint of the old gentleman, who knew well that for women politics was far too profound a subject; he was convinced that I was occupied with other matters, when in truth it was my business to imprint all upon my memory in order to copy it into my note-books. Frederick made no secret of his views, although he knew well what an unthankful *rôle* one plays in maintaining theories which by the world at large are regarded as fantastic and impracticable.

"I have an important piece of news to-day, my dear Tilling," said the minister as he came in one afternoon. "It is rumored in official circles that the war ministry are going to recommend a general obligation to military service."

"What? The same system which we so lately ridiculed when we talked about arming tailors' apprentices?" asked Frederick.

"We did have a prejudice against it, but Prussia has proved its value. From the moral, democratic and liberal standpoint, which you are lately talking about so much, it is the proper thing. Every citizen, without regard to condition or class, owes his country the same duty; and from the military point of view, why, Prussia proved that this was the reason of her success."

"You mean to say that if we had had a greater force the enemy could not have made his own so serviceable; ergo, if all nations carried out the system of general armament, no one would be the gainer. The war game of chess would be played with larger numbers, but the result would still depend upon the fortune and skill of those engaged, the only difference would be that where thousands are now slaughtered, hundreds of thousands would then suffer."

"Why, do you consider it just and right," exclaimed the diplomatist, "that only a part of the population should be sacrificed for the benefit of another class, who because they are sick can remain at home? No, no; with the new regulation this will all be changed. There will be no buying of substitutes—every one must serve. And these intelligent classes will make the finest material for soldiers."

"But the other side use the same educated class. There is another view of this question; both sides must suffer by the loss of priceless intellectual material, when the educated,—those who through invention, art, or any scientific investigation are materially advancing civilization,—are forced into the ranks as a target for the enemy's fire."

"Pshaw! what does invention, or art, or rummaging among dry bones, called scientific investigation, add to the power or influence of a state?"

"What!"exclaimed Frederick.

"Yes, how?"

"Oh, nothing of course, go on——"

"These men need to serve but a short time—a few years of strict discipline will not interfere with their other duties as good citizens. Blood tax we have all got to pay, so it might as well be divided equally."

"If through this division the blood tax were diminished, it would be a recommendation; but it is thereby increased. I hope the project will not succeed. One cannot calculate to what it may lead. One power will endeavor to surpass the other and it will end in the existence no longer of armies, but of armed nations. More and more men will be drawn into the service, the length of the time of service will be increased, the costs of maintenance will grow greater, and without actually coming to blows nations through this armed condition will be precipitated into ruin."

"You are looking too far ahead, Tilling."

"One cannot look too far ahead. Everything which man undertakes should be reasoned out to its logical conclusion, to its extreme consequences. We are fond of comparing war to a game of chess; politics is the same, your Excellency, and he is a poor player who does not calculate farther than one move, or who rejoices because he threatens only a pawn. Suppose, after every man regardless of age had been drawn up into line, some nation should conclude to arm its women and then its children,—think of battalions of children."

"Be quiet, Tilling. You are an impracticable dreamer. If you can tell me the way to prevent war it might be a good thing. But as that is not possible, every nation must look to it that in the inevitable struggle for existence (is not that one of Darwin's battle-cries?) it secures the best chance to win."

"If I were to tell you the way to prevent war you would think me a more impracticable dreamer than ever, and blinded by sentimentality and the 'humanity swindle,' as the war party denounces it."

"All practicable means fail to secure the attainment of your ideal. You can only reckon upon factors actually in existence. These are the passions of men, the rivalries, the antagonism of interests, the impossibility of agreeing upon all questions——"

"It is not necessary to agree," interrupted Frederick. "When differences arise a court of appeal —not a resort to force—could decide."

"Nations and people will never agree to an international tribunal."

"The people? Potentates and diplomats will be slow. But the people? Nowhere is the love of peace so earnest and sincere as among the people, while the protestations to that effect of diplomats and governments are mainly lies, hypocritical lies, or at least believed to be so by the antagonistic nation. More and more the people will cry for peace. With the growth of standing armies the dislike for war will increase in the same proportion. It is easy to conceive of enthusiasm for a class, and the soldier had an honorable position by reason of the halo of self-sacrifice surrounding him. But when this exceptional condition becomes the general one, all such distinction fades away. The admiring gratitude of those who remain at home disappears, because no one any longer remains at home. It will be difficult then to arouse the love of war so persistently ascribed to the soldier. Who were those who had so much to say of

the heroism of military service, and who glorified
the danger? Those who before were quite safe,
the college professors, the diplomatists, the pot-
house politicians, the chorus of the old men, as in
'Faust.' But with the loss of security for themselves these will all be hushed, and when not only
those who love the service, but those who cordially
detest it, are forced into the ranks, the situation
will then become more than serious and alarming.
Poets, thinkers, friends of humanity, gentle people,
timid people: all these will, from their own special
point of view, curse the whole thing."

"They will more likely keep quiet in order not
to be considered cowards, or for fear of getting
into disgrace with the powers that be."

"Keep quiet! Not always. I have kept silence
a long time, but the time has come for me to speak
out. When conviction drives, words come fast
enough. I was forty years old before my convictions assumed force sufficient to find expression.
And where I required two or three times ten years
to ripen conviction, the masses may need two or
three generations; but the time will come at last
and they will speak."

New Year, '67.

We celebrated St. Sylvester's Eve entirely alone,
Frederick and I. As it struck twelve o'clock I said,
sighing:

"Do you remember the toast that my poor father
offered at this hour a year ago? I do not dare to
wish you a happy New Year—the future hides in
her breast so much that is terrible, and no human
being can avert it."

"Then let us make use of the season to look
back instead of toward the future. How much
you have endured, my poor, brave wife! You have
buried so many of those you loved—and that
frightful day on the Bohemian battlefields——"

"I shall never regret being a witness of those
horrors. I can more thoroughly sympathize with
my whole soul in your undertaking."

"We must educate your—our—Rudolph to carry on these attempts; in his time, perhaps, the distant goal may be discerned on the horizon—in ours it is not visible. What a noise the people make upon the streets. They welcome in the new year as jubilantly as they did the last, which brought them such sorrow. Oh, how men forget!"

"Do not find fault with this forgetfulness. Already the anguish of the past seems to me a dream, and what I realize to-day is the happiness of the present, the happiness of having you, my love! I believe we have a sunny future before us —but we will not speak of the future. United, devoted, independent, rich—how much enjoyment life offers us; we will travel and see the world, the great, beautiful world. Beautiful so long as it rests in peace, and there seems now no prospect of war; and if there were, you are no longer obliged to serve, and Rudolph is in no danger, as he will not become a soldier."

"But suppose, as Minister 'Upon the Whole' reports, every man is liable to duty?"

"Nonsense; but what I meant to say was, we will travel, give Rudolph a model education and— we love each other."

The carnival of the same year brought with it balls and entertainments of all sorts. Naturally we took no part—my mourning kept me far from everything of the sort What surprised me was the zest with which society threw itself into every amusement. There must have been a loss by death in every family; but it seemed as though they had mastered grief. It is true a few houses remained closed, especially among the aristocracy, but the young people lost no opportunity to dance, and of course those who had returned safely from the Italian or Bohemian battlefields were great favorites; but the officers of the navy were courted the most—especially those who had seen service at Lissa. Half the women were in love with Tegethoff, the youthful admiral, (just as they were with the

handsome General Gablenz after the campaign
of Schleswig-Holstein). "Custozza" and "Lissa,"
they were the two trumps which were played in
every conversation upon the past war. Next in
order were the needle gun and militia service, two
institutions to be introduced as speedily as possible to secure future victories. Victories—when
and over whom? Of that no one had any particular idea; but the idea of revenge which every
person who has lost—even if only at a game of
cards—is accustomed to promise himself, pervaded
all the promises of politicians. If we did not ourselves choose to move against Prussia, perhaps
there were others who would take it upon themselves to revenge us. From appearances, France
would close an alliance with us, and much was
prophesied in diplomatic circles of a "Revenge
for Sadowa," so our old friend, Minister "Upon
the Whole" reported.

In the early part of the following spring one of
those famous "black spots" again appeared on the
political horizon. The matter in dispute was Luxemburg.

Luxemburg? How in the world could that be
so important? I began to study again, as I had in
earlier years endeavored to master the Schleswig-
Holstein question. The name had no meaning for
me beyond that suggested in Luppe's "Jolly Stu-
dent," where a "Count of Luxemburg wastes his
money—wastes it, wastes it." The result of my
investigation was as follows:

According to the treaties of 1814 and 1816 Luxemburg belonged to the King of the Netherlands
and at the same time to the German Bund. Prussia had the right to maintain a garrison in the
capital. Now, as Prussia had broken with the
Bund in 1866, how could it maintain its right to
garrison? That was the irritating question in dispute. The Treaty of Prague had recognized the
new system in Germany, and with this recognition

the old position of Luxemburg as a part of the Bund must be abandoned. Why, then, did Prussia maintain her right to garrison? The Hollanders never set great value upon the possession of the Grand Duchy; King William III. did not care for it and was willing enough to deliver it up to France for a certain amount, to go into his private purse. Secret negotiations began between the King and the French Cabinet. Quite right; secrecy is the kernel of all diplomacy. The people must not know anything of the differences; if matters come to blows they have the right to shed their blood. Why they shed it is of no consequence to them.

At the end of March the King officially reported his negotiations, and when he telegraphed his acceptance to France the Prussian embassador at the Hague was informed of it. Thereupon explanations began with Prussia. Prussia fell back upon the guaranties of the Treaty of 1859, the same upon which Holland relied. Public opinion in Prussia was outraged that ancient Germany was disrupted. Who is that—this public opinion? Is it the writer of the leading editorials? In the North German Parliament fiery resolutions were passed. Bismarck remained perfectly cool in regard to Luxemburg; he took occasion, however, to make preparations for war with France, which in turn made similar preparations. Oh! how I recognized this melody! At that time I was in terror of a fresh outbreak in Europe. Of instigators of mischief there was no lack: in Paris Cassagnac and Emile de Girardin; in Berlin Menzel and Heinrich Leo. One wonders if such fire-brands have any idea of the gigantic character of their criminality. I can scarcely believe it. It was about this time, though I did not know it until years later, that Professor Simon had a conversation with the Crown Prince Frederick of Prussia upon the disturbing question of the day.

"'If France and Holland have already made terms, that would indicate war.'

" Whereupon the Crown Prince, in the greatest excitement and with intense feeling, replied:

"'You have never seen war; if you had seen it you
could not utter the word so indifferently.   I have seen it
and I say to you, it is the highest duty to avoid it when
it is possible to do so.'"

This time it was avoided.   A conference was held
in London, which agreed upon a peaceful solution
of the difficulty.   Luxemburg was declared neutral
ground and Prussia withdrew her garrison.   The
friends of peace breathed freely, but there were
people enough to be found who complained of this
arrangement—not the Emperor of the French, who
wished for peace, but the French war party.   Voices
were raised in Germany, which muttered about
"the surrender of a bulwark," and the like.   But
every private individual who informed himself as
to the judgment of the conference was satisfied.
What this London conference had attained could
always be secured, and the rulers of states, by thus
avoiding war, could perform what Frederick III.,
Frederick the Noble, declared to be their highest
duty.

In May we went to Paris to see the great Exposition.

I had not yet seen the great cosmopolitan city,
and the brilliancy of its life dazzled me.   The empire was in the full flush of its existence, and many
of the crowned heads of Europe had gathered
there.   It did not impress me as the capital of one
country, but as a great international city.   Three
years later it was bombarded by its eastern neighbor.   All the nations of the earth had collected all
they could offer in this great tournament of indus-
try; so much that was wonderful, useful, or artis-
tic was brought together, that every observer must
have felt pride in the enormous progress of the
time in which he lived; and with this pride must
have been connected the hope that such development of civilization would no more be threatened

by the brutality of destruction. All the guests of the Emperor and Empress, kings, princes, and diplomatists, could not in the midst of accepted hospitalities, festivities, and congratulations, expect very shortly to exchange shots with their entertainers. No; I breathed easily. This whole brilliant Exposition was to me the pledge of a new era, the beginning of long, long years of peace. At the most it could only be an attack of Mongolian hordes which could make all these civilized nations draw the sword; but against each other—it was not to be thought of. My impressions were deepened by the intelligence brought us of a favorite plan of Napoleon III.—a general disarmament. Yes, Napoleon was then determined—I have been assured of it by his nearest friends and advisers— that at the earliest suitable opportunity he would present a plan to all European powers for reducing their armed force to a peace footing. That was a more sensible idea than general disarmament. The well known postulate of Kant would then be fulfilled, which is formulated in paragraph third of the "Preliminary Articles to Perpetual Peace":

"Standing armies must in time entirely cease to exist. They are a continual menace to other states, and by their apparent preparation will incite neighboring nations to range themselves in arms, a condition of things which will know no limits, and which, through the increased cost of maintaining peace, will become more oppressive than a short war; thus becoming a cause of war to escape this burden."

What government could refuse a suggestion made by France without unmasking itself as desirous of conquest? And what nation would not revolt against such an idea? The plan must succeed.

Frederick did not agree with me in my anticipations.

"First of all, I doubt whether Napoleon III. cherishes any such plan, and if he did the pressure of the war party is too strong for him to resist it.

And besides, the occupants of thrones are hindered by the great public opinion of their surroundings. In the second place one existent body will not allow itself to be ordered in this wise: 'Nothing for you, nothing for me.' It will take up arms at once."

"Of what body do you speak?"

"The regular army. This is an organization independent and capable of supporting itself. At present this organization is in the heighth of its power, and as you see—through the general militia system to be introduced in all countries—is even on the point of extending its influence."

"And yet you will fight against this spirit?

"Yes, but not by marching up to it and exclaiming: 'Die, monster!' for upon such an invitation the creature will scarce do me the pleasure to stretch itself out before me. But I wage war against it when I am striving for the growth of different, though now but a feeble order of life, which as it develops will press the other out of existence. For my metaphorical style of speech, you, Martha, are responsible. It was you who introduced me to the works of the modern scientists. I have learned to reason that the conditions of social life can only be understood, and their future course predicted, when we grasp the truth that they stand subject to the influence of the inexorable law of development. Of this, politicians and dignitaries of state have not the remotest conception, and the much vaunted military class of course none at all. A few years ago I myself had not reached this appreciation of truth."

We lived in the Grand Hotel on the Boulevard des Capucines. It was filled for the most part by Englishmen and Americans. Our own countrymen we rarely met; the Austrians are not fond of traveling. We did not seek acquaintances; I had not laid aside my mourning. My son Rudolph was of course with us. He was eight years old and an exceedingly clever little man. We had engaged a young Englishman, who occupied the double position of tutor and nursery maid. During our long visits to the Exposition we could not take Rudolph with us, and the time for instruction had come for him.

New—new—new was the whole great world as here displayed! People from all quarters of the globe, the richest and most famous—I was fairly bewildered by it. But interesting and enchanting as it all was, I longed for the quiet and peace of my own home, with my husband and children—for I again awaited the joy of becoming a mother—just as when we are shut out from the world we long for its stirring activity and life.

We had not entered society We had called upon our embassador, Metternich, and declined his offer to present us at court. We sought the acquaintance, however, of the most noted politicians and literary men, partly from personal interest, but largely to forward in every way the aim and object of Frederick's life. We occupied ourselves when at home in the collection of what we called a " Peace Protocol "—a sort of sketchy account for future use of the gradual growth of the anti-war sentiment. A feeble protest it was indeed, compared with the tons of war literature, but if there were no seed sown there could be no harvest. When one remembers this one need not fear the future.

Four hundred years before Christ, Aristophanes wrote a comedy, " Peace," in which the humane tendency is apparent.

Greek philosophy—later transplanted to Rome—suggested and defended the struggle for the unity of mankind. The idea was upheld from the time of Socrates, who called himself a citizen of the world, down to that of Terence, who was a "stranger to nothing human," and including Cicero, who declared the *caritas generis humani* the highest grade of perfection.

Next in time Virgil appeared with his famous Fourth Eclogue, that shepherds' poem, which represents the world enjoying eternal peace under the mythological image of the Golden Age.

During the Middle Ages the popes frequently offered themselves as arbitrators between states, but generally in vain.

In the fifteenth century George Podiebrad, King of Bohemia, conceived the idea of organizing a league of peace. He was anxious to end the struggles between the Pope and the Emperor, and appealed to Louis XI. of France, who declined to join him.

At the close of the sixteenth century Henry IV. of France suggested a plan for a European federation. After he had relieved his own kingdom from the horrors of a religious war, he wished to secure peace and tolerance for the future. He proposed to unite the sixteen states in which Europe was then divided (Russia and Turkey were considered a part of Asia) in one common federation. Each of the sixteen states was to send two members to a European parliament; these thirty-two members were to secure religious toleration and settle all international disagreements. As each state would pledge itself to abide by the decision of parliament, all danger of war would disappear. The King imparted his plan to his minister Sully, who received it with enthusiasm and began negotiations with other states. Elizabeth of England, the Pope, Holland, and several others, agreed to join the league; Austria refused because certain territorial concessions were demanded. A campaign seemed necessary to defeat this opposition. France organized an army with the declaration that the sole purpose of the war was in the interest of future peace. Henry was on the point of setting out to take command when he was murdered by an insane monk.

None of his successors and no future sovereign took up this plan for securing the happiness of their subjects. Regents and politicians remained faithful to the old war spirit, but the thinkers of all countries never lost sight of the idea.

In the year 1647 the sect of the Quakers was organized, whose foundation idea was the condemnation of war. The same year William Penn published his work upon the future peace of Europe, which is in the main the plan of Henry IV.

At the beginning of the eighteenth century appeared the famous book "La Paix perpétuelle," by the Abbe de St. Pierre. About the same time a Landgrave of Hesse developed the same plan and Leibnitz wrote a favorable commentary upon it.

Voltaire is the author of the expression, "Every European war is a civil war." Mirabeau, in the famous session of the twenty-fifth of August, 1790, says the following:

"Perhaps the hour is not far distant when Freedom as absolute sovereign of both worlds will fulfill the wish of the philosophers: relieve mankind from the crime of war and proclaim eternal peace. Then the happiness of the people will be the sole object of the legislature, the sole glory of the nations."

In the year 1795 Immanuel Kant, one of the greatest thinkers of all time, wrote his treatise upon "Eternal Peace." The Englishman Bentham joined the ranks of the representatives of peace, followed by Fourier, Saint-Simon, and others. Béranger wrote: "The Holy Alliance of Peoples"; Lamartine his "La Marseillaise de la Paix." In Geneva Count Cellon organized a peace union, in whose name he began a propaganda correspondence with all European powers. From America the learned blacksmith, Elihu Burritt, scattered his "Olive Branches" and "Sparks from an Anvil" in pamphlets throughout the world, and was the chairman of a convention of English friends of peace. At the Paris congress, which put an end to the Crimean war, the diplomatists conceived an idea in the interest of peace, when they introduced a clause into the treaty, by which the powers pledged themselves to consider conditions of peace before the beginning of future conflicts. This clause is the germ of the idea of international jurisdiction, but was never observed.

In the year 1863 the French government proposed to call a congress of the powers, to consider the means of bringing about general disarmament and a combined agreement to avoid future wars.

Few were the pages of my note-book. Later many were added to it. They only prove that the possibility of the peace of the world has not for centuries been entirely unconsidered. Here and there the voices have been heard, sometimes with long periods of time between, but never wholly silenced, though often unnoticed and unheard. It has from time immemorial been the same with all progress, all development, all discovery and all invention:

" From the south land spring approaches.
   At her coming, far and near
   Feeble twitterings in the branches
    Swell in chorus full and clear.
So, within time's great cathedral,
   Midnight watchers wait the hour,
And the sweet chime's silvery summons;
   Then the music bursts in power."

                        (*Märzroth.*)

Again my hour of trial approached.

But this time the husband was at my side—his proper place—where through his gentleness and his sympathy the suffering of the wife may be mitigated. The thought that he was with me made me almost forget my pain.

A girl! That had been our quiet wish. We knew, through our little Rudolph, the joy a son might bring us, and that our little Sylvia would become a model of beauty, cleverness, and sweetness, we did not doubt.

How selfish happiness makes us! A time followed when all else was forgotten outside our own domestic heaven. The terrors of the cholera week faded into a dream-like remembrance, and Frederick's energy in pursuit of his idea waxed somewhat faint. It was, in truth, discouraging whenever one broached the subject to be met by shrugs of the shoulder, a sort of pitying smile, and even condemnation. The world prefers, it seems, to be not only deceived, but made unhappy. When one proposes a means to put an end to misery and suffering one is met by "utopia!" "a childish dream!" and no one will listen.

But after all Frederick never lost sight of his ideal. He became absorbed in the study of human rights, opened a correspondence with Bluntschli, and projected the writing of a great work to be called "War and Peace."

" I am an old imperial officer," he said, "and most men belonging to my rank and station would be ashamed to begin to learn and study—a man of my age generally considers it beneath his dignity.

But as a new point of view was opened to me after I became imbued with the modern spirit, I was oppressed by my lack of knowledge. Now as the opportunity was not granted me in my youth, I must make up for the loss, even if I have silver threads in my hair."

The winter after Sylvia's birth we spent quietly in Vienna. In the following spring we visited Italy. To know the world belonged to our programme of life. Traveling with little children is something of a burden, but with a sufficient number of attendants it becomes possible. I had sent for an old servant who had been the nurse of my sisters, and who had subsequently married and become a widow.

Frau Anna was worthy of the utmost confidence, and with her I could safely leave my little Sylvia when Frederick and I undertook little journeys from our temporary headquarters. Rudolph was also safe with his tutor, Mr. Foster.

Lovely, beautiful days! It is a pity I kept no record of them.

I had the opportunity to add one bright page to our Protocol. It was a newspaper article signed "Desmoulins" in which a proposition was made that the French government set the example to European states of disarmament.

" By this means France will secure the alliance and friendship of all nations, who will then cease to fear her whose help they need. General disarmament will naturally follow, the principle of conquest will be abandoned, and the confederation of states will agree to an international court of justice, empowered to consider all questions which are now deemed cause of war. By such a course France would secure the only real durable power —that founded on right—and a new era would be opened to humanity."—*Opinion Nationale*, 25 July, 1868.

No influence was exerted by this article.

In the winter of 1868–9 we returned to Paris, and this time plunged into the great world of society.

It was an enjoyable though sometimes wearisome
season. We had rented a small furnished house in
the Champs Élysées, where we could entertain our
various friends, by whom we were daily invited
to numerous social events. Our embassador presented us at court and we became frequent guests
at the Monday receptions of the Empress. The
salons of all the foreign embassadors were open to
us, as well as those of the Princess Mathilde, the
Duchess de Mouchy and Queen Isabella of Spain.
All the literary notabilities of the time were entertained at our house, all except the greatest—Victor
Hugo—who was in exile. But we knew Renan, the
two Dumas, George Sand, and others. We went to
a masque ball given by the author of "Les Grandes
Dames," Arsène Houssaye. It was his custom to
give a Venetian masquerade once during the season
in his superb little hotel in the Avenue Friedland,
where, under the protection of a masque, the society women of the upper ranks had the opportunity of seeing the noted actresses and singers in
all the brilliancy of their diamonds and their wit.

In the whirl of so fascinating a place of amusement it is so easy to forget all except this heartless
and thoughtless life. We forget that the real world
lies outside of all this, and domestic happiness is
too apt to be shipwrecked. But we were determined not to lose our hold upon our own hearth-
stone, nor our deep interest in universal interests.

Much sympathy was always expressed in Paris
society with Austrians. Allusions were frequently
made to a possible future revenge for Sadowa, as if
the past could ever be made good by revenge. We
always rejected such suggestions and assured all
that we only desired perpetual peace.

Such was at this period—so it was said at least—
the earnest desire of Napoleon III. We were inti-
mately associated with those who surrounded him,
when we were assured of this and of his project
actually to propose a general disarmament. But
the most intense dissatisfaction existed amongst

the people, and close to the Emperor stood a party who considered it impossible to suppress this except by diverting toward a popular foreign war the dangerous antagonism against the throne—a sort of grand promenade on the Rhine, by which means the Napoleon dynasty was to be secured. It had been very unfortunate that the Luxemburg matter had failed, but it could no longer be made a cause of contention. But that in the long run war between Prussia and France was unavoidable was a mooted question, of which we read in the newspapers but were not influenced by its repetition.

The brilliant season reached its height in the spring months. It is the time of the drives in the Bois, the exhibition of the salon, the races, the picnics—besides the theatres, receptions, dinners and soirées, which were not less popular than in winter. We began to long for rest. This sort of a life has no charm unless love-making and flirting are added to it. Young ladies, looking for a suitable match, women who allow men to make love to them, and men hunting an adventure—for all these every new opportunity of meeting the object of one's dreams is eagerly sought—but Frederick and I? That I was faithful to my husband, that no one dared cherish any hopes of my interest, is a matter of course, which I mention without any special virtuous pride. Whether, under other circumstances, I should have been able to resist the temptations encompassing a young and pretty woman I do not pretend to say, but when one is possessed by so deep and happy a love as I felt for Frederick, one is armed against all danger.

As summer approached, the "Grand Prize" was won and the different members of society began to leave Paris—some to go to Trouville, to Biarritz and Vichy, others to Baden-Baden, others still to their estates—Princess Mathilde to St. Gratien, the court to Compiègne. We were overwhelmed with

invitations to join the travelers, and to visit the
houses of our friends. But we were determined
not to carry the social campaign of the winter into
the summer months. I did not desire to return as
yet to Grumitz, I feared the awakening of sorrowful memories, and on account of our many relatives and friends there we could not have secured
any privacy. We again chose a quiet spot in Switzerland for our abiding place. We promised our
Parisian friends to return the following winter, and
set out upon our journey.

Europe then seemed careless and quiet. At least
there were no "black spots," and we heard no more
of a revenge for Sadowa. The greatest annoyance
was that the general military service was then introduced in Austria. That Rudolph should ever
become a soldier was unendurable to me. And people will talk about liberty!

"A year a volunteer," Frederick said to comfort
me; "that is not much."

I shook my head.

"Not if it were but a day. No human being
should be compelled to a service which he detests,
even for a day, for on this day he must assume to
do with delight what he abhors—in short, he must
lie—and I mean to train my son for the truth."

"Then he ought to have been born a few centuries later!" replied Frederick. "It is true one
cannot be an entirely free man. Truth and freedom have a hard lot in our day—that I realize the
deeper I go in my studies."

Frederick now had more time to devote to his
special work, and he renewed it with redoubled
zeal. Happy as we were in our quiet nest, we
were determined to return to Paris in the winter,
not to enjoy ourselves as before, but to devote
ourselves to the object of our lives. We built all
our plans upon the furtherance of the idea of the
Emperor Napoleon, and hoped to get his ear
through our friends. Frederick desired to direct
his attention to the plan of Henry IV., which he

had found narrated at length in Sully's Memoirs; at the same time we hoped, through the Minister of Finance, our old friend, to secure the attention of the government of Austria, and Frederick had in Berlin a relative of influential position, popular at court, through whom it might be brought to the consideration of Prussia.

In December, when we were about to return to Paris we were somewhat hindered. Our treasure —our little Sylvia—was taken ill. Those were anxious hours, and with the fear of the death of our child, Napoleon III. and Henry IV. stepped into the background.

But she did not die. At the end of two weeks all danger was over. But it was not safe to travel and our departure was delayed until March.

SIXTH BOOK.

1870-71.

PRESENTIMENTS? There are none. Were it otherwise, Paris could never have made such a delightful impression upon me as it did that sunny afternoon of March, 1870, when we again entered it. We know to-day what frightful events followed close upon that time, but I felt then not the slightest misgiving.

Before our arrival we had engaged the same little palace which we had occupied the preceding year, and the same *maître d' hotel* greeted us at the station. As we crossed the Champs Élysées we met numerous acquaintances, for it was the hour for driving in the Bois—and exchanged cordial salutations. The many little violet carts, which at this time of the year are rolled about the streets of Paris, filled the air with a thousand promises of spring; the sunbeams sparkled and played with all the colors of the rainbow in the fountain of the circle, and glittered on the lamps and silver-trimmed harness of the procession of carriages. Among others, the beautiful Empress drove by waving her hand to me in recognition.

There are certain scenes and pictures which photograph and phonograph themselves upon the memory with their accompanying feelings and words. "How beautiful Paris is!" exclaimed Frederick, and my feelings were those of childish delight at the prospect of again living in this most charming spot. Had I but known what awaited me—what fate held in store for this thoughtless, brilliant city!

We had determined to avoid for this season the gay society into which we had plunged the few last months of our preceding visit. We declined all invitations to balls and visited the theatre but rarely, and so it chanced that our evenings were spent at home alone, or with some few friends who sought us there.

It was claimed that Napoleon III. had not abandoned his plan, but the time was not ripe for it. The throne was not, at best, on the surest foundations, and great dissatisfaction prevailed among the people. To prevent an outbreak all police regulations were sternly enforced—which only excited greater distrust. The only thing, the people were accustomed to say, which would secure the dynasty was a fortunate campaign. There seemed no prospect of war, but there was no more talk of disarmament; that would have utterly destroyed the halo surrounding the Bonapartes, which depended upon the inherited glory of the great Napoleon. We heard no encouraging report either from Prussia or Austria. It was the era of general increase of the armed force (the word army had become unfashionable), so that the suggestion of disarmament fell only upon deafened ears. To insure peace it appeared to be necessary to arm more men; the French were not to be trusted, neither were the Russians, nor most of all the Italians; they would fall upon Trieste and Trent, if they had half an opportunity—in short, the thing to do was to push the universal military-service system.

"The time is not yet ripe," said Frederick, when we received such reports; "and the hope that I personally may hasten the development of the idea of the peace of nations I must probably abandon. But from the hour that I dedicated myself to this work, even the little I could do became to me the most important. I bide my time."

If for the present the project of disarmament had to go by the board, I still had one satisfaction: there was no immediate prospect of war. The war party at court and among the people, which asserted that the dynasty should be re-baptized in blood, must give up all present hope of a cam-

paign on the Rhine boundaries. France had no
allies; the country suffered from a severe drought;
a failure of crops was anticipated and forage was
scarce; the horses of the army must be sold, the
contingent of recruits was declared unnecessary,
there was nowhere any political complication; in
short, Ollivier took occasion to declare from the
rostrum: "The peace of Europe is assured."

Assured! I rejoiced over this word. All the
papers repeated it and many thousands rejoiced
as I did. What greater good can be found for
most men than the certainty of peace?

What this security was worth, which was so
emphatically assured us by a noted statesman, we
all know now. We ought then to have known that
these diplomatic assertions which the public receive
with such simple confidence are no surety of truth.
The European situation presents no doubtful question; therefore peace is assured. What feeble logic!
Disturbing questions may be made to turn up any
day; the point would be to be prepared for some
other method of settlement than through war; then
we should be safely beyond the possibility of it.

Again Parisian society was scattered to the four
winds of heaven. We remained in town on account of business. We had the opportunity of
purchasing at an exceedingly profitable price a
new, half-completed hotel in the Avenue de l'Im-
peratrice. As we intended to spend a portion of
every year in Paris we preferred to own a home.
With the fascinating prospect ahead of furnishing
our own nest and completing the house according
to our mind we were content to spend the summer
in town.

Many pleasant friends owned country houses
in the neighborhood of Paris. The palace of the
Princess Mathilde, St. Gratien, the Palace Mouchy,
and Baron Rothschild's home, Ferrières, were at no
great distance, and once or twice a month we visited them all.

I distinctly remember it was in the parlors of the Princess that I first learned that there was another doubtful question floating in the air.

The party sat upon the terrace—after breakfast *à la fourchette*—with a charming view of the park. Who were there? Some I cannot remember; only two made a particular impression upon me—Taine and Renan. The intellectual hostess of St. Gratien loved to surround herself with distinguished literary and scientific personages.

The conversation was animated, and I remember that it was Renan chiefly who led the bright and witty talk. The author of "The Life of Jesus" is a remarkable example of how one can be inconceivably ugly and at the same time inconceivably fascinating.

Politics had its turn, for the Spanish throne was vacant. It was said that a prince of Hohenzollern was a candidate. I scarcely noticed even the name, for of what possible consequence could it be to any of us, who sat upon the Spanish throne. But some one said:

"A Hohenzollern? France will not tolerate that."

The remark cut me to the heart, for too well I knew what this "not tolerate" always meant. When that is said in the name of a nation, one sees in imagination the spirit of the country personified as a gigantic female statue, with her head thrown back defiantly and her hand on the sword hilt.

The subject was idly discussed and soon dropped, for not one of us could have the least presentiment of the fearful results of this question of the Spanish succession.

From this time on the Spanish question became more and more obtrusive. Daily the newspapers increased the space allotted to its discussion; most of them regarded it as an intentional provocation of war on the part of Prussia. Letters from Berlin, however, assured us that at court it was not regarded as of any importance whether a Hohenzollern occupied the Spanish throne or not.

Gradually we, too, became more attentive to the course of events. Like the rustle of the branches of trees before a storm, there was a premonitory murmur among the people. *Nous aurons la guerre—nous aurons la guerre!* resounded through the Parisian streets. Then I was seized with unspeakable terror—not on my own account, for we Austrians were beyond the reach of ill, though much was said to us about revenge for Sadowa. But we had forgotten to consider war from a national standpoint; for us the humane, the broad international view was the only possible one.

When the news arrived that Prim had offered the crown to Prince Leopold, the Duke de Grammont made an address in the French Chamber, which was received with great applause:

"We do not interfere in foreign affairs, but we do not believe that a respect for the rights of a neighboring state requires us to tolerate the attempts of a strange power to set a prince upon the throne of Charles V., a measure which would disturb the balance of power of all Europe (O this balance of power! what blood-thirsty diplomatic hypocrite invented this hollow phrase?), and thus put the interests and honor of France in danger."

I know a little story by George Sand, called "Gribouille." This Gribouille had the habit of throwing herself into the river at the approach of rain for fear of getting wet. When I hear that war must be carried on in order to ward off threatened danger I think of Gribouille. A whole race of Hohenzollerns could have been set upon the throne of Charles V., and a dozen other thrones, without disturbing the interests or honor of France, or doing one thousandth part of the damage which arose from this defiant "We cannot tolerate."

"We feel certain," continued the speaker, "that this event will not occur. We count in this respect upon the wisdom of the German and upon the friendship of the Spanish people. Should it happen otherwise, then, gentlemen, we shall understand how, through your support and that of the nation, to do our duty without hesitation and without timidity." [Storms of applause.]

From now on the war mania possessed the public press. It was Girardin, particularly, who could scarce do enough to fire the hearts of his country-men against the unheard-of impudence which was at the very bottom of this Spanish proposition. It would be the duty of France, in order to maintain her dignity, to put a veto upon it; naturally Prussia would not refrain even then, for it was her interest to foment war. Inflamed by the success of the campaign of 1866, Prussia now believed it possible to march over the Rhine to new conquests; but we are here, God be praised, to stem the passions of the pointed helmets. In this tone he kept it up. Napoleon III. himself wished for peace; but those about him were mainly of the opinion that war was unavoidable, especially as the people were dissatisfied with the government. The best that could be done to restore confidence was a successful campaign.

One after the other European cabinets declared themselves to be in favor of peace. In Germany a manifesto was published, signed by Liebknecht among others, wherein it was declared that the very thought of a war between France and Germany was a crime. Through this circular I became aware "that a great association existed of a hundred thousand members, whose object was the abolition of all injurious tendencies and prejudices of classes and of the nation." All this was in the line of modern thought, and the little sentence could be added to my peace protocol.

Benedetti was entrusted with the mission to demand of the King of Prussia that he forbid Prince Leopold to accept the crown. King William was at that time in Ems; Benedetti went there, and on the ninth of July was granted an audience.

The reply of the King was that as the Prince had arrived at years of discretion he could not forbid his doing anything.

This answer threw the war party into spasms of delight. "They are determined to drive us to extremities. How absurd! The head of the house cannot command the obedience of a member? it is a mere excuse. The Hohenzollerns are determined to get possession of Spain and then they will fall upon us from the north and south. Are we to wait for that? Are we to endure the humiliation that our protest is not respected? Never! we know what honor, what patriotism demands."

Louder and louder, more and more threatening muttered the approaching storm. At last, on the twelfth of July, a despatch was published which filled me with delight. Don Salusto Olozaga officially informed the French government that Prince Leopold of Hohenzollern, in order that there might be no pretext for war, had declined the Spanish crown. The announcement was made at twelve o'clock in the Chamber, and Ollivier declared that this was the end of the matter. On the same day, however (apparently the result of previous orders), troops and materials were despatched to Metz, and during the same session Clement Duvernois made the following interpellation:

" What security have we that Prussia will not again stir up complications similar to this pretension to the Spanish crown? We must be prepared to meet them."

Gribouille again bestirred herself: It is just possible—a little rain threatens to make us wet; let us jump into the river as quickly as possible. Again Benedetti was despatched to Ems to demand that the King of Prussia at once and for the future, forbid Prince Leopold from again presenting himself as a candidate. Was it possible under such provocation for the king to do otherwise than impatiently to shrug his shoulders?

On the fifteenth of July there was a remarkable session. Ollivier requested an appropriation of five hundred millions for the war. Thiers voted against it. Ollivier replied that he would be responsible to history. The King of Prussia had declined to receive the French embassador, who had by despatch informed the government of this fact. The Left demanded to see the despatch. The majority tumultuously and by vote forbade the publication of this despatch (which probably had no existence). The majority granted everything the government asked. Such patriotic willingness for sacrifice, which without a shudder welcomes ruin, was naturally immensely admired and described with all the euphonious, ready-made, customary phrases.

England made an attempt to prevent the war. In vain; if there had been a recognized international court of jurisdiction how easily this conflict might have been avoided.

On the nineteenth of July, the French embassador in Berlin presented the formal declaration of war to the Prussian government.

A declaration of war! We speak of it so coolly. What does it mean? The beginning of an action, the result of political intrigue, and incidentally the sentence of death of half a million human beings.

This document I copied into my red note-book:

"The government of his Majesty, the Emperor of the French, could only consider the elevation of a Prussian prince to the throne of Spain as an undertaking dangerous to the territorial security of France, and has therefore found it necessary to demand of the King of Prussia the assurance that a similar combination will not receive his support in the future. Since his Majesty declined to give this assurance, and, on the contrary, declared to our embassador that he reserved to himself the right of inquiry into such possible events, the imperial government must recognize in this declaration of the King a suppressed intention, which is threatening to France and the balance of power in Europe (there it is again, this famous balance of power). This declaration has become of more serious character through the report communicated to the ministry of the refusal to receive the Emperor's plenipotentiary and enter into further discussion of the subject (so it seems that a more or less friendly intercourse between regents and diplomatists settles the fate of peoples). As a result of this course the French government considers it its duty without delay to think of the defense (yes, yes, defense—never attack) of its outraged dignity and its outraged interests. Determined to adopt all measures to this end, which are offered it by existing circumstances, it considers itself from now on in the condition of war with Prussia."

Condition of war! Does he who sitting at the diplomatic table sets this word down on paper realize that he has dipped his pen in flames, in bloody tears, in the poison of disease?

So on account of a vacant throne seeking an occupant, and the consequent carefully nursed, unreasonable dissensions between two monarchs, the storm was brought upon us. Was Kant right when he set down, as the first definite stride to insure continual peace, that:

"The civil constitution of every state should be republican."

In truth, through the introduction of this system many causes of war would disappear, for history records that the great majority of wars are undertaken to settle some question of dynasty, and that all establishment of monarchical power rests upon martial conquest. Republics have made war to maintain national life. But in any case it is the old, barbaric spirit still, the taint of heredity, not yet over-mastered by development, which fans the flame of hate, and of love of victory and conquest.

I remember the peculiar frame of mind which took possession of me when this war broke out. The whole population was in a ferment and who could escape the infection? Naturally, according to old custom, the beginning of the campaign was regarded as a triumphant march; that is, of course, a patriotic duty. "*A Berlin, à Berlin!*" resounded through the streets and was chanted from the tops of the omnibuses; the Marseillaise was heard on every corner: *Le jour de gloire est arrivé!* At every theatrical performance the leading actress or singer —at the opera it was Marie Sass—must appear before the curtain in the costume of Joan of Arc and, carrying the national colors, must sing this battle song—the audience rising and generally joining in the chorus. Frederick and I realized

one evening the might of this popular enthusiasm,
and were compelled to rise to our feet—compelled
because we were electrified.

"See, Martha," exclaimed Frederick, " this spark
which spreads from one to another, uniting this
whole mass and making every heart beat higher,
is love——"

"Do you believe so? It is a song inspiring hate."

"That makes no difference; a common hatred is
but another form of love. When two or three or
more are bound together by the same feeling, they
love one another. When the time arrives for a
nobler, broader aspiration than the interests of
nationality, namely, the cause of humanity, then
our ideal will be attained."

"Ah, when will that time come?" I sighed.

"When? One can speak but relatively. As a
length of time compared with our personal existence—never; when compared with the existence of
our race—to-morrow."

When war breaks out the inhabitants of neutral
states divide into two camps; one siding with this,
the other with that party, as if there were a great
stake in which every one had a share. We were
unconsciously influenced by our earlier interests.
Frederick was of Prussian descent and the German language was my own. The declaration of war
had been made by the French on such insignificant
grounds—mere pretenses—that we must recognize
the cause of the Prussians as more justly representing that of defense, since they were forced into
the contest. It was inspiriting to note with what
enthusiasm the Germans, but so shortly before at
strife among themselves, now trooped together.

On the nineteenth of July, in his address from the
throne, King William said:

"The German and French nations, both in like degree
enjoying the blessings of Christian civilization and increasing prosperity, are called to a more beneficent rivalry
than the bloody one of arms. But the ruler of France,

instigated by personal interests and passions, has been able, through misleading statements, to excite the justifiable though excitable vanity of our great neighbors."

The Emperor Napoleon on his part issued the following proclamation:

"Because of the arrogant claims of Prussia we were obliged to protest. These protests have been met with ridicule. Events followed which indicated a contempt for us. Our country has been deeply incensed thereby and instantly the battle-cry has been heard from one end of France to the other. There is nothing to be done except to consign our fate to the lot drawn by war. We do not war against Germany, whose independence we respect. We have the most earnest desire that the people who compose the great German nation may be the arbiters of their own destiny. What we desire is the establishment of a condition of things which will insure our present security and make our future safe. We desire a permanent peace, founded upon the true interests of peoples; we wish that this miserable condition should end and that all nations use all possible means to secure general disarmament."

What a lesson, what a striking lesson this document is when we consider it in connection with the events which followed. In order to be sure of safety, in order to attain permanent peace this war was begun by France. And what was the result? "The Terrible Year" and enduring hatred. No, no; one does not use charcoal to paint a thing white, nor asafœtida to perfume a room, nor war to secure peace.

I could not believe that the war would be a long one. What were they fighting about? Really nothing at all. It was a sort of grand parade undertaken by the French from a spirit of adventure—by the Germans as a duty of defense. One might expect a few saber thrusts, and the antagonists would again shake hands. Fool that I was! As if the results of war bore any adequate relation to its cause. The course of it determines the result.

We would have gladly left Paris, for the enthusiasm of the population pained us immeasurably. But the way eastward was blocked; our house was not completed—in short, we remained. All of our acquaintances who could get away had fled, and excepting a few literary men, we had no visitors. Frederick was much interested at just this phase of the war to note the sentiment among the most noted of these men. A young writer, the later famous Guy de Maupassant, once expressed my own feelings so perfectly that I entered his words in my journal:

"War—when I think of this word I shudder as if one talked of the Inquisition, or of a distant, horrible, unnatural thing. War—to kill one another, cut each other down! And we have to-day—in our times, with our culture, with our extensive knowledge in the higher planes of development, which we flatter ourselves to have attained—we still have schools to teach men how to kill, to kill in the most scientific manner and as many as possible. It is wonderful that the people do not rise against this thing, that the whole of society does not revolt at the mere mention of war. He who rules is in duty bound to avoid war, as the captain of a ship is bound to avoid shipwreck. When a captain loses his ship he is required to answer for it, in case it is discovered that he has been remiss in duty. Why should not every government be called to account when it declares war? If the people understood how to refuse to allow themselves to be killed without just cause, war would cease."

Ernest Renan, also, let us hear from him:

"Is it not heart-breaking to think that all that we men of science have sought to accomplish the past fifty years is destroyed at a blow: the sympathy between peoples, the mutual understanding, the fruitful, united work? How such a war destroys the love of truth! What lies, what defamation of a nation will from now on, for the next fifty years, be believed by each of the other and divide them for an incalculable time! How it will retard the progress of Europe! We cannot build up in a hundred years what these men have torn down in one day."

I also had the opportunity of reading a letter which Gustave Flaubert wrote during those first July days to George Sand. Here it is:

"I am in despair at the stupidity of my countrymen. The incorrigible barbarism of humanity fills me with the deepest grief. This enthusiasm inspired by not one reasonable idea makes me long to die that I may not witness it. Our good Frenchmen will fight: first, because he believes himself called out by Prussia; secondly, because the natural condition of man is that of barbarism; thirdly, because war possesses a mystical element which carries mankind away. Have we returned to a war of races? I am afraid so. The horrible battles which we prepare for have not a single pretext to excuse them. It is simply the pleasure of fighting for fighting itself. I regret the bridges and tunnels that will be blown to pieces, all this superb work of man which will be destroyed. I notice that a member of the Chamber proposes the plundering of the Grand Duchy of Baden. Ah, I wish I were with the Bedouins."

"Oh!" I cried, as I read this letter, "if we had only been born five hundred years later—that would be better than the Bedouins."

"Mankind will not take so long to become reasonable," replied Frederick confidently.

It was now again the era of proclamations and army orders.

Always the same old song, and always the same enthusiasm and applause of the populace. There was the same rejoicing over promised victories as if they had been already won.

On the twenty-eighth of July Napoleon III. published the following proclamation from his headquarters in Metz. I copied this, not out of admiration, but because of anger over its everlasting hollow phrases:

"We defend the honor and soil of our native land. We will be victorious. Nothing is too great for the sturdy endurance of the soldiers of Africa, the Crimea, China, Italy, and Mexico. Once more they will show what a French army inspired by a love of country is capable of accomplishing. Whichever way we turn outside of our borders we find the marks of the valor of our fathers. We will prove ourselves worthy of them. Upon our success hangs the fate of freedom and civilization. Soldiers, do your duty, and the God of Battles will be with you."

Oh, of course, it would not do to leave out "the God of Battles." That the leaders of vanquished armies have a hundred times promised the same, does not prevent the claim of special protection being set up at every fresh campaign in order to awaken the same confidence. Is anything shorter than the memory of a people or anything feebler than their logic?

On the thirty-first of July King William left Berlin and issued the following manifesto:

" To-day, before I leave to join the army, to fight with it for the honor and preservation of all dearest to us, I proclaim a general amnesty for all political offenses. My people know that we were not guilty of enmity and breach of faith. But being attacked we are resolved, as were our fathers, in firm reliance upon God, to endure the struggle for the rescue of our country."

Defense, defense, that is the only dignified sort of death; therefore both sides cry: "I defend myself." Is that not a contradiction? Not quite—for over each a third power rules, the might of the old hereditary war spirit. If they would only defend themselves against that!

Next to the above-mentioned manifesto I find in my note-book a curious story with this singular heading:

"If Ollivier had married the daughter of Meyerbeer would this war have broken out?"

Among our Parisian acquaintances was the literary man, Alexander Weill, who asked the above question and answered it in the same breath:

"Meyerbeer sought a talented husband for his second daughter and his choice fell on my friend, Emile Ollivier. Ollivier is a widower. His first wife was a daughter of Liszt. This marriage was a happy one and Ollivier had the reputation of being a faithful husband. He had no fortune, but as an orator and statesman he was famous. Meyerbeer wished to know him personally, and with this object I gave a ball—in April of the year 1864 —where most of the celebrities of art and science

were assembled, and where Ollivier, who had been
informed by me of Meyerbeer's object, naturally
played the leading *rôle*. He pleased Meyerbeer.
The affair was not easy to manage. Meyerbeer
knew the independent originality of his daughter,
who could never be induced to marry a man except
of her own free choice. It had been decided that
Ollivier should go to Baden as if by chance, and
should be presented to the young lady, when fourteen days after the ball Meyerbeer suddenly died.
It was Ollivier, you remember, who delivered the
funeral oration at the Northern Railroad station.
Now, I insist that if Ollivier had married Meyerbeer's daughter this war would never have occurred. In the first place, Meyerbeer, who hated
the empire to the verge of contempt, would never
have allowed Ollivier to become a minister of the
Emperor. We all know that if Ollivier had threatened to resign if war were declared, the Chamber
would never have declared war. The present contest is the work of three intimate friends of the
Empress: Jerome David, Paul de Cassagnac, and
the Duke de Grammont. The Empress, incited by
the Pope, whose religious puppet she is, wished to
see this war, of whose success she never doubts,
in order to secure the succession of her son. She
said: '*C'est ma guerre à moi et à mon fils,*' and the
three above named were the secret tools who, by
means of false rumors and pretended despatches
from Germany, had compelled the Emperor, who
wished for peace, to consent to fight. The Chamber was ready to declare war, at any rate."

"That is called diplomacy!" I exclaimed.

"But hear the rest," continued Alexander Weill.
"On the fifteenth of July, Ollivier, whom I met
on the *Place de la Concorde*, said to me: 'Peace is
certain—or else I will resign.' How does it happen
that the same man, a few days later, instead of
sending in his resignation, supports the war with
all his heart, as he declared in the Chamber?"

"A frivolous heart!" I cried with a shudder.

"This is the secret, which I will tell you. The Emperor, who regards gold as of no value except to buy love and friendship—he believes, like Jugurtha of Rome, that all France is corrupt, men as well as women—is accustomed, when he appoints a minister who is not rich, to make him a present of a million of francs to bind him to himself. Daru, who told me this, would not accept this present: *timeo Danaos et dona ferentes.* And he alone, not being bound, tendered his resignation. So long as the Emperor vacillated, Ollivier declared himself neutral or for peace. So soon as the Emperor was over-persuaded by the Empress and her three ultramontane agents, Ollivier also declared himself for war and died to honor with a light heart and a full purse."

"O Monsieur, O Madame, what news!" With these words Frederick's valet and the cook behind him rushed into our sitting-room. It was the day of the Battle of Wörth.

"A despatch has arrived. The Prussians are as good as absolutely crushed. The city is being decorated with tri-colored flags, it will be illuminated to-night."

In the course of the afternoon further despatches proved that the first was false—a maneuver of the Bourse. Ollivier addressed a crowd from the balcony of his house. Fortunately we escaped the illumination, this method of expressing delight over beaten armies,—that is to say, over countless dead and crippled, and thousands of broken hearts, the bare thought of which moved me to wish with Flaubert that I were with the Bedouins.

On the seventh of August there was a rumor of disaster. The Emperor hastened from St. Cloud to the seat of war. The enemy had crossed the frontier and was marching inland. The papers could not express their indignation in strong enough terms. I had imagined that the shout *à Berlin!* meant a similar invasion. But that these

eastern barbarians should dare the same thing—
should march into beautiful and beloved France—
this seemed pure, audacious villainy, and must be
stopped at once.

The provisional Minister of War published an
order calling upon all able-bodied citizens between
thirty and forty years of age to enroll themselves in
the National Guard. A ministry for defense of the
interior was organized. The appropriation was
increased from five hundred to a thousand million
of francs. It is refreshing to notice how free the
authorities are with the money and lives of others.
An unpleasant little occurrence disturbed the convenience of the public; if one wanted to change a
bank-note he was obliged to pay a broker ten per
cent. There was not sufficient gold to keep the
notes of the Bank of France at par.

Now followed victory after victory on the part
of the Germans.

The aspect of Paris and its inhabitants under-
went an astonishing change. In the place of the
proud, boastful, war-loving humor, dismay and
vindictive anger appeared. The impression that
a horde of vandals were ready to devour the land
was widespread. That the French had called
down this storm upon themselves they never considered; or that they had done it to prevent some
Hohenzollern in the distant future from conceiv-
ing a fancy for the Spanish throne—that they also
forgot. The most astonishing stories were told
of the ferocity of the invaders, "The Uhlans, the
Uhlans!" the words had a sort of fantastic demoniac sound, as if they had talked about the armies
of Satan. In the imagination of the people these
troops became demons. Whenever a particularly
bold stroke was reported it was at once ascribed
to the Uhlans. They were said to be recruited
to serve for booty and without pay. Mixed up
with these recitals of terror were stories of occasional triumphs. To lie about success is naturally
the chief duty of the sensationalist, for of course

the courage of the populace must be kept up. The law of veracity—like many other laws of morality —loses its force in times of war. Frederick read to me from the *Le Volontaire*, the following, to be inscribed in my note-book:

"Up to the sixteenth of August the Germans have lost one hundred and forty-four thousand men, the remainder are on the verge of starvation. The reserves from Germany, the 'landwehr' and 'landsturm,' are arriving; old men of over sixty, with flint-lock muskets, carrying on one side a huge tobacco pouch, on the other a big flask of brandy, with a long clay pipe in the mouth, are staggering under the weight of the knapsacks, coffee-mills, and packages of elderberry tea. Coughing and groaning, they are crossing from the right to the left bank of the Rhine, cursing those who have torn them from the arms of their grandchildren to thrust them into the clutches of death. The reports we get from the German press of victorious battles are all the usual Prussian lies."

On the twentieth of August Count Palikao informed the Chamber that three army corps, which had united against Bazaine, had been thrown into the quarries of Jaumont. It is true no one had the remotest idea where these stone quarries were, or how it happened that the three army corps were kept there. From tongue to tongue the joyful tidings spread and everybody acted as if they had been born in the region of Jaumont and of course knew all about the quarries. At the same time there was a current report that the King of Prussia had become insane over the condition of his army.

All sorts of atrocities were reported; the excitement among the population increased hourly. The engagement of Bazaille near Metz was described as if the Bavarians had been guilty of most inhuman barbarity.

"Do you believe this?" I said to Frederick. "Do you believe these stories of the good-natured Bavarians?"

"They are possible. Whether a man is Bavarian or Turk, German, French, or Indian makes no particular difference; when he takes his life in his hands and fights to destroy others he ceases to be human. All that is awakened and strongest within him is the beast."

Metz is taken. The report resounded through the city like a shriek of terror.

To me the news of the capture of a fortress brought relief rather than dismay. Were we not probably nearer the end? But after every defeat each side strains itself to the utmost for a fresh trial of strength; possibly the fortune of war may turn. Usually the advantage is first on one side next on the other; on both sides there is certain sorrow and certain death.

Trochu felt himself called upon to arouse the courage of the population by a fresh proclamation, calling upon them with the motto of Bretagne, "With God's help for our native land." That does not sound quite new to me—I must have heard something similar to it in other proclamations. It did not fail of its effect, however; the people were encouraged. Next we were told Paris must be fortified. Paris a fortress! I could scarcely grasp the thought. The city which Victor Hugo called, "*la ville-lumière*", the loadstar of the whole civilized, rich, art- and life-loving world, the radiating point of splendor, of fashion, of the intellect—this city must fortify itself, that is, must be the aim of the enemy's attacks, the target of bombardment, and run the risk of destruction through fire and hunger. And these people proceeded to the work with gaiety of heart, with the zeal of pleasure, with self-sacrifice, as if they were bringing to completion the noblest, most useful work in the world. Ramparts to be manned by infantry were built with embrasures, earthworks were thrown up before the gates, canals were covered, and surmounted by parapets, powder magazines were built, and a flotilla of barges, carrying cannon, was put upon the Seine. What a fever of activity; what an expenditure of strength and nerve; what monstrous cost of labor and money! If all had only been so cheerfully and nobly devoted to works of true utility;—but for the purpose of destruction, which had no object except that of a strategic checkmate, it was inconceivable!

To be prepared for a long siege the city was amply provisioned. But it is the experience of ages that no fortification has existed which has been impregnable—capitulation is solely a matter of time. Yet fortifications are still erected, they are still provisioned, notwithstanding the mathematical impossibility of maintaining them, in the long run, against starvation.

The preparations were made on an enormous scale. Mills were erected and stockyards filled; yet the hour must come when the corn would all be ground and the flesh all eaten. But so far ahead as this no one thought; of what use? Long before that the enemy would be driven from the country. The entire male force of the city was enrolled in the National Guard and all possible were drawn from the country. What difference did it make if the provinces were laid in ashes? Such insignificant events were not to be considered, when there was prospect of a national disaster. On the seventeenth of August sixty thousand provincial troops had already arrived in Paris. The sailors were all ordered in, and daily new companies were organized under different names, such as *volontaires, éclaircurs,* or *franc-tireurs.*

With an ever-increasing activity events followed events. All around there was heard but one expression, "death to the Prussians." A storm of the wildest hatred was gathering—it had not yet broken out. In all the official reports, in all the street disturbances we heard of but one aim—"death to the Prussians." All these troops, regular and irregular, all these munitions of war, all these busy workmen with spade and barrow, all that one saw and heard, in form or tone, surged and threatened "death to the Prussians!" Or, in other words, it sounds really like the cry of love and inspires even tender hearts—"all for one country"—but it is one and the same thing.

"You are of Prussian descent," I said to Frederick one day, "how do these expressions of hatred affect you?"

"You asked me the same question in the year 1866, and then I answered, as I must to-day, that I suffer under these demonstrations of hatred, not as a Prussian, but as a man. When I reflect upon the feelings of these people from a national standpoint, I can only regard them as justifiable; they call it the sacred hatred of the enemy, and this sentiment forms an important incentive to military patriotism. They have but one thought—to free their country from the presence of the antagonist. They forget that they caused the invasion by their declaration of war. They did not do it themselves, but it was their government in which they believed. They waste no time in reflections or in recriminations; the misfortune is upon them and every muscle, every nerve is strained to meet it, or with reckless self-sacrifice they will all go to destruction together. Believe me, there is untold capacity in the love of mankind; the pity of it is that we waste it in the old rut of hatred. And the enemy, the 'red-haired, eastern barbarians!'—what are they doing? They were called out and they invade the land which threatened theirs. Do you remember how the cry, *à Berlin, à Berlin*, resounded through the streets?"

"Now the others march upon Paris! Why do the Parisian shouters call that a crime?"

"Because there is neither logic nor justice in that national feeling whose chief principle is, we are we—that is, the first,—the others are barbarians. That march of the Germans from victory to victory fills me with admiration. I have been a soldier and know what an inspiration the idea of victory has, what pride, what intense delight. It is the reward for all suffering, for the renunciation of rest and happiness, for the life at stake."

"Why do not the victors admire the vanquished, if they know all that victory means to those who are soldiers like themselves? Why do not the army reports of the losing party contain the sentence: the enemy has won a glorious victory?"

"Why? I repeat, the war spirit and patriotic egotism are the destruction of all justice."

On the twenty-eighth of August all Germans were ordered to leave Paris within three days. I had the opportunity to see the effect of this order. Many Germans had been citizens of Paris for ten and twenty years, had married Parisians, but were now compelled to leave everything—home, business and property.

Sedan! The Emperor had surrendered up his sword. The report overpowered us. Then truly a terrible catastrophe had occurred—Germany had won and the butchery was over.

"It is over," I cried. "If there are people who are citizens of the world, they may illuminate their windows; in the temples of humanity Te Deums can now be sung—the butchery is over."

"Do not rejoice too soon," Frederick warned me. "This war has long lost the character of a battle game of chess, the whole nation is in arms. For one army destroyed ten new ones will spring out of the soil."

"Is that just? These are only German soldiers, not the German nation."

"Why always talk of justice and reason in the presence of a madman. France is mad with pain and terror, and from the standpoint of the love of country her rage is just, her sorrow sacred. Personal interest is not considered, only the loftiest self-sacrifice. If the time would only come when the noble virtues common to humanity could be torn from the work of destruction and united for the blessing of the race! But this unholy war has again driven us back a long way from the attainment of this goal."

"No, no, I hope the war is at an end."

"If so, which I much doubt, the seeds of future wars are sown and the seeds of hate, which will outlast this generation."

On the fourth of September another great event occurred. The Emperor was deposed and France was declared a republic. With the destruction of the throne the leaves were torn out of the book of France which told the story of Metz and Sedan. It was Napoleon and his dismissed generals, who through cowardice, treachery, and bad tactics had been responsible for all this disaster—but not France. France would now carry on the war if the Germans still dared to continue the invasion.

"How would it have been had Napoleon and his generals been victorious?" I asked when Frederick told me this latest news.

"Then they would have accepted his success as the success of France."

"Is there any justice in that?"

"Why will you not break yourself of the habit of asking that question?"

My hope that with Sedan the war would end was soon dissipated. The frenzied orations, the atrocious pamphlets which were now made and published, and rained down upon the unfortunate Emperor and Empress and the unlucky generals, were absolutely disgusting. The rough masses held that they could lay upon these few the responsibility for the general disaster. The preparations for the defense of Paris were carried on with rapidity. Houses which might serve as protection to the approaching enemy were torn down and the region around the city became a desert. Crowds of country people filled up the already crowded city, and the streets were jammed with the wagons and pack horses of these people, laden with the remains of their household goods. I had seen the same sight in Bohemia, and now was fated to see the like misery and a similar terror in the beautiful streets of the most wonderful, most brilliant city of the world.

There came at last the news of the prospect of better things. Through the mediation of England an interview was arranged between Bismarck and Jules Favre. There was the chance that peace might be arranged.

On the contrary, the breach became much wider. For some time past German papers had suggested the retention of Alsace-Lorraine. The former German provinces were to be annexed. The historical argument was not quite tenable, therefore the strategical reason was made more prominent: as a rampart they were absolutely necessary in case of future wars. It is well known that the strategic grounds are the most important, the most incontestible—the ethical reasons must take second rank. On the other hand, as France had lost in the struggle, was it not fair that the winner should hold the prize? In case of the success of the French, they of course would have claimed the provinces of the Rhine. What is war for except for the extension of the territory of the one or the other antagonist?

In the meantime the victorious army did not halt in its march on Paris,—the Germans were already at her door. The consent to the cession of Alsace-Lorraine was officially demanded. In response the well known reply was given: "Not an inch of our territory—not a stone of our fortresses."

Yes, yes—a thousand lives—not an inch of earth. That is the foundation principle of the patriotic spirit. "They seek to humiliate us!" cried the French patriots. "We would rather be buried under the ruins of Paris."

We attempted to leave the city. Why should we stay among a people so embittered by hate that they clenched their fists if they heard us speak German. We had succeeded in making arrangements for departure, when I was seized by a nerv-

ous fever of so dangerous a character that the
family physician forbade any attempt at removal.

I lay upon my bed for many weeks, and only a
dreamy recollection of that time remains. In the
careful hands of my husband and the tender care
of my children, my Rudolph and my little Sylvia,
all knowledge of the fearful events then occurring
was shut out, and when I recovered winter had
set in.

Strassburg had been bombarded, the library
destroyed; four or five shots a minute were said to
have been fired—in all, one hundred and ninety-
three thousand, seven hundred and twenty-two.

Should Paris be starved into submission or bombarded?

Against the last the conscience of civilization
protested. Should this "*ville-lumière*," this rendezvous of all nations, this brilliant seat of art,
with its irrecoverable riches and treasures be bombarded as any common citadel? It was not to be
thought of; the whole neutral press, I learned afterwards, protested. The press of Berlin approved
the idea; considered it the only way to end the
war and conquer the city. No protest availed, and
on the twenty-eighth of December the bombardment began.

At first greeting it with terror, it was not long
before the Parisians chose for a promenade the
localities from which one could best hear the
music of cannon. Here and there a shell fell in
the street, but there was seldom a consequent
catastrophe. Rarely could any news from the outside world be obtained, and that only through car-
rier pigeons and balloons. The reports were most
contradictory; one day we were informed of successful sallies, the next, that the enemy was about
to storm the city, set fire to it, and lay it in ashes;
or we were assured that rather than see one German enter within the walls the commandant would
blow all Paris into atoms.

It became daily more and more difficult to obtain food. Meat was not to be had; cattle and sheep and horses were exhausted, and the period began when dogs, cats, rats, and mice were a rarity, and finally the beloved elephant at the *Jardin des Plantes* must be served up. Bread was scarce. People stood in rows, hours at a time, in front of the bakers in order to receive their tiny portion. Disease broke out, induced by famine. The mortality increased from the ordinary eleven hundred a week to between four and five thousand.

One day Frederick came into the house from his daily walk in an unusual state of excitement.

"Take up your note-book, my zealous historian," he cried. "To-day there is wonderful news."

"Which of my books?" I asked. "My Peace Protocol?"

Frederick shook his head.

"Oh, for that the time is past. The war now being carried on is of so mighty a character that it will drag its martial spirit long after it. It has sown broadcast such a store of hatred and revenge that future battle harvests must grow therefrom; and upon the other side it has produced for the victors such magnificent revolutionary results that a like harvest may be brought about by their haughty martial spirits."

"What is it that is so important?"

"King William has been proclaimed Emperor at Versailles. There is now really a Germany, one single empire—and a mighty one. That is a new event in the world's history. And you can easily perceive how this great result will redound to the honor of the work of war. The two most advanced representatives of civilization on the continent are the ones who from now on for some time to come will cultivate the war spirit—the one in order to return the blow, the other in order to maintain the position won; here out of hate, there out of love; here from a spirit of retaliation, on the other side out of gratitude. Shut up your

peace protocols—for a long time to come we shall
stand under the bloody and iron sign of Mars."

"Emperor of Germany!" I cried, "that is indeed glorious. I cannot help rejoicing over this
news. The whole barbarous slaughter has not
been in vain if a great, new empire has been born."

"From the French point of view the war is
doubly lost. And it is to be expected of us that
we should not regard this contest from the one-
sided German standpoint alone. Not only as human beings but from a narrower national feeling
we should be excused if we regretted the success
of our enemies of 1866. And yet I will acknowledge that the union of divided Germany is a
desirable thing, and that the readiness with which
all these German princes joined in offering the
imperial crown to the gray-haired victor is inspiring and admirable. Only it is a pity that this union
was not brought about through peaceful rather
than warlike measures. It may be that if Napoleon III. had not made his demand of the nineteenth of July there would not have been enough
patriotism among the Germans to bring about this
result. They may well rejoice; the poet's wish is
fulfilled—they are a band of brothers. Four years
ago they had each other by the throat and knew
but one common cause—hatred of Prussia."

"That word hate makes me shudder."

"Well it may. So long as this feeling is not
regarded as unjust and dishonorable, we shall have
no humane humanity. Religious hatred has about
disappeared, but national hatreds form a part of
the education of the citizen."

In the quiet of the next few days we had many
discussions as to our future. With the establishment of peace, which we could now hope for, we
might again dare to think of our personal happiness. During the eight years of our married life
there had been no discord, not a discourteous or
unkindly word or thought had passed between us;
as the years drew on we knew we should grow

nearer to each other, and we could look forward to an old age together—the golden evening of our lives—with sure content.

Many of the preceding pages I have turned over with a shudder. It is not without repulsion that I have recorded my visit to the battlefields of Bohemia and the scenes of the cholera week in Grumitz. I have done it as a duty. I had been told: "In case I die first take up my work and do what you can to further the cause of peace among men."

But I have now reached a point when I cannot go on.

I have tried; many half-written sheets lie on the floor beside me; but my heart fails and I can only fall to weeping—weeping bitterly like a child.

Some hours later I again made the attempt. But the particulars of the circumstances it is not possible for me to relate.

The fact is enough.

Frederick—my all! was seized by a fanatical mob who, finding a letter from Berlin upon his person, accused him of being a spy. He was dragged before a so-called patriotic tribunal, and on the first of February, 1871, was sentenced to be shot.

EPILOGUE.

WHEN I again awoke to consciousness peace had been declared, the Commune had been defeated. For months, attended by my faithful Frau Anna, I lived through an illness without knowing that I was alive. The character of my illness I have never known. Those about me tenderly called it typhus, but I believe it was simply insanity.

Dimly I remember that the latter part of the time seemed filled with the rattling of shot and the falling of burning walls; probably my fancies were influenced by the actual events, the skirmishes between the communists and the party of Versailles.

That when I recovered my reason and realized the circumstances of my profound unhappiness I did not kill myself, or that the anguish had not killed me, was owing to the existence of my children. For these I could, I must live. Even before my illness, on the day when the terrible event occurred, Rudolph had held me to life. I had sunk on my knees, weeping aloud while I repeated: "Die —die! I will die!" Two little arms were thrown around me and a sweet, piteous, pleading, childish face looked into mine:

"Mother!"

My little one had never called me anything but Mamma. That he at that moment, for the first time, used the word "Mother," said to me in two syllables: "You are not alone, you have a son who shares your pain, who loves you above all things, who has no one in the world but you. Do not leave your child, Mother!"

I pressed the precious being to my heart, and to

show him that I had understood him I murmured: "My son, my son!"

I then remembered my little girl—his child—and resolved to live.

But the anguish was unendurable, and I fell into mental darkness. For years—at longer and longer intervals—I was subject to these attacks of melancholy, of which upon my restoration to health I knew nothing. Now, at length, I have outlived them, and for several years have been free from the unconscious misery, though not from the bitterest, conscious sorrow. Eighteen years have passed since the first of February, 1871; but the deep anguish and the deepest mourning, which the tragedy of that day brought to me, I can never outlive though I should live a hundred years. If, in later times, the days are more frequent when I can take part in the events of the present, can forget the past unhappiness, can sympathize in the joys of my children, not a night passes when I escape my misery. It is a peculiar experience, hard for me to describe, and which can only be understood by those who have similarly suffered. It would seem to indicate a dual life of the soul. If the one is so occupied, when awake, with the things of the outer world as to forget, there yet remains that second nature which ever keeps faithfully in mind that dreadful memory; and this *I*—when the other is asleep—makes itself felt. Every night at the same hour I awake with this deep depression. My heart seems torn asunder and I feel as if I must relieve my agony in sighs and bitter weeping; this lasts for several seconds, without the awakened *I* knowing why the other is happy or unhappy. The next stage is a sentiment of universal sympathy, full of the tenderest compassion: "Oh, poor, poor humanity!" Then amidst a shower of bullets I see shrieking figures fall—and then I remember for the first time that my best-beloved met such a death.

But in dreams, singular to say, I never realize my loss. It often occurs that I seem to talk with Fred-

erick as if he were alive. Many circumstances of
the past—but no sad ones—are frequently alluded
to by us: our meeting after Schleswig-Holstein, our
joking over Sylvia's cradle, our walk through Switzerland, our studies of favorite books, and now and
then a certain picture of my white-haired husband
in the evening sunset-light, with his garden shears,
clipping his roses. "Is it not true," he says to me,
smiling, "that we are a happy old couple?"

My mourning I have never laid aside—not even
on my son's wedding day. The woman who has
loved, possessed, and lost—so lost—such a man,
must feel that love is indeed stronger than death.
With this may exist a longing for revenge which
can never grow cold.

But how should I seek revenge? The men who
were guilty of the act could not be personally
blamed. The sole responsibility rested upon the
spirit of war, and this was the only force with
which I could attempt—though in a feeble way—
to settle my account.

My son Rudolph shared my views in regard to
war—which did not, however, prevent his going
into camp for the annual military drill, nor would
it hinder his marching over the border, should that
gigantic European contest break out which we are
all anticipating. I might yet live to see the dearest
one left to me sacrificed to this relentless Moloch,
and the hearth of my old age fall in ruins.

Should I live to experience that and again be
driven to madness, or should I see the triumph of
justice and humanity, for which all nations and
alliances of peoples are now striving?

My red journals are closed, and under date of
1871 I marked with a great cross the record of my
life. My so-called protocol—my peace record—I
have again opened, and of late have added much
to the history of the growth of the international
idea of the settlement of the strifes of humanity by
peaceful methods.

For some years the two most influential nations of the continent have been watching each other, both absorbed in thoughts of war—the one in arrogant review of past successes, the other in burning hopes of revenge. Gradually these sentiments have somewhat cooled, and notwithstanding, or by reason of, the great increase of our standing armies, after ten years the voices petitioning for peace are once more heard. Bruntschli, the great advocate of civil rights, presented the just claims of peace to many influential persons and governments. It was at this time that the silent "Battle-thinker" uttered his well-known dictum, "Eternal peace is a dream, and not even a beautiful dream."

"Certainly, if Luther had asked the Pope what he thought of his defection from Rome, the answer would not have been particularly reassuring to the reformer," I wrote at the time under Moltke's words.

To-day there are few to whom this dream of peace seems an impossibility. There are sentinels on every hill, to wake humanity out of its long sleep of barbarism and to plant the white flag. Their battle-cry is "War against war"; their watchword, "Ground Arms!" The only thing which can now prevent the most appalling disaster to Europe is the universal cry, "Ground Arms!" Everywhere, in England and France, in Italy, in the northern countries, in Germany, in Switzerland, in America, societies have been formed with the common object to educate public opinion, and by the united expression of popular will to demand of governments that future dissensions shall be submitted to international arbitration, and by so doing to set justice forever in the place of rude force. That this is not the impossible fancy of a dreamer has been proved by facts: by the settlement of the Alabama claims, the affair of the Caroline Islands, and several other threatening questions, which in an earlier period would have been decided only by an appeal to arms. It is not only people of no influence and position, but members of Parliament, bishops, scholars, senators, embassadors, who stand on the list. To these is added that ever-growing party which will shortly number millions, the party of "Labor" and of the people, upon whose programme the demand for peace is a first condition.

I lately received the following letter, in reply to a request for information, from the President of the London Peace Society:

INTERNATIONAL ARBITRATION AND
PEACE ASSOCIATION,
LONDON, 41 OUTER TEMPLE, July, 1889.
MADAME:

You have honored me by inquiring as to the actual position of the great question to which you have devoted your life. Here is my answer: At no time, perhaps, in the history of the world, has the cause of peace and goodwill been more hopeful. It seems, at last, that the long night of death and destruction will pass away, and we who are on the mountain top of humanity think we see the first streaks of the dawn of the Kingdom of Heaven upon earth. It may seem strange that we should say this at a moment when the world has never seen so many armed men and such frightful engines of destruction ready for their accursed work; but when things are at their worst, they begin to mend. Indeed, the very ruin which these armies are bringing in their train, produces universal consternation, and soon the oppressed people must rise and with one voice say to their rulers: "Save us, and save our children from the famine which awaits us, if these things continue; save civilization and all the triumphs which the efforts of wise and great men have accomplished in its name; save the world from a return to barbarism, rapine, and terror!" "What indications," do you ask, "are there of such a dawn of a better day?" Well, let me ask in reply, is not the recent meeting in Paris of the representatives of one hundred societies for the declaration of international concord, for the substitution of a state of law and justice for that of force and wrong, an event unparalleled in history? Have we not seen men of many nations assembled on this occasion and elaborating with enthusiasm and unanimity practical schemes for this great end? Have we not seen for the first time in history a congress of representatives of the parliaments of free nations, declaring in favor of treaties being signed by all civilized states, whereby they shall bind themselves to defer their differences to the arbitrament of equity, pronounced by an authorized tribunal instead of a resort to wholesale murder?

Moreover, these representatives have pledged themselves to meet every year in some city of Europe, in order to consider every case of misunderstanding or conflict, and to exercise their influence upon governments in the cause of just and pacific settlements. Surely, the most hopeless pessimist must admit that these are signs of a future when war shall be regarded as the most foolish and most criminal blot upon man's record.

Accept, dear Madame, the expression of my profound respect. Yours truly,

HODGSON PRATT.

The international conference to which Mr. Pratt refers met in Paris. Jules Simon presided. In his opening address he said:

"I am happy to welcome in this hall the authorized representatives of the friends of peace of different nationalities. I wish the number were greater, or, more to the purpose, I wish it were much less and not a voluntary but an official, diplomatic congress. But what we cannot now carry out by legislative powers we may still make effective by popular education. As members of different states we can make the best use of the greatest power which exists—that power which we were elected to represent.

"For you must be aware, gentlemen, that the public sentiment of the majority of every nation is on the side of peace."

There were present at this conference members of the legislative bodies of Denmark, Spain and Italy, who pledged themselves to present to their governments during the next session the proposal for the establishment of an international court of arbitration.

The next international conference will meet in London in July, 1890.

I find a royal manifesto in the blue note-book, dated March, 1888—a manifesto which, so widely different from ancient precedent, breathes a peace-

ful instead of a martial spirit. But the noble man,
upon whose word his people could rely, the dying
monarch who with his failing powers grasped his
scepter which he would use as a palm branch,
remained chained to his bed of pain, and in a few
short days all was over.

Will his successor, who pants for great deeds, be
inspired by the ideals of peace? Nothing is impossible.

"Mother, will you lay aside your mourning day
after to-morrow?"

With these words Rudolph came into my room
this morning. For the day after to-morrow—the
thirtieth of July, 1889—the baptism of his first-
born son is to be celebrated.

"No, my child," I answered.

"But think, surely at such a festival you will
not be sad; why wear the outward sign of sorrow?"

"And you surely are not superstitious enough
to think that the black dress of the grandmother
will bring ill-luck to the grandchild?"

"Certainly not. But it is not suitable to the
occasion. Have you taken a vow?"

"No, it is only a quiet determination. But a
determination connected with such a memory has
all the force of a vow."

My son bowed his head and urged me no longer.

"I have disturbed you in your occupation. Were
you writing?"

"Yes—the story of my life. I am, thank God!
at the end. That was the last chapter."

"How can you write the close of your life? You
may live many years, many happy years, Mother.
With the birth of my little Frederick, whom I will
train to adore his grandmother, a new chapter is
begun for you."

"You are a good son, my Rudolph, I should be
ungrateful if I had not pride and happiness in
you; and I am also proud of my—his sweet Sylvia;

yes, I am entering on a happy old age—a quiet evening; but the story of the day is closed at sunset, is it not?"

He answered me with a quiet and sympathetic glance.

"Yes, the word 'end' under my biography is justified. When I conceived the idea of writing it, I determined to stop with the first of February, 1871. If you had been torn from me for service in the field—luckily during the Bosnian campaign you were not old enough—I might have been obliged to lengthen my book. As it is, it was painful enough to write."

"And also to read," answered Rudolph, turning over the leaves.

"I hope so. If the book shall cause such pain in the reading as to awaken a detestation of the source of all the unhappiness here described, I shall not have tormented myself in vain."

"Have you examined all sides of the question, Mother?" said my son. "Have you exhausted all the arguments, analyzed to the roots the spirit of war, and sufficiently brought out the scientific objections to it?"

"My dear, what are you thinking about? I have only written of my life. All sides of the question? Certainly not. What do I, the rich woman of high rank, know of the sorrows which war brings to the mass of the poor? What do I know of the plagues and evil tendencies of barrack life? And with the economic-social question involved I am not familiar—and yet these are all the very matters which finally determine all reformation. I do not offer a history of the past and future rights of nations—only the story of the individual."

"But do you not fear that the object will be recognized?"

"One is offended only by the veiled intention, which the author commonly seeks to hide. My aim is open as the day and is found in the words on the title page."

The baptism took place yesterday. The occasion was made doubly important by the betrothal of my daughter Sylvia and the old friend of her babyhood—Count Anton Delnitzky.

I am surrounded by the happiness of my children. Rudolph inherited the Dotzky estates six years ago and has been married four years to Beatrice Griesbach, promised to him in their childhood. She is a charming creature, and the birth of their son adds to their enviable, brilliant lot.

In the room looking out upon the garden the dinner was served. The glass doors were open and the air of the superb summer afternoon streamed in loaded with the perfume of roses.

Near me sat the Countess Lori Griesbach, Beatrice's mother. She is now a widow. Her husband fell in the Bosnian campaign. She has not taken his loss much to heart. On the contrary—for she is dressed in a ruby brocade and brilliant diamonds—she is exactly as superficial as in her youth. Matters of the toilet, a few French and English novels, the usual society gossip—these suffice to fill her horizon. She is as great a coquette as ever. For young men she has now no fancy, but personages of rank and position are the objects of her conquests. At present, it seems to me, she has our Minister "Upon the Whole" in hand. This gentleman has now changed his name; we now call him Minister "On the Other Hand," to conform to the latest expression adopted by him.

"I must make a confession to you," said Lori to me when we had congratulated each other upon our grandchild. "On this solemn occasion I must relieve my conscience. I was seriously in love with your husband."

"You have often told me that, dear Lori."

"But he was always absolutely indifferent to me."

"That is well known to me."

"You had a husband true as gold, Martha! I cannot say the same of mine. But nevertheless I was sorry to lose him. Well, he died a glorious

death, that is one comfort. Really it is a wearisome existence to be a widow, more especially as
one grows older—so long as one can flirt widowhood is not without its compensations. But now
I acknowledge I become quite melancholy. With
you it is different; you live with your son, but I
would not like to live with my Beatrice. She
would not wish it either. A mother-in-law in the
house—that does not go well; for one wants to be
mistress. One gets so provoked with the servants.
You may believe me, I am much inclined to marry
again. Of course a marriage with some one of
position——"

"A Minister of Finance, for instance," I interrupted laughing.

"O you sly one! You see through me at once.
Look there: do you see how Toni Delnitzky is
whispering to your Sylvia. That is compromising."

"Let them alone. The two have come to an understanding on the way from church. Sylvia has
confided to me that the young man will ask my
permission to-morrow."

"What do you say? Well, I congratulate you.
It is said the handsome Toni has been a little gay
—but all of them are that—it cannot be helped
and he is a splendid match."

"Of that my Sylvia has not thought."

"Well, so much the better; it is a charming
addition to marriage."

"Addition? Love is the sum of all."

One of the guests, an imperial colonel, had
knocked on his glass and: "Oh, dear—a toast!"
thought all, and discontentedly dropped their
special conversation to listen to the speaker. We
had good reason to sigh; three times the unlucky
man stuck fast and the choice of his good wishes
was unfortunate. The health of the young heir
was offered, who was born at a time when his country needed all her sons.

"May he wear the sword as his great-grandfather

and his grandfather did; may he bring many sons
into the world, who on their part may be an honor
to their ancestry, and as they have done who have
fallen, win fame on the field of honor. May they
for the honor of the land of their fathers conquer
—as their fathers' and fathers' fathers—in short:
Long life to Frederick Dotzky!"

The glasses rattled but the speech fell flat.
That this little creature just on the threshold of
life should be sentenced to the death-list on a battlefield did not make a pleasant impression.

To banish this dark picture, several guests made
the comforting remark that present circumstances
promised a long peace, that the Triple Alliance—
and with that general interest was carried into the
political arena, and our Minister "On the Other
Hand" led the conversation.

"In truth (Lori Griesbach listened with intense
interest), it cannot be denied that the perfection
which our weapons have attained is marvelous and
enough to terrify all breakers of the peace. The
law for general service allows us to put into the
field, on the first call, four million eight hundred
thousand men between the ages of nineteen and
forty, with officers up to sixty. On the other hand,
one must acknowledge, that the extraordinary attendant expenses will be a strain upon the finan-
ces. It will be an intolerable burden to the population; but it is encouraging to see with what
patriotic self-sacrifice the people respond to the
demands of the war ministry; they recognize what
all far-sighted politicians realize, that the general
armament of neighboring states and the difficulties
of the political situation demand that all other
considerations should be subordinated to the iron
pressure of military necessity."

"Sounds like the leading editorial," murmured
some one.

Minister "On the Other Hand" went on calmly:
"But such a system is surety for the preservation
of peace. For if to secure our border, as tradi-

tional patriotism demands of us, we do as our neighbors are doing, we are but fulfilling a sacred duty and hope to keep danger far from us. So I raise my glass to the toast in honor of the principle which lies so close to the heart of Frau Martha —a principle dear to the Peace League of Middle Europe—and I call upon all of you to drink to the maintenance of peace! May we long enjoy its blessings!"

"To such a toast I will not drink," I replied. "Armed peace is no benefaction; we do not want peace for a long time, but forever. If we set out upon a sea voyage, do we like the assurance that the ship will escape wreck for a long time? That the whole trip will be a fortunate one is what the honest captain vouches for."

Doctor Bresser, our intimate old friend, came to my help.

"Can you in truth, your Excellency, honestly believe in a desire for peace on the part of those who with enthusiasm and passion are soldiers? How could they find such delight in arsenals, fortresses, and maneuvers if these things were really regarded merely as scarecrows? Must the people give all their earnings in order to kiss hands across the border? Do you think the military class will willingly accept the position of mere custodians of the peace? Behind this mask—the *si vis pacem* mask—glitters the eye of understanding, and every member who votes for the war budget knows it."

"The representatives?" interrupted the minister. "We cannot enough praise the self-sacrifice which they have never failed to exhibit in serious times, and which finds expression in their willingness to vote the appropriations."

"Forgive me, your Excellency, I would call out to these willing representatives: 'Your "yes" will rob that mother of her only child; yours over there puts out the eyes of some poor wretch; yours sets in a blaze a fearful conflagration; yours stamps out the brain of a poet, who would have been an

honor to his country. But you have all voted
"yes" in order to prove that you are not cowards
—as if one had only oneself to consider. Are you
not there to represent the wishes of the people?
And the people wish profitable labor, wish relief,
wish peace.'

"I hope, dear Doctor," remarked the Colonel
bitterly, "that you may never be a member; the
whole house would spit upon you."

"I would soon prove that I am no coward. To
swim against the stream requires nerves of steel."

"But how would it be if a serious attack were
made and found us unprepared?"

"We must have a system of justice which will
make an attack impossible. But when the time for
action does come, and these tremendous armies with
their fearful new means of warfare are brought
into the field, it will be a serious, a gigantic catastrophe. Help and care will be an impossibility.
The endeavors of the Sanitary or Red Cross corps,
the means of provision, will prove a mere irony
of the demands; the next war of which people so
glibly and indifferently speak will not be a victory
for the one and a loss for the other, but destruction
for all. Who among us desires this serious attack?"

"I, certainly not," said the minister. "You, of
course not, dear Doctor, but men in general. Our
government, possibly not, but other states."

"With what right do you deem other people
worse and less intelligent than yourself and me? I
will tell you a little story:

"Once upon a time a thousand and one men stood
before the gate of a beautiful garden, longingly
looking over the wall, desiring to enter. The gate-
keeper had been ordered to admit the people, provided the majority wished admittance. He called
one man up: 'Tell me honestly, do you want to
come in?' 'Certainly,' he replied, 'but the other
thousand do not care about it.'

"The shrewd custodian wrote this answer in his
note-book. He then called a second. He made

the same reply. Again the wise man wrote under the word 'yes' the figure one, and under the word 'no' the figure one thousand. So he went on to the very last man. Then he added up the columns. The result was: One thousand and one 'yeas,' but over a million 'noes.' So the gate remained shut because the 'noes' had an immense majority. And that came about because each one not only answered for himself, but felt himself obliged to answer for all the others."

"It would be a noble thing," replied the minister reflectively, "if by general consent disarmament could be effected. But what government would dare to begin? There is nothing, upon the whole, more desirable than peace; but, on the other hand, how can we maintain it; how can we look for durable peace so long as human passions and diverse interests exist?"

"Allow me," said my son Rudolph. "Forty million inhabitants form a state. Why not one hundred millions? One could prove logically and mathematically that so long as forty millions, notwithstanding diverse interests and human passions, can restrain themselves from warring with one another —as the three states, the Triple Alliance, or five states, can form a league of peace—one hundred millions can do the same? But, in truth, the world nowadays calls itself immensely wise, and ridicules the barbarians; and yet in many things we cannot count five."

Several voices exclaimed: "What? barbarians— with our refined civilization? And the close of the nineteenth century?"

Rudolph stood up. "Yes, barbarians—I will not take back the name. And so long as we cling to the past we shall remain barbarians. But we stand upon the threshold of a new era—all eyes are looking forward, everything drives us on toward a higher civilization. Barbarism is already casting away its ancient idols and its antiquated weapons. Even though we stand nearer to bar-

baric ideas than many are willing to acknowledge,
we are also nearer to a nobler development than
many dare even hope. Possibly the prince or the
statesman is now alive who will figure in all future
history as the most famous, the most enlightened,
because he will have brought about this general
laying down of arms. Even now the insane idea
is dying out, notwithstanding that diplomatic egotism attempts to justify itself by its assertion—the
insane idea that the destruction of one person is
the security of another. Already the realization
that justice must be the foundation of all social
life is glimmering upon the world, and from an
acknowledgment of this truth humanity must gain
a nobler stature—that development of humanity
for which Frederick Tilling labored. Mother, I
drink to the memory of your devoted husband,
to whom I also owe it that I am what I am. Out
of this glass no other toast shall ever be drank"—
and he threw it against the wall where it fell shattered to pieces—"at this baptismal feast of the
first-born no other toast shall be offered. We
drink not to our fathers' fathers—as the old phrase
went—no; but to our grandsons. Mother—what
is it?" he stopped suddenly. "You are weeping.
What do you see there?"

My glance had fallen on the open door. The
rays of the setting sun fell on a rose bush, covering
it with its golden shimmer, and there stood—the
figure of my dreams. I saw the white hair, the
glitter of the garden shears.

"It is true, is it not?" he smiled at me—"we are
a happy old couple?"

Ah, me!

THE END.

THE STORY OF TONTY.

AN HISTORICAL ROMANCE.

BY MRS. MARY HARTWELL CATHERWOOD.

12mo, 224 pages.   Price, $1.25.

"The Story of Tonty" is eminently a Western story, beginning at Montreal, tarrying at Fort Frontenac, and ending at the old fort at Starved Rock, on the Illinois River. It weaves the adventures of the two great explorers, the intrepid La Salle and his faithful lieutenant, Tonty, into a tale as thrilling and romantic as the descriptive portions are brilliant and vivid. It is superbly illustrated with twenty-three masterly drawings by Mr. Enoch Ward.

Such tales as this render service past expression to the cause of history. They weave a spell in which old chronicles are vivified and breathe out human life. Mrs. Catherwood, in thus bringing out from the treasure-houses of half-forgotten historical record things new and old, has set herself one of the worthiest literary tasks of her generation, and is showing herself finely adequate to its fulfillment.—*Transcript, Boston.*

A powerful story by a writer newly sprung to fame.   .   .   .   All the century we have been waiting for the deft hand that could put flesh upon the dry bones of our early heroes. Here is a recreation indeed.   .   . One comes from the reading of the romance with a quickened interest in our early national history, and a profound admiration for the art that can so transport us to the dreamful realms where fancy is monarch of fact.—*Press, Philadelphia.*

"The Story of Tonty" is full of the atmosphere of its time. It betrays an intimate and sympathetic knowledge of the great age of explorers, and it is altogether a charming piece of work.—*Christian Union, New York.*

Original in treatment, in subject, and in all the details of *mise en scène*, it must stand unique among recent romances.—*News, Chicago.*

A vivid series of fascinating pictures.—*New York Observer.*

Sold by all booksellers, or mailed, on receipt of price, by

A. C. McCLURG & CO., PUBLISHERS,

COR. WABASH AVE. AND MADISON ST., CHICAGO.

www.ingramcontent.com/pod-product-compliance
Lightning Source LLC
Chambersburg PA
CBHW020901020726
47497CB00005B/1505